DREAM STATE

DREAM STATE

A NOVEL

ERIC PUCHNER

DOUBLEDAY

New York

Published by Doubleday, a division of Penguin Random House LLC, 1745 Broadway, New York, NY 10019.

DOUBLEDAY and the portrayal of an anchor with a dolphin are registered trademarks of Penguin Random House LLC.

Book design by Casey Hampton
Interior illustrations by Oliver Munday

Library of Congress Cataloging-in-Publication Data
Names: Puchner, Eric, author.
Title: Dream state : a novel / Eric Puchner.
Description: First edition. | New York: Doubleday, 2025.
Identifiers: LCCN 2024011435 (print) | LCCN 2024011436 (ebook) |
ISBN 9780385550666 (hardcover) | ISBN 9780385550673 (ebook)
Subjects: LCGFT: Novels.
Classification: LCC PS3616.U25 D74 2025 (print) |
LCC PS3616.U25 (ebook) | DDC 813/.6—dc23/eng/20240318
LC record available at https://lccn.loc.gov/2024011435
LC ebook record available at https://lccn.loc.gov/2024011436

penguinrandomhouse.com | doubleday.com

MANUFACTURED IN THE UNITED STATES OF AMERICA
1 3 5 7 9 10 8 6 4 2

The authorized representative in the EU for product safety and compliance is Penguin Random House Ireland, Morrison Chambers, 32 Nassau Street, Dublin DO2 YH68, Ireland, https://eu-contact.penguin.ie.

For Katharine,
and for Sy and Clem

I have had a dream—
past the wit of man to say what dream it was.

—Bottom, *A Midsummer Night's Dream*

The northwest Montana depicted in this book is
a blend of real and imagined geography.

I

JUNE–JULY 2004

ONE

A visitor to Charlie Margolis's house in Montana—which
really belonged to his parents, who spent their summers
there—might not have found it much to look at. The house was
cramped and musty and low ceilinged. There was beige carpet
from the seventies, bric-a-brac on every windowsill, secondhand furniture that smelled incurably of smoke. Someone had
taped a hand-drawn sketch of a mallard to the lintel above the
stairs, reminding you to duck. Board games, stacked into zig-
gurats, cluttered the floor. An antique sign—SWEET CHERRIES
U-PICK-M—hung on the wall of the narrow kitchen, where every
appliance was brown. Brown was the stove. Brown was the
refrigerator. Brown, brown were the microwave and dishwasher.
Brown was the toaster but rarely its toast, which popped up at
random, unforeseeable intervals, like a jack-in-the-box. There
was a charming porch—recently rebuilt, with a gorgeous prospect of the lake—and yet you couldn't soak in the view, or hear
the wakes of speedboats lapping the beach, because the yard was
cut off from the shore by a major trucking route. (The whoosh
of semis and logging trucks, the fart of Harleys speeding by, was
the sound of summer.)

Still, Cece loved it more than any place on earth. There
were orchards behind the house, ancient apple trees planted by
Mrs. Margolis's grandfather, varieties of fruit with names like
racehorses: Sweet Sixteen and Hidden Rose and Northern Spy.
There was a hammock where you could lie in the shade and
read while sun flickered through the pines. There were raspberry bushes, magically replenishing, like something in a fairy

tale. (In July you could go at them like a machine—fill six, seven buckets—and the bushes wouldn't look any different.) And the cherries! Somehow there always seemed to be a tree within reach. Fingers stained red, bloated with fruit, you'd run across Route 35 and jump into the lake to clean off, whooping lustily at the cold, feeling like a character in a Russian novel. At least that's the way Cece felt, as if she'd opened a door in her imagination, entered some pre-digital world where lusty whooping was all the rage. She loved the place as much as Charlie did. They loved it so much they were getting married there, more than a thousand miles from home. Some of their friends were upset—it was expensive to fly in from either coast, and not at all easy—but Cece didn't care. She couldn't imagine getting married anywhere else.

Now here she was, her first day in the house by herself. She'd flown out from LA a month early. Charlie's parents were back home in Culver City, and of course Charlie couldn't leave the hospital for more than a week: he was a cardiac anesthesiologist, fresh off his residency and tethered to the OR. So it was up to Cece to make sure the wedding came off. To save money—but mostly because it felt more genuine to her—she was planning the whole thing herself. She stared at her laptop, combing the pictures of square dance callers before snagging on one that featured a young guy in a cowboy hat looking vaguely hungover. She was attracted to the wedding band's name, Rod-O and the Feckless Fiddlers. That was the advice she'd been given about square dance bands: the more ridiculous the name, the better it would be.

"What does the 'O' stand for?" she asked Rod-O on the phone. A TV blared in the background. The band she'd originally booked—the Fiddle Faddle Stringtet—had canceled the week before.

"Nothing."

"What do you mean?"

"I just liked the way it sounded. I'm from Mamaroneck, New York. I needed something to stand out."

"You're not even a *real* Montanan?"

"What's 'real' even mean these days?"

Cece frowned. "Can you turn down your TV for a second? It's very loud." It sounded, from the British accents, like he was watching *Masterpiece Theatre.* At ten in the morning.

"I was a struggling nutritionist. Now I'm a square dance caller. It's all part of the cosmic wheel of life."

"Are you free on July seventeenth? That's the date of the wedding."

"I'll have to check my schedule. It's a busy summer. There's a festival in Burlap."

"Burlap?"

"That's the name that springs to mind."

"Can you look into it then and call me back?"

"Hang on. This will only take a second. Doot da doo. Okay, looks like, hmm, yes, might have to juggle some things around . . . I'll have to run it by the Fiddlers, but I can probably swing it."

Cece hung up, wondering if Rod-O was displacing his own fecklessness onto his fiddlers. But she was determined to give people the benefit of the doubt, particularly in a place she didn't know or live in.

Salish, Montana, was one of those western towns caught in a strange moment of transition. It had begun as a Native American trading post, then had reinvented itself for many years as a logging center, and recently had reinvented itself once again as a thriving tourist destination for outdoor recreators. There was a microbrewery and a sushi place called How We Roll and a cycle shop with an espresso bar, but there was also a gun store and a bar called the Stagger Inn and a pawnshop whose employees talked openly about "faggots." At the Lazy Bear Bar & Grill, you could go to Margarita Monday and find a sales consultant and a fishing guide or two and occasionally even an actual cowboy. But mostly you'd find people who'd washed in from larger cities—in search of fun or outdoorsiness or a different-but-not-too-different life—and didn't know quite what they were doing there. Like Rod-O on the phone, they had a bit of a tough time explaining who they were.

Cece changed into her bathing suit and walked down to the dock, darting across the highway when there was a gap in traffic. Even at ten o'clock, there was a steady stream of SUVs and semitrucks and rental cars. But the rush of the road evaporated as soon as she crossed the boatshed lawn and got to the lake, which steamed quietly in the sun. The water was so bright she had to squint. The Mission Mountains rose to the left of her, bristling with pines, and then farther across the blue expanse of water were the ghostly peaks of the Salish range, hovering in the distance. Before coming here three years ago, Cece had never seen anything like it. She'd grown up in LA, where the only "lakes" were artificial, the water—if you could even get to it—murky and opaque. The water in Salish Lake was so clear that you could see straight down to the rocks, picking out minnows and lost lures as if they were at the bottom of a swimming pool. The swim ladder shone as brightly below the surface as above it; in fact, the submerged half looked somehow sharper, truer to the eye, though the two halves didn't match up. It was like a more perfect world that had snapped off from the first.

Cece dove into the lake, then popped up hooting at the cold. In Montana, you hooted in the morning and whooped after lunch. Or so Cece postulated to herself. She enjoyed coming up with aphorisms like this and was indifferent, as a rule, to their truthfulness. She floated on her back for a while in the steaming water and then climbed up the ladder shivering in the sun. Vigorously, she grabbed a towel from one of the Adirondack chairs and dried her hair. A man was standing on the lawn, watching her from the base of the dock. She should have been startled, even frightened, except that the lake was so beautiful it seemed somehow rude—ungracious—to imagine anything sinister. The man was wearing coveralls and a trucker cap that looked like it had been chewed up by a donkey, then spat back onto his head. He had one of those pitiable mold-length beards, less a fashion choice than a flag of surrender. From his expression, it looked like he hadn't seen a woman in a bathing suit for a while.

"You're steaming," the man said.

"Excuse me?" Cece said.

"There's, um, smoke coming off you."

It was true. Steam rippled from her arms. The man kept his distance, standing there with his near-beard, and so Cece wrapped the towel around her waist before warily approaching him. Garrett Meek, Charlie's best friend from college. He'd grown up in Missoula and had recently moved nearby, to an apartment in Woods Bay. Cece, who'd been hearing about Garrett for three years, eulogized in comic anecdotes, had not pictured a dour-looking guy dressed like a mechanic.

"I was on my way to work, so I thought I'd stop by and see if you needed anything."

She crossed her arms, partly to hide herself. "You mean Charlie called you and made you come by."

He blushed. "No. I mean, he called, yes, and told me you might need some help with a few things." He glanced at her arms. "You'll freeze to death swimming in the morning. It warms up by noon."

"A person afraid of cold water is a bystander of life."

"Who said that?"

"Me. I did. Anyway, the lake is so beautiful in the morning."

"It's a graveyard," Garrett said. "The native fish have all disappeared. They stocked some lakes with Mysis shrimp, back in the eighties, and now they've invaded everything and fucked up the food web for good."

Cece frowned. Who was this guy? Why he'd moved back to

Montana from the Bay Area was unclear, and Cece didn't ask. Charlie had said Garrett was having a bit of a hard time—what that meant exactly, Cece wasn't sure, except that in guy-talk "a bit of a hard time" generally meant something much worse. It meant depression or addiction or both. She knew a friend of theirs had died in college, a skiing accident. The death had been rough enough on Charlie, but apparently Garrett had never really recovered. Now he was working at the airport, which spoke for itself.

"Charlie had me lower the boat lift for you," Garrett said, nodding at the old Crestliner moored in its slip. "I did it last weekend. It's good to go."

"Why?"

"I think he had the idea I might take you fishing or something, in case you got bored."

"I thought you said it was a graveyard."

"There's more than enough lake trout," Garrett said, frowning. He said "lake trout" the way someone might say "child rapist."

"Well, it's so great to finally meet you," Cece said. "Charlie won't shut up about you, you'll be happy to know. Especially if he's had a beer or two." She checked her watch. "I've got the caterer coming at ten thirty."

Garrett stared at her.

"We're supposed to discuss some things—the menu—so I'd better get changed."

"Oh. Here. Almost forgot."

Garrett reached into his pocket and pulled out a plastic baggie, which he handed to Cece. Weed. An eighth or so, it looked like. She used it for a sleep aid, mostly, but of course hadn't dared to take any on the plane. So Charlie had arranged this favor and hooked her up. He was the cardiac anesthesiologist with weed connections. Cece thanked Garrett Meek and offered him some money, explaining that her wallet was in the house, but he mumbled something she couldn't make out, shaking his head. Incredibly, Charlie had asked this morose baggage handler to be the officiant at their wedding, insisting that he had a way with words. "The most eloquent man you'll ever meet," Charlie had called him. "Eloquent man," in Cece's experience, tended to be a bit of an oxymoron. She had objected—strenuously—but it seemed to mean a lot to Charlie, and Cece was arranging every other detail of the ceremony, so she'd given in.

Now she wished she'd stuck to her guns. Just standing in front of Garrett was like a flash of bad news. The light sort of got sucked out of the sky. She wanted to get rid of him, to say goodbye in a way that might discourage further visits, but he was staring impolitely into space.

"You've got an osprey on your property," he said.

"Where?"

Garrett pointed at the trees along the beach. Sure enough, wedged in the crotch of a dying pine, as if a beaver's dam had lodged there in a flood, was a tangle of sticks—a nest—from which a beautiful bird gazed back at them. A band of brown striped the bird's eyes, like a tiny blindfold. Its beak, bent straight down at the tip, seemed to be melting. Peeking from the nest were two chicks, homely as dinosaurs.

"How long before they're big enough to fly?"

"Seven, eight weeks," Garrett said.

"So they'll be there for the wedding," she said happily.

"Unless a bald eagle gets them first."

Cece looked at him. "What are you talking about?"

"Baldies like to pluck them out of the nest sometimes. Makes for a good fight."

"How awful!"

Garrett shrugged. "Eagles need to eat too. They don't have the same, what do you call it . . . cuteness response."

Did he mean to be so insulting? Cece gazed out at the lake, searching for bald eagles. A stand of cumulus clouds, darkened underneath like charred biscuits, had banked over the mountains. As she scanned the horizon, a beam of sunlight spoked through one of the clouds, projecting a distant movie onto the lake.

"Holy smokes," she said, wishing Charlie were there to witness it. From their apartment in LA, you could see a mini-mall with a Kentucky Fried Chicken.

"I wonder when it was that a caveman, Australopithecus or whoever, first looked at the sky and thought, *That's beautiful. I'm going to stop what I'm doing and look at it.*"

"I don't know," she said. "It could have been a woman."

"A woman?"

"A she-Australopithecus."

Garrett looked at her and frowned. Was he sexist? The last thing she needed in her life was some dorm-room philosopher from Charlie's past. What a strange and awful man, she thought. His coveralls smelled like BO. She felt suddenly depressed, as if the Eden she'd looked forward to all winter and spring had been contaminated by this smelly man who'd forgotten how to smile.

"I'll check back in a day or two," he said. "To make sure you haven't gone crazy or something."

Cece had the sense Garrett was doing this—keeping an eye on her—out of an obligation to Charlie. She smiled vaguely, watching him cross the boatshed lawn to his pickup, which made a truck-show rumble when he started it. How did someone pissed off about Mysis shrimp justify driving that thing around? And what did it mean that Charlie liked him so much? Not "liked," but *adored*? Cece would have been surprised to learn they were second cousins, let alone best friends. For a moment, the man she was about to marry seemed like a stranger.

Cece went up to the house, shivering in earnest now. Once inside, she felt immediately better. The cedary smell. The warm rug on her feet. The view of the old wire clothesline in the backyard, a forgotten sweatshirt swinging like an acrobat in the wind.

Yellowflower, the house was called. It actually had a name. (There was a notebook on the coffee table called *The Yellowflower Bible*, filled with divine instructions.)

Cece opened her laptop and checked her email: two from Charlie, both in the last hour. *Miss you already, about to head into the OR.* At work he killed people and brought them back to life. More specifically, he froze people's hearts so that a cardiac surgeon could repair them, then thawed the hearts again to see whether the surgery had been a success. *Did Garrett M come by? I told him to bring you a present. Cool guy, right?*

Actually he depressed the shit out of me, Cece wrote back, then came to her senses and deleted what she'd written. It was clearly important to Charlie that the pair of them get along. She'd do her best to be polite.

He seems great, she wrote instead. *Maybe a bit lonely?*

Cece went up to the bedroom, where she struggled to unstick the door. None of the doors shut properly; when you pried one open, another would telekinetically open in a distant room of the house. She loved this too. She changed into some jeans, and an old ragg-wool sweater she'd stolen from Charlie's closet at home, before starting to unpack the last things from her suitcase. She'd lied about the caterer; he wasn't coming till the afternoon. She had the whole day to relax and recover from getting in late last night; with the layover, the drives to and from the airport, the trip had taken six and a half hours.

She coiled a pair of brown socks into a cinnamon bun and then put it in the top drawer of the Margolises' dresser, which smelled like mothballs. A woman with a messy sock drawer was a woman in crisis, she thought to herself. Or maybe the opposite was true: a woman who coiled her socks was secretly unraveling. Cece pondered this. It was at times like these—when her life snagged for a second, the distractions of the wedding momentarily deserting her—that she felt a vertiginous panic in her chest, as if she were about to leap from a plane.

She reached into her pocket and took out the baggie Garrett Meek had given her. In general, she regarded people who got high before noon as hopeless losers. Why? She had no idea. Anyway, it was a medical thing. She plucked a couple buds from the plastic bag and packed them in the little pipe she'd cleaned out scrupulously before sticking it in her Dopp kit. Then she lit the bowl with a Blue Tip match she found in the bedside table, sucking in the flame so that it looked like a magic trick, the match burning upside down.

She felt immediately calmer. The sun poured through its hole in the clouds, fracturing into crepuscular rays. The silver movie, so vast and luminous it looked like a mirage, was still playing out there on the lake. Cece thought about the Australopithecus, glancing around to see if any sabertooths were on her trail and then forgetting herself for a moment because the sky looked strange and beautiful. Yes. The Australopithecus might die soon, she's in grave danger, and yet she stops for no animal reason to take in the view. *Hey, stupid!* the other Australopithecuses grunt. *You're going to get yourself killed!* But she doesn't care. She risks her life to stare at it. Then she runs back to her cave, feeling this new, perilous strangeness inside her.

"Hey, stupid," Cece said out loud, to herself, then messed up the socks in her drawer.

TWO

Garrett knelt in the pit of the 737, watching Burelli load bags of various shapes and sizes onto the belt loader. There were six ramp agents who worked for Maverick Air, but Burelli was the most sadistic, choosing to load even the bulkiest duffels horizontally on the belt. It was like some diabolical video game. Garrett would kneel at the top of the belt while the bags came at him, one after another, an assembly line of suitcases and backpacks and garment bags, some of them as heavy as slain deer, and in the split second between them decide—depending on the airport code on their tags—whether to stack them with the pieces going through to Houston or to heave them deeper into the pit, where they'd get unloaded in Vegas and carted off to their connecting flights.

That was the idea anyway. Hunched in the bowels of the pit was Félix, a French Canadian who'd moved here from the Magdalen Islands, on the heels of a girlfriend who worked as a ranger at Glacier National Park. His English consisted primarily of the word "fuck." He did his best to field the volley of bags Garrett threw at him and stack them into successive walls of luggage, greeting each bag with courtly wrath. "Fuck you, Vegas," he said. "Fuck you, Denver. Fuck you, Boise." (He pronounced "Boise" to rhyme with "blasé.") If he couldn't see the tag, he'd say, "Fuck you, Samso*neet*," and then continue his excoriation of America.

Sweat stung Garrett's eyes, but he didn't have time to wipe them. His knees throbbed, he was sick from exertion, he couldn't swallow from the dryness in his throat. Bag after bag came at him, some upside down so that he couldn't read the tags; by the time he hefted each bag around to plot its destiny and heaved it in the right direction, another one had smashed him in the face. It was like being buried alive. Eventually he gave up looking at the tags and just started tossing all the bags to the left. If a bag destined for Tucson got stranded in Houston, so be it. Attachment was the root of suffering.

When the belt was empty, Garrett sat back on his ass, panting for breath. His coveralls stuck to him like Kleenex. As a discount airline, Maverick Air prided itself on forty-minute turnovers, but lately to cut losses they'd been scheduling more flights and trying to get them out even faster. Garrett sat there rubbing his knees. He'd left his kneepads in the pit of a Chicago-bound plane and hadn't had the guts to tell Mr. Purifoy, his boss. His back was killing him too, from heaving bags around on his knees.

He climbed out of the pit and walked down the belt loader to where Burelli was standing. Burelli took off his earmuffs and revealed his bad ear, which he'd damaged in a bar fight before Garrett knew him. It swelled up now and then and began to close, like a tulip at dusk. As usual, when confronted with its source, Garrett's anger dried up immediately.

"You're burying us up there," Garrett said, trying not to look at Burelli's ear.

Burelli eyed him suspiciously. "You don't seem too peeved about it."

"I'm not."

"Maybe you should be."

"Perhaps," Garrett said.

"'Perhaps.' Jesus. Did you grow up in Wizardpants, England?"

"I grew up in Missoula."

"You don't talk like it," Burelli said.

Garrett shrugged. "I'll try to enrich my vocabulary."

Disappointingly, Garrett did not get punched. He put his earmuffs back on and then walked over to the baggage cart, where he'd left his wands. He preferred it inside the earmuffs, where the world had the fragile quality of a dream. It was like wearing a space helmet. He tended to feel this way anyway, as if he were visiting from another planet, but the earmuffs made the feeling especially pronounced.

Garrett sat in the baggage cart, waiting for the passengers to board. Soon the engines would start up and they'd have to unchock the wheels and Burelli would man the tug to push the plane out—but for now Garrett could dream undisturbed. He could see the passengers in the terminal, lined up at the gate and preparing to fly back to Denver or Paris or maybe even Tokyo, carrying whatever they'd unwittingly picked up: bacteria in their stomachs or insects in their luggage or seed pods stuck to their socks. They were redistributing the world's flora and fauna, creating a single ecosystem like the one that existed in the days of Pangaea, when the earth's continents were one. Which meant that most of the world's species were dying off. And, of course, Garrett was helping them. Why? Because it was the only job he could find, given his résumé: a college dropout with an erratic work history, whose most promising reference was the counselor at a halfway house.

Garrett watched the first passengers funnel through the gate. It was a small enough airport that there wasn't a Jetway, and something about the people parading across the tarmac, half-blinded by the sun, made them seem cinematically doomed. And then it happened. The sky flattened like a TV screen; the people herding toward the boarding ramp began to look funny, bobbing up and down as they walked; a nauseating implausibility washed over everything, as if it were coming not from Garrett but from some cosmic leak in the sky. How outlandish they looked, teetering along on two legs: the bald man with the scabs on his head; the boy with the peeling pink gumdrop of a nose; the pregnant woman waddling along, palming her stomach like a basketball. Garrett took off his earmuffs, but it didn't help. "Onion," the people said, chatting on the ramp. "Onion onion onion onion onion." Snow began to fall. Always the snow: huge flaked, snowier than the real thing, like angels having a pillow fight. It was pretty and abominable at the same time.

———

After his shift, Garrett showered at home and then drove out to his father's place, following the Swan Highway toward the mirage of sunlit mountains in the distance. Even with his sunglasses on, the snowcapped peak of Mount Aeneas blinded him. He had his window down—it was ninety degrees out—and the air smelled dank and viscous, musky from the chartreuse fields of canola. Fences everywhere, undulating like waves; behind them grazed long-necked horses, their heads planted in the grass, so that from a distance they looked like headless, two-tailed beasts. The ranches were all fake these days, owned by one-percenters—Realtors called them "lifestyle ranches"—but this didn't make them any less beautiful. Garrett had moved here ten months ago and had yet to become hardened to the landscape. Of course, it was tough to separate the beauty of the place from his nostalgia for it. Especially this stretch of road. His dad lived in his grandparents' old house—Garrett had driven this way countless times as a boy, from Missoula—and so it was like seeing two things at once wherever he looked. It made his heart ache with longing, though what it was he longed for he couldn't say.

He turned up the road that led to his dad's house, crunching through gravel that pinged the bottom of his pickup. Garrett rolled up his window to keep out the dust. His father was dying; there was no way around it. Pulmonary fibrosis. IPF: the kind nobody could figure out why you got. Anyone else would have sunk into despair, but fortunately Garrett's father had no interest in being depressed or reckoning with his place on earth or making amends for the mistakes he'd made during his fifty-seven years on the planet. He wanted to get laid. He'd spent the sixteen months since his diagnosis driving out to Snookums Lounge in Kalispell—the nearest gay bar—and trying to get lucky. More than once Garrett had come out to the house unannounced and been greeted by a potbellied ex-linebacker type with afternoon bedhead. Garrett did not know what to make of this carnal turn, or of the linebackers, except that it made a kind of sense given what was happening to his father's body.

Garrett parked next to his dad's Mustang convertible. He'd leased it the day after his diagnosis. Cautiously, so as not to surprise his lower back, Garrett reached behind his seat and pulled out a twelve-pack and a savory pie he'd bought at the IGA in Salish.

"Pie and Budweiser," his father said, greeting him on the porch. He was wearing a bathrobe at four thirty in the afternoon. "I forgive you."

"For what?"

"I don't know. For being so much younger than me."

"It's a Dorito-and-onion pie."

"Dorito and onions?"

"It's better than it sounds."

"That would be impossible," his dad said. He took the pie from Garrett's hands. "Whoa, it's still warm. Fresh from the oven."

"Actually, I bought it before work," Garrett explained. "It was kind of sitting in the truck."

He made an undistinguished mother, but Garrett was new to the role and so cut himself some slack. It helped that his dad shared these low expectations for him. They walked into the living room, which doubled as his father's studio—or used to, when he was still painting. The only remnants of its former life were a few drips on the floorboards where the drop cloth hadn't met the wall. That, and the couch shredded into a hairy avant-garde sculpture by his cat, Barnabas, the most pathetic feline Garrett had ever seen. Barnabas had lost a leg in an incident with a motorbike but didn't seem to realize he was crippled, meaning that he was forever leaping onto things, then falling off.

His father disappeared into the kitchen with the Dorito pie, stifling a cough that happily didn't turn into an attack. Garrett had a feeling he was the only man to have visited the house for a while. His father didn't look his best. He was skinny and slow-moving and his cheeks had started to hollow, as if he were sucking on a straw. Also, a weird thing was happening to his fingers. They were swelling at the tips and beginning to look like miniature tennis rackets. This was not uncommon, apparently. (Dr. Shrayber called it "clubbing.") The change had seemed gradual at first, but recently Garrett had noticed old acquaintances gawking at his dad or keeping their distance, wondering if he was contagious. His father was convinced half of Salish thought that he was lying about having IPF, that God was punishing him with "gay cancer."

His father came back with two slices of the pie, and they sat out on the porch with the plates on their laps. The beer was lukewarm, but they drank it anyway. What did you do with your dying father whose midlife coming-out had ruined your mother's life? Apparently you got drunk. You sat on the porch of the house, as if your childhood had happened to someone else, in a far-off land, and behaved like old friends. It helped that Garrett felt like he was dying himself.

"Tastes kind of like piss," he said, sipping from his beer.

"Do not insult the king of beers," his father said. He was a staunch defender of Budweiser. Anything with actual flavor he deemed "hipster beer," part of his Ironic Cretin act. "Anyway, it tastes nothing like piss."

"How would you know?"

His father looked at him.

"On second thought, don't answer that."

Barnabas scaled the fence separating the yard from the driveway and started to gimp along the top of it on three legs, making his way to the corner post.

"Bet you he'll make it this time," his father said.

"How much?"

"Five bucks?"

They watched the animal totter along the fence. Two-thirds of the way along, he fell off dramatically and landed in a hydrangea bush. Whoever said cats always land on their feet had an inadequate sample size.

"Crap," said his father, whose belief in Barnabas had cost him a fair bit of money. Barnabas hobbled out of the hydrangeas and then lay belly-up in the sun with his legs splayed in exhaustion. His stump pointed at the fence.

"Do you think he believes he's a person?" Garrett asked.

"On the contrary," his father said. "He believes we're cats."

"How do you know?"

"He stares at me during my coughing fits sometimes. I swear he thinks I have a hairball."

His dad went inside again and emerged with a five-dollar bill. Garrett might have felt guilty if he didn't suspect his father *wanted* to slip him money. What else was he going to spend his pension on? The restless man had left Missoula and moved up here to his own father's house, where he wouldn't have to pay rent and could work undisturbed, though what this disturbance back home consisted of Garrett couldn't imagine. It wasn't like he was spending time with Garrett; he'd been a rotten father, or at least an absent one, more interested in escaping his life than living it. He'd taught fine art at the university for thirty years, forever talking about the day he'd retire and move to New York City, where he could get out of "academic prison" and work on his own paintings—"fictories," his father called them, encaustics of old sawmills and copper mines, layered with wax until they looked ghostly and half-remembered—and yet this had turned out to be another story, a myth in the larger fictory of his life, like the "conferences" he was perpetually running off to or the nights he claimed to be painting but was really out cruising for men, sometimes entertaining them in the studio he'd built in the old stables behind the house. He'd admitted everything, soon after Garrett went off to college. Garrett's mother—living now in Albuquerque, remarried to a periodontist—would never forgive him.

"I met Charlie Margolis's fiancée," Garrett said, pocketing the money. "She's here for a month, planning the wedding."

"Where's Charlie Margolis?"

"In LA. Saving people's lives."

His father nodded. "Interesting."

"What's that supposed to mean?"

"Is she a babe?"

"No. Jesus." His father used vintage words like this—"babe"—on purpose. It was an older-person joke. "Anyway, I'm officiating the wedding, so her 'babeness' is irrelevant."

His father laughed. The laugh coarsened into a coughing fit, then dwindled to a wheeze before abruptly begetting another fit. You just had to wait it out. Sometimes it took ten minutes for him to weather an attack. Meanwhile, Garrett opened a fresh beer and handed it to him.

"I thought you didn't believe in marriage," his father said finally.

"I don't," Garrett said.

"What are you going to do? Talk about the anesthetization of the soul?"

"Charlie asked me to do it. We were college roommates for two years. With that whole gang of guys at the Mill. Everyone will be at the wedding." This wasn't true, of course—the "everyone" lingered for a second, like an unpleasant smell.

"And?"

"What could I do, say no?"

"The answer to that particular question—'What could I do, say no?'—is always yes."

Garrett frowned. It was too late to refuse now: the wedding was in a month; he'd filled out the ordination request form on the internet; he was an official Universal Life Church minister. He had the certificate at home—signed by one Chaplain Br. Martin—to prove it. True, he despised the idea of marriage, but Charlie had asked him so fervently, as if he were conferring upon him some rare and special honor, that to avoid alienating him Garrett had said yes. He didn't have too many friends left in the world.

"Anyway," his dad said, "what makes you think you have any ministerial skills?"

"Everyone has a spark of divine wisdom inside them."

"Says who?"

"The Universal Life Church. Or at least their website."

"Sounds like a day to remember." His father picked up the last morsel of Dorito pie on his plate and shoved it into his mouth. "Just download one of those wedding scripts—you'll be fine. Anyway, it's only the vows that matter."

"Like yours and Mom's, you mean?"

His father looked at him. "I loved your mother," he said. "That's not fair."

Garrett ignored this. It had taken him years of incremental forgiveness to reach this perch of acceptance. He didn't want to fuck it up now. The fact that his father had married his mother knowing full well he was gay, that he'd lived with her for eighteen years while they raised a son together, pretending all the while he was a happy husband with a libido problem—Garrett could put this into context. It was a different time, the eighties, and we were talking *Missoula* after all, not as far from Matthew Shepard country as the vegans on Higgins Avenue made it seem. Garrett had seen enough queer bashing at Missoula High to understand why someone might not admit that he was gay, perhaps even to himself. And it did seem that Garrett's dad and mom had been, if not romantically entwined, *entangled*. It was one of the reasons Garrett hated marriage so much—that it could force people, basically good and decent ones, to cheat and lie and wound each other for life.

He fished another Budweiser from the twelve-pack, aware that his dad was watching him.

"That's your third beer already," his father said.

"Would you like to see some ID?"

"I'm just worried about you. Look at your hat."

"What's wrong with my hat?" Garrett said.

"Just be careful, all right? You don't want to end up like one of those college dropouts whose best friend is his dad."

This was so obviously already true—that Garrett's dying father, who'd deserted his mother twelve years ago, was his best friend—that they didn't dare look at each other. His dad coughed, once, like a normal person. Garrett suspected it was to hide his embarrassment.

"Look," his dad said, clearing his throat. "I know you've had a rough time. Your friend dying like that. I can only imagine. And all the . . . *trouble* you had in San Francisco. I can understand wanting to get out of there."

Garrett peered into the keyhole of his beer can.

"I mean, it's not like you moved here just because I did."

Garrett blushed. He could feel his father's eyes upon him.

"You *did* get the job at the airport first, right?"

"That's right," Garrett lied.

His father looked relieved. "Good. Because I feel some"—he held up his clubbed fingers—"*urgency* about this. I want to make sure you're okay." He stared into his own can now. "I didn't do the best job of that, when you were younger."

"You were . . . distracted."

"I should have gone to more Little League games."

"One would have been nice. Like when we made it to regionals."

"You made it to regionals?"

"Wow. You could at least *pretend* to know that."

"I taught you to ski," his father said defensively. "You're a damn fine skier. We had some nice times out on the slopes, didn't we? I used to stick hand warmers in your boots to keep them warm in the Jeep."

"I think Mom stuck those warmers in my boots."

Garrett said this to annoy him—also, it was true—though in all honesty he'd loved those ski trips and looked forward to them more than anything. They were the one time he felt close to his father—or that he had a father at all. (And the skiing too; the skiing! How harmless it had seemed, like dreaming you could fly.) But he was feeling a bit hurt. Shouldn't his dad feel, well, *touched* that he'd settled ten miles from his house, in a crappy apartment in Woods Bay? Grateful that his son was around to check on him? Instead, his dad seemed worried about *him*, Garrett, as if he were one of those thirty-year-old shipwrecks who move back in with their parents.

His father coughed for real this time, covering his mouth with his fingers. Much to Garrett's dismay, the world began to flatten again, that cosmic disgust settling over the porch and making his dying father seem like a facsimile in a museum. The angels resumed their pillow fight. It was his dad's fingers—their strangeness—that had sent Garrett over the edge. Hümanz! In the inpatient ward, he'd been surrounded by them twenty-four/ seven, these revolting creatures who'd made him sit in their onion-groups and say onion onion onion. It had snowed from the ceiling, for weeks, though not enough to make them shut up. Depressive psychosis, they'd diagnosed it as—or psychotic depression, one of those fun terms you can reverse like a belt. Curable, supposedly, thanks to Eli Lilly and Company. Comparatively speaking, he was as sane as a cheerleader. And yet the episodes persisted; they'd never gone away entirely; the only full cure, it seemed, was to avoid his fellow species.

His father stood up (outlandish) and then walked over to the railing (outlandisher) to spit into the bushes. Even Barnabas, marooned on his back in the yard, seemed less alive than the grass he was lying in.

"I worry about you, that's all," his father said, sitting down again. "You wear that hat and you're not always the, I don't know . . . *sunniest* guy to be around. I think you scare people."

Direly, Garrett crunched his beer can and threw it at Barnabas, who startled from his nap and rolled onto his legs. The snow evaporated.

"See?" his dad said. "Even Barnabas is afraid of you."

"That's not true."

"It's the hat."

"He sits in my lap!"

"Strictly out of pity."

"It is not pity! He purrs with delight."

"Let's see whose lap he chooses right now," Garrett's dad said. "Yours or mine. Bet you a ten-spot."

"Barnabas," Garrett called, taking off his hat.

Barnabas, responding to his name, hobbled closer.

"Here, Barney!" his father called. "Come on, kitty! Meow."

"Meow meow."

Barnabas mounted the first step to the porch. In the distance, looming above the house, Mount Aeneas began to take on that magic-hour glow that seemed brighter than the sky, illuminated somehow from within, as if the earth were using it for a lantern. Barnabas paid no attention to this. He looked at the two enormous cats on the porch, meowing at him. He wanted nothing to do with them and scoped a path to the house that would evade them both. The sick cat, Fills the Bowl When Scratched, had sudden retching fits. Plus his lap was bony. But the other one, the healthy cat, gave off something strange. Barnabas could smell it from the steps. A tang of fear, as if he expected to be eaten.

THREE

Go away!" Cece yelled out the window.

"We're supposed to go hiking? Remember? I rang the doorbell three times."

"Four," Cece said. "You rang it *four* times."

"It's seven o'clock."

"Exactly!"

"When I said I'd be here," Garrett elaborated.

He'd found his way to the backyard and was standing next to the clothesline, from which a row of colored underwear drooped like a chain of prayer flags. The underwear might have embarrassed Cece if she'd been less tired, or if Garrett himself looked any less ridiculous. He was wearing a new cap—was it actually denim?—and a pair of shorts that covered one knee but not the other. It looked like he'd cut the legs off some chinos, paramedics-style, after a car crash. She leaned out the window.

"Wow. You look awful," he said.

"Please go away."

"I don't mean awful in a, you know . . . bad way. You look great usually." He frowned, chewing his lip. "Not *great* great. I didn't mean it like that. Just a lot better than you do now." He chewed his lip again. "Not that you don't look good now. You look totally fine." God, his poor lip! "I mean 'fine' as in 'okay.' 'Adequate.' The literal meaning."

Cece told him she'd be down in ten minutes, mostly to keep him from devouring his own face. Was he really yelling at her from the backyard, telling her how awful she looked? Why the hell had she agreed to go hiking so early? And who, when they said seven o'clock in the morning, actually meant *seven o'clock in the morning*? Served her right for agreeing to it, even if she'd been grateful to Garrett for giving her a tour of the local thrift stores. Instead of renting dinnerware for the wedding, she'd had the idea of buying vintage dishes: how quaint and charming it would be, for everyone to eat off mismatched plates! Charlie, of course, had immediately enlisted Garrett, which, given the man's taste in apparel, made a certain amount of sense. He was a Goodwill connoisseur. To Cece's surprise, he'd been patient and unglowering, driving her around town, waiting in his truck while she scoured every junk shop in Salish. It helped that he barely spoke to her, more interested in listening to the local news on the radio, which had something to do with "sustainable timber harvests." So it surprised her when he asked her on a hike. Cece had been standing in the Margolises' driveway, holding a circus tower of vintage plates. It had seemed easiest, at the time, to say yes.

Also, what else was she going to do? Cece was feeling a bit unemployed. She'd been in Montana two weeks now and had already met with the caterer, the florist, the photographer; she'd found a hairdresser she liked in town; she'd approved the playlist sent to her by the DJ, who was to come on after the Feckless Fiddlers. Her dress, sized and fitted, was hanging in a closet. She'd written her vows, revised them several times. Why had she imagined she needed a month to prepare for the wedding? She'd imagined it because life often failed to match her perception of it, and because the aphorisms in her head (*A Montana wedding can only be planned in Montana!*) were often unrelated to fact.

Cece got dressed in shorts and a T-shirt and the floppy felt hat that Charlie said made her look like Faye Dunaway. Then she sat on the bed, worried she might cry. It was the tenth anniversary of her mother's death. Incredibly, they'd originally planned to have the wedding *today*, but Cece had come to her senses and realized that what in theory seemed like an homage to her mother would be the worst idea ever, an emotional suicide vest. It still felt that way, her mother's death: like something she strapped on every morning, concealing it craftily from others. Cece had been seventeen. Her father, a computer-chip broker who woke up at one every morning to do business with China, had explained that her mother had stage-four cancer and might not make it through the summer. Cece had not believed a word. Her mother was an air force psychiatrist, a captain; she wore fatigues to work, went to the gym three times a week, drank snot-green smoothies that smelled like manure. Cece responded to the preposterousness of the news by going on a bender. She'd already been experimenting with drugs and alcohol, strictly on the weekends; now she applied herself. Her mom had brain cancer, and it was time to party. With the help of Paige, her best friend, she drained her parents' liquor cabinet, drove drunk to parties, passed out on the stairs. Once a guy she'd never met turned up at her school, claiming he'd held her hair the night before while she puked. Cece had no recollection of him at all. Meanwhile, her mother embarrassed her, always on the couch and greeting people in her bathrobe. She lost her hair and eyebrows and looked like a seal. She barked like a seal as well; the radiation had done something to her diaphragm, and she hiccupped exuberantly in a way she couldn't control.

Even after her mother was taken to a hospice—even after the case manager had called the house one Sunday at five a.m., telling her father to come in—Cece believed everything would be fine. It was all a stupid misunderstanding. Cotton-mouthed, hungover from a night of tequila shots with Paige, she'd entered her mother's room and thought she'd opened the wrong door. But no. This terrible creature was her mother. She stared at Cece with watery eyes, opaque and unseeing, the way a lizard might. For the first time, Cece recognized that something was happening not only to herself but to the woman lying in front of her. She forced herself to approach the bed. Her mother plucked at

her sheets with one hand, peacefully almost, as if she were picking buttercups. Yet she wasn't at peace; she was deeply distressed.
Her lips trembled. She held out her hand, as if inviting Cece to
arm wrestle. Cece grabbed it. "Come closer," she said, surprising Cece with her strength. Her breath smelled like scorched
butter. Cece leaned in close, expecting a secret. "Come closer,"
her mother said again, clutching Cece's hand so hard it hurt.
Cece leaned in closer, as close as she could possibly get, hugging
her mother so tightly she worried her bones—like kindling, like
Popsicle sticks—might break. And yet her mother said it again,
"Come closer," as if she had something vital to tell her, something urgent and remarkable, if only Cece would obey her. But
Cece couldn't do it. Unless she dissolved into a gas, got sucked
up somehow into her lungs, there was no way to get closer. She
tried to explain this to her mother, but she just repeated her
command, gently but firmly, as if she were imploring Cece to
clean her room. *Come closer.*

By the time it occurred to Cece that her mother was dying,
she was dead. Even then, it seemed like possibly a mistake, like
there was no way in hell her mother would have agreed to it.
Cece hunched through the memorial service, unable to speak or
move or smile. People hugged her, one after another, a series of
random blows. At the national cemetery, she stood on the perfect lawn rolling down to a smudge of ocean in the distance, the
tombstones a run of dominoes waiting to be tipped, feeling like
she'd been beamed to an alien planet. She could not fathom her
own fingers. It was a military burial, with guards of honor and a
flag-folding ceremony and a lone bugler playing taps. The long,
sorrowful notes floated over the cemetery, turning everything
into the tragic plot point in a movie: the gravesites and their
wilting flowers, the guards of honor frozen like statues, the hole
in the ground where her mother would be lowered and transformed into a skeleton. Such was the grace and beauty of the
bugler's playing that Cece, returning to Earth for a moment,

couldn't help being moved. It seemed to give form to the precious void inside her. Then the bugler stopped in midnote, as if he'd forgotten what song he was performing. He turned red with embarrassment. Finally, he took the bugle from his lips and shook it, and it played the lost note for a second, as if possessed by a ghost. It wasn't a real instrument at all, Cece realized, but a stereo made to look like one. The thing had run out of charge. A couple of the mourners giggled. Cece glanced behind her, startled. Later, in the middle of the eulogy, the bugle began playing again from its case.

Strangeness and sorrow. Strangeness and sorrow. Cece went back to school, amazed that her life still existed. *My mother is dead*, she told herself, over and over, not immune to its dramatic value. It was precisely this sense of being in a play or a movie that made her death feel temporary. At any minute the play would end and her mother would be alive again, taking her to the beach like she used to every weekend; Cece would massage her head while they watched stupid shows together, dizzy with the smell of sweat and jojoba oil. (That smell! When Cece was little, she used to suck on her mother's hair, put strands of it in her mouth.) Cece missed her so much it howled through her like a wind. She stopped eating. On the soccer field she stood there shivering, staring at the grass. Her friends, understanding at first, eventually gave up on her, stopped asking her to parties and the Galleria, to bonfires at the beach. When her father wasn't home, Cece sometimes sneaked into his room and stripped the mattress, gazing at the orphaned sweat stain, pale as a shadow, where her mother used to sleep.

Once, the phone rang and Cece picked it up: her mother's hair salon asking to confirm an appointment. "She died," Cece said, perhaps too softly to be heard, because the woman on the phone said, "I believe so, yes. A coloring. Missed the last one, so wanted to confirm." The next day, Cece drove to the hair salon and showed up for the appointment. The hairdresser didn't question who she was. He led her to a chair, then grabbed a book of color swatches and handed it to her. Cece flipped through the book—a rainbow of tiny rabbit's feet—and found one that matched her mother's hair. She smelled the swatch, but of course it smelled like nothing. She cried and cried, for the first time since the funeral. The hairdresser, perhaps used to such things, ignored her. He painted and foiled Cece's hair, then rinsed it out and revealed the hideous product of her grief.

———————

"You're different than Charlie," Garrett said now, driving up Route 35 on their way to Glacier Park. She was beginning to feel half-awake, mostly because of the "expresso" in her hand. Montana's tendency to misread the cues of gentrification—to transform everything, essentially, into fast food—was refreshing to her, heartening even, but only after ten a.m. (When Cece had tried to order an Americano, the teenager at the coffee stand had raised her voice and begun enunciating carefully, as if she were a foreign exchange student.)

"How do you mean?" Cece said.

"In college, he used to leap out of bed every morning like it was on fire."

"He still does that."

"Does he still yell 'Rise and shine!' at the top of his lungs?"

"Not anymore," Cece said ominously.

Garrett laughed. She immediately felt guilty about ganging up on Charlie, then stupid for feeling guilty when they were just joking and it was actually a tribute to Charlie's wonderfulness that they were poking a bit of fun at him. And that *was* the wonderful thing about Charlie: he made you excited about getting out of bed. Well, maybe not about getting out of bed, but definitely about the rest of your day. It was the "shine" part that chiefly interested him. He woke up and did things, which inspired you to do things too.

"Actually, it's something I admire about Charlie. He's a man of action."

Garrett took off his denim cap and set it on the dash. "Yep. One of them."

"What's that supposed to mean?"

He shrugged.

"I mean, yes, he can sometimes seem a bit . . . *overeager*," Cece said, annoyed. "It can feel strange to an introvert."

"You're an introvert?"

"No. Not really. I just mean it can sometimes feel . . . I don't know. Like he's turned inside out." Garrett glanced at her. What was she talking about? She'd never thought of Charlie as being "turned inside out" before—the words themselves had never crossed her mind—and yet the phrase had plunked out of her, fully formed, like a gumball.

"What do you mean?"

"After we see a movie, Charlie always wants to talk about it right away. Like as soon as we're walking out. But I need to let it sit for a while. Especially if it's a good movie. Like it's over, but not *actually* over."

"You're still dreaming," he said practically. "You haven't fully woken up."

"Yeah. Something like that."

"He did the same thing in college. Used to drive me crazy. We'd go see something great, part of the film series, you know— *McCabe & Mrs. Miller*—and he'd start dissecting it the second it finished. Sometimes he couldn't even wait for the credits to roll."

Cece frowned, feeling even guiltier than before. She felt tricked and disloyal, bamboozled into bad-mouthing her fiancé. Why hadn't she kept her mouth shut—or better yet, stayed in bed and avoided this whole stupid trip? She could have been waking up right now and having an actual coffee, one that could spell.

"How did you guys meet anyway?" Garrett asked. "Charlie didn't tell me."

"In med school. Johns Hopkins. Or rather, he was a resident and *I* was in med school. We bonded over missing LA."

"You're a doctor too?"

"Don't act so surprised," she said. "But actually, no. I'm not. I dropped out second semester."

Garrett nodded, as if dropping out of one of the best med schools in the world was a perfectly reasonable thing to do. He didn't seem shocked or appalled or worried for her future. Even Charlie, who'd supported her decision and wanted her to be happy, always seemed embarrassed when she told people about it, rushing to clarify that she had other ambitions for herself, she wouldn't be temping for an architecture firm for the rest of her life. (She'd solved this already by quitting a month ago.)

"You know how Charlie's so passionate about working in the OR? I just never felt that way. Like it was my calling in life. Mostly I just felt, I don't know . . . *exhausted* all the time. Exhausted and stressed and like I was missing the best years of my life." She frowned. "I looked at the students a bit older than me—Charlie's friends, who'd started their residencies—and their hair was all going gray. In their *twenties.*"

Garrett sneaked a look in the rearview mirror. His hair was thinning on top, tapering to the hidden glade of a bald spot. Perhaps he was vainer than Cece thought. "Charlie's not going gray already, is he?"

"Charlie! No. He sleeps like a baby, even on call. He's like designed by NASA or something."

The tone of Cece's voice surprised her. She didn't tell Garrett about suffering through four years of premed in college—all that chem and bio and, sadistically, *biochem*—thinking the whole time that med school would be different, would flip some magic switch in her soul and make it all seem worthwhile, all the books and movies and happy hours she'd missed, the beach trips and road trips and camping trips, and then sitting in Genes to Society one day, bored to tears and half-delirious from four hours' sleep, and realizing that she had no interest at all in being a pediatric neurosurgeon, even though she'd wanted to be one since she was fourteen. It was all a big misunderstanding. Something about the words themselves—"pediatric neurosurgeon"—had appealed to her, she'd seen them in a book somewhere and they'd sparked her curiosity, an interest that was immediately affirmed by the grown-ups around her, eliciting misty-eyed looks of pride—*Cece here, on the honor roll for the third time in a row, wants to be a pediatric neurosurgeon!*—which encouraged her to seek further approval and start telling everybody that she wanted to be one when she grew up.

It had been the same thing, strangely, with baboons. Ever since Cece was a little girl, she'd claimed to love baboons. She'd had baboon T-shirts and a baboon lunch box and even a stuffed baboon as big as an armchair sitting in the corner of her room. Her father had given her the stuffed baboon when she was five, because he'd asked her what her favorite animal was and he'd misheard her when she said "raccoons." She'd meant to correct him, but he seemed so taken with the idea that she loved baboons that she didn't want to disappoint him. He'd bought her the baboon for Christmas, joking about how long it had taken him to track one down—by then, of course, it was too late to speak up. Soon everybody was giving her baboon things. It became part of who she was, so much so that she convinced herself she really *did* love them, dressing up as one for Halloween and drawing them obsessively at school. She even had an imaginary friend: Oonie the Baboon. But it was all a mistake. If her father had thought she'd said "wombats," or "beluga whales," she'd be a completely different person.

She ended up telling Garrett this last part, about the baboons, and what did he do? Laughed, his mouth a strip mine of fillings.

Practically ran off the road. It was the first time she'd seen him look even slightly happy.

"What's so funny?" she said.

"It just makes perfect sense."

"Charlie thinks it's hilarious too," Cece lied, realizing only as the words left her mouth that she'd never told him about it. Why hadn't she? Well, he wouldn't have understood. He would have asked, very reasonably, why she hadn't just corrected her dad from the beginning. "Then my mom died, and going to med school became about, I don't know, this earth-shattering thing. Like I could make up for it or something. But of course, that's ridiculous. Why are you wincing?"

"Just that term. 'Earth-shattering.'"

"What about it?"

"Nothing."

"Nothing what?"

"It's just a . . . pet peeve."

"A pet *peeve*?"

"Sorry. Nothing to do with you. It's just that we're destroying the planet for real and no one seems to give a shit—and then something bad happens to one of *us*, a human being, and it's 'earth-shattering.'"

It was not her imagination: he was a major fucking asshole. How the fuck did Charlie tolerate him? Cece closed her eyes, doing some full yogic breathing—or whatever it was called when you were driving to Glacier with a sanctimonious asswipe instead of doing yoga. She just had to get through the next couple weeks. Prove her eternal love for Charlie—make sure the wedding was fun, lovely, free of surprises—by not calling his best friend in the world a prick. It was a kind of test. A challenge. Like one of those fairy-tale things, where the suitor has to kill the dragon to prove himself worthy.

When she opened her eyes, Garrett was watching her instead of the road. She forced herself to smile. This must not have been a complete success, because Garrett regarded her with mild concern.

"What is it you want to do then? With your life?"

"Good question," Cece mumbled. Also a strange one, as if your life were a tool that had only one function. (Someone had handed you this weird thing, your life, and now everyone kept asking—quite reasonably, perhaps—"So what are you going to do with *that*?") She knew what she didn't want to do with it. But what did she *want*? Well, she wanted to marry Charlie, but that wasn't a real answer—she wasn't so shallow, so *nineteenth century*, as to think that marriage was the mysterious function her life was designed for. It was merely a bonus feature: a lovely one, but not the reason she was put on earth. She'd hoped her love for Charlie might clarify things, help her figure out what to do with her life, but so far it had only confused it. She saw how people reacted to him—an ambitious young doctor, out saving lives—and it left her feeling more marooned than ever. Not just marooned, but occasionally a little bit *vexed*. Annoyed at Charlie through no fault of his own. She didn't want to be a doctor; but even more than that, she did not want to be "a doctor's wife."

She was sure she had something great to offer the world, something big and pure-hearted and indispensable. If only she could figure out what it was.

In the meantime, she was planning a wedding. A relief, really, to dodge the question of her future for a while. You might even call it an avoidance strategy. But why had she insisted on having it out *here*? Cece suspected it had to do with Charlie's family. With the Margolises. It was here, in this wonderful house, that she'd seen them together for the first time: Charlie and Mr. and Mrs. Margolis and his brothers. (His brothers! She was a little in love with his brothers.) They were everything she'd always wanted from a family: warm and jokey and unburdened by grief. They had Ping-Pong tournaments. They Hail Mary–ed sodas to each other. Random words—"colander," say, or "sticky bun"—

made them burst into hysterics. They had rituals no one could explain, like touching the roof of the car when they passed a tractor. They had Wednesday game nights, beloved second-rate movies that made them cry, a fridge so stuffed with food that opening it was a concussion hazard. A country unto themselves, with their own customs and traditions. (Cece especially loved the leader of this country, Mrs. Margolis.) Just being around them made Cece instantly happy, even delirious. It was like the click that Tennessee Williams talked about, when you've drunk enough that you begin to feel okay in the world. Something clicked for Cece in the Margolises' presence, made the strangeness and sorrow dissolve into a buzz of well-being. She got drunk on Charlie's family. And so she'd come to the place where she'd felt so at peace: this lake; this gabby clubhouse; this museum of happy summers.

"Well, what do you like to do with your time?" Garrett persisted. "When you're not planning weddings."

"Are you always this nosy?"

He shrugged. "Hard to say. I don't really talk to people."

"I like to read books," Cece said, because it was true. In college, she'd been happiest in the library, reading thousand-page monsters for her Golden Age of Russian Lit class. Not just reading them but discussing them with other people. Saying smart things about them and hearing smart things back. She'd taken every lit course she could fit into her schedule, and not only because her premed classes bored her to tears.

"What's your favorite novel?"

She thought of trying to impress him with something from left field: *Independent People*, say, or *We Have Always Lived in the Castle*. "*Anna Karenina*," she said finally.

Garrett smiled. "I knew it."

"No, you didn't," she said angrily. It wasn't enough that he'd ruined her favorite spot on earth; now he was trying to ruin her favorite novel. Probably he'd never even read it.

"Do you have a favorite scene?"

"Do *you*?" Cece said, calling his bluff.

"I asked you first."

"When Kitty gives birth and Levin expects to be, you know, madly in love with the baby. But then he sees it for the first time and is repulsed."

Garrett looked genuinely startled.

"I guess you didn't expect me to say that."

"No," he said. "Kitty and Levin, I got that. But I thought you might say the dinner party scene, when he asks her to marry him again. While they're playing secretary."

"Well, I love that scene too."

"But it's sentimental. They read each other's thoughts perfectly. It's not life."

"They're *both* life."

Garrett studied the road, seeming weirdly unsettled. She'd been trying to be provocative, choosing the birth, so it surprised her to realize the scene really *was* her favorite. (Or up there anyway.) Of course, Cece would never have admitted such a thing to Charlie. The idea that you might be disgusted by your own baby would be as alien to him as jumping off the Golden Gate Bridge—or finding a marriage proposal, enacted through a word game, anything but romantic. A bad taste entered her mouth, like the ghost of a burp.

"Oh god," she said. "Tell me you're not one of those down-with-marriage people."

Garrett shifted in his seat.

"You're officiating our wedding!"

He frowned. "Uh-huh. Well. That wasn't my idea."

"Mine either!" Cece said. "Why didn't you say no?"

"I don't know. It seemed so important to Charlie. He kept saying how much it would mean to him. I mean, he never asks for *anything*—he's always the one helping me out. It didn't seem polite to bring up my, um . . . philosophical objections."

Cece snorted. She was beginning to wonder, dismally, if the wedding would be a disaster. "And what are those?"

Garrett flipped his sun visor down. "I'm not sure I should tell you."

"Look, Charlie and I love each other. Our marriage isn't going to be derailed by one person's opinion." Especially a baggage handler in homemade shorts, she almost added. "Anyway, it's not like I don't know it will be hard sometimes. It's supposed to be an adventure, right?"

"'The only adventure open to the cowardly,'" Garrett mumbled.

"What sad lonely fuck said that?"

"Voltaire."

Cece laughed. "Didn't Voltaire, like, write dirty letters to his own niece?"

"Have you actually thought about what it will mean?" Garrett said. "Devoting your life to another person?"

"Of course," she said.

"How long do you think real attraction lasts, before the mystification wears off?"

"If you're talking about my attraction to Charlie, I can't imagine it ever wearing off."

"Everyone says that."

"In our case it's true," Cece fired back.

"Everyone says that too." He flipped his visor back up. "Is there something right now—a weird quirky habit of his—that you find endearing?"

"Well, sure," she said, playing along.

"What is it?"

"He shakes his sandwich before eating it. Between bites, I mean. Like he's weighing it in his hand."

"Three years from now, that's going to drive you up the wall. You'll see Charlie shaking his sandwich and be like, *Eat your fucking lunch already.*"

"You're wrong."

"And then, let's see, the babies will start coming, and you'll be too wiped out to do anything. You'll never be able to travel or see a movie or read a real book. I've seen it happen to my friends from college—*Charlie's* friends. You know how you'll spend most of your time on earth? Trying to get your kids to stop fighting. *Conflict mediation.* There's your great adventure for you. You'll be so bored inside from devoting your life to babysitting that you'll do something pointless, like remodel your kitchen. Just to distract you from your boredom. Maybe you'll remodel it over and over. And you'll have a big fat mortgage, you'll have to send your kids through college, you'll sacrifice Life at the altar of your children. It's the American dream."

Cece stared at Garrett. Why wasn't she more offended? Mostly she felt sorry for him. His "objections," such as they were, weren't even original. It was like he'd been preparing for an oral exam—possibly even hoarding quotations, the way a squirrel collects acorns.

"I'm guessing you weren't born this way," she said.

"What do you mean?"

"I mean, something must have happened to make you so anti-love."

Garrett looked at her in surprise. "I'm not anti-love. Just anti-marriage. Two completely different things. *Opposites,* in fact."

"Love and marriage are not opposites!"

"'Marriage is the tomb of love.'"

"Not more Voltaire," she said.

"Casanova, I think."

Cece rolled her eyes, though in truth this was the first thing he'd said that gave her pause. She had never thought about her love for Charlie this way: that there was something particular about *marriage*, the institution itself, that might destroy it. "I think we'd better find another officiant," she said.

Garrett, who'd been going eighty miles per hour, slowed up

on the gas, as if he were thinking about maybe turning around. "I'm an idiot. I shouldn't have told you all this."

"You're right," Cece said flatly.

"Hey. I'll say all the beautiful things, I promise. Marriage-is-beautiful things."

"But you'll be *lying*."

"I'll *want* it to be true," he said. "That's the important thing. I'm not about to sabotage my best friend's wedding."

He said this so sincerely, with such urgent tender feeling, that Cece had a mysterious reaction. A strange kind of disappointment. Not that she wanted him to sabotage the wedding, of course—just that she hadn't expected him to disown his convictions so easily.

Garrett kept his face to the road, one eye squinched up like a pirate's. There was a sadness about him that seemed almost disfiguring. She wanted to ask him about what had happened to him in college, about the death of his and Charlie's friend, about his mysterious troubles in San Francisco, but she was worried he'd dislike her for prying. Or worse: he'd tell her all about them. Anyway, it was there already in his face, like mineral locked inside a rock. It was not a bad face; in fact, it was kind of handsome, or maybe a better word for it was "striking," if you ignored the slight snowman-crookedness of his eyes and focused on the darker depths. Cece—so used to looking at Charlie, who was mineralogically all on the surface—had forgotten there were people who walked around like that, as if waiting for someone to smash them open.

They passed a roadside attraction advertising a LIVE GRIZZLY ENCOUNTER, which made Cece wonder what Garrett looked like naked. Not because she *wanted* to see him naked—dear god, no, she'd rather encounter a live grizzly—but because she remembered a story Charlie liked to tell about his college days, how he and Garrett and some equally stupid friends would get drunk sometimes and stage their own, as he called it, "roadside attraction." This involved stripping out of their clothes and posing like Greek statuary by the side of the highway, surprising drivers as they turned a bend and caught them in their headlights. Naked discus throwers, but with Frisbees. Charlie couldn't tell the story, even to Cece, without crying from laughter. The idea of Garrett taking part in such a thing seemed impossible; even picturing him with a Frisbee, fully clothed, was beyond her powers.

Garrett rolled down his window while they waited behind a string of cars to get into Glacier Park. Cece imagined asking him to play the Movie Game—or maybe Fortunately/Unfortunately, like she and Charlie did when they were stuck in traffic—but it was as hard to picture him doing this as it was to imagine him having fun in college. In front of them was an RV whose fender was plastered with bumper stickers: CHOOSE HAPPY; HAPPINESS IS A WARM TENT; HAPPINESS IS BEING IN MONTANA.

"Let's put them out of their happiness," Garrett said.

Cece stared at him.

"Why are you looking at me like that?" he said.

"It's just . . . I've never heard you make a joke before. That was even kind of funny."

"Thanks?"

"Charlie told me that," she said. "How funny you were."

"You're still looking at me."

"How did you get that little scar there? On your cheek?"

"Frostbite," he mumbled, in a way that precluded follow-up questions. She afflicted him with her gaze—or so it seemed. Unlike pretty much every other man on the planet, he did not like to be looked at. "Anyway, Montana has the second-highest suicide rate per capita in the nation."

"They're bumper stickers!" Cece said.

"What's your point?"

"No point! Just that you don't like marriage. Or happiness. You must be the most cynical person I've ever met."

He glanced at her, his eyebrows clamped into a vise. My god, was he hurt?

"I'm not cynical," he said earnestly. "I just don't trust people who advertise how happy they are. The happiness cult."

"I'm happy," she said, trying to lighten things up. "And you're somehow tolerating *me*."

"That's true." He smiled, or did his best impersonation of someone smiling. "Maybe you're not as happy as you look."

Inside the park, Garrett pulled over to the Lake McDonald Lodge so they could use the bathrooms, parking beside a van with a LEGALIZE JESUS magnet stuck to its door. When Cece emerged from the ladies' room, Garrett was nowhere to be found. She waited for him in the lobby, which was gargoyled with the heads of majestic beasts: moose, elk, bighorn sheep. She wasn't sure this set the right tone for a national park. While Cece waited for Garrett to emerge, a group of children with compasses dangling from their necks gathered in front of the fireplace. The children were dressed like British military commanders, in knee-high socks and khaki shorts. One of them blew into a pitch pipe, tentatively, and they broke into song. "O Everlasting Light." Their voices were beautiful, breathtaking, angelic as a church choir's. They beamed at the crowd of visitors, impressed by their own virtuosity. People stopped what they were doing and gathered to watch. *Brightest of all on earth that's bright / Come, shine away my sin.* Cece found herself thinking of her mother—always her mother!—of the musty, agonizing pews in the Episcopal church they went to when she was a girl. Still, she loved singing the hymns, mostly because her mother's voice was so beautiful; it seemed to come from somebody else, a different mother entirely, like a ventriloquist's trick. Cece knew nothing about this other mother except that God did something to her, made her shining and mysterious, which aroused Cece's jealousy. She pictured

Him in black orthopedic shoes and Bermuda shorts, like the old men they saw at the beach. She was sad, at age five, when her dad—much more of a believer than her mom was, despite the singing—snatched Cece from this secret mother and began sending her to Sunday school. Hearing the name, she'd thought it would be a school where they learned about Sunday. Instead, they'd learned about Adam and Eve and Noah's ark and the various things God did to his children who misbehaved. Sometimes Ms. Sissel, their teacher, would read to them from the actual Bible. Cece still remembered the second verse of Genesis, which had made little sense to her but struck some gong of terror in her heart. *And the earth was without form, and void, and darkness was upon the face of the deep.* She lay in bed at night, thinking about the Deep and its hideous face and wondering, too, what would have happened—where Cece herself would be—if God hadn't said "Let there be light." What if He'd simply forgotten? Or overslept? Or had laryngitis? After reading aloud, Ms. Sissel had asked them to draw Creation, the beginning of the world, and Cece had colored her piece of paper black.

Ms. Sissel hadn't liked this. Another time, she'd handed out a worksheet called "Words to Describe Yourself," and Cece had spent a long time, longer than anyone else, trying to figure out what to put down. Nothing that popped into her mind seemed right. If she said "fearless," she also meant "scared." If "joyful," then "gloomy" too. Whatever she thought of, the opposite seemed equally true. So Cece made up some words to describe herself: "blahphoric," "selfishless." When Ms. Sissel saw them, she seemed offended, angry, even—which surprised Cece—and threw the worksheet in the trash. So Cece wrote what everyone else wrote: "friendly," "adventurous," "helpful." It was the first time she realized people didn't really care who you were; in fact, they were happier when you lied about yourself.

Garrett emerged from the men's room at last but then seemed to have some trouble navigating past the gift shop. He froze under a sheep mount, staring at the identically dressed children assembled by the fireplace, their faces lifted in song. Cece watched him from across the lobby. Was she imagining it, or was he rooted in fright?

"Are you okay?" she asked after they were back on the road.

"Yeah," he said unconvincingly. "Why?"

"In the lodge you looked—I don't know."

Garrett blushed, staring at the windshield. He fiddled with the radio, though he'd told her earlier there wasn't reception in the park. They'd begun to climb now, looping east and leaving the river behind. "It's something that happens to me sometimes. Things start to look sort of, I don't know . . . *impossible*. I can't really explain it. People are the worst. It's like they don't belong. I'll see them standing on two legs, wearing these freaky lace-up things on their feet, and think: Who invited *them*?"

Cece laughed. "You don't think that about yourself?"

"That's just the feeling I get. I'm trying to describe it. You know how Levin feels disgusted by his own baby? Imagine if *everyone* made you feel that way. Like they're supposed to be related to you, right? But there's been a terrible mistake." He grimaced. "I just want to spray them with something, to reverse the error."

"Like what?"

He shrugged. "A can of something. Human Off! or whatever. Something to make them disappear." He glanced at her. "I don't actually want to kill people," he explained.

"That's good." She stared at the uneven legs of his shorts.

"Probably it was the animal heads in there. There's generally a trigger."

It occurred to Cece, for the first time, that he might be mentally ill. But something was happening to her. The hairs on her arms felt strange, astir, like filings under a magnet. It had begun when Garrett told her she wasn't as happy as she looked. They drove up the Going-to-the-Sun Road, which was so crowded with vehicles that Garrett could drive only about five miles per hour. This was the national park experience now, he told her: an endless clusterfuck. Most people didn't even bother to get out of their cars—or if they did, it was to pull over at a viewing area and snap a few pictures.

"I can see why they want to, though," Cece said, crouching down to see as much through the windshield as possible. The road had been blasted right out of the mountain and taken eleven years to build, which seemed like a hell of a lot of work, even for a road that went to the sun. Three people had died building it, Garrett explained; in places, they'd had to use so much dynamite that the crew wore socks over their boots to prevent sparks. She had the sense he was telling her all this to impress her—not with his knowledge but with his dullness. He was trying to sound as uncrazy as possible. Though he also seemed to genuinely love the place, hanging from the steering wheel to gawk at views he must have seen a hundred times before.

They passed a sign for something called the Weeping Wall. Just as the name suggested, it seemed to be in tears, water streaming down its face. A crowd of tourists was taking pictures. Towering above the wall, so high it looked like a painted backdrop, was an enormous saw-toothed ridge, as finely ribbed as the sail of a dinosaur.

"Zowie," Cece said. "Look at the size of those cliffs."

"That's the hike we're doing," Garrett joked.

"Charlie was right. You're hilarious."

"Should have seen this place when I was a kid," Garrett said. "Talk about zowie. There were a hundred and fifty glaciers."

"How many are there now?"

"Twenty-five, I think."

"God."

"Soon they'll have to change its name—Slush National Park—or doom it with tragic irony for the next thousand years."

Cece was sad about this—the wall, it dawned on her, was

weeping glacier tears—though honestly she couldn't imagine the place being any more glorious than it was. People might look at it and drop dead. OD on beauty. Peaks soared all around them, as if competing for God's attention; one of them, so big it gave you the feeling of an alien arrival, was wearing a necklace of clouds. A silver waterfall dangled beneath the clouds, fine and glittering and still as thread. At the bottom of the valley, far, far below them, the river was no more than a squiggle; a hawk wheeled back and forth, puny enough to trap in your fist. For a moment Cece was borne aloft, released, the demands of her life as small and distant as the river.

Then she started to feel dizzy, not borne aloft at all. Cece pinned her eyes to the road. She was a little scared of heights. Okay, more than a little. She tended to forget this in LA. The fear only popped up occasionally, typically on vacation—climbing the stairs of the Eiffel Tower, say, or soaring over a gulch in a chairlift—so she had a habit of forgetting it was there.

They got to Logan Pass and drove around searching for a space. After twenty minutes of sharking the lot, Cece felt the elation of the drive up melting away. It was hot in Garrett's pickup: the air-conditioning didn't work very well. After about the tenth trip around the parking lot, they lucked into a spot by the visitors' center, next to a Chevy Suburban the size of a house, inside of which a cage match appeared to have broken out. A boy, maybe five years old, was screaming at the top of his lungs, trying to yank something away from his older sister, who was yelling out the opposite window for her father. The mother sat in the passenger seat with her hands over her ears. Eventually, the father burst out of the bathroom as if from a starting gate: three hundred pounds maybe, and yet he sprinted at full tilt across the parking lot, the ice in his drink shaking like a maraca. The effect was mesmerizing. The kids stopped fighting and watched him through the window. At the car, the man flung open the door to the backseat and pulled the boy out with his free hand before sitting him on top of the roof. "SHUT UP! SHUT UP! SHUT UP!" the father yelled, practically in tears.

"Should we report him or something?" Cece asked after the family had trooped, tear-streaked, to the visitors' center, weirdly united by the scene they'd put on.

"Report what?" Garrett said, sitting beside her on the gate of the pickup to retie his hiking boots.

Cece stared at him. "That father!"

"I don't think you can report a father for having a bad day."

"'Bad day'? That guy was abusive!"

Garrett looked up from his boots. "You can't imagine ever losing your shit like that?"

"My god. *No.* Not like that."

"Ever?"

Cece stood up from the tailgate. "I can promise you I'll never scream 'Shut up!' in my child's face."

Garrett smiled.

"I won't," she said, annoyed.

"Want to bet?"

"Sure. A million dollars."

"A hundred," Garrett said, sticking his hand out. "Let's make it reasonable."

Cece took his hand and then released it almost immediately, in midshake. They had never touched before. His hand was slender, more girlish than she'd expected—a shock. She cleared her throat.

"Anyway, if I don't win, I would like you and Charlie to kill me."

"I hope you do win," he said seriously.

At the trailhead, Garrett led her onto a dirt path that wound through a meadow of purple daisies, billions of them, as if all the flowers on earth had flown there for a convention. Cece had a hard time believing her eyes. She'd heard the word "purple" all her life, had arrogantly presumed she knew what it meant, but clearly there'd been some kind of misunderstanding. She'd been a prisoner in a cave. Before long they were walking along the edge of a cliff, steep enough that you could see straight down to the road, all the miniature rental cars lined up like a row of candy buttons. A terrible thought chilled her scalp.

"Wait, is this the hike you pointed out from the road?"

Garrett nodded.

"You said you were joking!"

He looked at her curiously. "Why would I joke about that?"

Cece felt faint. Phantom hands materialized at her back, aching for a push. She did her best to ignore them. The trick was not to look down, to keep her eyes locked on the Nalgene bottles going *slish slosh slish* on Garrett's hips. He had on a kind of fanny pack that doubled as a holster for water bottles, like a cowboy who'd taken a wrong turn at the Alamo and ended up at Angkor Wat. When she got tired of staring at Garrett's hips, there were other things to distract her, alpine vistas and little splashing waterfalls and glacier lilies drooping obscenely in the sun, petals peeled back to expose their genitals. Bear grass—that's what Garrett called it—bobbled in the breeze. Each stalk of grass foamed with tiny flowers, exploding in a plume of white. Cece slipped her camera from her pocket to take a picture.

"Don't ruin it," Garrett said.

"I'm not going to *ruin* it."

"Photos make beautiful things uglier and more boring," he said. "And ugly things less ugly and more interesting."

Cece laughed. "Is that an aphorism?"

The path narrowed significantly, until they were edging along an actual precipice. It wasn't a trail so much as a bas-relief. Cece's knees went weak. A green rope had been eye-bolted to the rock. She grabbed on to it. The hands on her back were less ghostly now, seemed to be exerting palpable force. She inched along the cliff, trying to ignore the preschool wobble in her legs, clenching the rope as if it were a literal lifeline. A line of life. The back of her T-shirt, drenched with sweat, had turned to ice. The trail followed a bend in the cliff; she closed her eyes and inched around it as best she could, summoning years of expensive yoga coaching to silence the Voice of Doubt, to become as mindful as possible, but she was full of mind already, or at least the mental image of herself bouncing like a Barbie doll down to the road. Her mind was kind of the trouble.

When she opened her eyes again, she was staring at a mountain goat. It was white and woolly and blocking their way, eating some needlegrass growing along the fringe of the trail. One of the goat's horns had fractured at the root but hadn't fallen off completely, still dangling from its head. The broken horn hung rakishly over one eye.

"Wow," Garrett said. "That's one ugly goat."

Cece tried to smile.

"Even a mother couldn't love that goat," he said.

Garrett swung his waist pack off and unzipped the pocket to take out his camera. As he was doing this, Cece made the mistake of glancing down. The world seesawed, trying to dump her off the cliff of its own accord.

"Want to test my hypothesis?" he asked, holding out his camera.

She shook her head, clutching the rope with two hands.

"Hey, are you all right?"

"Make it move," Cece said quietly.

"I'll try. But this is his home. *We're* the wildlife to him."

"Please!" she said. "No fucking nature sermons."

Garrett looked at her in concern. He tried to shoo the goat away, doing a kind of plane-rescue thing with his arms, waving them in the air, but the ugly creature only continued to graze, its head bent to the ground. Flies buzzed around its broken horn. They were trapped. There was no way to get past—the trail was too narrow—and Cece didn't think she had it in her to turn around. The mountain goat inched closer to get at some lichen, causing a landslide of pebbles. Cece sat down on the trail, close to tears.

"This isn't a great place for a picnic," Garrett said.

"You think this is *fucking funny*? That goat almost killed us!"

"That goat did not almost kill us."

"It caused a landslide!"

"That was a pebble hitting some other pebbles." He took off his hat and peered valiantly past the ugly goat, which had flumped down on the trail as well. "Okay, here's what we're going to do."

"What?"

He paused. "Actually, I don't know. It's just what people say in situations like this. Why didn't you tell me you were so scared of heights?"

"Why didn't you tell me you were a fuckface?"

Garrett frowned. "You don't actually like me very much, do you?"

"No shit! I don't like you at all! I've been pretending for Charlie's sake."

"I'm that awful?"

"You told me my mother's death was a pet peeve!"

"I'm sorry," he said sincerely. He tugged his hat back on, then fiddled with his stupid water holster, tightening the strap until it cinched him like a girdle. Jesus, was he going to cry? "I don't know why I said that. There's something wrong with me."

"Ha! You think?"

"My father's dying too," he said.

"Boo-hoo! Who gives a shit!"

A breeze picked up, tickling Cece's armpit. She gripped the rope tightly, like someone on a runaway bus. She was hanging on for dear life. Garrett tried to get her to stand up, explaining that they could return the way they'd come, nice and easy, *Imagine you're on a big flat beach*, but her fingers wouldn't let go of the rope, even when he tried hoisting her up himself. They were like someone else's fingers, far stronger than her own. The goat looked at Cece and Garrett, as if they'd finally captured its interest. They were mounting a play for its entertainment. Eventually, Garrett sat down beside her.

"I'm going to kill that ugly goat!" Cece said.

"If you're going to kill something, it should probably be me."

"Okay," she said earnestly. She looked down at the tiny, sunbound cars—a grave error—and felt the trail pitch like a boat.

"Here, grab my hand instead of that rope," Garrett said. "We'll stand up together."

She refused, then refused again, and then—acknowledging that she had no other option but to let go of the rope, the sooner the better—refused once more. Finally, after the fuckface continued to badger her, sitting there on his fuckass and holding up his fuckhand for her to grab, Cece took a deep breath and dropped the rope and gripped him instead. They sat there for a minute, holding hands. Judging from the look on Garrett's face, she was squeezing hard. Was he bleeding? Probably it was just sweat. Patiently, Garrett knelt on the trail and then asked her to do the same—deep breaths, prayers to a God she didn't believe in—and then he got to his feet very slowly and pulled her up with him, supporting her so her legs wouldn't buckle, Cece clinging to him like a toddler. Garrett said something in a calm voice—she didn't catch a word of it, nor did she care—and then he very gradually and delicately transferred her weight to the ground, forcing her to trust her own feet.

Cece stood there panting. Garrett began to coax her in the direction they'd come from, away from the triumphant goat, leading her by the hand while she clutched the guide rope with the other, doing everything in her power not to look down. It was harrowing and then merely distressing and then kind of doably uncool. She was aging in reverse, gaining limberness with every step. By the time they reached the end of the guide rope, the trail widening into a slope gentle enough for flowers to grow on, Cece felt almost bipedal again.

She just about kissed the ground. How horizontal it was! For the first time in her life, it occurred to her that Flat Earthers might not be lunatics.

She was still holding on to Garrett's hand. Squeezing it, actually, just as hard. Of course, she would have held anyone's hand on that cliff: Idi Amin's or Jack the Ripper's.

Then something strange happened. Garrett relaxed his grip, trying to release her, but she continued to hold on to his hand. She didn't let go of it. Was she trying to hurt him? It had stopped being a fear thing, or maybe it was a different fear entirely, something impervious to rescue. His hand was thin and sweaty and full of hand parts. He quit trying to let go, squeezed hesitantly back. *Come closer*, her mother had said, as if some secret might be imparted to her. She was waiting, still; waiting and waiting. A ground squirrel peeped at them from a hole in the dirt. Cece let go of Garrett's hand, as if she'd been bitten.

Her hand ached. She was trembling. It felt like that: a bite.

She sniffed her fingers when Garrett wasn't looking. Why? They smelled like the rest of him: vaguely of food, like the ice at the bottom of a cooler. Garrett, blushing, stuffed his hand into his pocket. Perhaps he'd seen her from the corner of his eye.

They hiked back without speaking. One of those silences that dug itself deeper and deeper, each step like the pitch of a shovel. Cece trailed a few yards behind, tasting the dust from Garrett's boots. The water sloshed in his holster thing. She was thirsty. Totally parched. But the silence was too thick to breach. Anyway, he didn't seem interested in stopping to offer her a drink. And why would he be? She'd called him a fuckface. Even scoffed at the news that his father was dying. She'd started—now that she could walk again—to feel somewhat guilty.

Cece stopped, finally, waiting for Garrett to notice. She thought he might keep going without her, just slosh back to the parking lot on his own, but instead he slowed after a few steps and turned in her direction. He did not look insulted. He looked dazed, stricken, almost as if he were ill. He walked back to where she stood. A dragonfly was perched on the button of his cap, like a propeller. It had all happened before, or seemed to have, in precisely this way.

"Could I maybe get some water?" she asked.

He gazed at her, squinting in the sun. She might as well have spoken Bulgarian.

"Water?" she tried again.

"Yes!"

Cece took the bottle from his hand, careful to avoid his fingers. Raising it to her lips, she was distracted by some approaching hikers, an out-of-shape couple and their kids. The screaming family from the parking lot. The son was perched on the dad's shoulders, smiling like it was the greatest day of his life.

Garrett slipped out of the house while Cece was upstairs, knowing he'd drunk too much wine, that as soon as he got into his truck he would technically become a *drunk driver*, one of the least appealing things a drunk person could become—but he'd stayed too long already. He pulled his car keys from his pocket, almost dropping them on the porch; his hand felt heavier than usual, dense with the memory of Cece's grip.

She'd hardly said a word to him on the way back from Glacier, staring crossly out the window, still fuming, Garrett imagined, over "the death hike." Probably it was a relief: not to have to pretend to enjoy his company. He'd had to pee terribly but was afraid to disrupt Cece's silence. So he was surprised—after he'd dashed into the Margolises' to use the bathroom—when she asked if he wanted a drink. Charlie had sent her some wines to taste; no doubt he'd value Garrett's opinion. Also, drinking alone depressed her. Garrett knew nothing about wine but pretended to, noting that one called Half Past a Freckle had "some earth to it" but agreeing, emphatically, that something was missing. ("Wind? Fire?" he'd said, finally making her laugh.) They'd tried a Côtes du Rhône that made his mouth pucker, then something that tasted like a Jolly Rancher—all on an empty stomach. Garrett waited for Cece to kick him out, or at least to nudge him tactfully out the door, suspecting she was simply absolving a guilty conscience. And yet she poured them another wine, and another. Meanwhile, her hand—the same one that had squeezed his up at Glacier, refusing to let go—did not creep away in shame. It did not crawl under the porch to die. Garrett kept sneaking glances at it, as if it were a rare and bashful creature. At some point Charlie called, and Cece had taken the phone upstairs to talk to him.

Garrett climbed into the truck, steadying himself, then dropped his keys before he could get them into the ignition. He switched on the dome light and found them sitting in the thermos he'd parked in the cup holder. They were soaking in the coffee at the bottom. He tried to retrieve them with his fingers, from the heeltap of coffee, but the thermos was too narrow. He drank the cold coffee, extracting the keys with his teeth.

When he glanced up again, through the windshield, Cece had reappeared downstairs. She searched the living room, then stuck her head into the kitchen. How wonderful this was: to be looked for. He was invisible; he could spy on her from his vehicle. Then she opened the front door and went out to the porch and saw him, because of course he wasn't invisible. He was sitting in a truck with the dome light on. For no earthly reason, Cece pretended not to notice him and then picked up the binoculars from the table and pointed them in his direction, jumping back as though she'd seen a bear. A dopey thing, a joke, and yet all was lost. It was like a compass finding north: a happiness as pure and sudden as that. She even *looked* different: new and strange and somehow in focus. The wild shrub of hair; the slanty, jack-o'-lantern eyebrows; the dimple in her chin that looked like a poke. None of these features was particularly attractive—on their own, in fact, they were sort of funny-looking—but put together they were beautiful, heart-walloping, a face he'd missed his whole life without knowing it.

Cece, who'd lowered the binoculars, stared at him in concern. Garrett realized he still had the keys in his teeth. He dropped them in his lap, like a golden retriever. "I have to go!" he shouted, essentially to himself. He had some trouble hand-eyeing the key into its slot. Then he switched off the dome light and reversed down the driveway and backed into a corner of the fence, which made a sound like a firecracker. Garrett sped off in his truck, then slowed once he realized how fast he was going. The empty road seemed to dangle in front of him. Good god, what had he done? The moon, that lighthouse in the sky, guided him home. *I'm sorry*, he said to Charlie in his head, because he'd damaged something and couldn't remember feeling so happy.

FIVE

What a simple story this would be, if we paid no attention to Charlie. But here he is, unlatching the gate to the orchard. He looks a bit lost too—or at least misplaced. He's wearing a trucker's cap, something he does only in Montana, which, combined with his pale legs and designer eyeglasses, makes him look faintly ridiculous. He knows this, of course, but it doesn't bother him. He has on a tie-dye shirt, not because he likes the Grateful Dead but because he found one in the mothbally dresser in his room and it reminds him of being sixteen, the last time he felt this happy. He takes a deep breath of Montana air. Pine needles, a faint crawfish-y smell from the lake, a hint of sweetness from the cherries bubbling in the trees. Charlie spends so much time in the hospital that it's always the air he notices first, the smell of it moving through things. The opposite of death.

Second thing he notices is the boredom. Even now, with the wedding in less than a week, he isn't quite sure what to do with himself. Sometimes he finds himself standing around the yard in a kind of trance, waiting for god knows what, befuddled by the fact that he isn't even on call. In LA he often complained about not having enough time—but wasn't that the whole purpose of time? To *spend* it? Charlie liked having the currency to spend, even to waste, but he also felt lost and a bit freaked out by its abundance, as if he'd inherited something that wasn't his. He liked vacations—knew, rather, he was *supposed* to like them—but they seemed to expose him to pesky existential riddles, like why he was on earth to begin with.

Of course, he wasn't on vacation now. He was getting married. Surely there were a hundred things to do before Saturday. But Cece seemed to have taken care of them all. The caterer, the florist, the square dance music (band) and the later *unsquare* dance music (DJ). Even Charlie's bachelor party, on Wednesday night, was being arranged by other people.

He couldn't tell Cece this, but he didn't really care about the wedding at all. He wanted to *be married* to her—wanted this more than anything he'd ever wanted in his life. The actual wedding part seemed somehow beside the point. Honestly, he couldn't help feeling like all the material parts—the flowers, the gourmet taco station, the photographer and his interest in "visual storytelling"—cheapened their love a bit, made it seem like everyone else's.

Anyway, he was glad to have a task now, which was picking raspberries for Cece's extended family, most of whom were arriving at the Salish Inn this afternoon. Once in the orchard, Charlie made sure to chain the fence behind him in case a stealth deer tried to sneak in and devour all of his mother's vegetables. His mother despised deer for this reason and had been known to run into the orchard with her father's old shotgun, not to kill them of course but to scare them off with the noise. Some ancestral hillbilly possessed her when her kale was threatened.

He carried his bucket to the row of irrigated bushes and began plucking the berries from their thorny white middles, like bees from their stingers, plopping half of them in the bucket, the rest in his mouth. He'd done this every summer of his life and it never ceased to make him feel like a kid again, not just the Huck Finn–y pleasure of it but the lonely pioneer feeling of everyone else being in the house, his ears adjusting to the frequency of birds and breeze. Charlie looked up from his bucket and saw Mr. Petersdorf watching him from his backyard. Mr. Petersdorf, the Margolises' neighbor, was a retired patent lawyer ideologically opposed to the sharing of resources. He had an enormous collection of traffic cones, which he liked to arrange along the boundaries of his driveway and lake access to ensure that no one was encroaching on his property. How the hell he got so many orange cones, or why he needed to reconfigure them on a daily basis, no one in the Margolis family could figure out.

"Hello!" Charlie called.

Mr. Petersdorf nodded at him.

"I'm getting married on Saturday!" Charlie said.

His libertarian neighbor regarded him gravely. "I hope you've figured out parking. That's an awful small driveway you got. And the shoulder of the highway, you know, is illegal to park on, unless the standing vehicle is visible from two hundred feet—in *each* direction."

"It's a casual thing, like with square dancing. You're welcome to stop by."

"Blinkers don't work either. They attract motorists. There's something called 'the moth effect.' "

"Got it!" Charlie said cheerfully.

He went inside with his bucket of berries, wondering where everyone would park. Charlie decided not to mention his interaction with Mr. Petersdorf to Cece, who seemed stressed enough as it was. She was sitting in the rocking chair where she could reach the Ethernet cable, hunched over her laptop in his favorite sweater, a speckled Donegal thing with leather patches on the elbows. The only one he'd packed. Noisily, Charlie put down his bucket and kissed the top of his fiancée's head.

"We need welcome bags," Cece said without glancing up.

"Welcome bags?"

"Or baskets! Every one of these wedding sites, they all mention them."

"We talked about this months ago, didn't we? I thought welcome bags were 'cheesy.' "

"They are," she said, "but people are going to expect them! Montana-themed welcome bags. They came all this way."

Charlie laughed. "Like, filled with jars of huckleberry jam?"

"Mmmm. Maybe some bear bells."

He realized she was serious. The wedding was in six days. "Neither of us is even *from* Montana," he said. "We live in Los Feliz."

"Don't they make fir-scented candles?"

"Babe, why do our guests need a bag of touristy crap?"

"Because that's what you do!"

Perhaps encouraging her to come out here alone had been a bad idea. She'd gone hotel caretaker on him. Still, she was a beautiful lunatic: his eyes wandered to the miraculous dimple on her chin.

"Maybe we should just elope," he said, only half-joking.

Cece looked at him for the first time. She seemed startled. "What are you wearing?" she asked.

"A trucker's cap."

"You never wear caps."

"I does in Montana, ma'am," Charlie drawled. He tipped his hat to the lady.

She scowled at him, then reached up and removed the cap from his head.

"It's not you," she said quietly.

The screen door opened, and Charlie's brothers barged in, hefting plastic bags of groceries. (Paper was not an option in Salish, or at least the risk of asking for it outweighed the reward.) Behind them came his mother, beaming in triumph. She was in her element, basking in her good fortune, glancing from one son to the other like a dog back from the kennel. She was thrilled about the wedding, of course, hosting it by the lake was a dream, but Charlie couldn't help feeling that *this* was the main event for her. The Margolises under one roof. They'd gotten in yesterday, converging from various California locations—Jake from San Francisco, Bradley from UC Santa Cruz, his parents from LA— and she'd already made them play a buggy game of croquet and a half round of Trivial Pursuit.

Mrs. Margolis approached the couch and kissed Cece in the same spot Charlie had and then rested her hands on her shoulders, kneading them with her fingertips. She was always kissing Cece or whispering things in her ear. Sometimes Charlie felt like he was being cuckolded by his own mother.

"Where's your father?" she asked Charlie.

"Still in bed," he said. "He says he's gravely ill. Claims you refuse to take him to the hospital."

"Your father is a hypochondriac."

"He made me check him for appendicitis."

"What if he's actually dying or something?" Jake asked, kicking his sandals across the room. He had a belligerent relationship to shoes. He was the tallest of the three of them and wore size 14 sneakers.

"If I took him to the hospital every time he was dying," Charlie's mother explained, "we wouldn't ever be able to go on vacation."

Jake laughed at this, then pulled some OJ from a grocery bag and took a swig right from the container. Barefoot, he looked like a Maurice Sendak character. Bradley and Charlie swigged from the jug as well, as if they were sharing a flask. "Don't hog it, Woody," Jake said, because this was Montana, a picturesque Neverland where Charlie would forever be thirteen. He stepped off the plane as Dr. Charles Margolis but was soon being referred to as Woody, short for Morning Wood, because Jake had ripped the covers off him one morning when they were teenagers, seen him lying there at full mast in his Fruit of the Looms. The calumny, Charlie suspected, was closely aligned with love. (His brothers had met him at baggage claim yesterday, holding a sign that said DR. M. WOOD.)

His mother knew nothing of this, thought "Woody" was some cute term of endearment Jake had come up with, like "Slugger" or "Wiggleworm." Something you'd call your baby cousin. And in fact they looked more like cousins than brothers, spanning a middle range of complexions between their mother and their father, whose parents were Ashkenazi Jews. Charlie, the only one who'd stayed blond, had the fairest skin and freckled haphazardly when he went out in the sun. Jake, the oldest, burned himself to a crisp every summer before starting to tan. And then there was Bradley, who had the same build as his brothers—lean as a rock star, shoulders so broad and bony they looked like wings—but turned nut brown at the lake, the color of his hair. Girls ogled him in restaurants, followed him, like bumbling movie spies, around the supermarket. Mrs. Margolis almost didn't like seeing her sons together, as it made Jake and Charlie seem so much less handsome.

A window popped open behind her, startling her half to death—but of course no one was there. These casement windows! They were prone to opening for no reason, so water-damaged that half of them no longer latched.

"Dagfinn's up," Jake said.

"Who's Dagfinn?" Cece asked, taking the bait.

"Our great-grandfather. Or rather, his ghost. I'm surprised you haven't met him yet."

"Don't listen to them," Charlie said. "There are no ghosts in this house."

Jake plopped down beside Cece on the couch. "Don't worry, sis. We'll protect you. Even if Woody refuses to."

"It's the least we can do," Bradley said. "Given your sacrifice."

"Sacrifice?" Cece said.

"We never imagined anyone would marry him. Maybe someone diseased?"

"Or physically deformed?"

"Or with hair all over her face! Like one of those wolf babies."

"Or an actual baby."

"No offense," Bradley clarified.

"I feel like we can confide in you like this," Jake said, throwing his arm around her. "Now that you're officially a Margolis."

Ordinarily Cece would have played along—she loved kidding around with Charlie's brothers—but it seemed to Charlie that she looked weirdly flustered. More than flustered: on edge. Charlie couldn't wait for the wedding to be over so she could return to herself again. He carried a bag of groceries into the kitchen, plopping it on the counter beneath the picture of his grandparents in front of the old boathouse, long since torn down. The house had been his grandparents', and before that his great-grandfather's, who'd emigrated from Norway and lived briefly in a packing crate before making enough money as a dry goods purveyor to build a humble vacation home on Salish Lake. He'd named it after the wild yellow bells growing behind the house. How astonished he'd be to see it now! Each generation had expanded the house to fit their needs, building outward from both floors, adding more and more petals. And now Charlie was getting married, set to continue this expansion—this labor of love—with kids of his own.

He straightened the picture, which had been knocked askew on the wall. In the middle of it, Charlie's grandfather dandled his mother on one knee, gazing down at her as if she were the Second Coming. His grandmother, too, seemed utterly besotted, though Charlie knew from his mom that they'd briefly disowned her when she got engaged to his father. They'd come around eventually—or at least devised a strategy of "don't ask, don't tell." Simply by ignoring it completely, they'd decided to treat his father's Jewishness like a toxin they could extract, the way sunflowers are said to absorb radioactive metals. They paid for the wedding; treated him like a family friend, if not precisely a son; were loving, generous, toddler-smitten grandparents. That their grandchildren had any Jewish blood in them never came up. Why would it? Charlie's dad was a Reform Jew, not overly observant, though it was important to him that the boys go to Hebrew school twice a week so they could get bar mitzvahed. There was a menorah every year, but also a Christmas tree. When Charlie's parents decided to send Bradley to the JCC for preschool, his grandmother made remarks about the Shabbat sing-alongs, how they were teaching him to dislike her cooking. It was a joke and not a joke. Even now, long widowed and too sick to travel, she sometimes complained about "the Heebs" in her nursing home, as if completely forgetting her own grandchildren—not to mention her son-in-law—identified as Jewish.

Charlie and his brothers put away the groceries, refusing to let their mother help. This sounded generous but was really a subtle form of torture. Out of perversity, Jake stuck the Grape-Nuts in the snack cupboard instead of on the cereal shelf. Charlie's mother suffered in silence. "Oh, don't be a crumbum!" his mother said when Jake snatched some deli meat from her hand, insisting she relax. Her sons laughed with delight. It wasn't really a reunion until she'd called someone a crumbum.

"Cece," Jake said when they'd finished, "has Mom called you a crumbum yet?"

"I don't think so."

"Not even a pain in the wazoo?"

Cece shook her head, as if this were a serious question and she'd failed somehow as a daughter-in-law. Charlie had the exotic feeling of being more fun than his fiancée. From his parents' room upstairs came the thudding of feet, then the clunk of the toilet seat in the bathroom. They all looked at the ceiling. Bradley, who was listening to his iPod, took out an earbud. The sound of retching was simulcast through the air vent.

Cece gripped Charlie's arm. "Tell me it's not this super-contagious stomach thing you were talking about."

"What stomach thing?" Jake asked.

"Norovirus," Charlie said. "A contagious gastroenteritis. It's going around."

"Don't tell Dad that. He'll want a blood transfusion."

"I'm sure it's food poisoning," Charlie said confidently, though he wasn't a hundred percent sure. "Dad said it himself—that his shrimp fajitas tasted funny."

"Can we, like, call the restaurant?"

"We could. They might deny it." Charlie shrugged. "The only way to know for sure is to get a stool sample and have it tested."

"Not it," Bradley said, putting his earbud back in.

Cece stared at Charlie, clutching his trucker cap with two hands. "Hey," Charlie said. He squatted in front of Cece. "My dad's sick. So what? Everything will be fine."

"You always say that."

"What do you want to do," he joked, "call off the wedding?"

His fiancée gave him a look of such distress and bewilderment that he feared she'd taken him seriously. She hadn't, though, because she managed a smile. A strange, limp, puppet-y smile, but a thing of beauty nonetheless. How he'd missed her those three weeks of living alone! In LA, doing his rounds in the cardiac care unit, he'd conceived a vision of her that was impossible to live up to, according her a gorgeousness that did full justice to his love. Sometimes it was all that kept him from having a nervous breakdown. The night before his flight, he'd faced what the team called a Full Monty, a heart so ravaged from hypertension that it was splashing blood all over the operating room. Everyone in the OR was dripping wet, like a Monty Python sketch. Just to keep the guy from flatlining, they'd had to pump *forty times* the normal units of blood into his veins. Even after the surgeon put in an LVAD, the stuff was filling the guy like a water balloon, finding any exit it could. At one point blood began spraying out of the end of his penis. Charlie had had to do an emergency cautery. Changing his bloody scrubs afterward, he thought of Cece's face, trying to hose down his mind by picturing her beauty.

As always, then, when she'd picked him up from the airport yesterday, there was the slight disappointment of seeing her in the flesh: she was not Ms. Universe, and her breath when they kissed was sort of bad—mushroomy in a familiar way he'd forgotten about—and she even had a bit of a strange thing going on with her teeth, which looked occasionally when she smiled like they were too big for her mouth, like those candy teeth you wear on Halloween. But there was also a poignancy to her imperfections and to the fact that Charlie's love for her had embellished her beauty, or at least transformed her prettiness into something as rare as his feelings for her. He was head over heels. They were about to spend the rest of their lives together.

So why, driving home from the airport, had they struggled a bit to make conversation? They'd kissed, yes, and had said *I missed you* to each other, but then a murky drizzle of embarrassment seemed to descend upon them, as if they had to live up to the momentousness of the occasion. For the first time in his life, Charlie felt a brush of terror that everything tethering him to the world—everything he believed in and held dearly, including his love for Cece—was as flimsy as a cobweb. What did his life even mean, if their intimacy could be destroyed so easily?

They'd had sex last night—quietly, uninventively, with his family in the house—but they were shy about whispering dirty things and didn't talk about it afterward like they usually did. (He'd felt closer to her, strangely, on the phone.) Charlie fell asleep with his hand inside her hair, as always, but woke up in the middle of the night to discover Cece gone. He switched on the light. On her bedside table, open like a hymnal, was a stupid novelty book that had been at the house ever since Charlie could remember and that he used to pore over as a kid. *The Bathroom Trivia Book.* She'd been reading it before bed.

Jellyfish sometimes evaporate, the book claimed, without explanation.

Charlie found her sitting on the dock, staring at the sky and smelling like weed. She seemed to be smoking more than she used to, which he wasn't crazy about and which contributed to his dangling-cobweb feeling. (He couldn't imagine wanting to feel better—*higher*—than she already made him.) It was late enough that there was no music trampolining off the lake, only the splash of waves slurping the dock. A shooting star whistled across the sky. When he asked her what she was doing, she claimed she was thinking about Cinque Terre, where they were going on their honeymoon. She was worried about the hiking they'd planned. Were there mountain goats in Italy? Charlie laughed, because she was stoned and talking crazy. Without a word, she'd stood up and led him back to the house and did various things to him she'd never done before, things that he would have been embarrassed to ask for, begging him to do things in return he hadn't known she'd wanted. She no longer seemed to care about waking up his parents. It had been incredible, but also like fucking a stranger.

The doorbell rang now; Charlie stood to get it, hoping it was Garrett. He'd left him two voicemails since getting to Salish, but his old friend hadn't returned his calls. This was troubling, given that Garrett was supposed to officiate the wedding. Troubling, too, in light of what Cece had reported: that Garrett had come by a couple times and then abruptly disappeared. She hadn't seemed upset by this one way or another, presumably because she had enough weed. Charlie didn't blame her for not making more of an effort; he knew Garrett wasn't the most *charismatic* guy in the world. He had a way of depressing people. (Okay: of making them want to hide under their beds.) Still, Charlie had hoped Cece and Garrett would hit it off a bit, the way you hoped old friends from different phases of your life would get along and make it seem like the moon, each phase congruous with the next.

The truth was, too, Charlie felt guilty for not being there for Garrett during the difficulties he'd had in San Francisco. His hospitalization. It had been a couple weeks before Step 2 boards—Charlie's fourth year of med school—and he'd been too overwhelmed to drop everything and fly out there. This was why he'd had the bravely foolish idea of asking Garrett to officiate the wedding, why he'd urged his troubled friend to visit Cece.

Charlie answered the door, disappointed to find a stranger in a safari vest, a half-smoked cigarette dangling from his mouth. The wedding photographer. He wanted to scout for locations and get to know the venue before "the big day." Cece joined Charlie at the door, and they led the lumbering man—who looked, with his mournful face and safari vest, more like a war photographer—toward the boatshed lawn, where the ceremony was going to be. It was a hot day, the buzz of cicadas throbbing in the trees. The photographer glanced around as he walked, as if searching for something. He seemed unimpressed. Charlie began to size up the property, viewing it through his eyes.

"What happened to that fence post?" Charlie asked, opening the gate to the road. "Was it always too short like that?"

Cece glanced at him. "Your friend the baggage handler. He backed into it with his truck."

Charlie laughed. "Classic Garrett! You didn't tell me he'd done that."

"I thought I had."

"He fixed it himself?"

"I guess so," Cece said, unconcerned.

"And now he's too embarrassed to call me back," Charlie said, feeling relieved. It was just like Garrett to let some stupid mishap get in the way of their friendship. He blew things so out of proportion.

Down by the water, the photographer made them stand in various spots—grass, beach, perched on the bow of the Crestliner—looking for a suitable backdrop. He seemed less interested in Cece and Charlie than in the light itself, pointing his camera at the sky and then checking its readings, cigarette bouncing in his mouth. Charlie was thinking about the man's heart. A vocational side effect. He couldn't look at a smoker without imagining the astonishing time bomb inside his chest, collecting and pumping blood at the same time, its tiny doors opening and shutting with the crack timing of a Broadway farce. How could anyone treat it with such disrespect?

"You're not going to smoke during the wedding, are you?" Cece asked.

"Why?" the photographer said. "You pregnant or something?"

"No!"

"No skin off my teeth if you were. Believe me, I've seen it all. Do this long enough and you get some pretty good stories. Once I saw an expectant bride snort a bump of cocaine. Poor girl was uglier than a barber's cat." He ushered Cece and Charlie into the rosebushes. "Also shot a nude wedding once—some hippies like you out in Livingston."

"Oh," Charlie said, glancing down at his tie-dye. "Well, we're having welcome bags."

"That's a baldie up there," the man said, ignoring him.

Charlie peered in the direction his camera was pointing. Sure enough, an enormous bird was circling the lake, its wings pinned vertically against the sky. Its tail, white against the blue, looked like a jet of smoke.

"What's he doing? Riding the thermals?"

"Hunting, actually," the photographer said.

Cece stepped out of the rose brambles. "Oh my god," she said, squinting at the dying pine that used to shade the beach.

There was a nest up there, at the top of the tree. A mother and, what? Two chicks? Charlie was familiar with ospreys—they were the dogs, the construction trucks, of his toddlerhood. The bald eagle banked suddenly and came swooping toward the nest, wings caped back in a V, swift as a projectile, as if it might miss the tree entirely and splash into the lake. But it didn't. It was right on target, legs thrust forward like a baseball player sliding into base. The mother osprey watched it from her nest, seemingly unconcerned, then shot *chereek*ing from her perch at the last second and flew straight at the plunging bird's talons and fought with it in midair, pecking and flapping her wings, emitting a strange sound like a teakettle, an awful whistling scream, until the eagle gave up and retreated to a nearby branch, its beady eyes fixed on the nest. Charlie asked the photographer if it would attack again.

"They're determined predators," he said. "I know that much."

Cece grabbed his sleeve. "We need to do something!"

"Like what?" Charlie said.

"Scare it away from the nest!"

She said this so fervently—with such *anguish*—that he agreed. Charlie jogged across the lawn to the boatshed, hardly aware of what he was doing. Some squirrels had wintered in the shed and it was full of acorns, which crunched underfoot. Bushwhacking through some fly rods in the corner, he found his grandfather's old bird gun, the one his mother used to scare away deer from the garden. He took the gun out of its case and grabbed a shell from the leather ammo pouch at his feet. Charlie had shot skeet with his grandpa a few times as a kid and knew how to fire a shotgun, or at least a twenty-gauge break-action, or at least a something-gauge something—he couldn't recall.

When he emerged from the shed, he had the shotgun in his hands, locked and loaded, though the chamber was rusty enough he wasn't sure it would work. He rushed down to the end of the dock, as close as he could get to the eagle's perch; he got a good cheek weld on the stock and closed his eyes and fired the gun straight into the air, the recoil kicking him so hard he almost fell. The sound of it cracked across the lake. When Charlie opened his eyes again, the bald eagle was gone from its perch, flying southward over some fishermen cowering in their rowboat. The patrons at the Lazy Bear, whose patio was down shore from the dock, had stood up from their tables and were staring in Charlie's direction. He waved at them. They didn't wave back.

"I'm not dangerous!" he called to them.

"The fuck are you aiming at?" one of them shouted.

"Nothing! I had my eyes closed!" Charlie squeezed his eyes shut and aimed at the sky, demonstrating.

"Put that thing down!" the guy said, scrambling behind his table. The wedding photographer, crouched between some hydrangeas, was snapping pictures of Charlie with the gun.

"Is this for the *wedding album*?" Charlie's mother asked, alarmed. She'd run down to the dock, followed by Bradley and Jake, naked except for a towel around his waist.

"I always thought it was Bradley who'd have the shotgun wedding."

"He saved an osprey chick's life!" Cece said.

They all squinted at the nest. Impressively, the mother osprey had remained with her young, perched on one edge of it like a statue.

"Why are you looking at me like that?" Charlie asked Cece. She was beaming at him.

"I don't know. You're just, like . . . a man of action."

She grinned stupidly, lopsidedly, in that way that made Charlie feel like he'd done something remarkable just by being born—the first time since his arrival that she'd looked at him this way. Cece hugged him, which hurt the new bruise on his shoulder. Charlie didn't really give a shit about baby birds, and in fact often groused about people who cared more about saving African elephants than members of their own species languishing in underfunded hospitals right down the street—but he couldn't help it. That he could draw such delirious fulfillment from pleasing a single person, a woman with occasionally bad breath, amazed him.

They watched for a while to make sure the eagle wouldn't come back, then Charlie returned the shotgun to the shed and they all went up to the main lawn of the house. The photographer rumbled off on his motorcycle just as a black-and-white

SUV with the word SHERIFF on it crunched up the driveway. There had been a report of a gun going off at the lake. Mr. Petersdorf, no doubt. Charlie, too pleased with himself to care, did his best to explain what had happened.

"Let me get this straight," said the sheriff, who was considerably less pleased than Charlie and wore a cap with a star silkscreened on it. A gray ponytail spouted from the back of her cap. Smiling did not appear to be high on her list of job requirements. "You were shooting at an osprey?"

"Actually, it was a bald eagle," Charlie explained. "I was trying to save the osprey's family."

The sheriff stared at him. "A bald eagle?"

"Well, not *at it* or anything. I was just trying to scare it."

"Are you familiar with the Bald and Golden Eagle Protection Act?"

"No, ma'am."

"It prohibits the hunting, catching, or *disturbing* of a bald eagle."

"That eagle was already disturbed," Cece said.

"I could arrest you right now," the sheriff said. "You could spend a year in prison."

"I'm getting married on Saturday," Charlie said.

"You could also face a hundred-thousand-dollar fine."

"It's my fault," Cece said valiantly. "I told him to disturb the eagle."

The sheriff looked at her. "And where are you two from?"

"Los Angeles."

The sheriff brightened. This seemed to clarify the situation in a way that was immensely helpful to her. She walked back to her truck and made a call on her radio. While they waited, Cece put her arm around Charlie's waist, squeezing him so hard his ribs hurt. She did this sometimes, as if she were trying to play him like a bagpipe. It was a kind of joke—though in this case, Cece was hardly aware she was squeezing him. She'd forgotten he could make her feel this way: as if she were the luckiest person on earth. Something—an acorn?—pachinkoed down the roof of the porch.

"She's just trying to spook us. She's not even talking to anyone! Look."

"How do you know?" Charlie asked.

"Just do," Cece said, and she was right. The sheriff, an abysmal actor, kept glancing out the window to see if they were scared. After giving them a warning, she started her truck and backed down the driveway, past the mismatched fence post Cece had watched Garrett pound into the ground. Cece pictured him in his tool belt, the boyish pride on his face when he'd searched the windows of the house for her approval. Cece had ducked down, pretending she wasn't home. She was not proud of this, or of continuing to hide when Garrett rang the doorbell. This was a week ago, the last time she'd seen him in person—not that she was keeping track. (There had been a cameo in her dreams, a disturbing one, in which he was wearing a prison cap.)

Cece and Charlie headed up to the house. A cloud of no-see-ums had formed at the base of the steps. They hovered in place, frantic as molecules. Charlie jogged through the luminous curtain of bugs, which distorted her view of him. How strange he looked! Like a mirage. "Come on!" he said from the porch, laughing. Cece followed him up the stairs, bugs fizzing in her nose, a wild feeling inside of her.

SIX

1.

Cece unbuttoned her shirt. It was like she was letting something out of it, a bird or a snake, she did it so carefully. Garrett could see the trompe l'oeil of a bikini where her skin wasn't tan, could smell the fermented-juice smell of the lake, but it was as if he was experiencing these things indirectly, through the derangement of his happiness. He did not know he could be happy like this. They were on a beach of polished stones. He stepped toward Cece and his heart sloshed, spilling its sides. Until this moment, it had been an empty thing. He'd been window-shopping at the store of life. She smiled at him, in that lopsided way, and kissed Garrett on the mouth.

He woke up in his bed, feeling a loss that made him gasp. Dark outside, or almost dark: the edges of his windows, where the blinds let in light, were blue. Garrett touched himself, an act of despair. Any brief pleasure he felt was immediately negated by the mess he made of his boxers. Was there anything in the world as wretched as a man coming on himself? It was the opposite of praying. Garrett wormed out of his boxers and walked them to his laundry basket.

He glanced at the clock on his dresser. Eight sixteen p.m. He was late to Charlie's bachelor party. Charlie, his best friend. *Only* friend, at this point, besides his father. Garrett had been so exhausted after work—he'd been up till three a.m. the night before, his head filled with visions of Charlie's fiancée—that he'd lain down to rest and must have fallen asleep.

Garrett opened the blinds. Despite the complex's name—Elm Creek Apartments—there were no creeks nearby or anything resembling an elm. Instead there was a view of some abandoned train cars, going slowly to rust. Droughty weeds grew in the stretches of track and around the rusted couplers of the train cars. It was the sort of view that would make for a quaintly evocative photo in a San Francisco art gallery but that in real life was depressing as shit. Someone had had the bright idea of paving a bike path in front of the abandoned railroad tracks, so that occasionally Garrett would look up from his dinner and see someone zipping by his window on Rollerblades, peering in at him as if at an animal in the zoo.

He retreated to the bathroom, remembering how giddy he'd felt after that day at Glacier: tasting wines with Cece, watching her face light up when she'd seen him sitting in his truck. How she'd put the binoculars to her face and jumped back in surprise. He'd driven home with the windows down, his heart filling like a sail, singing along to some atrocious song on the radio. "Rock You Like a Hurricane." The memory of her hand gripping his, refusing to let go even after he'd released it, squeezing for so long it became almost *verbal*, a silent confession, like a note being passed under the desk—seconds? years? it was impossible to tell—more intimate, somehow, than a kiss. Had he lost his fucking mind? Had he thought, somehow, the wedding wouldn't happen? That Cece would . . . what? Run away with him? *Charlie's best friend?* It wasn't like he'd forgotten about the wedding. Just that it no longer seemed real to him—or if it seemed real, it was mysteriously irrelevant.

He splashed his face with cold water and watched it drip from his chin. Of course, he'd invented it all: Cece's desire for his company, her reluctance to see him go that night. She hadn't held on to his hand after he'd escorted her from the cliff. He'd imagined this too. He might as well have been a guide dog. In fact, she'd called him a fuckface. How idiotic could he be? She was furious at him for dragging her up there. When he'd come back to fix the Margolises' fence, she'd made a point of not being home—or pretending not to be, since her car was sitting in the driveway.

She'd felt sorry for him—who wouldn't?—but could barely stomach talking to him.

Garrett studied his hair in the mirror, the way you could see through to the scalp when he bowed his head. In a few years there'd be little left. The mole on the side of his chin, too, was getting molier. Not to mention the frostbite scar on his cheek, which she couldn't help pointing out. It turned white in winter, like a ptarmigan.

No doubt he disgusted her. He was like that goat they'd seen on the trail. Why else would she have sniffed her fingers?

Driving to the Margolises' house, Garrett kept his eyes on a logging truck stacked with cedar trunks, which stuck out the back like unsharpened pencils. He had no desire to go to a bachelor party, Charlie's or anybody else's, but he knew from past experience that reneging on the basic requirements of friendship was a slippery slope. It's why he had only one friend left to begin with. Now that Garrett had survived his own misery, he felt a clammy airsick foreboding that he recognized as guilt. Not just for falling *in happiness* with Charlie's fiancée—he refused to call it "love"; it couldn't be love; he wasn't a monster—but for being such a shit friend. Charlie had called him how many times since flying in? Six? Garrett hadn't even managed to listen to the voicemails, perhaps because he'd worried Charlie might become real again. He'd forgotten, for a brief period, that Charles Isaac Margolis existed. But he did exist; he did; Garrett was driving to his house, suddenly petrified of seeing him in person.

And it wasn't just Charlie he feared. The whole gang would be there, everyone he'd lived with at Middlebury. Garrett had avoided them, more or less successfully, since college. He couldn't bear to talk about Elias—or worse, watch them dance around the subject, pretending their friend had never existed.

Garrett had to keep himself from veering into the parked cars in the driveway, so accustomed was he to pulling right up to the door. He parked on the side of the road instead, listening to the tangle of drunken voices on the porch. The house blazed with light. What had he been thinking? A party? Garrett felt a twirl of anger, as if the people on the porch had no right to be there—as if, in fact, they'd stolen something precious from him. His time alone with Cece seemed as distant, as improbable, as his dream.

How strange it was to walk up the steps of the porch, where she'd stared at him that night through binoculars. The same ones now resting on the railing.

"You look like hell," Brig Atherton said fondly after locking Garrett in a hug. He was wearing an enormous cowboy hat, as if he'd ridden in a cattle drive from New York City. Brig did something with rich people's money, helping them come up with "risk management strategies." He had an apartment on the Upper West Side. This was a guy who'd occasionally shat his pants from drunkenness in college. "What? Do they keep those airline counters open all night?"

"I'm a ramp agent," Garrett said.

"I thought you worked behind the counter, taking tickets."

"Nope."

Brig took off his hat. "So you're like one of those guys on the runway? Holding the sticks?"

"Wands. Yeah."

"Cool," he said unconvincingly.

Garrett appreciated, at least, that he'd asked. The other old acquaintances he'd run into who knew something about his life had been reluctant to even ask about it, assuming he'd be embarrassed. Brig, however, was too drunk to care. He offered Garrett a cup of beer. Garrett accepted it. Marcus Porter offered him one too, which he was forced to accept as well. Johnny Hyong—

navigating the porch in a deliberate way, as if it were the deck of a boat—hugged him vigorously, though with both hands full Garrett could only stand there like a robot. His old friends laughed. Unlike Garrett, they all had wives and families and fully functional stoves that weren't portable electric burners salvaged from Goodwill. Somehow this had not prevented them from aging poorly. Johnny's hairline was faring worse than Garrett's and had shrunk to a landing strip on top, as if it had been bikini-waxed. Brig had a potbelly and the nascent mudslide of a double chin, which he'd failed to disguise under a beard. Marcus, an athlete in college, was as trim as ever—though he currently walked like someone's grandpa, hobbling to the keg for another beer. A torn meniscus, he explained.

"You seemed fine last night at the Lazy Bear," Brig said, "talking to those female river guides."

"Ask Brig about his hat," Marcus said.

"What's with the hat?" Garrett asked.

"I won it in a pool game."

" 'Won,' in this case, means 'lost,' " said Johnny.

"I didn't say I won the *game*," Brig said. "Just the hat. Some rancher dude gave it to me."

"The term is 'dude rancher,' " Marcus said.

" 'Gave,' in this case, means 'left it on the table while he went to the bathroom,' " Johnny explained.

Garrett couldn't help relaxing somewhat, remembering how much fun he used to have with his old housemates. They'd played in a band together at the Mill, Beastly Baby, which was mostly an excuse to get drunk and come up with dopey cock-rock riffs to crack each other up. (Their best song, "Katzenjammer Morning," was only fractionally better than their worst, "Poststructuralist Jockstrap.") They'd skied together at the ancient resort near campus, shouting at each other from the wooden bouncy chairs of its lift and forcing Brig and Marcus, both beginners, down expert runs. They were smart enough not to have to study very hard and generally regarded life as a thing impossible to fuck up, like some foolproof joke. When it turned out not to be a joke—turned out, in fact, to be unsuitably tragic—Garrett's friends adjusted to this new unsuitable life and did what they could to suit *it*. After all, it wasn't that difficult. You just did what people expected of you, fueled by the fear of what would happen if you didn't. You graduated from college, then went to med school or found an internship in the right company, and the rest just sort of scripted itself.

What had surprised Garrett was how easy it was *not* to follow the script. To blue-pencil yourself from it completely. That fear and happiness might have something in common.

Now, double-fisted, Garrett felt a stirring of warmth toward these old friends he barely knew anymore. A comforting pity too. They were like children, children who had children. He asked them where Charlie was.

"Good question," Marcus said. "I think he smoked too much kush."

Charlie's brothers emerged from the house, wearing matching T-shirts with vintage woodie wagons on them.

"Hey, where's the man of the hour?" Brig asked. Charlie's brothers shrugged in unison. Garrett barely recognized them. He'd spent a Thanksgiving at the Margolises' in college when Bradley was still playing with light sabers; now the onetime aspiring Jedi accepted a pipe from Johnny's hand and took a supersized hit. The smoke, when he eventually exhaled, was ectoplasmic. Garrett tried to give his extra beer to Jake, who declined the offer.

"I'm sticking to Tums right now," Jake said, touching his stomach.

They all stared at him.

"It's not *that*! I've got an acid reflux thing. Acts up when I'm drinking."

"Thank god," Marcus said.

"Anyway, I avoided Dad like the plague—Mom was the one

in the trenches." Jake looked at his brother. "Isn't that what Woody said? It only spreads through direct contact."

"Fecal-oral route," Bradley said, nodding. "Though infected particles can end up on doorknobs. Oh, and toilet plumes? He mentioned that too. Those are plumes from the toilet."

Brig, who'd ended up with the pipe, examined the mouthpiece.

"You guys all lived together at Middlebury?" Jake asked, changing the subject.

"Nauseating, isn't it?" Marcus said. "Like a college catalog."

"Just not Middlebury's," Johnny said.

"We had to lure Marcus away from the tennis team."

"They warned me I'd be the only Black person living at the Mill."

Brig took a hit and smogged the porch with smoke. "Just like you're currently the only Black person in Montana."

"That cannot be true."

"If you spend more than two weeks here you turn white. It's the water. Even your shit comes out white."

Johnny took the pipe from Brig. "Actually, I saw a Korean kid at the IGA today."

"Probably adopted."

"*Definitely* adopted. Dad's name was Tanner."

"Or they stole it."

"The mother kept looking at me," Johnny said, "as if I was the birth father come to claim it."

"I wouldn't be surprised," Brig said. "Did she have a fanny pack?" This was a joke, referring to a famous hookup of Johnny's who'd apparently come to a party at the Mill wearing a fanny pack. It only occurred to Garrett now, ten years later, that the accessory might have been *functional*: contained something vital to her well-being, like insulin pens. "The important thing is that everybody's here."

"Well, almost everybody," Marcus said.

The revelers went quiet. Brig flashed Marcus a dirty look, one Garrett wasn't supposed to see, then stared into his cup. Everyone, in fact, seemed abundantly interested in their beers. Garrett waited for the sickening snowstorm to begin. Had he really believed he could do this? Consort with human beings, old friends? His heart was a haunted doll living in a box. One of the windows of the house popped open, suddenly, of its own accord. The men on the porch stared at it.

Brig lifted his beer to the open window, like a toast, and then the rest of Garrett's friends did too. Garrett, incredibly, did this as well. He had two beers still and lifted them both. "Speech!" Marcus said to the window. It did not respond.

"Where the fuck *is* Charlie?" Jake said finally.

Brig shrugged. "Probably ran off into the woods."

"Are you kidding? Guy's madly in love."

"Well, monogamy will cure that soon enough," Johnny said bitterly. Garrett faintly remembered hearing, probably from Charlie, that the guy had separated from his wife. They had twins: identical boys.

"If he went anywhere," Marcus said, "it was to go find Cece."

Garrett's heart leapt. "She's here?"

Brig gave him an affronted look. "Have you been to a *bachelor* party before?"

"No."

Garrett's old housemates glanced at one another. He'd declined to attend their weddings.

"Cece's down at Finley Point," Marcus said. "The women all went camping and are, you know, *womanizing*."

"Poor Charles," Johnny said. "It's not too late for an intervention. He hasn't started talking about sump pumps yet. As soon as he gets a sump pump, it's all lost." He took a hit from the pipe in his hand. "You know what H. L. Mencken said about marriage, right?"

"Here we go again."

" 'The longest sentence you can form with two words is *I do*.' "

Garrett smiled vaguely. It was strange to hear his own opinions echoing from someone else's mouth. Stranger still, they annoyed him. Not for the first time, he wondered whether his opinions were based on anything he truly believed. What if his whole belief system was just, like, an advanced form of Tourette's? He said one thing without thinking about it, maybe just to fill the silence, which forced him to defend the thing with another, which forced him to defend *this* with another, and so on, until he had to explain these meaningless noises to himself by pretending he'd made them for a reason.

He went to the second floor in search of Charlie and passed a door with a homemade sign on it that read BIOHAZARD AREA—god, was he actually back in college?—then found his way into a bedroom that smelled like mothballs. A lace bra hung from the post of the antique bed, fluttering in the breeze from the casement window. Cece's, no doubt. Garrett stared at it. Perhaps Charlie had taken it off himself. Garrett unthreaded the bra from the post and stuffed it into the front pocket of his jeans. This was not a conscious perverted choice but a mad spasm, a burst of jealousy. He would have some forbidden piece of her. What an animal he was! Cece was right. He was basically a goat.

He wandered over to the open window, recognizing it as the same one he'd yelled up to from the backyard, that morning when Cece had refused to get out of bed. Garrett squinted out the window. Charlie was perched at the edge of the roof in the moonlight, standing with his back to the house. The guy—a doctor, an anesthesiologist—was smoking a cigarette.

Garrett crawled through the window onto the roof. His armpits were sweaty. Had he forgotten deodorant? Charlie, absorbed in his cigarette, did not seem to notice him. Garrett had a strange thought. He could sneak up goatishly on his hands and knees and butt Charlie off the roof, whereupon he might very well break his neck. How easy it would be! Bump, oopsy-daisy, over the edge. Charlie, drunk, might easily have lost his footing . . .

Wasn't this a plot—a movie—he'd seen before? Young widow, devastated by grief, winds up in the arms of the groom's best friend.

At the very least, Charlie would be seriously hurt. The wedding would have to be postponed.

Garrett's mouth tasted like chalk. He pictured Cece in the bedroom: her face, fogged with lust, as Charlie unhooked her bra. It played in Garrett's mind, choking him with jealousy. The roof seemed to have steepened. Mountain goats laughed at gravity; their hooves were like suction cups. Lowering his head, chafing his knees on the uneven shingles, Garrett tried creeping down the roof on all fours before realizing this was humanly impossible and shifting onto his butt and sliding down that way, toddler-style, imagining Cece and Charlie on their wedding night—how ghastly this was, monstrous, as if he were imagining a crime—until at last, practically within reach, Garrett stopped. Dear god, what was he doing? Crickets chirred in the trees. He stood up quickly. Startled, Charlie reeled around drunkenly and stepped into the rain gutter. Garrett grabbed him with both hands, keeping him from tumbling off the roof.

"You almost killed me!" Charlie shouted.

"Don't you mean 'saved your life'?"

Charlie peered over the edge, cigarette tweezed between two fingers. In reality, the drop wasn't far enough to do much damage. "Oh," he said gratefully. "In that case. Cece would just about kill me if I died." Charlie looked at Garrett, then down at his feet. "Sorry," he mumbled.

"For what?"

"The thing, you know, about being killed."

Garrett frowned, wondering if he should make him say Elias's name directly. It would be worth it, almost, to see him squirm. But then Charlie would just say the thing he always said, about as convincing a lie as saying your phone's been acting up. *You didn't kill him. It wasn't your fault.*

Garrett sat down on the shingles. He felt suddenly exhausted. Charlie—very carefully, or drunkenly, or carefully-drunkenly—sat down beside him.

"What the hell are you doing out here anyway?" Garrett asked.

"I didn't want anyone to see me smoking." Charlie took a drag, then blew the smoke expertly out his nose. "I hate people who smoke. It's like the worst thing you can do to your heart. Basically starves it of oxygen."

"I know the feeling."

Charlie laughed. He offered him a smoke, holding out a soft pack of Marlboros. Garrett took one. Charlie insisted he take the whole pack—he didn't want it in his possession.

"You know, it sounds exciting, being a doctor, but mostly what I do is fill out forms. I'm a bureaucrat, basically. Bartleby, the anesthesiologist!" Charlie shouted.

"Shut the hell up over there!" someone yelled.

"I would prefer not to!"

There was a slam from the house next door, followed by the groan of a screen door.

"That's Mr. Petersdorf," Charlie explained. "He collects traffic cones."

"Wow," Garrett said, failing to make a joke. His jealousy had alchemized into guilt. "Your brother's not feeling great."

"Oh god," Charlie said. "Bradley?" He looked stricken.

"Jake."

"If he's got norovirus, I'll kill *him*."

"I'm sure it's not that," Garrett said.

"I'm glad you're here," Charlie said, in what sounded like genuine relief. "It's like old times, smoking on the roof of the Mill."

"Except we'd be smoking Viceroys."

"Why the fuck didn't you return my calls?"

"My phone's been acting up," Garrett said.

"You're still going to officiate the wedding, right? Cece's *freaking out.*"

Garrett nodded, staring at the smoke from his cigarette.

"I'm counting on you," Charlie said earnestly. "I told her you always come through in the end. You're like the Rocky Balboa of friendship." He dropped his hand from Garrett's shoulder. "You've written it, right? What you're going to say?"

"Of course."

"I bet it's fucking timeless. Is it fucking timeless?"

Garrett opened his mouth to tell him the truth—that in fact it was so timeless it didn't even exist—but Charlie raised his hand to shush him.

"I don't want to ruin it. Surprise us."

Garrett looked above him, at the galactic scar tissue of the Milky Way. It seemed like a figuration of his guilt. He blew some smoke at it. Laughter rose from the front porch, eerily amplified by the lake.

"You're missing your bachelor party," Garrett said.

Charlie shrugged. "Do you want the embarrassing truth?"

"Sure."

"Johnny keeps telling me to enjoy my last gasp of freedom, whatever that means, but I don't give a rat's ass about that. Only people with traffic cones care about that stuff." He flicked his cigarette off the roof. "You know in those old cartoons, where somebody gets shot with a cannonball and it just leaves that big gaping hole in their stomach? That's what I feel like when I get drunk without Cece. I start to miss her terribly. I'd do anything to hear her voice. Like if someone told me to, I don't know, *cut off my nose* and she'd have cell service in her tent right now, I'd probably do it."

"I know what you mean," Garrett said.

Charlie looked at him. "You do?"

"I mean, she seems like a real find. One in a million." He blushed at these platitudes.

"Has she been acting weird to you at all?" Charlie said. "When you helped out with the fence and stuff?"

"What do you mean?"

"She's just so distracted all the time. I talk to her and it's like talking to the wall. She's always going out to the orchard, but there's nothing to pick. Plus she can't sleep. The other night I woke up at three in the morning and she wasn't in bed."

"Where was she?"

"Down at the dock. She was high as a kite, checking out the stars in the middle of the night."

Garrett could picture her perfectly, curled in an Adirondack chair with a flip-flop dangling from one foot. "Probably it's the stress of the wedding," he managed.

"You think so?"

"Everyone acts weird before they get married."

"She does this thing, where she chews her lip and smiles at the same time. It should be illegal. Even when she's mad at me, I just want to kiss her. *Especially* when she's mad. She says the most amazing things. Like she told me I was 'a pisspot.' A pisspot!"

"When did she call you a pisspot?"

"I tried to take her skiing last year," Charlie said, "and she freaked out on the traverse."

"Did she sit down and refuse to move?"

"How'd you know?"

"She did the same thing up at Glacier. When we went hiking. She insulted a goat."

Charlie straightened. "You went hiking together?"

"Yeah," Garrett said, surprised she hadn't told him. "Like over a week ago?" Charlie's eyes, in the moonlight, looked newly alert. "On the Highline Trail? I had to drag her up there."

"Probably she told me," Charlie said. "I just forgot."

"There's a lot going on."

Charlie stared at the blizzard of stars. "What a pisspot," he muttered. "A piss-*barrel*." He frowned at Garrett. "What did you do with my cigarettes?"

"You told me to take them away from you."

"Some bachelor party. Don't be an asshole."

Garrett reached into the wrong pocket of his jeans and pulled out a strap of Cece's bra.

"What's that?" Charlie asked.

"Nothing."

"A fanny pack?"

"No."

"You and Johnny."

Charlie threw his arm around him affectionately, as if they were still in college. Garrett handed him the Marlboros, and he plucked one out before hunching over to light it. While he was busy with the cigarette, Garrett sneaked Cece's bra from his pocket and threw it off the roof. He watched it parachute into the dark. Something spread out mystically before him: an alternate future, in which he rejoined the world and stopped neglecting his friends, possibly even did something with his life. All he had to do was leap. There was some laughter from the bedroom. Garrett turned to see Johnny and Marcus grinning at them from the window, Johnny holding up a jewelry bag of coke.

"Hey, they're out here on the roof!" Johnny called behind him. "Rekindling their friendship!"

2.

Cece followed Paige, her best friend from high school, to the rockiest site in the campground. Cece couldn't complain— or didn't feel like she could—since Paige had organized this whole camping trip herself, driving the six hundred miles from Portland on what seemed like the gale of her own enthusiasm.

What Paige's enthusiasm could *not* do was pitch a proper tent, at least the one she and Cece were sharing. Fitting the fiberglass poles together proved more difficult than she'd imagined. She refused to let Cece help. Eventually, after watching the other bachelorettes easily erect theirs, Paige wrestled the tent into a domeless brown shape that resembled a giant turd. She picked up the nylon bag the tent had come in and shook out a few remaining pebbles.

"Shit," Paige said. "Where are the spike thingies?"

"The stakes?"

"They were supposed to be in the bag."

Cece laughed. "You brought an inflatable sofa but no tent stakes?"

Paige found some rocks and began securing the corners of the tent with them. "It's okay! These will do it!"

Perhaps she was right: there wasn't much wind, just a light breeze feathering Paige's hair. She still wore the same scarlet lipstick she'd worn in tenth grade—still had the same unfortunate tattoo, a bracelet of barbed wire, that she'd gotten in 1994, hoping to impress a UCLA student she'd met at a Smashing Pumpkins concert. The only thing missing was the joint hidden in her bra. Cece half-expected her to start talking about Señor Ramirez, the Spanish teacher they used to concoct perverted fantasies about. And yet this girl with a barbed wire tattoo was a successful executive—did market research for Nike—and had a one-year-old at home who'd just learned to walk. (She'd shown Cece a video of his first steps, the kid staggering to his crib like a drunk.)

They sat on a log together, sharing some bourbon from Paige's thermos. "What do you think the boys are doing right now?" Paige asked, clearly delighted that Charlie's friends were stuck having their bachelor party at the house while they did the stereotypically manlier thing. She was one of those people, handy to know, who saw life as a competition that could only be won through aggressive remarketing. "I mean, besides talking about pussy."

"I kind of doubt Charlie's talking about pussy," Cece said.

"You're right. They're probably just watching porn."

"Charlie doesn't watch porn."

Paige laughed. "All men watch porn."

"I really don't think Charlie does," Cece said. Why did she sound, god, *disappointed*?

"Well, just wait till you're married," Paige said.

"Said watches porn?"

"Dunno. I hope so. I know *I* would, if I had any time. I only get to do it on business trips." Said, Paige's husband, was a stay-at-home dad. She laughed at Cece's face, whatever involuntary expression it was making. "Oh, it's not *his* fault. We're so exhausted all the time we can hardly kiss each other good night."

Cece took a swig of bourbon, feeling sick to her stomach. Growing up, Paige had been the girl in the class who always had a boyfriend, sometimes two: the sort of serial romancer who thought little of stealing someone's lover for good or just hooking up with him behind the gymnasium at a dance while his girlfriend drunkenly bellowed his name. There'd been a joke in eleventh grade: *Don't let your boyfriend get Paiged.* Cece had enjoyed watching Paige run rampant. Though she'd worried about her too, in a smugly superior way: what it portended for her future. Certainly Cece had never imagined her getting married. It seemed about as likely as Paige becoming a high-powered executive.

"How did you know you wanted to get married?" Cece asked her now.

Paige looked at her. "Oh dear," she said seriously. "Shit. Are you getting cold feet?"

"No. I mean, I just never thought, you know, when we were kids—you seemed to like twisting guys around your finger so much and then, well . . ."

"Dumping them on their ass?"

"Yeah."

"Promwrecker, they called me," Paige said nostalgically. She threw an arm around Cece. "I was just joking about the porn. Being a stinkwad. Charlie's going to be an amazing husband."

"I know."

"What's wrong? You're worried about his mother?"

Cece nodded, happy to change the subject.

"Look, it's probably just a coincidence."

"A coincidence that she's throwing up, two days after his dad got sick?"

"Well, maybe not. But it doesn't mean it's going to turn into a puke-fest. They found a hotel room, did they not?"

"*Motel*," Cece said. Charlie's parents had moved into quarantine yesterday, when they realized it wasn't food poisoning. Both the Salish Inn and the Serenity Shore Cabins were booked through the weekend, mostly with wedding guests, so they'd had to take a room at a Motel 6.

"The wedding's not for three days," Paige said. "Everything will be fine."

She dipped into the woods behind their tent, presumably to pee. "Come on!" she said to Cece. Paige pulled down her shorts and squatted there half-naked, waiting for Cece, who yanked her jeans down as well and squatted beside her. She held Paige's hand. They used to do this as kids, peeing together at the beach during a bonfire or else at the golf course after sneaking over the fence to slam vodka shots. (The litter box, Paige used to call the sand pit at the golf course.) The smell of urine and pine needles evoked precisely itself. It was so stupid and gross, but Cece felt like she might start crying. Paige was married. She was about to get married too. Eventually they'd be dead.

Pulling her shorts back on, Paige cursed herself for forgetting to bring her boric acid capsules. She worried she might be getting a yeast infection. Concealing her tears, Cece said that she might have some in her Dopp kit.

"Hey," Paige said, waggling her eyebrows.

"What?"

"We're talking about pussy."

They walked over to join the others: Esther and Ushi and Colleen and Akriti, all friends of Cece's from Pitzer except for Akriti, whom she'd met in med school. Paige grabbed some portable speakers from the car, eager to get the bachelorette party started. Or *maiden party*, since Esther objected to the term "bachelorette." "You don't call female mail carriers mailmanettes," she explained.

"But 'maiden' is even *worse*," Akriti said. "It means you're a virgin."

"How about 'damsel'?" Colleen said.

"Ew."

"Are there really no unsexist terms for an unmarried woman?"

The six of them thought about this.

"Good thing you're getting married," Colleen said.

"Yeah," Ushi said, "answering to the term 'wife' will complete your liberation."

"Does Said call you his wife?" Cece asked Paige. "Because I'm struggling a bit with that. 'My fiancée' is bad enough."

"Who's Said?" Paige said in front of the group. As an "honorary bachelorette," she insisted on banning all references to her husband and child. She cued up some music on her laptop: pop hits from summers past, transforming the woods into a roller rink. At least she hadn't brought an actual DJ. Cece hoped they weren't disturbing the family at the next campsite, where a little girl was skipping rocks in the river. Colleen, a former bartender, made margaritas from supplies she'd brought and everyone drank them in front of the fire, reminiscing about Cece's old boyfriends. Ushi told a story about Cece's hooking up with a boy in college and then waking up the next morning and accidentally clogging the toilet so that the whole bathroom flooded with fecal water. She'd been so embarrassed she'd escaped out the window. The story was met with raucous laughter. Cece laughed too, of course, trying to be a good sport, but she also thought about how crazy she'd been about the boy—his favorite movie, she remembered, was *Duck Soup*—and how, except for a stupid quirk of fate, they might have become an item. Who knows? They might even still be together. Lots of undergrads at Pitzer ended up married to each other.

Cece suddenly felt depressed. It was getting dark, stars beginning to fill the sky like snow. She got up and walked toward the river, pretending she needed to grab something from the tent. Why this unditchable sadness? Would it hound her to the grave? Couldn't she have a bachelorette party, for fuck's sake, without it trailing her like a pet? Paige must have left a flashlight on when they were laying out their sleeping bags, because their tent was glowing eerily, lit from the inside out, as if an alien were in there waiting for a snack. The tent seemed to be in a different spot than before. Had it moved? Cece sat on a stump, feeling dizzy. She wondered if the norovirus had infected her, was replicating in her bloodstream.

Cece thought of her father's wedding to Lillian, her step-mom, how it had seemed like a major betrayal even though it had been three years after her mother's death. How Cece had despised the bride, watching her walk down the aisle in a beaded flapper dress and headband, an honest-to-god *egret feather* sticking out of her head. She'd escaped the reception and found her grandmother outside, sitting on the steps of the ballroom, such sadness in her face that Cece didn't recognize her at first. To her astonishment, her grandmother pulled a bottle of tequila from her purse, explaining she'd nabbed it from the open bar when no one was looking. She took a swig, then offered some to Cece. *Don't tell your father.* They passed the tequila back and forth. Inside the ballroom the toasts had begun; the guests rippled with laughter. Cece was supposed to give a toast herself—a tribute to her father, to a bond forged in the crucible of tragedy—but she was outside instead. Getting shitty with her grandma. At some point, she climbed into her grandmother's lap, imagining it was her mother's.

She'd expected her father's marriage to fall apart after a year, or at least had prayed for this to happen, but her dad and Lillian were still together. They were flying into Kalispell tomorrow, too late for Lillian to get sick herself. Of course, they were staying at some fancy lodge in Somers because Lillian couldn't bear to stay anywhere that wasn't a five-star hotel.

After Cece headed back to the campfire, where her friends were dancing to OutKast, the glowing tent resumed its escape. It seemed to be sneaking away of its own accord. Had the wind picked up? Hesitantly, without a sound, the tent slipped down to the river. The little girl at the next campsite thought about alerting the women, but she was far more scared of them than the wandering tent, which anyway was the most interesting thing to happen all day. It drifted out to the middle of the river and got picked up by the current, glowing like a water lantern, spinning slowly under the stars.

3.

At some point in the evening, a point both inevitable and impossible to pin down, Charlie's friends—pallbearers of his bachelorhood—decided to go swimming. Lack of swimwear was not an issue. Had you driven by the house at the perfect moment, you would have seen four men dashing across the road, fully clothed but already beginning to yank off their shirts, tugging them over their heads or unbuttoning them midsprint, like Superman on his way to a phone booth. You might have believed them too old to go skinny-dipping, or at least to behave in such a childish way, and they might on a different night have agreed with you. And yet a strange thing happened when they reached the water and finished stripping out of their clothes, hopping around on one leg while they tugged off their shoes and socks, struggling a bit to get out of their jeans—freshly laundered, these jeans, and in some cases two sizes bigger than the ones they wore in college—a strange thing happened when they stormed the dock, dicks flapping, and whooped into the lake: the beer and the drugs and the attempted sorcery of pretending to be young made them *actually young*. Water was the missing ingredient. It was what the spell needed. The imperfections of their bodies dissolved into the lake. They lost their beer guts and their spare tires, their shin splints and torn menisceses, anything that made them look half-comic when they ran. They were twenty again, svelte and handsome and bombed out of their minds. Bill Clinton was in the White House. The internet wasn't much, a new thing, and people argued about whether it was just a fad. The Twin Towers stood as they always would, till the end of time.

And so the Bachelors hollered. They climbed the ladder and fucked the air for no reason and cannonballed into the lake. They splashed one another and woke up the neighbors and did things that would have made them call the cops themselves had they been awakened by the same racket while at home with their wives. Even Garrett, who'd followed at a distance and was still fully clothed, content to watch, felt the embrace of nostalgia, the mysterious goodwill that alights on people who've spent countless hours together in various rooms and cars and ski lodges, laughing like idiots. It hadn't seemed particularly newsworthy at the time, this laughter, just something you did between one event and the next—but of course it was. It was the event itself.

"Jump in!" the Bachelors shouted.

"Ha ha," Garrett said. "I don't think so."

"Come on! Let's see that ass!"

"I'll need another line for that. Maybe two."

"Help yourself! It's in my jeans!"

"I wouldn't touch Johnny's jeans if I were you! If you value your health!"

"Scabies, scabies, burning bright! In the trousers of the night!"

"What's the matter, Minister? Need a life vest?"

"Afraid we'll handle your baggage?"

"We're all naked in the eyes of God!"

"Oh my god. Wow. I can't believe I was friends with any of you."

"Holy shit! He's taking off his shirt!"

"The minister disrobes!"

"Jump in! The water's freezing!"

Garrett walked to the edge of the dock, fighting the urge to conceal himself. It had been a long time since he'd been naked in front of someone, and he couldn't help wondering how he looked, if anyone noticed the furry sinkhole of his belly button, which seemed to get furrier every year. Specifically, he wondered how he compared to Charlie. Garrett stretched as if he were performing an Olympic dive, canting his hips back and forth with his arms akimbo. Everyone laughed, thinking he was trying to be funny. Because he *was*. He was stark naked, cracking people up. No one was more surprised than Garrett himself.

Charlie swam under the dock, frogman style, then sneaked up to Garrett from behind and pushed him in the lake. They came up together, spitting mouthfuls of water at each other. Charlie's face bobbed in the moonlight. The cartoon funk of "Give It Away" by the Red Hot Chili Peppers drifted over the lake, played by a cover band at the Lazy Bear—the dreadful song had become, yes, classic rock—and Brig got out of the lake and scatted along to the music, playing his dick like a guitar. The remaining Bachelors expressed their disgust. They insulted the size of his guitar. Marcus referred to it as a ukulele. Johnny squinted and wondered if he was playing air guitar. Garrett joined in the insults, feeling transformed back to a former shape. He had friends who weren't his father.

He and Charlie swam out twenty or thirty yards from the

dock, then flipped onto their backs so that they were floating side by side, their ears corked with water. The music disappeared, replaced by the infinite silence of the lake. He couldn't see Charlie but knew he was listening to the bottomless silence too. It contained Elias, Garrett's grief, everything they would ever need to say to each other. They floated on top of it, like debris from a wreck. They'd found each other again. The sky bristled with stars. If only this could be his wedding speech. A wedding *silence*, with their whole lives cradling them.

They stopped floating and peered at the moonlit docks along the shore, which looked like the teeth of a giant comb. Garrett could not believe that he'd been jealous of this man, or lusted after his fiancée, or done anything but call him daily on the phone.

"What's the name of that church?" Charlie said.

"What church?"

"The online one! Where you got ordained for the wedding?"

"Universal Life," Garrett said.

Charlie laughed. "How do I join?"

"You're in it already. We're all part of its flock."

The band at the Lazy Bear had launched into "Smells Like Teen Spirit." Tragically, this was classic rock now too. Garrett and Charlie swam back to the dock and then, teeth chattering, climbed the ladder to gather their clothes. But they did not find their clothes. The other Bachelors had taken them up to the house. This was their idea of fun. Garrett and Charlie cursed them bitterly. They put on their shoes, which had been graciously left behind. In this peculiar fashion the two of them walked back to the house, crossing the highway not as heroic young nudists but in shivering disgrace, hunched and cowering, glancing back over their shoulders toward the lake. They covered their genitals with two hands. The spell had been broken.

The remaining Bachelors jeered at them from the porch.

"You stole our clothes!" Charlie yelled at them.

"And yet you're wearing shoes," Marcus said philosophically.

"Yes, strange things are afoot," Brig said.

"Earlier it was raining bras," Bradley said. "In the backyard. One almost landed on me while I was taking a whiz."

"Also, the Bachelorettes have returned a day early!"

"For real?" Charlie said happily.

"One of their tents floated down the river!"

Sure enough, the Bachelorettes began to emerge from the house, one after the other, like clowns from a car. A succession of Cece's friends. They made it seem like the real party—the one the Bachelors had all secretly dreamed of having—had finally begun. Cece appeared last of all, wearing a flannel shirt that hung to her knees. She stopped in her tracks when she saw the two naked men on the lawn, sporting sensible footwear. Her eyes widened; she burst into laughter. As soon as Garrett saw her, laughing on the porch in one of Charlie's shirts, something happened. The nostalgic affection he'd been feeling for his old friend dried up at once. It might as well never have existed. He was lost again, murderous, a naked goat on the roof.

Cece caught Garrett's eye and then peered at her feet, pretending not to have seen him. Garrett's heart lurched. He would need to do something drastic. He couldn't kill Charlie, but he would need to do something. Time was running out.

"Ceeeece!" Charlie called to her, clutching the whereabouts of his heart with two hands, but she'd already covered her eyes.

SEVEN

From: garrettmeek74@yahoo.com
To: ceciliabedelia15@hotmail.com
Subject: I have to tell you this I'm sorry
Date: Thur 7/15/04
Time: 2:58 AM

Cece,

   You know how some lights have those dimmer switches? Where you can adjust them to any brightness? I used to think that aliveness was about being on or off alive or dead but I realize now that it's like one of those switches, that being alive has many brightnesses to it. you can be dim for so many years that you dont even know it, you mistake it for bright, like for the only bright you're capable of, but then something happens that turns up the switch and youre like oh right this is life. This is what people have been talking about.

   Is that corny? good, I'm trying to be. I'm trying to be a normal human being who other people recognize as a fellow creature and say: hey there's a human being who might even I don't know own a spice rack or a leaf blower. Obviously, I own neither but I want to be mistaken for someone who does. Ive been in the Land of Hümanz for too long and I want to get out before it's too late and they lock the gates on me forever.

   You never asked what happened to me in San Francisco but I should probably tell you now because thats what people with spice racks do, tell things to each other. I don't really know why I ended up there except my dad was living with this guy I couldn't

stand and I'd dropped out of college and I wanted to move someplace where I didn't know a soul, where no one would hug me
and rub my back and insist I hadn't killed anybody. San Francisco
was as far from Middlebury as you could get, at least without
going to Alaska. also I wanted to be somewhere that didn't have
snow. Back then snow to me was like kryptonite. It was the ash
of my old life coming down. I dreamed about it all night long. Id
close my eyes and it would immediately start blizzarding like the
fuzz on a TV set.

So I moved to sf and got a job canvassing for the Wildlife
Conservation Society because I needed to pay my rent and that's
what I'd always cared about most in life, animals I mean. (Well
skiing too but I was never going to ski again for as long as I lived.)
Starting when I was a kid I loved animals, not in the sentimental
way that most people love them but in a deep trueheartedmonk-
like way that had to do with not being very impressed by human
beings, probably because the human beings I knew i.e. my parents were often yelling at each other. even back then I hated the
way people sentimentalized penguins and pandas and dolphins,
all the charismatic megafauna, preferring the ugly weird animals
that did incredible comic book things to survive, like the Malaysian ant that explodes like a bomb and sprays deadly toxic goo
all over its enemies or the blue-tailed skink which can break off
its own tail just by thinking about it and leave it squirming on
the ground so it looks like a tasty snake. Or the hooded seal! i
had books and books about these weird amazing animals, I had
them all memorized, like a catechism or something, and it was a
kind of worship now that I think about it if you define worship as
wanting to get as close as possible to the mystery of creation.

Anyway I was out canvassing for the Wildlife Conservation
Society trying to get people to sign a petition about stopping
the shark fin trade or protecting polar bears from seismic testing in the Arctic, something like that, but first you had to talk to
people and explain why the petition was important and I was no

good at that. In fact I was probably the last person in the world youd want approaching strangers on behalf of the polar bear (Mr. Charismatic Megafauna himself) and asking for their addresses. I was sleeping two hours a night because all I saw was snow, I'd lie down in bed and my heart would start going, the panic would begin, but even this was better than actually sleeping because I always had the same dream, I was up on the mountain again except it was clear flawless ice at my feet instead of snow and i could see Elias's face, see it turning blue however many yards below me, I had fifteen minutes fifteen minutes fifteen minutes, I would have to watch him die while I dug. what's more I couldnt shower very often because the roommate I'd found on a flyer at some taqueria was this mildly epileptic guy who played fantasy games on his computer all the time and walked on the balls of his feet and took half hour showers every morning when I needed to get ready for work.

So I stood there with my clipboard looking like a lunatic. People crossed the street to avoid me. I could see them coming down the sidewalk and they'd do a little whoa-there swerve and get as much distance from me as they could. And that's when I had my first episode, the kind Ive told you about. the light turned gross and everyone started to bounce when they walked and to look like impossible creatures and I felt that bug on the face feeling, felt this disgust come over me not just for the pedestrians on the street but for pedestrians everywhere, on every street in the world, blah blah blah. I wanted to spray them with a giant can of Raid or better yet explode deadly toxic goo everywhere like the malaysian ant and die in the process because I was human too. The strange impossible feeling went away after a while but not the disgust and I stood there on the sidewalk without moving for the rest of my shift, like a Beefeater or something, and something wonderful happened which was that people stopped avoiding me and began brushing past me as if I wasn't there, I didnt exist, and I began to wish that they were right.

After that I quit my job and began to stay home all day long, surfing the internet for the first time in my life, one of those dial-up connections that was like waiting for water to boil—I wouldn't have even known what a webpage was except for my roommate—and feeling more and more disgusted with people. It wasn't just what I saw on the newsfeeds, the ways in which we were destroying the planet, the burning of fossil fuels of course but also the soil erosion deforestation plastic pollution ocean acidification overpopulation habitat degradation wastewater contamination, one -tion after another, so wholesale the destruction that it was almost funny: the strip mining for kitty litter, the estrogen leaking into lakes and making male fish produce eggs, the songbirds too stoned on Prozac waste to eat or mate, the deadly bits of glitter in the oceans that fish gobble up because they think they're food. disco balls in their stomachs! But it wasnt just this, it was the internet itself, which seemed like a gigantic endless shopping mall beamed into our homes to get people to buy more shit, more more more, stuff stuff stuff, which of course human beings couldn't actually throw away. That was the internet's actual real purpose: to spread our shit all over the planet. Or so it seemed like to me. if it wasn't getting human beings to buy more shit it was devoted to their mating, which honestly disgusted me most of all.

That was the real problem: I couldn't stand to be human. So I decided to stop. I found the phenobarbital my roommate kept in his bedside table and took the whole bottle or whatever was left of it and drank a beer for good measure and waited for the snow to bury me alive. And it would have buried me except my dad called me out of the blue. I don't think I'd talked to him for a few months, i'd stopped returning his calls, but he had some kind of premonition and called me and I answered the phone and he could tell something was wrong, I was slurring my words, I think i might have even told him Id been eating glitter, and he called

911. So the doctors saved me. they gave me activated charcoal and dug me out but I was still a danger to myself I guess because they 5150ed me. I was in the psych unit for a while, in a halfway house for a lot longer than that. Suffice it to say Ive flushed my fair share of SSRIs into the ecosystem. and then the odd jobs busing tables and taping drywall where I had to totter around on these long metal stilts and now of course throwing bags at the airport, basically a hydrocarbon bonfire, helping people destroy the planet so they can see a glacier or two before they're gone. But that's another story.

You're getting married in two days, to my best friend in college, and you know what's demented is that Im looking forward to the wedding even though it's going to be one of the worst days of my life. I'm looking forward to it because i get to see your face again. Isnt that fucked up? When I see you it fills me with the opposite of disgust, which I know doesn't sound exactly like high praise but for me is sort of like the return of the world. It's like I stop being a mess of exploded thoughts for a second and am just happy to be a human, a human looking at another human. i used to feel something like it when I was skiing and I wasn't thinking about anything except the sun on my face and the softness lifting me like a hand and i was floating through the world in a way that was a rare special thing. On my computer keyboard I can maybe describe it this way: [!!!] > ∞ . I haven't felt like that in a long long time.

I'm drunk I'm sorry. It's 2:43 in the morning. I think ive lost my mind again. I can't sleep or eat or even watch TV because my only ambition in life is to see your face again as soon as possible. I don't know if Im miserable or happy.

I know I said those things about marriage being a fascist institution. I have these beliefs I feel very strongly about when I'm talking to other people out in the world but when I think about them in private they start to seem kind of arbitrary. like they could just as easily be the opposite. The truth is you make me feel like I could actually do something with my life, maybe finish up my degree and go to grad school and become a wildlife biologist, focus on something else's survival instead of my own.

Why am I telling you this? I dont know. You probably think I'm crazy. (well, that cats out of the bag.) I guess what I'm saying is that I probably had a vESTED interest in telling you what I thought about marriage that day. And then later you smiled at me. I saw you looking for me downstairs even after Id been such an asshole and you saw me and your whole face kind of changed like you'd been climbing a mountain for a long time and youd seen a view finally, remembering why you were even there, and that was basically the last time I slept. Did I imagine it, that your face looked like that?

i'm going to confess something to you: I BACKED INTO CHAR-LIE'S FENCE ON PURPOSE BECAUSE I WANTED TO HAVE AN EXCUSE TO COME BACK.

Charlie told me that he found you on the porch in the middle of the night looking at the stars. Are you maybe awake right now too? Is it possible youve chosen I don't know *baboons* instead of *raccoons,* all because of a misunderstanding?

G

EIGHT

From: garrettmeek74@yahoo.com
To: ceciliabedelia15@hotmail.com
Subject: PLEASE DO NOT READ EMAIL I JUST SENT!!!!!!!
Date: Thur 7/15/04
Time: 3:06 AM

PLEASE PLEASE DO NOT READ THE EMAIL I JUST SENT AND DELETE IT ASAP **WITHOUT READING IT!!!!** PLEASE! I CAN'T SLEEP AND IT'S NOT TRUE AND PLEASE TRUST ME, DELETE! PROMISE ME??????

NINE

G arrett tried to focus on the bags moving toward him on the belt loader, to mentally process their tags before they got to him, but it was like trying to keep track of someone else's thoughts or being trapped in a dream where everything eluded him. He was so tired he couldn't see straight. Félix wasn't helping matters, reporting every time Garrett threw a bag in the wrong direction.

"Another Boise," he said indifferently from the depths of the pit. As usual, he pronounced it "Bwa-zé." "Wrong side."

"It's pronounced '*Boys*-ee,'" Garrett said angrily, after he'd caught his breath. They were waiting for the next baggage cart to pull up. It was ninety-three degrees and the pit reeked of BO and jet fuel and the charred-marshmallow smell of the shimmering tarmac.

"Ha ha," Félix said.

"I'm not joking! It's true!"

"It is an interesting controversy."

Félix turned from him and began to look for duffel bags from Vegas that might contain rolls of quarters. He liked to steal the rolls and hide them in his socks. For the third time that day, Garrett excused himself to pee, then jogged across the tarmac when Burelli wasn't looking and used his badge to slip inside the terminal. As usual, it was easy to find an open computer. Garrett logged in and checked his Yahoo! account. His heart pounded, he was clutched with fear, he trembled once again with dread and half hope, lobbing Hail Marys to a God he didn't believe in. He waited for his email to load, staring at the little hourglass on the screen. It seemed to hold his life in the balance, to contain his salvation or destruction.

Nothing. Some spam for "FASTER CHEAPER MEDS."

Garrett logged out of the computer. His face burned with shame. He'd sent the email to Cece at some godforsaken hour, then sent the second email, both of which mortified him now, filled him with a feeling of humiliation and doom. What had he been thinking? At first there'd been a shred of actual hope: the idea that she might read his first email, powerless to resist, and write him back with an astonishing confession of her own. The shred of hope persisted into the morning, with the ancillary hope that she had yet to check her email. But as the day wore on, as Garrett found himself choking down a few bites of cereal and getting dressed for work and then doing his best to focus on the luggage riding up the belt loader, trying not to get creamed by a duffel bag or screamed at by Burelli, he realized she must have seen the emails already and been too aghast to write back. It had been ridiculous to hope otherwise. Who did he think he was? When he imagined the look of disgust and astonishment on Cece's face as she read his email, his trite, childish, melodramatic confession—"my only ambition in life is to see your face again," he'd written!—he had to keep himself from purposefully getting sucked into a turbofan.

Baboons! What was he, an idiot?

Most likely she'd talked to Charlie about it. Or maybe Charlie was the one who'd found the emails first—for all Garrett knew, they shared an account. Probably they were laughing over the most embarrassing bits. They didn't want to laugh (*Oh, god, we shouldn't laugh!*), but they couldn't help themselves. No, worse than laughing: they pitied him. Poor Garrett Meek, baggage handler in love.

He'd never thrown up from shame before, but a sour taste curdled in his throat.

The tarmac seemed to writhe in the heat. Another cart had

arrived and Burelli was tossing bags onto the belt loader, one on top of another, exhibiting his usual disdain for the humanly possible. "The hell you been?" he demanded. His bad ear, normally abloom this time of day, was still swollen shut.

"In the restroom," Garrett said, breathing slowly.

"Christ. What are you, an old man?"

"I think I ate something funny. For lunch."

"I don't care if someone shat in your Post Toasties. No breaks before pushback—Mr. P's orders. Get your ass up there before those bags do!"

"Too late," Garrett said matter-of-factly. The bags had reached the top of the belt and formed a kind of luggage jam in the mouth of the pit; suitcases began to plummet off the belt and smash on the tarmac, one of them exploding in a burst of clothes. T-shirts, caught by a gust of wind, scuttled under the plane. Burelli shut off the belt loader.

"Are you looking to get fired?" he said furiously.

Garrett pondered this, treating the question nonrhetorically, which seemed to throw Burelli for a loop. Was there a flash of envy on his face?

"Go clean up those clothes," Burelli said quietly, "or I'll make sure your next potty break is your last."

After work, Garrett sped down the highway, heading god knows where. One of his wipers had broken midswipe, when he was spritzing his windshield with fluid, and now it stood at two o'clock in front of him, bisected by the ghoulish rainbow of a smeared moth. Garrett hardly noticed. He'd checked his email one more time after his shift, stopping by the Maverick counter on his way out.

Still nothing. Zilch. Exactly what he deserved.

A buzzard hovered in the sky ahead, occupying the segment of windshield he could see through. Garrett, who was straddling the yellow line, moved back into his lane. He'd lost his mind, his pride, and probably his best friend. At least now he wouldn't have to officiate the wedding.

Of course, there was another possibility. The other possibility was that she'd read the email and was secretly in love with Garrett and didn't know what to do about it. Maybe she'd even written him back, on the eve of her wedding, but was too frightened to send it.

The idea, no matter how far-fetched, simmered in the back of his brain. It was unlikely—though far less unlikely than, say, the existence of angels, which supposedly 77 percent of Americans believed in. Garrett had read that somewhere. If angels existed, perhaps Cece was in love with him too.

His truck turned off the highway of its own accord, heading up the road toward his father's house, which is generally what happened when Garrett wasn't sure where he was going. This was true of his thoughts as well. Washing the dishes, or gazing at the train cars outside his window, he would turn a corner sometimes in his mind and end up suddenly on his father's porch. It was the secret terminus of his dreams.

"Who are you supposed to be?" his father said, greeting him at the door.

"Very funny."

"I've left you five voicemails."

"I'm sorry, Dad. I've been super busy."

His father scoffed. "With *what*? Hat shopping?"

"Important stuff."

"What's more important than visiting your sick father?"

"Well, I've had that speech to write," Garrett said. "For the wedding."

His father stared at him.

"And . . . I drove up to Glacier. To go hiking."

"By yourself?"

"No."

"Aha," his father said. "I knew something was up. When I saw your new hat. Who's the lucky girl?"

Garrett didn't respond to this.

"Must be hot and heavy, if you can't even return my calls."

Garrett nodded, letting him persist in this misunderstanding. It was a convenient excuse for neglecting him the past couple weeks. They grabbed some Budweisers from the fridge and settled on the porch. It was a beautiful day, cloudless and hot, the smell of wildfire merely a tartness in the breeze. His father avoided his eyes. Garrett was touched by his resentment, though also annoyed; if his father wanted to talk about neglect, they should back up a bit and start with Garrett's childhood. They should get some historical perspective.

His father met his gaze finally. "I don't know who this new *acquaintance* of yours is, but it looks like you haven't slept in two days."

"More like a week and a half," Garrett said.

His father turned to the yard, as if he didn't want Garrett to see his face. My god, was he jealous? He seemed skinnier than ever, maybe because he was wearing shorts, his legs as frail, as dainty, as a little girl's. Were these really his father's legs? The same ones that had held Garrett in place, secure as a vise, when he was learning to ski? It was one of his earliest memories: nestled in his father's thighs as they snowplowed the bunny slope together, weaving miraculously downhill, Garrett smiling so big that his teeth turned to icicles. His dad had gripped him under the arms, hard enough that it hurt—but Garrett didn't mind, so exotic was it to be held. The only time, really, that his father touched him. Once, he'd zipped ahead by accident, his father's mittens tucked inside his armpits. What joy and terror he'd felt! Later, at eight or nine, the thrill of blasting past his father on a mogul run, of finding that perfect line where he was skimming the top of each bump, skipping like a stone on a lake, showing off for all the tourists on the chairlift, who cheered and whooped and made him feel like the best skier they'd ever seen. The powder days when his dad rousted him out of bed so they could be first in line for the bowls to open, boot-packing along the ridge till his goggles fogged with steam, his long johns soaked with sweat, the Adam-and-Eve thrill of dropping into virgin snow. The pure tethering delight of looking back at their tracks. Neither of them wanted to take a break, to lose a fresh line, so his dad filled his pockets with Almond Joys they could share on the lift. "Joy?" he'd ask, and they'd laugh. The snow coming down fat and beautiful. How could Garrett have forgotten all this? He'd pushed it out of his mind. He'd turned to backcountry skiing as a teenager, traded his father in for his high school buddies—early pioneers, they'd used telemark gear and didn't even have beacons—coming to disdain the resorts his dad had taken him to as a kid, the whole corporate rape of land and wallet. At the time it had never occurred to Garrett, caught up in self-righteous disdain, to wonder if his dad missed skiing with him.

His father bent over to tie his shoe—he was wearing brand-new running shoes without socks—and when he sat up again he seemed winded, breathing through his mouth. Garrett, braced for a coughing fit, watched him uneasily. For some reason, the new shoes saddened him.

"I ran into your friend Charlie," his father said after a moment.

"You did?"

"At the IGA. He recognized me, if you can believe that." He stretched his legs, unfolding them one at a time. "Was he always that handsome?"

Garrett frowned. "I'm not sure what you mean."

His father eyed him curiously. "His fiancée was with him."

"So?"

"You were right. She's kind of weird-looking."

"I never said that."

"She's got that thing where each feature looks like it came from a different face. Like one of those flip books where you mix up the parts of different animals."

Garrett felt himself redden. "Everyone looks weird in the supermarket."

Barnabas was creeping across the lawn on three legs, attempting to stalk a chickadee, which seemed to realize that it was in no real danger and continued to pick seeds from the grass. Garrett, trying not to betray his feelings, could feel his father's eyes on him. When he finally looked back, his dad's face had changed completely, sprouted the tiny bud of a smile, as if he'd put two and two together in his head. Cece was the woman—the "acquaintance"—who'd been sleeping in his apartment. Garrett and Cece were having an affair. The triumphant certainty was written all over his face. He seemed, in fact, strangely impressed. Garrett was not immune to his father's pride, no matter how misplaced. To disabuse him of the notion, Garrett would have to delve into the details of his infatuation, which he had no interest in doing.

"You probably don't want to hear this," his father said.

"You're right. No 'probably' about it."

"Before I met your mother," he said, ignoring Garrett, "there was a boy I knew in high school. Bobby Malpas. In fact, he was my first kiss. We used to meet behind the groundskeeper's shed sometimes and, you know, do things together. The problem is, he was going out with Kristen Segal, a cheerleader. Yes, an actual cheerleader! They still existed back then, in an indigenous state. Pom-poms and everything. They were like an ethnicity unto themselves. Kristen Segal and Bobby Malpas were on the homecoming court, if you can believe that. A gay homecoming prince! He made me swear on my life not to tell anyone. I was madly in love with him and would have killed Principal Weaver if he'd asked me to. Then one day Kristen saw us together, fooling around behind the auditorium at a dance, and she threatened

to report me to the police for *sexual perversion*. So I never talked
to him again. Bobby wrote me a letter after they broke up, a
couple months later, but I never responded to it. I was too scared
of what might happen."

"Why are you telling me this?"

"I don't know. I just find myself thinking sometimes about
what-if. About Bobby Malpas."

Garrett tried not to think too hard about this what-if, maybe
because it precluded his own birth. "You're just romanticizing.
It only means something because you *didn't* respond to his letter.
Probably if you'd ended up with him—like you'd moved to San
Francisco together, wine and roses—you'd have grown com-
pletely sick of him. You'd hate his guts right now."

His father sighed. He seemed to lose interest in the topic,
or perhaps Garrett himself, as if he'd disappointed him in some
way. "You've never forgiven me, have you, for your mother's
happiness. Unlike me, she found the love of her life."

"*Kirby?* Jesus, Dad. He's a fucking *periodontist*."

"That's hardly the point, is it? Whether you like him or not."

He started to cough, muffling it in the crook of his elbow. The
coughing flared and died down, several times, before mounting
a sustained attack.

"I'll get you some water," Garrett said, standing up.

"You won't!" he wheezed. "I can still get my own water."

His father cursed himself, as if disgusted by his own infirmity,
and then walked into the house, leaving Garrett alone with Barnabas. The cat yawned in the sunlight. He eyed Garrett from the
lawn, as if aware of being watched, then sprang onto the fence
and climbed up to the top and began to funambulate across it
as best he could, as if this time he thoroughly intended to get
all the way across. A relief that Garrett's father wasn't around
to wager on his chances. The betting was just a pretense to give
Garrett money, they both knew it, and Garrett was sick of the
whole charade.

Barnabas teetered along the fence, past the safety net of hydrangeas he usually fell into. Garrett watched his progress, worried the cat would drop into the rosebushes and get impaled on some thorns. The cat swayed a bit but hung on, righting his balance. Incredibly, he passed the roses. He passed the wild strawberry patch. He passed the trellis of overgrown vine weed. Garrett stood from his chair. His heart was in his throat. Barnabas wobbled the last few feet, serenely, then made it to the end of the fence. Garrett cheered from the porch. The cat seemed as surprised as anyone, enthroned atop the corner post, as if wondering what to conquer next.

Garrett turned to his father, hoisting his Budweiser, and was met with an empty chair. He'd forgotten he wasn't there. Garrett called into the house. Silence. He wandered inside, pissed at his father for missing Barnabas's triumph. It seemed emblematic somehow: he was never around when it mattered.

Garrett stepped through the clutter of the living room, his eyes adjusting to the dim house. It smelled like cat shit; no doubt the litter box hadn't been cleaned in a week. He turned into the kitchen and almost tripped over his father, who was lying on the floor.

TEN

Cece lay in bed after the rehearsal picnic, listening to Charlie's half-drunken snores. He'd fallen asleep a while ago, having drunk a bit too much at the picnic, on the heels of having drunk *a lot* too much at his bachelor party. He was not a big drinker in LA—he was too busy saving lives—so she didn't begrudge him a bit of fun. So long as he wasn't hungover for the wedding tomorrow. "Dear husband," she whispered in his ear, taking the words for a test drive, but as usual he slept like a drowned man, leaving her to suffer alone. The guy hadn't had a night of insomnia in his life. He never even remembered his dreams. Cece skipped through burning houses, discovered her own name on tombstones, fucked high school boyfriends while their faces turned into demons'—and Charlie lay there calmly, as still as death.

The wall had a picture of the window on it, composed by the moon. Cece stared at the blank storyboard of panes. She rearranged the sheets, trying to find the holy grail of positions that would make her sleepy, and a faint smell of farts escaped from their blanket. Cece didn't mind it really. It was the inside of him—why shouldn't she smell it? She was marrying this too.

"Dear husband," she said to the smell, though they'd never met. Charlie still did not stir. In fact, he was blissfully ignorant of Cece the Insomniac, though she spent a good chunk of her life this way, lying miserably in the dark while her brain gusted around like a kite.

Cece felt an itch in her throat, a dewy quiver, as if she might start crying. What was wrong with her? She'd hoped getting married would answer some basic questions about, well, *marriage*. Specifically: What the hell was it? A romantic comedy, where there was a Mr. Right and a Mr. Wrong? Where love and happiness were the same thing? Or was it a Russian novel, where you could marry the person of your dreams, get in fact everything you ever longed for from life—true love, riches, a beautiful family—only to discover, like Levin, that you had to hide all the rope in the house so you wouldn't hang yourself? Where there was no right or wrong choice, just varieties of sadness?

At least neither of them was ill. They'd given up trying to quarantine the norovirus sufferers: Bradley was sick now too, along with Jake and Mrs. Margolis. Luckily, Mr. Margolis was in recovery, and had even managed to roast Cece and Charlie at the picnic, using a visual aid "to demonstrate the dynamic between the lucky couple." In front of all the guests, he'd blown up a balloon—"This is Charlie," he'd said—and then had slipped a sewing needle from his pocket—"Cece"—before popping the balloon. Everyone laughed, of course, including Cece's dad and stepmother, who didn't know Charlie well enough to get the joke. Cece laughed as well, though in truth she felt sick to her stomach. Charlie's thing was to be big, to inflate himself like a balloon, and her thing was to bring him back down to size? Who'd *hired* her for this job? Cece hadn't ever conceived of their relationship like this before, and yet now it had been demonstrated for her, whimsically, using props. She looked at her grandmother, sitting by herself in a camp chair—heroic, exhausted-looking Grammy, who'd made it in on a red-eye after a delayed flight—and wanted to climb into her lap.

But when Charlie sensed this—no, even *before* he sensed that Cece wasn't altogether down with this characterization—he set the record straight. He said to the guests at the picnic, in his unfailingly polite and charming way, that this wasn't true. That Cece was going to be the balloon soon enough, and that he, Charlie, would have to be the needle—although Charlie might have to grab a scalpel from work, given how famous she was going to get. Somehow, he said all this without condescension. Everyone laughed and cheered, sitting at picnic tables spread with hamburgers and hot dogs and potato chips, the Salish Dam roaring softly behind them, sending up a gentle mist that made a rainbow, and Cece was so happy and proud that she hardly cared if Charlie was exaggerating or if she still hadn't figured out exactly what to do with her life. So what if no one else believed it? Everyone adored Charlie; she did too. For a second she was too happy to breathe. She could hardly believe that he'd consented to marry her. All the misgivings she'd had on her bachelorette night, when she'd worried that she was getting married for the wrong reasons—to collect an IMPORTANT MOMENT for the Museum of Life or, worse, fill an emptiness she'd mistaken for love—seemed stupid and childish, a result of looking at too many square dance videos online.

Secretly, she was glad that Garrett hadn't shown up at the picnic, just as he hadn't shown up at the Margolises' dock at one thirty, for the wedding rehearsal. His dad was in the hospital—a stroke or a hemorrhage, somehow connected to the illness in his lungs. Charlie had told her this, insisting Garrett would be there for the wedding itself. He had his speech all written; someone could coax him through the logistics on the big day if need be. Cece had just nodded, worried for Garrett's sake but also relieved, as if a plane she'd been sitting on for a long time had finally left the ground. Besides, the rehearsal was pretty much a wash, seeing as only half the groomsmen were healthy enough to participate. Charlie, walking through the mock ceremony, pretending that his brothers and best friend were actually present, seemed for the first time a bit depressed. By "the first time," Cece meant *ever, in his entire life.*

"I'm sorry about Garrett," Charlie said. "I should never have asked him to do it."

Cece smiled. "It doesn't matter."

Charlie looked at her in amazement. "You're not worried that our wedding officiant is AWOL?"

She shook her head. Why was she so relieved? It didn't occur to her to examine it. "Your father can do it if need be. I don't care what happens anymore—whether it's perfect or not."

He peered at her suspiciously.

"Maybe it's because I haven't been online," she explained. "I'm off the grid. Haven't even checked my email in two days."

"Seriously?"

"It was making me crazy, remember? All those wedding lists." She'd kissed him, devoutly, on the forehead. "At this point, I'd rather not know what else we've done wrong."

So why, now, couldn't she sleep? Cece stripped the covers from her body, forming a moat of comforter between her and Charlie and staring at the ceiling, naked and unmoving, like a garden waiting for rain. Charlie, roaming the void of his sleep, stopped snoring for a moment and moaned happily. *Having insomnia next to a happy sleeper,* Cece thought, *is like attending an AA meeting in a bar.* Aphorisms were coming to her unbidden. It promised to be a long night. Her laptop sat on the wardrobe, where she'd put it deliberately out of reach; from her vantage in bed, she could just see the corner of it, a silver triangle gleaming in the dark. She thought about giving in to temptation and taking the thing into the living room, logging in to MySpace for a bit, but knew she'd regret it. Besides, all her friends and family were *here.* For the wedding. She'd check her email in the morning, just to make sure there weren't any emergencies.

If only there were some weed in the house! Cece considered getting up and rooting around the place, just in case Charlie's friends hadn't smoked it all—but the house wasn't hers anymore. She and the house had broken up. Or rather, it had left her for the Margolises. Earlier this morning, Mr. Margolis had pleasantly scolded her for leaving the porch gate open, and the porch, its gate creaking back and forth in the wind, seemed to agree with him. She'd gone out to close it, feeling strangely bereft. It made no sense. She was getting married at the house, tomorrow! They would have plenty of time—an entire life—to get reacquainted.

She was happy and sure. She was happy and sure.

ELEVEN

Garrett listened to his father breathe, the steady rhythm of it broken every so often by an alarming in-suck of air. Oxygen tubes snaked into his nose and wrapped around his ears, cinching under his chin. He looked spiritually debased, like a cat dressed up in a bonnet. Plus his hospital gown kept riding up his legs. Garrett, who'd never seen it before yesterday, had become familiar with his father's scrotum, a dark veiny thing that seemed to be a different color than the rest of him. Garrett took the sight of it basically in stride, chalking it up to his father's downward climb, the latest stop in his multipitch descent from god to mortal.

Mercifully, it had not been a major stroke. Garrett had known the risk was there; the lungs of IPF sufferers scarred and started to fail, which taxed the heart and led, in some cases, to blood clots. Or so Dr. Shrayber had told him. Garrett had rushed to the hospital—running red lights while his father slumped in the passenger seat, throwing up on himself—because that's what you did with stroke victims. You drove like a maniac. You teleported them to the ER. A supernatural composure had possessed him, guiding Garrett invincibly through the streets. He'd even had the sense to call ahead. An ER team had greeted them at the curb, like a pit crew.

He'd spent the night at the hospital, worried this was it. But now his father, drifting in and out of sleep, seemed better. He'd stopped throwing up; he knew what year it was; he could close his eyes and touch his nose with the forefinger of each hand. When asked, he could lift his palms symmetrically in the air, like someone delivering a pizza. He had not tried to walk yet, but his brain seemed to be there, still curating memories into a self.

Even so, it was the beginning of the end.

The patient in the room next door began to howl. A kind of despondent moan-bellow, as if he were calling for the rest of his brain to come home. The poor guy had been doing this for hours, ever since he'd returned from neurosurgery. It was the only sound he could make. Walking by his room earlier, Garrett had caught a glimpse of an old man trembling like an infant, wearing what looked like a marching band hat: an enormous bandage, held in place by a strip under the chin. Meanwhile, in a room down the hall, a nurse shouted, "Rosa, can you hear me?" at the top of his lungs. Over and over again the nurse shouted this, and over and over again Rosa failed to answer. A typical day, it seemed, in the Neuro ICU.

Garrett was the implausible one here. He looked at his father's sleeping face, its quaint impersonation of death, and his heart went sideways in his chest.

His dad woke up eventually, then brightened when he saw Garrett there. A coquettish smile, courtesy of Dilaudid.

"How are you feeling?" Garrett asked.

"Like one of those blind skiers."

Garrett laughed. This was the thing they didn't tell you on all those TV hospital dramas—that the patients were all as high as a kite. "What are you talking about?"

"Haven't you seen them? At Big Sky? They have those orange vests that say 'blind' on them. The guide skis in front of them and yells out commands through this PA thing. 'Turn a left!' 'Turn right!' They have no idea where they're going—just swoosh down in the dark."

Garrett frowned. It occurred to him, suddenly, that he had no idea if his father believed in a higher power. He'd always assumed he was an atheist, though they'd never discussed his religious beliefs; for all Garrett knew, he was Zoroastrian. Garrett stood up from his chair. Outside the window, ten stories down, a guy in scrubs was playing Hacky Sack by himself in the green space across the street, ponytail wagging as he hopped from foot to foot. Could he possibly be a *doctor*? A *neurosurgeon*?

"Remember when we were skiing that time and you asked to borrow that guy's sunblock, then dropped it off the lift by accident?"

Garrett's father, still smiling, looked at him blankly.

"The guy was furious. He was German or something and didn't speak much English."

"Must have been your mother," his father said.

"It was you!" Garrett said. "We laughed about it the whole ride home. '*Mein* face stick!'"

His father shook his head. He closed his eyes again, following the Dilaudid drift of his thoughts. Garrett's sadness curdled into despair. A stupid little thing, nothing at all really, but he'd never laughed so hard with his father, exhausted from a long day of skiing and remembering the poor German's face when they'd offered him an Almond Joy in return. And yet his dad had forgotten it completely.

Garrett fiddled with his father's leg massager, Velcro-ing it more tightly around his calf to make sure it was working properly, preventing another blood clot from firing into his brain. How small and helpless his father seemed. And yet to Garrett he was the most powerful king on earth. All he had to do was ditch his family—joyously, as soon as his son went off to college—to be enthroned forever. What did Garrett want from him? An apology? An *I love you, son, I always have*, like in the movies? Watching his dad's heartbeat on the monitor, transmuted into peaks and canyons, Garrett realized he'd been waiting for something all this time, waiting since that day his father called him from a motel to say he wasn't coming back—realized that he might have even moved back to Montana, ten miles from his father's house, specifically to hear it.

The nurse came in to do her hourly test—"Close your eyes and hold your hands in the air"—and Garrett's dad obeyed her, doing his invisible-pizza routine. Garrett's nose prickled inside. It occurred to him that no one else was coming to visit his father—even knew, needless to say, that he was in the hospital. Garrett was all he had. He thought about calling Chad, his ex-boyfriend, but based on his dad's nickname for him ("Chad the Impaler"), Garrett decided he wouldn't want to see him.

The nurse left, and the moaning started up again next door, ranging expressively in pitch. Really it was more of a song, as complex and mournful as a whale's, which Garrett remembered from one of his childhood books could travel ten thousand miles.

"What's the big guy from *Star Wars*?" his father said. "Cowardly Lion?"

"You mean Chewbacca?"

"Yes." He smiled. "Sounds like that."

"Shhh," Garrett said, getting up to close the door. "His family might hear you."

His father watched him tenderly. For a moment, Garrett thought he was about to speak. Instead, his father let out a slow, earnest, forlorn-sounding moan. Was he making fun of the guy next door? Impersonating Chewbacca? Impossible to tell. Either way, he kept a straight face, staring into Garrett's eyes. Garrett, interpreting it as a joke, moaned sorrowfully back to him. His father stared at him without blinking. The room felt different somehow, as if they'd been away for a while and come back to it. Garrett cleared his throat. It was the most they'd ever said to each other.

He had the urge, suddenly, to tell Cece about this. How he'd moaned along with his father and didn't know if it was a joke. Amazingly, he hadn't thought about her—or about the shame of her reading his email—all day.

His father closed his eyes once again, exposing the veins of his eyelids. They looked like cracks in an eggshell. Garrett peered around the empty room, then back at his father, wondering if they shared a terminal gene of loneliness—if he was destined, like his father, to end up alone. After all, he'd had plenty of friends in college, just as his father, at one point, had been the life of the party. Charlie and Elias had been like brothers to him.

His father's breathing deepened. Exhausted, Garrett slumped down in his chair and closed his eyes too, falling half-asleep himself, imagining he was one of those blind skiers swooshing through the dark. Except where were the instructions? No one was telling him what to do.

TWELVE

1.

Charlie sat in class, trying to listen to what Professor Yamamoto had to say about Kierkegaard's *Concluding Unscientific Postscript*. The problem was the student sitting next to him. The guy kept answering Yamamoto's questions as soon as they left his mouth, as if he were sitting in Yamamoto's office with him and the rest of the class didn't exist. Charlie could see the other students rolling their eyes. The student next to him, the know-it-all, had messy black hair and a very wrinkled shirt and what looked like a coffee stain on his nose, perhaps from drinking from a thermos. He also had an adversarial relationship with his desk: one of those long-legged guys who were always shifting around in their seat, as if holding in a fart. He'd use some word Charlie had never heard before—"ontological," say, or "ineluctable"—squirming all the while inside the prison of his desk. Even Yamamoto seemed a bit put off by him, though it was clear, too, that he was impressed. Charlie would have been more annoyed by the guy if he didn't recognize something in his restlessness, an aspirational quality that seemed at odds with his confidence. He wasn't one of the prep schoolers from Exeter or Andover. He was from the West, like him. Probably not California. There was a Rocky Mountain drift to his vowels. Plus he had a way about him—an eagerness, cool for not giving a shit whether it was cool or not—that suggested he'd spent his life dreaming about going to a college like Middlebury and was determined to squeeze every last drop he could out of it.

The beautiful girl sitting on the other side of the guy's desk must have seen something in him too, because she introduced herself after class. Charlie eavesdropped while zipping up his backpack. Sabina, she introduced herself as—though Charlie already knew her name. Sabina Gonzales was one of those goddesses who, miraculously, also seem to be warm and approachable and friendly to mortals. They'd made a kind of altar to her in the bathroom on Charlie's hall, her class picture taped to the mirror above the sink. The graffiti surrounding it was more chaste than obscene: a couple marriage proposals, a cartoon wolf with an enormous heart trampolining from his chest, the poignant YOU GIVE ME HOPE TO CARRY ON that nobody would own up to.

The know-it-all stayed to chat with Dr. Yamamoto while he erased his notes from the board, and Charlie deliberately lagged in the hall, waiting by the stairs. He couldn't say why he wanted to meet the boy so much. It was an instinctive thing, a vague tingling promise, as if some of the boy's galling confidence would rub off on him. In the three months he'd been at Middlebury, Charlie had met lots of fun, likable guys who enjoyed playing foosball or knew how to get a bottle cap off without an opener or maybe even whose favorite movie was *A Clockwork Orange*—but nobody Charlie could really talk to about things. He'd imagined college would be like it was in certain movies he'd seen, that he'd be staying up all night debating the existence of God, or at least doing inspired and memorable things, but so far it was just like high school. In some ways, in fact, it felt *more* like high school than high school itself. Kahlúa was humiliating enough, but Jell-O shots? Charlie had always assumed they were a hoax, like the left-handed Whopper. But no—they actually existed. Not that he didn't like to get loaded; he just wanted to get loaded with brilliant, funny, exceptional people.

"Did you get that girl's number?" Charlie asked the guy when he finally left class, feeling how supremely unexceptional a question this was. He'd rushed to catch up with him. The guy started a bit, as if surprised to be spoken to.

"She's not really my type."

"Not your type! She's everyone's type."

The guy stopped to open the door. "I'm not sure that exists. Unless you're talking about, I don't know, Ingrid Bergman."

Charlie followed him outside, the air numbing his face. What sort of kid made Ingrid Bergman references? Charlie had only a vague idea who she was. The December sky was flat and pitiless, so gray that looking at it felt like a kind of blindness. Recently the snow on the ground had melted a bit during a brief last gasp of fall and then frozen again overnight, turning every walkway on campus into a bobsled run. It was the season of the embarrassing injury. All over campus people were slipping and bruising their tailbones, sometimes worse. Charlie had already fallen twice, landing cartoonishly on his ass. It was so cold in the morning that he'd stopped showering before class, worried his wet hair would freeze into a helmet; he'd heard about a freshman who'd gone bald because an upperclassman had smacked his hair, shattering it clean off his head.

Now Charlie did something he hadn't expected to do. He slipped on the ice again. Or rather, he pretended to slip, knowing that the guy from Yamamoto's class would stop and help him up, that they'd be forced to shake hands. It was a freaky thing to do—he'd never pretended to fall before, even to meet a girl—but Charlie did it anyway.

Sure enough, the guy leaned down and helped him up, their breath merging into a single cloud. Charlie proceeded to be grateful. "You've got to watch out for the ice," he said, brushing the snow off himself. "It's a real pain in the wazoo."

The guy smiled. "Did you just say 'wazoo'?"

"I guess so. Why?"

"I've just never heard anyone say that before. In the wild."

Charlie blushed. His mother was the one who said "wazoo"

and "crumbum" and "har-dee-har"; for years Charlie had been trying to shed her influence, a kind of congenital dorkiness. But in this case it seemed to pique the know-it-all's interest. He was suddenly looking at Charlie in a curious, attentive way. Often, years later, Charlie would credit the birth of their friendship to that fact that he'd used the word "wazoo" instead of "ass."

"I just mean you've got to watch your step," he said.

"I'm acquainted with ice. We've got plenty of it in Missoula."

"You're from Montana?"

The guy nodded.

"I go to Salish every summer," Charlie said happily, unable to contain himself. "We've got a house on the lake. I mean, my parents do. My great-grandfather built it. I've been going there since I was a baby." He stopped, realizing how this must sound. *There's a major trucking route in front of the house,* he wanted to say, but that would only have sounded worse.

"My grandparents live near Jewel Basin. Not too far from there."

"Amazing!" Charlie said, though his new acquaintance didn't seem to find the connection particularly impressive. Perhaps he had deeper things on his mind. They introduced themselves, the guy presenting his name—Garrett—as if it were perfectly in tune with the Trips and Blakelys and Campbells they went to school with. Charlie hadn't known how lost he felt on the sea of Eastern preppiness he'd been navigating for the past three months until he heard the Western homeliness of that name. It was like the sight of land on the horizon. They walked toward the dining hall, hunched together for warmth. It was so cold that you had to think about moving your lips when you talked. Garrett asked if he was planning to be a philosophy major.

"Are you kidding?" Charlie said. "I'm premed."

"You want to be a doctor?"

"A cardiac anesthesiologist."

Garrett laughed. "That's very specific."

"Well, I'm into saving people's lives, but I don't think I have the nerves to be a surgeon. Those guys are like the fighter pilots of medicine. It's all about going into combat. I'm more of a, I don't know, *tactician*. Plus I loved making potions as a kid."

Garrett laughed again, perhaps assuming this was a joke. Charlie felt vaguely hurt. He asked Garrett what he wanted to major in.

"I'm thinking about a triple major, actually," he said. "Philosophy, English, environmental studies."

This time it was Charlie who laughed. Was he *serious*? Did triple majors even exist?

The trees around them had frozen into glass replicas of themselves, some of their branches glued to the ground. Charlie and Garrett passed a snowman that had been rained on overnight and then refrozen into a volcano. Just beyond it, the path slanted downhill at what was usually an inconsequential pitch, made harrowing now by a sheen of ice. The slope was long and ran all the way to the road; rather than imperil their lives, previous travelers had cut a bootleg trail through the snow.

Garrett stopped at the top of the hill for a second, as if taking in the view. Then, flashing Charlie a grin, he leapt flat-footed onto the slope, sliding down the iced-over path in his snow boots. He picked up speed, gradually at first and then more and more rapidly, managing somehow to stay upright, bending his knees and thrusting his arms behind him as if he were tucking down a ski jump. He barreled toward the road, where a line of cars had stopped at a traffic light. Charlie yelled out. He would crash! Split his head open and die! Garrett sailed toward the wall of traffic—Charlie bellowing now, sure he would smash his brains all over the road—but then Garrett sprang off the path at the last minute, arms outstretched like wings, and landed gracefully in the snow.

"Come on!" Garrett called up the hill. "It's a blast!"

"No way!"

"It's just like skiing!"

His face looked demented. It seemed impossible that this was the same guy just talking about Kierkegaard's refutation of Hegelian determinism in class. Charlie was scared to do it but also knew that he'd look like a chickenshit if he didn't. He was an accomplished skier, though only when he was on skis. Why did he want to impress Garrett so badly?

In the end, he did what he did when working up the courage to drop into a treacherous chute: he imagined that his body was on fire. Skiing downhill was the only way to put it out. He inched forward, one Sorel at a time, doing a kind of rehab shuffle until the path steepened and he found himself bending his knees and precipitously taking flight, sliding down the ice at a speed he hadn't imagined possible without something strapped to his feet. The air froze his face, squeezing tears from his eyes even though he was laughing, savoring the pride of his own daring while realizing at the same time what a dumbass he was, that what he was doing was profoundly stupid, nothing to be proud of at all, possibly even a cry for help—*I'm in college and I still say "wazoo"!*—and yet he hurtled toward the road, whooping like an idiot.

———

Elias waited in the infirmary, subjected to death by Muzak. An instrumental version of "Afternoon Delight." Actually, the feeling it gave him was less like death and more like birth, or rather pre-birth, as if he were floating in an amniotic sac. To entertain himself, Elias imagined the musicians recording the song in the studio, the bassist laying down a fat, righteous groove while his bandmates in the control room passed around a spliff. It was what he always did when listening to elevator music. *Fuck yeah*, the electric harpist would say, nodding with his eyes closed.

The nurse practitioner had disappeared some time ago. Down the hallway, Elias could only see the closed door of the room where she'd taken two freshman guys, one of them holding the other around the waist to help him walk. It seemed weird that they'd gone into the examination room together. Maybe they were lovers. Elias was cool with that. He was cool with just about everything, save for being strangled to death. That was what his roommate had tried to do to him this morning. He'd pounced on Elias while he was half-dozing in bed and gripped him by the throat with both hands, squeezing so hard Elias thought for a second he might croak. Gunnar, his roommate, had come to his senses finally and let go. The two of them did not get along—rooming together had been a disaster from day one—but Elias had not pegged the guy for a murderer.

Now his neck was turning the color of an eggplant. Plus it hurt to turn to the left. And to the right. And not to turn it at all. The girl he was seeing, Hannah, had made him promise to have it looked at.

Presently the door to the examination room opened and the nurse practitioner emerged, looking put out, trailed at some distance by the two freshmen. One was holding an ice pack to his elbow, his arm done up in a sling. They sat beside Elias in the waiting room while the nurse practitioner prepared something for them on the computer.

"Hey there," Elias said, to be friendly. He made a point to be nice to gay people and freshmen, both common victims of bullying.

"What happened to your neck?" the unhurt one asked. Elias told them the story of almost being strangled to death.

"Jesus. That's messed up. You should get him kicked out of school."

"I don't want to get him kicked out," Elias said, feeling the bruise on his neck. "We used to be buddies. Before we moved in together, I mean." He looked at the two boys, one of whom was carrying both of their backpacks. "Are you guys roommates?"

"Actually, we just met!" the guy with the sling said.

"What?"

"About an hour ago," No Sling concurred.

"I fell down and he helped me up," Sling said.

"A man falls on his wazoo, it stirs me to chivalry."

Elias laughed. "At least you haven't attacked each other yet."

"Actually, he did this to my arm," Sling said. "Talked me into sliding down a ski jump of ice. Then he tackled me and sprained my elbow."

"I tackled him because he was about to fly into a semitruck. Also because he looked terrified. Also because he was yelling, 'Stop me!'"

Elias laughed again. There was something wrong with these goofballs. But also something not wrong at all. Elias couldn't look at them without feeling like a window somewhere had been cracked. Maybe his problem was hanging out with sophomores like himself; all they did was slump around, depressed, and complain about their midterms.

The nurse practitioner handed a prescription to Sling, then disappeared into the back again. It seemed to be a one-person operation. The two freshmen zipped up their jackets—No Sling helping Sling—then retrieved their winter hats from the coatrack. Elias introduced himself, hoping to prolong their company.

"Why did your roommate try to strangle you anyway?" the one named Charlie asked.

"Long story," Elias said. He told them about turning Gunnar's underwear pink because he'd failed to separate darks from lights, which led to Gunnar's refusing to take turns doing the laundry, which led to Elias's going on strike and refusing to wash the dishes in the sink of their suite, which led to Gunnar's picking all of Elias's dirty dishes out of the sink and tossing them into a pile next to the dumpster behind Gifford, where they got covered in snow (last week) and then irretrievably encased in ice (last night). Gunnar had discovered Elias eating instant ramen for breakfast out of his favorite mug, which had sent him into a homicidal rage. "What else was I supposed to do?" Elias explained. "The dishes are trapped till spring."

"You're not on the meal plan?"

Elias shook his head. "I haven't eaten a real meal for a week."

"We can sneak you into the dining hall," Garrett said.

"How?"

"You're speaking to an operative of Dining Services." He checked his watch. "Proctor's still open for a couple three minutes."

"A couple three? What does that mean?"

"Beats me," Charlie said happily. "He's from Montana."

Elias grabbed his coat from the rack.

"What about your neck?" Charlie asked.

"Screw it. I'm going to strangle *myself* if I have to listen to this music any longer."

At Proctor Hall, Garrett sneaked Elias through the door where the kitchen staff took out the trash while Charlie went in the normal way, handing his ID card to the doorkeeper on duty. He didn't like breaking rules and was nervous they'd all be caught and sent to the dean's office. Maybe even suspended. But Elias and Garrett were already in line when he got to the taco bar, happily loading up their trays, as if they'd been friends for years. And Charlie felt that way too, that the three of them had known each other for years instead of minutes. They'd been bewitched somehow, like the trees.

Garrett helped Charlie carry his tray, since he was still icing his elbow. They sat down with a couple of friends from Charlie's hall, Johnny and Marcus, who were playing a game of shuffle-board with the saltshaker. Johnny and Marcus were not hard to spot, given that the rest of the tables were filled with Trips and Corkys. Also, they were wearing Hawaiian shirts in the middle of winter. They'd begun to do this last week, as a form of psyops against the cold. As far as he'd thought about it, which wasn't

very far at all, Charlie assumed he'd befriended the two freshmen of color on his hall purely by chance, though it occurred to
him now, introducing them to Garrett and Elias, that maybe it
wasn't as random as he thought. Just seeing them warmed the
homesick Californian in his soul.

"What happened to your arm?" Johnny asked.

"I fell on the ice," Charlie said.

"So you're putting more ice on it."

"Yep."

"You're the doctor."

Johnny peered at the food on Elias's tray. "Jesus. Has it been,
like, a week since you've eaten?"

"Actually, yes."

The four of them watched Elias attack his food. It felt like an
event, something you might charge admission for. The bruise on
his neck had continued to spread, darkening like a cloud. Given
that Elias was so handsome—and it was clear, even with the
gargantuan hickey on his neck, that he was threateningly handsome, with his brown skin and Roman nose and green eyes the
color of Easter grass—it did not surprise Charlie that another
guy, a competitor in the Middlebury game of musical beds, had
attacked him. Sharing a room with him was probably not the
easiest thing in the world. So Charlie was taken aback when the
beautiful girl from philosophy class, happening to pass their
table while busing her tray, paid no attention to Elias but smiled
conspicuously at Garrett, revealing a speck of cilantro between
her teeth. Garrett nodded back, as if greeting a stranger.

"Who was *that*?" Elias asked. He'd stopped eating and seemed
to have forgotten about the boiled potato at the end of his fork.

"I forget her name," Garrett said.

"Sabina Gonzales," Charlie said.

Elias stared after her, holding his potato aloft.

"Are you all right?" Charlie asked him.

"He's not moving," Johnny said.

"Maybe he ate himself to death," Marcus said.

After lunch, the five of them walked back to their dorms. The sun had magically appeared—the first they'd seen of it in weeks—and the trees were painful to look at, seeming to shine from the inside out. Elias stopped outside his dorm room to show them the mound of dirty dishes floating in a pristine dome of ice, like one of those glass weights with a tarantula inside. Not only spoons and knives and bowls, but the crust from a piece of toast and what looked like a half-eaten meatball levitating over a plate. Garrett squatted beside it and knocked on the ice.

"Wow," he said.

"It's like one of those Jell-O salads with the fruit inside them," Charlie said.

"Have you tried peeing on it?" Marcus said.

"On my own dishes?" Elias said.

"I'm just thinking about survival. It's going to be a long winter."

Elias peered at the window of his room, where the light was on. A languid guitar solo, all roll and no rock, burbled from inside.

"Smells Phish-y," Johnny said.

"The psycho's home," Elias lamented. "I can't go inside."

"Stay with me," Garrett said, or perhaps demanded.

"Don't you have a roommate?"

"Nope. The guy never showed up for school." He did a victory thing on the ice—a moonwalk?—that was hard to interpret. "I've got a double to myself."

"Okay," Elias said. "I mean, if it's cool with your friends."

"What friends?"

"You don't have friends?"

Garrett shrugged. "You're the first people I've met here that I've liked."

2.

For Halloween sophomore year, the three of them—Charlie, Garrett, and Elias—dressed up as speed bumps. This involved wearing all yellow and then lying on the floor without moving. They did this at several dorm parties, stretching across the hallway so everyone had to step over them. It was a convincing costume in that it authentically congested traffic.

"We're speed bumps," Charlie said for the umpteenth time, because the costumes required a fair bit of explanation.

"So it's okay if I step on your faces?" a Jedi knight asked them.

"No," Charlie said.

"You can *drive* over our faces," Elias clarified. Somehow, dressed in matching yellow sweats—which, like Charlie and Garrett's, were stuffed with dirty laundry—he was still handsome. Elias tried to drink supinely from his cup and found that half its contents ended up on his face. "Whose idea was this anyway?"

"Garrett's."

Garrett shrugged. "I'm sort of a genius."

"Is that why everyone thinks we're ducks?"

"I don't expect to be understood in my own time."

Eventually someone came along dressed as a car. This seemed highly propitious. It took a moment for Charlie to recognize who it was, given that she was wearing a cardboard box pimped into a roadster, then spray-painted silver to look like the Monopoly token. The smell from the floor was narcotic. She honked at them rather than step over Charlie without his permission.

"We're speed bumps," he said. "This is a five-mile-per-hour zone."

"I'm just trying to get to Vermont Avenue."

"Greetings," Garrett said. "You were in our philosophy class freshman year."

"I remember," the Monopoly token said, resting her hands on

her hood as if she were pregnant. "Dr. Yamamoto. You looked pretty different."

"We were too shy to talk to you."

"Hmmm. I don't remember you being too shy to talk in class."

Garrett blushed, perhaps the first time he'd ever been embarrassed about speaking too much. "I have a speed bump that would like to meet you."

Elias, who hadn't said a word, nodded at her. Charlie had seen him seduce countless girls, but now he lay there with his arms clapped to his sides, refusing to break character. He roused himself eventually and tried to shake her hand, reaching up from the floor, but it was impossible for her to reciprocate, and so there was nothing for Elias to do but drop his arm and lie there again in a municipal way. Sabina Gonzales left in bemusement.

"What's the matter with you?" Charlie asked Elias.

"I'm not sure."

"A speed bump in love with a car," Garrett said. "It's like *Romeo and Juliet*."

Later, the three of them staggered home beneath a blizzard of stars. Charlie and Garrett, both drunk, walked with their arms around each other, leaving a trail of dirty laundry behind them. It was late enough that the dormitories were mostly dark, a single window lit up here and there among the black ones, like a gold tooth. Elias wedged his way between Charlie and Garrett, sharing the weight of their drunkenness. How Charlie loved them, these nights when it felt like the three of them were basically one person, when everything they said was funny and perfect and also somehow nostalgically aware of itself, as if they could already hear the stories they'd tell about it the next morning, making everything they did seem larger than it was and confirming for Charlie in a lyrically poignant way that his vision for their future was correct. They would be famous, and financially okay, and would end up with beautiful, horny, brilliantly intelligent wives.

They rounded the student union in the dark and ran into the rest of their tribe: Marcus, Johnny, Brig. The six boys hugged tearfully, as if they hadn't seen each other in years. Marcus and Johnny, who'd glued a bunch of trash to their shirts, were supposed to be flotsam and jetsam. But Brig had outdone them all, dressed as a businessman caught in a storm. His umbrella had been turned inside out, exposing its ribs, and he'd shellacked his hair so that it looked like it was gusting back; even his tie was sticking up in the air, molded to seem like it was blowing over one shoulder. He staggered around, hunched and bandy-legged, as if walking into a gale. The speed bumps felt strangely exalted. Occasionally someone executed a costume so perfectly that it made you wonder whether you'd undersold what life had to offer.

Elias, at any rate, had sprung the cage to his soul. He wandered into the quad and lifted his yellow shirt up to his chin, baring his chest to the night. "Sabina!" he howled. "Where are you?" Charlie tried to shush him, forgetting that two thirty in the morning was the hour of drunken howling, that all across campus boys and girls—serious students, many of them, with excellent GPAs—were yelling names into the night. It was like a rite of affliction. Elias howled Sabina Gonzales's name so pathetically, with such drunkenness and despair, that Charlie half-expected her to run out of her dorm room and leap, Scooby-Doo–style, into his arms. On such a beautiful night, anything seemed possible.

And in fact something did happen. One of the darkened windows squealed open. It was not Sabina Gonzales, but someone with a beard.

"Shut the fuck up!" he yelled from the third floor, and began throwing baseballs at them.

"Sorry!" Charlie said. "He's looking for someone else."

"Let me take a wild fucking guess. Her name's Sabina."

He threw another baseball. Charlie ducked and covered his head. The guy, though pitching from the third floor, had excellent aim.

"How many baseballs do you own?"

"Tell your friend, Scrooge McDuck, that she's not interested."

"What are you, her fucking father?" Brig said.

"He's my boyfriend, actually," Sabina Gonzales said, because she'd appeared at the window now as well. She was not dressed as a car anymore, which flattered her. In fact, she was wearing a knee-length jersey and possibly nothing else. The bearded guy put his arm around her, scowling half-heartedly at Charlie and his friends, as if unsure whether to bask in their envy or sprint down there and kick their asses. Charlie and Garrett tugged at Elias, who was staring at the window as if the world had collapsed.

"I need those balls back!" Sabina's boyfriend called after them. "They're school property!"

In front of the New Dorms, the six friends split off again, the speed bumps heading back to their suite in Atwater North. Elias wove back and forth on the grass, like a wounded duckling. Charlie and Garrett knew he'd be fine in a couple days—possibly even tomorrow—yet said scurrilous things about Sabina Gonzales, trying to buck him up. Already they were composing the story of tonight, archiving it for future retellings: the howling, the baseballs, the mystical appearance of Sabina in the window. It was the sort of story you laughed about for years, that gave birth to nicknames. Elias, from now on—*for the rest of his life, probably*—would be "McDuck." He took a baseball from his sweatpants and threw it at Charlie, as if in protest, then waddled off to bed.

Charlie and Garrett sat in their favorite place to smoke, a bench outside Atwater North with a relief map of gum stuck to one armrest. Who put the first piece there, no one knew, but it was a landform in expansion. Charlie pulled a pack of Viceroys

out of the kangaroo pocket of his sweatshirt and offered one
to Garrett, though not before complaining that Garrett never
bought packs for himself. They smoked only on special occasions, when they were drunk, which meant they smoked a lot.

"You're my tobacco mule," Garrett said.

"Tobacco duck," Charlie said, lighting their cigarettes. "You
could at least throw me some cash once in a while."

Garrett reached into his own front pocket and pulled out
some change and threw it at Charlie. It bounced off Charlie's
chest and landed in his lap. Some pennies, maybe a dime. Charlie leapt up from the bench.

"Don't ever fucking do that again," he said quietly.

Garrett stared at him. "Do what?"

"Throw pennies at me."

"You told me to!" He looked dumbfounded, astonished by
Charlie's anger, though no more astonished than Charlie himself.

"I know they don't have Jews in Montana, but don't be a
shithead."

Garrett looked stricken. Of course he hadn't meant anything.
He was clueless. Clueless and drunk. Charlie's rage evaporated.
He felt suddenly like he might cry. He wanted to tell Garrett he
was sorry, that he loved him like a brother, but you didn't say
these things out loud. They were nineteen-year-old men. They
were dressed like ducks. Male friendship was all about rhythm. It
was a kind of song without words, an instrumental you knew by
heart, you learned the rhythm together and practiced it all the
time, for days and months and years, perfecting it by feel, it was
the swing of your silences, the karaoke track behind the gibberish you sang. The rhythm itself said the important things, the
non-jokey things, so you wouldn't have to. Still, there were times
like this, rare ones, when it wasn't enough. Charlie sat down on
the bench, drunkenly, and told Garrett about going to a largely
Jewish elementary school when he was a kid, how he never felt
like he completely fit in—he could sing the songs at Chanukah,

sure, finish the sentence "*Baruch atah Adonai . . . ,*" but that was about it—and how once when they scrimmaged another team in basketball, at a fancy prep school in Orange County, some kids in the bleachers had thrown pennies at them. Charlie hadn't even known what it meant. His father had had to explain it to him, that the kids in the stand were insulting him. Weirdly, he'd been angrier at his dad than anyone. It was all a mistake! They hung stockings at Christmas! The next year, for high school, he'd gone to a fancy prep school himself, and though there were some other Jewish kids there, or at least a few, Charlie never mentioned he was Jewish, or raised that way, and did everything he humanly could to fit in. It helped that he was good at sports. He joined every team he could: soccer, squash, water polo. Head of the ski club. He had to excel at everything. "I was class president. I was in the Admirals. I was on the honor roll. Homecoming king junior year! Oh man, the glory. I soaked it up. I had to be the most popular kid in school, but also the smartest, the funniest, the best athlete. Like I always had to prove myself worthy." Charlie flicked his cigarette to the ground, where it throbbed like a firefly. "That's why I wanted to be your friend so badly. That day in Intro to Philosophy. People were rolling their eyes when you talked, but you didn't care. You don't give a fuck what people think, about fitting in."

"They were rolling their eyes?" Garrett said.

"That's why I admire you," Charlie said. "You never want to be anyone but yourself!"

"That's not true."

"Yes, it is."

"I wish I was you all the time," Garrett said casually.

Charlie looked at him. "Yeah, right. Don't be a putz."

"Last night, when you were on the phone with your parents."

"What about it?" Charlie said.

"I was listening to you. How could I help it? Your family's so fucking loud. You were talking about something really stupid, like how your dad had a flat tire on his car and the tire guy said that he might have a leaky nipple, and how funny this was, that your dad had a leaky nipple, and I kept thinking, like, when have I ever talked to either of my parents about anything like that? We're lucky if we talk once a month. I mean my mom's got three stepkids; she hasn't even officially invited me for Thanksgiving. My dad's basically AWOL. And I could hear your brothers in the background, wanting to talk to you too, joking about your dad's leaky nipples." Garrett crashed his cigarette butt into the mountain of gum. "And your mom. She's always asking you how I'm doing and then saying how smart I am, because I used the word 'schadenfreude' in front of her one time. Sometimes, when I hear her voice on the phone, I get a boner."

Charlie offered him another cigarette. They were both lonely. They were far from home. They got infelicitous boners. Charlie looked at his best friend, feeling a love he could barely distinguish from the source of that love (himself).

"What's the worst thing you could do to me?"

" 'Worst' as in shitty?"

"As in despicable."

Garrett shrugged. "Have anal sex with your mother?"

Charlie nodded. "Let's make a vow, right now, to always be best friends, even if we fuck each other's moms in the wazoo."

"You mean like on Parents' Weekend?"

"Exactly!"

"I'm not sure that's fair," Garrett said finally. "Since you could probably fuck both my parents if you wanted to."

"True. What else could we do to each other?"

"Try to strangle each other in our sleep?"

"Yes! Like Elias's psycho roommate." Charlie lifted his chin. "Here, put your hands around my throat."

Garrett did as he was told. Then Charlie copied him, clutching Garrett's windpipe. They sat that way on the bench, affectionately gripping each other's throats.

"Repeat after me," Charlie said. "'I promise to stay friends even if you try to strangle me in my sleep.'"

"I promise to stay friends even if you try to strangle me in my sleep."

"'Forever and ever.'"

They let go. "I've never understood that. How can you have more than 'forever'?"

3.

They'd skinned up to an old mining hut, hauling two sleds of food and beer. The hut was so buried in snow it looked like part of the landscape until you found the front of it, and even then it looked a bit like a snow cave someone had barricaded with logs. The three of them—Charlie, Garrett, Elias—took off their skis and packs and rested to catch their breath. Even in January, the sun felt different from the one in Vermont, not just warmer but more companionable somehow, as if it were closer to the earth. It sniffed Charlie's face, fogging his sunglasses. He cleaned them with the pulled-out pocket of his fleece. Looming all around him, buried under sixty inches of snow, were the chutes and bowls and tree-candled glades of McMillan Peak, sparkling below the great scalloped cornice that ran along its ridge. Not a soul anywhere in sight. You couldn't even see a track. Charlie, who'd grown up skiing at Mammoth and Squaw Valley, trapped for hours in lift lines or waiting torturously on powder days for ski patrollers to howitzer the slopes, then watching those slopes get skied out in half an hour, felt almost deliriously happy.

They were on winter break—amazingly, Charlie and Garrett were juniors now, taking 400-level courses—and had come to southern Colorado to go backcountry skiing. It was the easiest place for them to meet: Garrett was in Albuquerque already, spending the holidays with his mom, so Charlie and Elias flew in from opposite coasts and he picked them up from the airport, the car loaded with supplies. The guy was like a scoutmaster. Not only did he have the sleds packed, Tetrised into the back of his mother's Subaru, but he'd found a beacon, shovel, and probe for each of them, even drummed up some AT gear from a guy he knew in Silverton. This wasn't telemarking—which Garrett had taught Charlie to do in Vermont—but a new genius thing where you could lock down your heels and ski alpine turns, as if you'd never left the resort. Charlie couldn't wait to try it.

They'd had some fine times in the Breadloaf Wilderness. But this was the West, the Rockies. The Appalachians were to the Rockies as, well . . . what? Snorkeling was to deep-sea diving? Charlie had never been on a hut trip before, and certainly not at twelve thousand feet.

Garrett went into the hut to get the woodstove going while Charlie and Elias unpacked the sleds, following him inside with bags of groceries. The hut was small and low-ceilinged and smelled dangerously of gas from the vintage Alcazar range hooked up to a propane tank outside the window. Charlie had to stoop to keep his head from grazing the ceiling, as if the miners who'd lived here long ago were the seven dwarfs. Waiting for the stove to heat up, Charlie rubbed his gloves together, trying to get the feeling back into his fingers. His sweat-soaked thermal had frozen solid, like a bulletproof vest. He loved this. He loved all of it. He was a huge proponent of frozen underwear and nineteenth-century mining huts.

"Man, it's fucking cold," Elias said. "I miss the lodge."

"What lodge?"

"Any lodge. A ski lodge. With overpriced cheeseburgers."

"But do ski lodges have *this*," Garrett said, lifting a ceramic sculpture from a shelf. The sculpture, the hut's lone decoration, depicted a naked woman fucking a skeleton.

"Wow. That is completely disturbing."

"What's it even supposed to mean?" Charlie asked.

"Means if a skeleton can get laid, there's hope for McDuck."

Charlie laughed. This was a joke that they'd had ever since Elias started seeing Sabina Gonzales. He refused to talk about their sex life, or even if they were sleeping together, so Garrett and Charlie had begun pretending she was saving herself for marriage.

"Anyway, you can never find a table at those places," Charlie said seriously.

"At least they *have* tables."

"What do you call this?" Charlie said, patting the giant stump someone had dragged into the center of the hut.

"Is there anything you don't enjoy?" Elias asked.

"Sure."

"Besides going to the dentist?"

Charlie shrugged. "Actually, I like having clean teeth."

Garrett put his hand on Elias's shoulder. "It will all make sense once we get up there skiing."

Elias looked at him skeptically. He'd grown up in Vermont and was probably the best skier of the three of them, having coped with eastern crud his entire life. But he'd never so much as boot-packed to a run before and had griped the whole way up to the hut, lagging behind Charlie and Garrett even though he wasn't towing a sled. The very idea of skiing uphill, rather than down, seemed to offend him. "Just think of it as a mountaineering trip," Charlie told him, which didn't do much to boost his spirits.

They ate a quick lunch—peanut butter and honey sandwiches, which Charlie had forgotten existed—then filled the stockpot with snow and melted it on the woodstove while Elias popped outside to the outhouse. He came back after a minute, looking shaken. The outhouse had not been cleaned all winter.

"There's like a stalactite of frozen shit, higher than the toilet seat."

"Stalagmite," Garrett corrected him.

"What the hell does it matter?"

"A stalactite would be hanging from the ceiling."

Elias frowned. "My larger point is that you can't *sit*."

"We can't be the first skiers to encounter this problem."

"We're not," Elias said despondently. "There's an ice pick leaning in the corner of the outhouse."

He looked at Garrett and Charlie. Garrett and Charlie looked at him back.

"Remember when you had to dig out all your dishes that time?" Charlie said.

Garrett kneaded his shoulder. "There's no hill for a climber."

Elias strapped on his goggles and returned to the outhouse. Charlie didn't feel too sorry for him. The guy was so madly in love—at school, he was basically orbiting in space—that it was hard to take his unhappiness seriously. Garrett had planned the trip partly as a way of spending some time with Elias, of extracting him for a few days from Sabina's dorm room, so there was bound to be a bit of resentment. The three of them were best friends and supposedly housemates, and yet he never slept at the Mill anymore and Charlie and Garrett had the wounded feeling they'd been replaced, or at least that Elias had moved on to a higher plane. Not to mention that he was a senior, graduating in a few months' time. Charlie didn't blame him, really—the guy had been in love with Sabina Gonzales for, oh, *two and a half years*—but there was the niggling worry, shared by Garrett too, that he'd already begun his departure.

Later, the three of them geared up and tested their avalanche beacons, pairing off and taking turns switching them to SEARCH, walking out of sight and then returning to make sure the beeps sped up as they approached their partner's signal. Then they double-checked that they were all on SEND and snapped into their skis and began the ascent toward McMillan Peak, skinning up single file, climbing gently through a copse of pines before eventually cresting the tree line and getting a panoramic view of the mountain for the first time, gazing upon the immaculate white bowl that seemed to trap the air in a new kind of stillness. Charlie's heart blew open like a door. He smiled at Elias behind him, who'd lost his grumpiness in the presence of all that snow and was smiling now too, his face glowing inside the hood of his jacket.

Charlie stopped to drink some water, but his Nalgene bottle was frozen shut. He'd forgotten to pack it upside down. Ahead of him, Garrett turned his skis peakward and cut more or less straight uphill toward the ridge. Charlie kept inside Garrett's tracks, where it was easier to skin. His head pounded from the altitude, he was dying of thirst, his toes and fingers were numb. Yet Charlie couldn't have been happier. At some point in the last three years, cold weather had ceased to bother him. He preferred it, in fact, to the seasonless warmth of California. It reminded him that he was on a planet, ninety-three million miles from the sun, and that something had collided with it a long time ago and made it lopsided, and therefore cold as shit in the winters. Back home in LA for the holidays, walking the dog in a T-shirt, he found himself feeling strangely uneasy, glancing around aimlessly or gazing at the snowless peaks of the San Gabriels in the distance.

After what felt like an hour of climbing, they reached the ridge and then rested a bit before transitioning. The air was thin enough that it was hard to catch their breath. The cornice smoldered in the wind, powder blowing off it like smoke that stung Charlie's lungs. They ripped their climbing skins off—Garrett did this without removing his skis, reaching back to the tail of each one and stripping the skin in a single fluid motion as if he were tearing off a Band-Aid—then folded them carefully and stuck them in their packs. Charlie snapped back into his bindings, locking his heels in place for the descent. Goggles on, they traversed in the shadow of the cornice, following the ridgeline in order to find the best pitch without losing too much vertical. Anything over thirty degrees, and you were in avalanche danger.

Garrett stopped at a wind-sheltered cirque that funneled at the tree line into a beautiful glade and took out his slope meter, then rested it on the snow to see where the little ball inside it stopped. Twenty-nine degrees. Just about perfect. No other skiers anywhere to be seen; they had the mountain—the whole universe, really—to themselves.

"Okay, fellas," Garrett said, grinning like a maniac. "Cold smoke as far as the eye can see."

"What are you talking about?" Elias asked.

"Pow-pow! That's what I'm talking about. Soft as a bunny's ass."

Elias turned to Charlie. "Why is he speaking that way?"

"It's like a brain injury or something. It always happens when we ski."

They let Elias get the first line, watching him push off into the knee-deep powder and then rise magically to the top of it as he picked up speed, floating in and out of the snow, bobbing up and down in a perfect gliding slalom that wasn't skiing or flying but somehow both of them at the same time, half-lost in the snow he sent up. His tracks seemed to unspool from a cloud of smoke, like a wick burning in reverse. He stopped at the edge of some krummholz and whooped up at them. Charlie traversed a bit to find a fresh line, his throat sore with excitement, hesitating because he almost didn't want to spoil the thrill he was about to have by having it.

But then he swallowed hard and pushed off with his poles, feeling that first lift of freedom, of leaving gravity behind, and he was floating downhill through snow light as flour, aiming straight down the fall line and shaping each turn into a perfect C, dragging one pole behind him, borne aloft by his own speed, as if a giant hand were lifting him up and down, up and down, bouncing him out of each turn, the easiest skiing in the world, one of the few things in life that were actually *better* than your dreams of them, which were already the best dreams Charlie had, but of course he wasn't thinking this but only feeling that seamless swerving hand underneath him, getting face shots every time he pitted a turn, eating snow because he was laughing out loud, or maybe whooping, lost in a white room of powder, until finally his quads began to burn so badly he was glad to stop beside Elias and slump over his poles and gasp for breath, wincing, the pain seeping from his thighs.

When he looked up at last, he was met with a beaming snow-man, Elias's beard flocked with snow. They grinned like children, like idiots. They couldn't help themselves. Garrett skied down after them, grinning stupidly as well. Charlie got that feeling he had occasionally: that life was a Christmas present, your only job to unwrap it. The three of them gazed uphill together, admiring the identical sine waves of their tracks.

They did laps for a while, trekking back up the cirque and then carving tracks again to the krummholz of the tree line instead of heading all the way down to the gully. Eventually, when there were no more fresh lines to be had, they called it a day and skied back to the hut, weak with hunger. Garrett made spaghetti for dinner while Charlie and Elias warmed themselves by the wood-stove. Elias was a changed man, the morning's grouchiness only a distant memory. They ate from plates on their laps.

"I was worried after the outhouse debacle," Garrett said, drinking from one of the Sierra Nevadas they'd brought. It was only dusk, though it felt like the middle of the night with the windows all blocked with snow. "You looked like a broken man coming out of there."

"Plus I was covered in shit."

"That too."

"By the way, this is the best spaghetti I've ever eaten," Elias said. "Is it a family recipe or something?"

"Ragú," Garrett said. "Old World Style."

"I'm going to serve this at my wedding."

"It's the one that says 'flavored with meat,'" Garrett said.

"May I suggest a warm-weather wedding?" Charlie said. "If you're going to have porta potties."

Elias stared at his plate, then peeked at them shyly. "We're thinking not this summer but next, after Sabina graduates."

Charlie and Garrett looked at each other.

"You haven't actually *proposed*?" Garrett said.

"Of course not. I mean, not *directly*. We just talk about it sometimes."

"Whoa."

"Holy shit, McDuck."

"You know you can't break up with her now like you do everyone else," Charlie said. "Only a douchebag would discuss wedding plans with someone and then dump her."

"Do I look like a douchebag to you?"

"Yeah. A little bit."

"I thought it was intentional," Garrett said.

Elias laughed. Then he set his beer on the stump and looked at them mistily. Perhaps it was the exhaustion from touring all day, or the altitude, but there may have been tears in his eyes.

"Can someone have two best men?"

"Why not?"

"I want you both to be up there with me. When it happens."

"So long as Sabina has two maids of honor," Garrett said.

"And they look a lot like her," Charlie said.

"Preferably her sisters."

"And their names are Sabina too."

That night, curled up on an old bunk in his sleeping bag, Charlie had trouble falling asleep, his head pounding from the altitude or perhaps the faint eggy smell of propane from the range. Across the room, Elias was snoring so loudly it sounded like the hut might collapse. Charlie's heart went out to Sabina Gonzales, if they were truly getting married. He closed his eyes again and drifted into a half dream he couldn't command or direct, though he was aware he was dreaming it, just as he was aware of Elias's snoring and the throb of his headache and the Rembrandt-y glow of the woodstove in the corner, nursing its embers. He saw a woman, naked, sitting with her back to him in the kitchen. She was levitating somehow a few feet off the ground. Then the naked woman turned sideways, coyly, and he saw that she wasn't levitating at all. She was having sex with something. A skeleton. Her legs were wrapped around its pelvis, head tossed back so that her hair touched the floor. The woman bucked and groaned. Charlie, still dreaming, was gripped by dread. Luckily, he didn't wake; the feeling dissipated into the corners of his sleep. It was lost somewhere inside of him.

The next morning, the three of them got up early and skinned up the same side of McMillan Peak. Another bluebird day, but colder, *Vermont* cold, the wind numbing the crack of forehead between Charlie's hat and goggles. The sun, dim as a thought, seemed to have been left in the sky by mistake. The snow had crusted over in the night, and their poles postholed through the crust. They followed their skin track from yesterday but then traversed farther along the ridge to a north-facing glade protected from the wind. Garrett thought the snow would be better. Also, Elias wanted something steeper. He was used to resort skiing, where he could schuss down the most perilous chutes.

Garrett took out his slope meter and measured the angle. Thirty-one degrees. Right on the edge. To be safe, they dug a snow pit with their shovels and Garrett cut out a tall column of snow with his saw and then did a compression test on it, something he'd learned from a ski patroller back home, laying his shovel blade on top of the column and tapping it gently at first with his fingers, then his palm, then increasing the strengths of his pats until he was using the full leverage of his elbow. No failures. He cut another column and repeated the test, just to make sure. Elias, shivering in the cold, watched in amusement.

"All this for a blue run?"

They skied it for a while, doing laps. The snow was almost as good as yesterday's. As the day warmed a bit, and the aching stiffness in his limbs seemed to thaw, Charlie felt the exhaustion from his bad night's sleep ebb away and leave him in the same sort of blissful daze he'd felt yesterday. Even his head had stopped hurting. Elias and Garrett seemed to feel the same way, too snow-drunk to speak. They were basically dogs, romping in the water. When the glade was skied out, they ate lunch and then skinned over the top of the ridge to the back side of McMillan Peak, where an enormous bowl funneled into a V-shaped valley with the pines all flagging to one side. It was glorious, a mist of snow ghosting across it. Garrett measured it at thirty-three.

"Rats," Charlie said.

Elias frowned. "Why rats?"

"Too steep."

"It's *two* degrees steeper than the last one."

"Which was already steeper than what we agreed to ski."

They looked at Garrett, who shrugged.

"At least do another test," Charlie said.

Elias groaned. "*Another* snow pit?"

Garrett knelt in the snow and dug a little hole with his glove, then probed the walls of it with his fingers, hunting for weak layers. It looked sound.

"I meant dig it out," Charlie said. "Shouldn't we do a real test?"

"We've tested it once."

"But this is the back side. Different snow."

"Temperature's been consistent," Garrett said equably, "and it hasn't snowed since Sunday."

Charlie looked at him. He knew this was exactly when you needed to be careful: when you'd been skiing all morning, floating through harmless powder, and began to feel invincible. How could something so fun be dangerous? Charlie felt this himself. And yet he also felt that forgotten dread from last night, that fathomless orphaned feeling, creep across his scalp. He didn't remember the dream itself—only its presence.

But Garrett seemed so confident and relaxed, so at ease in this world of endless snow—so, well, *Montanan*—that Charlie second-guessed himself. The feeling faded. He remembered the way Garrett had looked the first day they'd met, before sliding down that icy path in his boots. The same invincible playground grin. And nothing had happened then. Well, Charlie had sprained his arm, yes—but he'd also made the best friends of his life.

Elias, impatient, lowered his goggles. He looked at Garrett, waiting for the okay.

And Garrett nodded back, a bit pleased with himself, magnanimous even, as if he were handing him a present.

And of course it was only a ski run, no different from the rest they'd done, Elias whooping as he dropped his line and sent up a cloud of powder, carving each turn perfectly, ornamentally, as if engraving something in the snow. Charlie was suddenly ashamed of his own cowardice. Elias wove down the mountain. So effortless were his turns that he seemed almost bored. But he wasn't. He was whooping. He skied into the shade cast by a spur of the peak and a slab *whumpf*ed loose from the snowpack above him, small and harmless-looking, almost pretty to watch, like something sliding off the bed of a truck. Then the slab turned into a raft of debris that found Elias and swept him off his skis so that for a moment he was floating on top of it, yelling in a different way, skis pointing at the sky, but then he managed to get halfway upright again, dragging his ass along the snow before tumbling forward onto his stomach, bodysurfing the wave of debris, which reached the shallow base of the bowl and crested into a heap and came gently to a stop. The whole ride had lasted several seconds.

Charlie looked around, thinking that Elias had managed to stand up again and ski to one side of it. But he was gone. The bowl was deserted. It was only when Charlie looked at Garrett—

saw the dumb panicked stillness of his face—that he realized what had happened.

Garrett, who wasn't really there. Who'd left his body and was watching from above. Everything looked flat, implausible, like the leaves of a pop-up book.

A sickness, inside and out.

Charlie said something to him, but he didn't recognize the sounds Charlie was making, or even that they were meant to be different from each other. *Onion onion onion*, he seemed to be saying.

Rousing himself, Garrett skied down to where he thought Elias had gone under and ripped off his glove with his teeth and unzipped the beacon from his pocket, almost dropping it in the snow. His fingers stung in the cold, but the pain seemed to be happening to someone else. Fifteen minutes. Thirty at most, if Elias had made an air pocket for himself. Garrett switched his beacon to SEARCH. Even the thoughts he was having—*fifteen minutes, air pocket*—failed to seem real. He was shaking. Holding the beacon in one hand, he watched it carefully and crisscrossed the slide path on his skis, following the flux line on his screen, skiing like a beginner on a bunny slope, except through blocks of uneven snow, and then when it told him he was close he popped out of his skis and knelt in the runout zone and did a fine search, checking his distance reading, holding his beacon right over the snow until he found the lowest reading he could get. He did this alone, forgetting that Charlie was with him. Then he remembered. He yelled for Charlie's help, startled to see Charlie there beside him already, then got his probe out of his pack and assembled it shakily and plunged the probe into the snow as he'd been taught, probing in a small circle of plunges first and then moving concentrically outward, making a bit bigger circle, then a bigger one, the whole time thinking, *This isn't real, this isn't real, this isn't real*, but there were no hits, he couldn't find him, it seemed impossible that Elias had ever been on the mountain at all, and Garrett was about to give up and do another beacon search when he hit something hard, far down, nearly two meters, the hard lifeless *thunk* of it clutching him in a type of fear he hadn't known existed in the world. He got his shovel out of his pack and yelled at Charlie to dig behind him, farther downhill, and Garrett began to dig as swiftly as he could, shoveling snow so dense it felt like cement, his arms burning, tossing each bladeful as far downhill as possible, not daring to stop even for a second, the wind biting a hole into his cheek, and he dug and dropped out of college and wandered between rooms and fell in love with his only friend's fiancée and was still digging.

THIRTEEN

The day of the wedding was clear and beautiful, a few vaporous clouds draped across the sky like streamers. You couldn't have asked for better weather. The lake was as flat as a mirror. The boatshed lawn, where the bridesmaids in red were setting up chairs, smelled of hydrangeas and fresh-cut grass. The white chairs bisected by an aisle of lawn looked like snow.

At least they looked that way to the osprey, staring down from her nest. A trout moldered beneath her claws. Someone fussed with the microphone, testing to see if it worked, and an ungodly squeal pierced her ears. An eagle—or something that would eat an eagle. The osprey, afraid for her chicks, spread her wings over them.

Meanwhile, down the road at the Serenity Shore Cabins, where many of the guests were staying, people were throwing up. Norovirus had felled a third of the groom's party. They sheltered inside, too ill to come out. The place was like an isolation ward. Guests lay on the floor with buckets or slept curled around the toilet between attacks. You could hear groaning through the windows, unspeakable sounds. Vacationers passing by the cabins on a lakeside stroll, oblivious to the nuptials down the road, had the impression of something evil—potentially even devil related—going on.

Charlie's father, the source of all this despair, stood sheepishly on a stepladder, hanging paper lanterns from a fishing line strung between bamboo poles. He motioned to Garrett to join him on the lawn. The wedding would begin in an hour, and there was a general sense of looming disaster. Garrett had no choice but to assist. The bridesmaids setting up chairs kept their distance from Mr. Margolis; even though he'd recovered, there was a common feeling of wariness and distrust.

The Wedding Plague, as it had become known, had put a strain on the mingling of tribes.

Garrett, who might have nursed a desperate hope due to the wedding's misfortunes if he hadn't been sick himself, not with norovirus but with the sense that his life was ending, or about to end, felt only exhausted. He'd stayed at the hospital till one in the morning, needing to convince himself that his father wouldn't die in the middle of the night, that this wasn't the main event but only a preview. Then he'd lain in bed as usual, wondering for the umpteenth time if Cece had read his email. But of course she hadn't read it. It was impossible. If she had, she would have told Charlie, who would have barred Garrett from the wedding. Certainly, at the very least, he would have found another officiant. Instead, when Garrett had called him yesterday from the hospital, half-terrified and explaining why he had to miss the rehearsal, Charlie was all kindness and concern, peppering Garrett with medical questions and asking whether there was anything he could do.

This would have been an opportune time to bow out of the wedding as well. After all, he had a pretty good excuse. But given that half the groomsmen were too sick to attend, Garrett hadn't had the heart.

Needless to say, he still hadn't come up with a speech for his opening words. He had no idea what he was going to say. He was convinced, as well, that everyone would know what was wrong, that the source of his misery was written across his face. The fact that he was wearing his father's ill-fitting tux only made him feel more conspicuous.

"You've lost a button," Mr. Margolis said, pointing at Garrett's stomach. Sure enough, the tuxedo shirt had puckered open above the cummerbund, exposing a lune of skin.

"Shit," Garrett said. He reached into his pants pocket, hoping by some miracle his dad had stuck a safety pin in there.

"Murphy's Law," Mr. Margolis said. "Nothing to be done."

Garrett frowned. "Well, I'll have to do something."

"Nope. You look like a vagrant. Might as well accept your fate and wear it with pride." It dawned on Garrett that Mr. Margolis was drunk. Not just a little drunk, either, but on his way to being soused. Perhaps the vilification of being a disease vector was too much for him. "Charlie's having a bit of a meltdown. You know, his brothers are too sick to leave the cabin, and his friend Brigley isn't doing much better."

"Brig," Garrett said.

"Have you met the bride?"

Garrett nodded.

"Lovely girl. Smart as hell too. Were you aware that she has strong feelings about adjectives?"

Garrett looked at him, speechless. He shook his head.

"I said I had an 'earth-shattering' headache, and she told me not to use the word lightly." Mr. Margolis reached up to hang a lantern, teetering on the stepladder. "Apparently the earth has bigger problems than I do."

Garrett helped Mr. Margolis move the ladder and then handed him up some more lanterns, unsure what to do with this information. He stared at the bridesmaids—he recognized them from Charlie's bachelor party—as they told the caterers where to set up their stations. Despite the Wedding Plague and its discontents, they seemed to be in good spirits. When the caterers weren't watching, one of them grabbed an hors d'oeuvre from a chafing dish, threw it into the air, and caught it deftly in her mouth. The other bridesmaids, ablaze in red dresses, clapped.

"I should go practice my opening remarks," Garrett said.

Mr. Margolis studied him from the stepladder. "Ah yes, the minister. Of my namesake's wedding."

Garrett, inexplicably, gave him a thumbs-up.

"What words of wisdom will you impart?" he asked.

"Oh, you know. Your basic wisdoms."

"Uh-oh," Mr. Margolis said.

"I don't want to ruin the surprise."

"On second thought, I urge you to get your button fixed. Or maybe find a new outfit entirely."

Garrett agreed. He crossed the highway and went up to the house, hoping to bump into someone who could help him. How strange it was to step foot on the porch, knowing Cece was inside somewhere—that she might know how he felt about her. But of course she didn't. The effect of Cece's virtue, on Garrett, was profound. She'd read the second email he'd sent and then deleted the original, his confession of love, as he'd asked her to. Who else would have the moral strength to resist peeking at it? Certainly not Garrett himself. He was more in love with her than ever.

The screen door squealed when he opened it, but there was so much commotion inside that no one seemed to notice him. People—Mrs. Margolis, someone's grandfather, a harried, fit-looking man who he could only imagine was Cece's father—were rushing around the house, attending to mysterious tasks. Two caterers stood in the kitchen, shouting at each other. Garrett opened random drawers, unnoticed, searching for a safety pin. Aimlessly, he walked upstairs and ran into the groom, who was sitting at the top of the steps in his tuxedo shirt and no jacket. He had his sleeves rolled up, as if he were about to mow the lawn.

"Garrett!" Charlie said feebly. His sideburns were damp, and there were beads of sweat shining on his forehead.

"Are you all right?"

Charlie shook his head.

"Hey, it's your big day. Feel happy."

"I wish I could," Charlie said.

Garrett felt a rush of anger. Wanted to clock Charlie in the face. *If you're going to marry this woman, hoard her monogamously for the rest of her life, then at least don't be a wuss about it.* "It's natural to be nervous, right?"

"It's not that," Charlie said. "I feel sick. Like I've got the thing."

"Oh Jesus."

"Don't tell anyone! I don't want Cece to find out!" He looked pale, his eyes darting around the room. "She's already losing her shit."

"I won't," Garrett said.

"It would ruin her entire wedding day."

Garrett touched Charlie's forehead, which was warm and sticky. He felt a wave of sympathy, keen and uncomplicated. He remembered the day they'd met, how he'd tackled Charlie in the snow to keep him from sliding into traffic and almost broken the guy's arm. Charlie had never blamed him for it, or gotten angry when he'd had to quit the squash team, even though the stunt had been Garrett's idea to begin with.

"You're going to be fine. I bet it's just nerves. Anyway, all you have to do is stand there."

Charlie looked at him.

"Repeat after me," Garrett said. "'I'm getting married.'"

"I'm getting married," Charlie mumbled.

"'*I'm getting the fuck married!*'"

"I'm getting the fuck married!"

"That's the spirit."

He helped Charlie up, who seemed better once he was on his feet. He even laughed at Garrett's shirt. He led Garrett into his father's upstairs office, where they found a stapler sitting on the desk. Shakily, Charlie knelt on the floor and stapled Garrett's shirt through the buttonhole so that the placket stood awning-like from his stomach, making him look pregnant. Charlie tried to bend the placket flat, but it sprang up again. He bit his lip, trying not to laugh.

"You don't look so great yourself," Charlie said, staring at Garrett's face.

"That's just my everyday appearance," Garrett said.

"My comb's in the bathroom—second door on the right—if you want to spruce up a bit."

Charlie opened a drawer in his dad's desk and pulled out a bottle of scotch, something with an unpronounceable name. It looked expensive. He uncorked the top and handed the bottle to Garrett, who took a swig. Wincing, Charlie closed his eyes and took a swig too.

"Thank god you're here," he said, slinging his free arm around Garrett's shoulder. "I don't know what I'd do without you."

Charlie left to finish getting dressed. Alone, Garrett sat down in front of a yellow legal pad that was sitting on Mr. Margolis's desk, then grabbed a pen from a cup on the windowsill. He tried to summon at least one or two inspiring thoughts for his speech. He just needed a few words to get him started. Anything. Why had he never even begun? What was wrong with him? Why did he fail at everything he did—*will* himself to fail? In college, he used to write term papers in a single night, words spilling out of him faster than he could type. *We're gathered here to celebrate two remarkable people*, Garrett wrote, then froze in place. He felt like he was composing his own obituary.

He grabbed the scotch out of the drawer and took a longer swig. He needed to take a leak. Dispirited, he got up and poked down the hallway, trying to remember his way around from Charlie's bachelor party, and opened what he imagined was the door to the bathroom. But it was not the bathroom. It was a bedroom smelling of perfume, tense as a greenroom before a play; several women in red, the bridesmaids he'd seen outside, were gathered around a stranger in a wedding dress. Cece, sitting with her back to the door. So resplendent did she look, even from behind, that Garrett hadn't recognized her. An elderly woman with a dimple on her chin—her grandmother?—stood nearby. One of the bridesmaids squatted in front of Cece, dabbing at her face with a tissue. The others all stared at Garrett, as if he'd walked into a church service. For a moment, confronted by this tableau of protective women—stern and hushed and emitting inscrutable tribal power, gathered around Cece as though guarding a fire that might go out—he was speechless.

Cece turned in her chair and noticed him for the first time, her face opening in surprise. Had she been crying? Her eyes were bloodshot, her makeup smeared. Seeing her lovely, tear-stained face, Garrett forgot where he was for a second—forgot that he was searching for a bathroom, or that he looked pregnant, or that he had a dying father in the hospital. Until that moment, Garrett had associated weddings with "Pachelbel's Canon," froufrou-looking cakes, maybe *The Graduate*. But he realized, all at once, that he'd completely misconstrued what they were about. They were about stopping time. They were about making the world conform, if only for a few hours, to the parameters of your desire, that secret part of you that sang out to perfection and rescued you from ordinary life.

What if the world had a dream, and it was miraculously about you?

And now Cece stared at him, in tears. A red rose floated in her hair. Who wouldn't cry, with a third of the guests quarantined in their rooms? He wanted only to console her. It didn't even matter who she was marrying. Garrett didn't believe in a soul, at least in the ordinary sense, and yet something soul-like seemed to spring out of him—to strain toward this weeping bride, this human being, and because he was a human being too. He hadn't felt this sort of thing in years. It was a strange feeling, like rejoining a flock.

Garrett took a step toward her, instinctively, and an extraordinary thing happened. She curled her lip at him; the tendons in her neck stiffened like cables. The effect was mesmerizing. She stood from her chair, baring her teeth like a cat. Then she raised her right hand and thrust it toward him, hooking the air with one finger, as if it were perched on the button of something. A spray can. "Pshhhhhhhhhhh!" she hissed, spraying the imaginary can in his face.

II

SUMMER TIME

On the way to the Margolises' house, or should she say "Charlie's" now, Cece watched the familiar sights flash by her window: Fred's Bait and Tackle, the concrete teepee that used to be a motel, the blue lake strobing through the trees. She wasn't sleepy at all but couldn't stop yawning. Her stomach hurt from dread, nerves, possibly hunger. She'd been unable to eat breakfast, staring at her bowl of oatmeal this morning as if it were prison gruel. Garrett seemed as nervous as she was, gazing silently ahead, his hands clenching the wheel. Every so often he glanced at the mirror and fussed with his hair, so thin on top it looked like a baby's.

It had taken Charlie years to forgive them—nine, in fact—and now they were driving to the house that she'd once loved, the place where Charlie and Cece had intended to take their children every summer. Where they'd had their wedding and vowed to love and to cherish, till death did them part. How strange to be headed there, now, for a visit. Cece had driven by it before, of course, though only once when she had to get to Missoula for a flight; she generally did everything in her power—took the long way around the lake—to avoid it.

Lana seemed to have absorbed the nervousness of her parents, sitting in the backseat with her hands clasped, thumbs steepled together. She hadn't said a word since they left. This was uncharacteristic enough to seem like an omen: a sign that they shouldn't have accepted Charlie's invitation. Cece had only explained to her, of course, that he was an old friend. Lana knew nothing of the history, the wedding, Cece getting so sick she couldn't fly back to LA with Charlie—and then never flying back to California at all.

"Honey, we need to tell you something," Cece said, turning around in the front seat. Her daughter, seven years old and preposterously beautiful, like a child in a French movie, seemed strangely obedient.

"All right."

"The man we're visiting, Charlie, he and I used to be—well, we were engaged to be married. But I fell in love with your father."

Lana nodded. "I know."

"You *know*?"

"You ran away with Daddy after your wedding."

Cece blinked at her. "How do you know that?"

"Daddy told me."

Cece looked at Garrett, doing her best to convey her annoyance without telegraphing it to their daughter.

"She asked me about it last night," he said, shrugging. "Wondered why she'd never met Charlie before, since he has a kid her age. And a house ten minutes away. Did you really expect me to lie?"

"Yes," Cece said. "What else do you know?" she asked Lana.

"You and the man we're going to see weren't full-way married yet. When you ran away with Dad. You never turned in the certificate to get it certificated."

"*Certified*," Garrett said.

"Plus the man has a whole new family. So it's cool."

Cece looked at Garrett again. "Right. Extremely cool. Coolest thing I've ever done in my life." This was meant to be a joke. Her throat clogged and she looked out the window.

"Also, Dad was refereeing the wedding and he was supposed to say a speech, but he was too in love with you to write it beforehand and had to make up something on the spot."

"You *told* her that?" Cece said.

"Well, not the referee part. She might be confusing marriage with competitive sport."

"What did the speech say?" Lana asked.

"Oh, it was really . . . ," Cece began, but found herself at a loss for words. *Beautiful? Appalling? Like a knife, now, in the heart?*

"I'll tell you about it sometime," Garrett said. "When you're older."

Cece stared at him, wondering whether to be mad or not. There was so much agony there—so much guilt and second-guessing and trapdoor ambivalence opening to regret—that she didn't know where to begin. The thing was, she loved Garrett, still desired him on some molecular level she didn't fully understand. But of course being married to him was a lot different from *not* being married to him. Not being married was the easiest thing in the world. It was as impossible for her to imagine the hunger she'd felt, the dark aching madness that had caused her to blow up her life, as it was to imagine a stranger's. *More* impossible, perhaps. The things that had seemed so irresistible to her—Garrett's tragic sadness, his distrust of pieties, his gimlet-eyed way of looking at the whole American project—were less alluring when you had to live with them on a daily basis. Nonconformity, when you're married to it, ends up looking more and more like inertia. And yet there were surprising compensations: she would never, for example, have imagined him being such a good father.

She touched his leg now, choosing to forgive him. Garrett, stiff as a statue, smiled back. Yes, he was sick with fear too. When Charlie had emailed him a month ago, out of the blue, it had seemed like a miracle; neither of them could believe it, that Charlie had invited them back into his life. A long letter, mostly about himself: his wife and kids, how happy he was. He'd lost a transplant patient during post-op; the guy's best friend, whom he'd fought with in Vietnam, had been in the room when he died. *I don't want to go the rest of my life not speaking to my best friend.* Garrett, reading the email aloud to Cece, had stopped after this line, overwhelmed. It was one of the few times she'd seen him choke up.

They rounded the bend to the Margolises' and there it was: the dock, the electric lake, the house making its guttersnipe face at them, porch sticking out like a tongue. Other than some rose-bushes on the front lawn, blooming as yellow as the house, the place looked the same. Even the fence post that Garrett had put in was still there, shorter than the rest. It angered her, for some reason, that Charlie hadn't replaced it.

Garrett parked by the side of the road—the driveway was blocked—and Cece got out first and walked down to the lake without thinking to bring Lana with her or to tell either of them where she was going. She felt it in her legs: an almost physical tug. The boat creaked gently in the water, dock lines straining against their cleats. She'd forgotten this sound existed in the world. A sound she loved. A daytime moon hung over the Lazy Bear, which had yet to open. Cece stepped out of her thongs and warmed the soles of her feet. The huge lake, glazed by the sun, shone bright as a movie. Beyond the western shore loomed the peak of Baldy Mountain, wearing its green gown of trees, unzipped down the middle from an avalanche last winter.

She'd given all this up. Oh god, what had she done?

Charlie met them at the door, looking fit and happy, astonish-ingly the same except for a reddish beard that shouldn't have suited him but did, maybe because it made him appear less boy-ish. He introduced them to his wife, Angeliki, who said she'd encouraged Charlie with the beard; of course, he would never do something without it being carefully focus-grouped. Shak-ing hands with this beautiful Greek wife, who had a beautiful half-Greek toddler clinging to her leg—Charlie's youngest—Cece felt the twinge of something she wasn't used to feeling in Montana. Frumpiness. She wished she'd had her hair cut in the last six months.

"And this little fellow is Jasper," Charlie said, in a proud-parent voice she wouldn't have expected. Somehow this suited him too. A tan-faced boy with Charlie's slender, rocket-fin nose smiled politely up at them. Something crumbled in Cece's chest. No: came down all at once. The toddler hugging Angeliki's leg mimed some squeezing motions with her hand, as if she were milking a cow, and Angeliki sat down on the edge of the couch and promptly began to breastfeed her. Unlike Cece's Montana neighbors—who used what they called "hooter hiders"—the woman didn't feel the need to conceal herself.

"And how old are you?" she asked Lana, who did not smile politely like Jasper but stared brazenly at Angeliki's breast.

"Eight."

"Actually, she's seven," Garrett said. "She's been lying about her age since she was six."

"*I'm* seven too," Jasper said.

Lana gave him a withering look.

"Do you like mushrooms?" Charlie asked her.

"No."

"How about hot dogs?"

"No. They taste like airport."

"Lana!" Cece said, blushing. "Be polite."

"I dislike them very much, thank you," Lana said.

"Why don't you put some pasta on the stove," Angeliki said from the couch, "for anyone who doesn't like airport."

At dinner, she set up a booster seat for little Těa, who proceeded to calmly suck peas from her fingers. She had to be the mellowest two-year-old Cece had ever met. Lana, at her age, was flying around like a pinball, breaking things left and right. Cece wondered why it had taken Charlie and Angeliki so long to have a second child, whether there'd been some kind of hidden trouble in their marriage. Infidelity? Depression? She found herself dwelling on the possibilities.

"So when I was older than you, sixteen years old," Angeliki said to Lana, though everyone at the table was listening, "my parents sent me to this summer camp in Oregon. We'd just moved to the States and I didn't really like American food." She explained how they'd gone on a camping trip and one of the counselors had found some chicken-of-the-woods mushrooms growing out of a tree and cooked them up for all the campers. Those big, orange, ugly-looking mushrooms that supposedly taste like chicken. Well, they convinced her to try one, because all the campers were eating them, and then suddenly one of the girls said she didn't feel very well and threw up in the woods. And the counselors were like, 'Poor kid! Has the flu!' But then another kid clutched her stomach and had to go throw up. And then all of them were suddenly groaning and hugging themselves and rolling around on the ground. They had to take everyone to the hospital. "We were all passing a cardboard box around in the bus and throwing up into it. We made up a song about it: 'Puke Box Hero.' Turns out the counselor had picked some mushrooms growing out of the wrong kind of tree! The kind that grows on conifers or hemlocks, I don't remember which, can make you really ill."

"Hemlocks are a kind of conifer," Cece said. "They're conifers already."

"Oh yes, well," Angeliki said graciously. "You're right. Something else then."

Lana looked at Cece—wondering why she was being such a bitch, probably. Cece blamed it on the rock slide in her chest. Angeliki's story had made her think of the wedding, of course, how Mr. Margolis had given half the wedding party norovirus all those years ago. Judging from the awkward silence, Charlie and Garrett were thinking about this too; only Angeliki, cleaning Těa's face with her napkin, seemed unfazed by the connection. Perhaps she didn't know about the wedding at all. Was it possible Charlie hadn't told her?

It didn't help that she was lovely: olive skin and big stage-struck eyes and the kind of symmetrically perfect face that flipped a switch inside you, one you wished didn't exist. It was one of those faces that seemed kind *because* it was beautiful. This had always seemed ludicrous to Cece—a literal interpretation of moral beauty, exploited by Victorian novelists—but in this case it seemed to be true. The woman was genuinely kind. Cece had not counted on this. She had prepared herself for anger, brittleness, even open hostility. But this hearty indifferent friendliness—somehow it was worse.

Charlie put his hand on the back of Angeliki's neck, massaging it gently. He used to do the same thing to Cece whenever they had company over, as if showing everyone in the room how lucky he was—had done this during their rehearsal picnic, in fact, little knowing what lay in store. If Cece hadn't been felled by norovirus after the wedding, too sick to fly home with Charlie, they might still be together. He'd wept on the phone when she told him she wasn't coming back to LA, that she was in love with Garrett and staying in Montana: wept and wept. How horrific it had been! Charlie had done his share of screaming, of course, but mostly Cece remembered how crushed he'd sounded, how small and broken and abandoned, like a little boy. He'd pleaded for her to come back, made himself sickening and pathetic, then when that hadn't worked vowed never to forgive her. And Cece really thought she'd done something unforgivable, that she was some kind of monster. She despised herself, but at the time this seemed like an acceptable price to pay. Or, if not exactly acceptable, *bearable.* She could be a good human being and marry the wrong person, or be a monster who ran off with his best friend, the man she'd fallen in love with.

But now, of course, Charlie had forgiven her. And why not? It had worked out in the best possible way for him. He'd found someone better.

"And, Garrett?" Charlie said in his friendliest voice. "Catch me up on your life."

"Okay," Garrett said, then fell silent.

"You're a wildlife biologist now?"

"Sounds a bit more glamorous than it is. And lucrative."

"Well, last time we were in touch"—a bit of awkwardness here, a pause, but he seemed so at peace it may have only been a hiccup—"you were working at the airport."

Garrett blushed. "Everything's relative, I guess. But yeah, fieldwork mostly. Population ecology. I'm out in the trenches."

"Studying what?"

"I did fishers for a bit. That was for Defenders of Wildlife. Then mountain caribou, up in northern Idaho. For the past couple winters, we've been tracking wolverines in Glacier."

"Wolverines are endangered?"

"In the lower forty-eight they are. Or should be. That's one of the study objectives—we're trying to get them designated."

"There are only about three hundred left," Lana said informatively.

"Is that so?"

Lana glanced at Téa and leaned forward, lowering her voice. "Sometimes they kill each other too. Their own offspring."

She adored her father and had adopted his sociopathic way of describing animal behavior. Well, not sociopathic exactly—just free of the cuddly Disney-isms Californians used when talking about animals, particularly ones they wanted to keep roaming the earth. (Cece and Garrett's neighbors, who hunted elk with rifles and crossbows and weird primitive muskets you had to load with a rod, anything that would allow them to keep killing things all year round, talked about animals in the same way Garrett did.)

"It's the shorter winters that are really killing them," Garrett said. "The decline in snowpack. They build snow dens for their young, ten feet deep sometimes—for insulation, but also to hide them from predators. I mean, have you ever seen a wolverine's feet?"

Charlie shook his head.

"They're as big as Ping-Pong paddles."

"Really?"

"You'd be hard-pressed to find an animal," Garrett said, "that evolved more thoroughly for snow."

Charlie smiled at him.

"What?"

"Just amazed. A wolverine expert. Last thing I heard, Cece, you'd married a baggage handler."

There was an awkward silence. What did he mean by this? Nothing. Everything. Cece looked at her daughter, who was staring at her in astonishment.

"You were married to a baggage handler?" Lana asked excitedly.

"Yep," Garrett said. "A real loser."

"So you're away from home a lot?" Angeliki asked Garrett.

"Just a few weeks at a time."

Angeliki shook her head. "Must be hard," she said sympathetically. She'd turned to Lana, but Cece felt like she was addressing her.

"We manage okay," Cece said. "Don't we, Lana?"

"I'm kind of a latchkey kid," Lana said provocatively. Where did she get these terms?

"You're *not* a latchkey kid."

"I am. I come home after school to an empty house. I watch TV by myself."

"Only for a half hour!"

"I want to be a Latchki kid," Jasper said. It was the first thing he'd said all dinner.

"Mom forgot to put the spare key in the mailbox one time, and I had to wait for her to come home. It was below freezing outside. My ears fell off."

"Your ears did not fall off. You had a wool hat in your backpack the whole time and didn't even take it out. Besides,

I told you to go to the Washburns' if anything like that ever happened."

"The Washburn kids chew tobacco. Plus they set their little cousin on fire."

"That was an accident."

"Can we go to the Washburns'?" Jasper asked his mom.

"No," she said calmly, with that noirish unflappability certain moms had and that always made Cece feel like a mass of nerve endings. Angeliki looked at Jasper for a second, as if wondering whether Lana was a bad influence. "And where do you work, Cece?"

"At the Trout and Tackle. Next to the playhouse."

Angeliki looked at her blankly.

"That's her restaurant," Garrett explained.

"Oh, wow. You have your own restaurant?"

"No no," Cece said. "It's not *mine*, thank god. I'm just a server."

"Actually, she's going back to school," Garrett said. "To get her PhD. It's just a matter of when we can get our lives in order."

Cece looked at him, suddenly furious. Why was he so intent on making her life seem less small? Probably he just didn't want her to feel humiliated, but in fact his rushing to her defense had the opposite effect. It made sense that she would have supported his career first, given how unhappy he was working at the airport. They'd rented an apartment in Missoula those first few years so he could finish up his bachelor's, then his master's, while she tried to map out a future for herself, something that would allow him to continue doing fieldwork in the Rockies. All the English grad programs were on the coasts—at least if she wanted a PhD worth its salt, that might actually translate into a career. Regardless, he'd agreed to follow her wherever she wanted. They'd make it work.

Except she'd gotten pregnant. A mistake: she'd gone off the pill, suspecting it was giving her migraines, and they'd become a bit complacent. She'd always imagined having kids, just not quite so soon. There were complications: six months of bed rest *with bathroom privileges* (thank god). She had an "incompetent cervix"—this always made Garrett laugh, though in med school you got used to the slanderous dissing of body parts—and a doctor sewed it up. Cerclage. Every day Cece took to the couch, worried the feckless organ would pop its stitches. The worry and boredom and confinement were unspeakable. It was the sort of ordeal that sweeps you out to sea and then crashes you back to shore half a year later, your bones turned to coral, your hopes and dreams worn down to basic human demands. You just want a healthy baby. You want to get off the couch again. You want to smell something other than your armpits. She would not trade Lana for anything—she was determined to be a great mother, who would never die—but Cece couldn't help feeling her dreams had failed to recover from those months of bed rest. They'd never fully made it off the couch.

Broke, having burned through the meager savings Garrett had inherited from his father, the dregs of his TIAA-CREF account, they moved back to Salish—or rather to his father's house, which he'd failed after his dad's death to even rent out. They needed more space, Garrett had begun working at Glacier, so it made sense. Plus they both missed it up here, though it didn't take long for Cece to realize she'd confused the place in general with her very limited experience of it: i.e., the lake. The lake, in summer, with no money problems to speak of. How divine it was, to splash around in the water! She felt hopelessly naïve. Not that the landscape didn't move her—she couldn't drive home from work, the Swan Mountains white with snow, hovering like shot-down clouds in the distance, without feeling a lump in her throat—just that she didn't know who she was. That was the trouble. Money, she realized now, had protected her from this startling fact.

She did her best not to obsess about it, but sometimes Cece

couldn't help imagining the life she would have led if she'd never left LA. In this alternate universe, she'd gone back to med school and become a doctor: a radiologist, with humanely regular hours, living in a nice suburb somewhere where the neighbor children didn't chew tobacco. She was happy and professionally fulfilled. Cece knew this was bunk—she'd been miserable in med school, ill-suited to the whole endeavor—but in her weakest moments blamed Garrett for everything she'd lost.

After dinner, she helped Charlie and Garrett clean up, since Charlie insisted that Angeliki—who'd spent the afternoon cooking—relax. Apparently, "relax" in Angeliki's case meant happily agreeing to play Monopoly when Lana and Jasper asked her to, a game Cece refused to play at home. (She loved her daughter but would rather have killed them both in a murder-suicide.) Lana, who did not realize mothers played Monopoly—or board games at all, really, except under duress—was delighted. It was like she'd discovered a new kind of life-form. She even got to insist on being banker, making things proceed even more glacially than usual.

Cece watched the Monopoly game from the kitchen, where she was helping to do the dishes, Garrett scrubbing each one in the sink and then handing it to her to dry before she passed it to Charlie to put away. Charlie chatted about the renovations they'd done to the house, seemingly oblivious to the awkwardness of the three of them doing dishes together. It was as if he and Cece had never so much as kissed each other on the cheek. She kept glancing at Garrett, wondering what he made of Charlie's happiness. Did he feel as depressed as she did? Full of disdain for his old friend's restless waste of money? Or—because anything was possible with Garrett—was he just happy to be there at all, too humbled by Charlie's forgiveness to say much?

"Remember the old kitchen?" Charlie said, to Cece in particular. He looked away when she met his eyes, the first time he'd seemed at all uncomfortable.

"Yes."

"We just gutted it completely. Knocked the wall with the pass-through in it down—remember that?—knocked the whole damn thing down and just went ahead and absorbed the old dining room. It was all Angeliki, really. I mean, my brothers had a say, of course, but she came up with the design herself."

Cece tried to picture exactly where the wall used to be, envisioning the kitchen as it once was, brown and cramped and windowless. It was twice the size now, and objectively speaking a hundred times better, with a stainless-steel fridge and a separate island for the sink and those quartz countertops that looked like marble but didn't stain. There was even a built-in wine cooler. Everything was in perfect taste. And yet Cece much preferred the old kitchen: its brown appliances and jack-in-the-box toaster and breakfast table with its plastic tablecloth. God, that tablecloth! She could see it perfectly in her mind. At least the living room looked the same, probably because they hadn't gotten around to renovating it yet: beige carpet. Musty furniture. Haunted windows that popped open for no reason, impossible to latch. Cece, twisting around to look, was relieved to find the hand-drawn duck still taped above the stairs. Relieved and heartsick. She dropped the glass tumbler she was drying, but miraculously it hit the quartz without causing so much as a crack.

She excused herself and went to the bathroom, where she sat on the edge of the tub for a minute to recover. Even the bathroom, its familiar ugliness, stabbed her heart. Probably they shouldn't have come. She'd thought about rejecting Charlie's invitation—why reopen the wound?—but it was important to Garrett, whose guilt, perhaps more than hers, kept him up at night. A pardon they'd never expected, dropped into their laps.

But it wasn't just Garrett. She'd felt pulled here herself, drawn treacherously to the house, the way a murderer might be drawn back to the scene of the crime. She'd wanted to see what she was missing.

Cece hadn't smoked weed in a long time—years—but suddenly craved a joint. She could almost smell it, the sweet mildewy funk. She wondered if Charlie had any lying around—or maybe his brothers?—but remembered the sparkling kitchen and came to her senses.

After cleaning up, they walked down to the lake for an after-dinner swim. Cece was worried Lana would throw a fit about quitting Monopoly—at home, she tantrumed if you didn't finish a board game in a single sitting—but somehow Angeliki was able to convince her to abandon her miniature collie on Marvin Gardens. Clearly, the woman had cast a spell. Angeliki brought Tẻa down to the lake, dressing her in a sunbonnet with little birds on it, which the toddler suffered without complaint. Lana, starstruck, insisted on holding Angeliki's hand. Cece walked along beside them. The evening was warm and breezeless, the dock still hot on Cece's feet though the sun on the lake was beginning to congeal, frosting it like a cake. The fish jumping looked like invisible rain. Before long the sun would sink below the mountains, swallows strafing the water.

Angeliki went swimming first, handing Tẻa to Charlie. Of course she looked good in a bathing suit. A bit heavier than Cece—but she knew that Charlie was susceptible to this, so long as the plumpness was where he liked it (especially up top, where Cece was more, well, *streamlined*). Impatient, Garrett jumped in too, hooting as always when he hit the water. He'd gotten this from Cece.

"Come on!" Garrett said to her.

"In a minute."

She sat next to Charlie on the dock. Garrett swam to where his feet could reach bottom and hoisted Lana onto his shoulders, dunking her underwater and then springing up suddenly so that she toppled like a tree. He did the same thing to Jasper, who laughed and laughed. Garrett laughed too. He looked balder when his hair was wet, Cece noticed.

"He's turned into quite the dad," Charlie said, holding Tẽa on his lap. She did not like the water, or perhaps was intimidated by Lana. "I never would have expected it."

"Me neither," Cece said.

She looked at him and blushed. He'd kept all his hair: not even a widow's peak. Tẽa asked for her mother, the first grumble from the girl she'd heard all day, and Charlie pointed at Angeliki in the water, who was bobbing in the wake of a speedboat. Cece would have loved to do that too—it looked, honestly, like bliss—but something gravitational was keeping her here. Partly she wanted to face the lake and not the lawn, where they'd had the wedding. Walking across it had been upsetting enough.

Angeliki waved at them from the water, and Tẽa and Charlie waved back. He looked tan, besotted, invincibly happy. "Lana's an amazing girl," he said suddenly. "One of a kind."

"Yes, well, that's one way of putting it."

"She's got a lot of . . . I don't know. Spark."

"I think the reigning euphemism is 'spirited.'"

Charlie laughed. "Same old Cece," he said, as if he were her folksy hayseed uncle or something. When did he start talking this way? Tẽa whispered something in Charlie's ear; he reached into the swim bag by his feet and handed her a juice box. Was his hand, ever so slightly, trembling?

"Is there a reason you guys waited five years? Between kids?"

Charlie shrugged. "Happiness? I think we worried we'd screw it up."

She ignored the smugness of this. Or tried to.

"And you?" he said quietly. "You always said you wanted two children."

"With *you*."

She'd just meant to be truthful, but it sounded different than she'd intended. In any case, he glanced in Angeliki's direction. A loyal husband. They sat there in silence, watching Tẽa sip demurely at her juice box. (Lana still sucked them down in one go, as if she were huffing hair spray.)

"How are Jake and Bradley?" Cece asked.

"They'd never forgive me, if they knew I'd invited you here."

"They hate me that much."

Charlie nodded. That meant his parents did too. They were a family that, once betrayed, took no prisoners. Of course she'd known his brothers hated her, but hearing it from Charlie's lips gutted her anew. Charlie must have felt something as well, because the breezy expression on his face wavered, straining at the guy-wires holding it in place. The happiness, the holiday-card platitudes, the children who gleefully ate mushrooms . . . Cece had the sense, if only for a second, that it was all some kind of hoax. That he'd ordered Angeliki from a catalog called *Monopoly-Playing Moms.* But of course she was imagining this.

"I forgot to put on sunscreen," he said finally, without looking at Cece. "Shit. Do you mind watching Téa for a second? She's not wearing a life vest."

"It's seven thirty at night."

"As long as the sun's putting out UVs, you can burn," he said.

She'd forgotten how fair-skinned he was—and how fastidious. Cece took the child in her lap. Téa fussed and reached for her father, but then Cece dandled her on one knee and jiggled it like a pony, making her laugh. Anyone would have thought she was the child's mother.

Charlie put some sunscreen on, doing that thing where you smear it on your palms first and then rub it two-handed all over your face, like a monk performing ablutions. Cece stared at his wedding ring. A simple band, like the one Cece had bought for him. No doubt engraved on the inside was a secret message. God, could it be the same thing she and Charlie had engraved in each of *their* rings? The corny lyric from *Singin' in the Rain,* Charlie's favorite movie? Cece shuddered inside just thinking of it. Couldn't even bear to say the lyric to herself.

He must have caught her staring at the ring because he began to fiddle with it self-consciously, twisting it back and forth. Before their ceremony, she'd read about the origin of wedding rings: a vein, it was believed, ran straight from the ring finger to the heart.

She handed Těa back, feeling a strange aversion to the girl. Almost a disgust. Charlie's face, greasy with sunscreen, shone like a painting. "This is the life, isn't it?"

It sounded like an accusation. Or a boast. Or both.

Cece took off her T-shirt and grabbed the swim goggles out of her bag—she hated not being able to see underwater—and dove into the lake, feeling the cold grab her like a fist. It held her for a few seconds before releasing its grip. She came up panting. She'd swum countless times since her last summer here, in this very same lake, driving to the public-access beach with Lana. So why did this feel so different? So much more, well, *correct*?

This is the life. What an absurd expression. As if there were a single life and the others didn't count.

Garrett called to her but she ignored him, leaving him with Lana and swimming farther out than she was used to, prey to the Jet Skis hot-rodding the lake. She floated on her back like a seal. There'd been a time when Garrett's voice had quickened her pulse, when she would have obeyed it at once. How madly in love they'd been at first! A form of derangement. Certainly she'd felt deranged after the wedding, stranded at the Margolises' house, too ill to do much of anything but lie in bed, head roaring with pain, as if her brain were literally on fire. All she could think about was Garrett's email. She'd read it again and again, committing it basically to memory, imagining that her fever had been caused by it—Garrett's drunken confession—and not a virus at all. Emerging from her sickness, she'd felt emptied of everything, all the gunk in her brain replaced by a pristine ruthless clarity she hadn't felt in years. Charlie's mother, whom she'd always adored—and who'd taken care of her in Charlie's

absence, helping her sip ginger ale through a bendy straw—
seemed to her a sad, lonely woman stuck in a moribund marriage,
pining for the sons who no longer needed her. Cece had urged
Charlie's parents to fly home on their original flight. It was the
height of the tourist season, everything sold out; Cece was stuck
there for another week. The thought of flying home, of officially
beginning her marriage, filled her with ineffable dread. She lay
in bed for two days, staring at the portrait of Charlie's great-
grandfather on the Margolises' wall (muttonchops, eyes of God).
At last, trembling, she'd written Garrett back, ostensibly to ask
how his father was; he'd offered to come by with more weed . . .

Terrible, wonderful, a treachery so deep it felt like being rescued. It really was just as he'd said, like a dimmer switch: you
thought the world had a certain wattage, that it would forever
be the same, and then suddenly it went even brighter and you
thought, *What was I missing?* Those first weeks in Garrett's
apartment, hiding out on his lumpy roadkill of a futon—Cece
remembered them like a single day. The fallout hardly mattered.
Or rather, it was atrocious, it mattered immensely, but it was
happening on a different planet. They lived on Planet Futon.
The place was dingy, it smelled like an old sponge; mice raided
the cupboards every night and left their spoor in the rice. But
they didn't need to eat. They feasted on each other. She'd never
felt this before, this hunger for another person, as if she might
actually starve without him. Parting from him was like pulling a
tooth. When he had to go to work, or visit his dad at the hospice,
she held on to his wrist so he wouldn't leave. It was a joke and it
wasn't. She felt delirious, actually had to remind herself that she
was a separate person. When they went out together, everything
seemed new to her, wondrous. A trip to the IGA was like going
to an amusement park; they reeled around the aisles, arm in arm,
giggling at the things in other people's carts. One night they'd
gone to a bowling alley—bowling!—and she'd gotten her thumb
stuck in the ball. This was not a disaster but the funniest thing

ever. To get it off, the guy at the concession stand had to soak the ball in a vat of cooking oil. When Garrett's father finally died, it made them even closer; their world shrank to the dimensions of his grief. That first winter, he'd taken her down to the bay, where the lake had frozen over. *December's the best, when the ice is expanding.* They walked right off the end of the marina, onto the lake. Nighttime: a dome of stars. He told her to put her ear to the ice. What sounds! Like ghosts being shot by a slingshot. She had no idea ice could sing. They lay there face-to-face, listening to the same secret music. Even afterward—eating, say, in comfortable silence—she got marvelously spooked sometimes, felt a bigness between them, as if they were still out there listening to the ice.

And then it dimmed: the delirium, the sense of being in on a marvelous secret. The doubts began. Things Garrett did started to annoy her, just as he'd predicted so long ago: the way he used up the toilet paper and didn't replace it, the weird silent burping he did after drinking a beer. They began to fight, often over money. And of course Lana, in her "spirited" way, ground them down, depleted the stores of affection they had for each other. Not that Cece didn't love Garrett. She did! Just that this love failed to solve their problems. Sometimes she'd hear him rant about "the self-help industrial complex," or watch him do that thing where he sniffed his boots before putting them on, and it would bewilder her—actually seem borderline insane—that she'd chosen him.

Cece closed her eyes, suspended in the heated blanket of water at the surface. When she righted herself again, she could see someone swimming toward her from the dock. Charlie. She could tell by his full head of hair. No doubt he was showing off, eager to prove he'd forgiven her. To flaunt his happiness. Angeliki, who'd perhaps taken Tëa back to the house, was nowhere to be seen.

Charlie swam to where she was treading water and stopped

right in front of her. But he didn't look happy. Quite the opposite. He was trembling, his mouth wide as a gash. The water had
done something to the sunscreen on his face, turned it filmy and
opaque, as if he'd been painted with primer. Cece's heart stamped
in her chest. For the rest of her life, replaying the scene in her
head, she would see each and every detail of it, as vivid as a clip
from a movie: His white-painted face, the tiny pink coastline of
his gums. He peers into Cece's eyes. Then he grabs her arm, right
above the wrist, making it hard to tread water. He keeps his grip
on her, squeezing so hard that it hurts. He dips below the surface, yanking her with him. Cece doesn't struggle. Somehow she
knows he won't drown her. And yet it seems possible he might try
to, given how angry he looks underwater, how pale and strange
and alien, his hair floating above him, as white as his face. It looks
like an old man's. Through the prism of her swim goggles, he
seems to age before her eyes, turning older and older, his face
growing stranger by the second, more wrinkled and toothless,
his grip on her arm weakening to a pinch. He's frail, shriveled,
ninety years old. The air leaving his mouth looks to Cece like
his own soul. And she can feel herself aging as well. She's turning
into an old woman, her body shriveling like his. She can barely
breathe. He's holding her; they will die in each other's arms.

He let go of her and she swam to the surface, gasping. She
could have broken his grip earlier but didn't. She'd stayed down
there with him. Cece began to swim back with her head above
water. At the dock, Lana and Jasper were fighting over Garrett,
who was waist-deep in the lake, looking brown and beautiful in
the dampening sun. He watched Cece swim back, ignoring the
kids tugging at his arm.

Then they were packing up to go home, herding Lana into the
car and bidding farewell to Charlie and Angeliki. Charlie hugged
Cece gently, smiling in his new avuncular way, as if the episode

in the lake had never happened. Someone, Angeliki no doubt, had managed to get the sunscreen off his face. *Yes, so much fun! Let's see each other soon.* They waved from the car and then were on the road again, the house disappearing behind them, driving into a magic-hour sky. The clouds glowing in the west were like the way Cece once imagined them as a kid: purple airships, powered by great sails or mechanical wings. The lake seemed to brighten as the daylight faded. A transference, a Magritte painting, as if the lake and sky had traded places.

Garrett drove without speaking, distracted by something or maybe just tired. Three kids at once had been too much for him, and his mood, as sometimes happened, had turned. He was thinking of disappearing back into the mountains, to his wolverines.

"Angeliki is beautiful," Cece said, mainly to break the silence.

Garrett glanced at her. "If you find Muppets beautiful, I suppose. She's like Jim Henson's wet dream." Cece flicked her eyes toward Lana but was too pleased to care. "Big eyes. And all mouth. And those cheeks! I thought she might start subtracting cookies. Lana, doesn't Angeliki look like a Muppet to you?"

"Who's Angeliki?"

"Jasper's mother!"

"I liked her," Lana said. "She let me trade Baltic Avenue for Park Place."

"Also Muppet-like, in terms of IQ."

Lana giggled. Cece had been completely wrong about Garrett's mood. He was a total mystery to her, after nine years.

"What's a wet dream?" Lana asked.

Cece and Garrett looked at each other.

"It's a dream you have," Garrett said, "but extra intense."

"About Muppets?"

"They're not typically about Muppets. No."

"Good. I despise Muppets. All they do is complain about their life. Mom used to make me watch their show."

"I never *made* you watch anything," Cece said.

Lana started to hum the *Muppet Show* theme song. Actually, she'd loved the show and used to beg to take out the DVDs from the library. Why did her experience of something have nothing to do with her later opinion of it? Cece felt a disconcerting poke of recognition.

"Well, Charlie at least seems besotted with her," Cece said to Garrett. "Muppet or no."

Garrett shook his head. "That wasn't Charlie."

"What are you talking about?"

"It was like a play he was putting on for us. He'd spent a long time casting it, blocking out the scenes, but I think he realized about halfway through that we weren't buying it."

"Maybe it was the goop all over his face."

"Stage makeup!"

It was almost dusk now, only a thin flare of pink on the horizon. Her throat swelled a bit. This is partly why she'd fallen in love with Garrett to begin with: that he could see into things this way, confirm what had already been half-formed in her heart, written in a kind of invisible ink. Garrett had the magic light. And it made sense to her, as it sometimes did—*often* did—that she'd run away with him. Upended her life.

She slid over in her seat and put her hand on Garrett's leg. It was lean and whittled, from all the time he was spending in the mountains. She could feel his thigh muscle, the animal shape of it. She loved these moments, when she was certain that the choice she'd made—easily the riskiest thing she'd ever done in her life, and hands-down the bravest—was the right one. Cece squeezed his leg. This was the life. *This* one. It was precious, this certainty, because she knew it wouldn't last.

FIFTEEN

G arrett clicked into his skis outside the ranger station—
Bengt Isaksson, his field partner, was already geared up
and waiting—and began the early-morning trip out to Fishercap,
where a wolverine was trapped. Or hopefully trapped. Occasionally the furious beasts chewed their way through the thick log
boxes and got out before daylight. P2, in fact, had done this once
before. Chewed a hole right through the timber and escaped
with beaver bait in his jaws. Garrett had rebuilt more than one
trap himself. An imperfect system, but the only one that didn't
risk injuring its quarry; if they used a cable snare or steel trap,
the gulos might chew off their own feet to escape.

The sun had crested the Great Divide but wasn't doing anything yet to warm Garrett, whose face was so numb he couldn't
feel the spindrift off the lake. Bengt drafted behind him, following in his tracks. Garrett herringboned up a knoll to stay
warm, then refound the eroded outline of his tracks and skied
down to the lake in them, listening to the ice sing to him as he
crossed it, the eerie pings and pongs and pyoos, like a gunfight
in outer space. Even in technical gear, hundred-dollar mittens,
he couldn't feel his fingers gripping the poles. Still, it had been
worse in the middle of the night. The radio signal had come in
sometime around two in the morning, telling them the trap had
been triggered. They'd flipped a coin to see who'd do the night
run, which once again Garrett had lost. He wondered if Bengt
was using a trick quarter. He'd had no choice but to head out, in
an exhausted dream-trance, to check the trap. Sometimes it was
a marten or a lynx, staring back at you with sapphire eyes. But

usually it was a wolverine, P2 or P3 or P7, and you had to wire
down the lid and pack snow into the cracks to lessen the chance
of escape, since it was too dangerous to sedate the thing at night.
Then you had to ski back, in an even deeper trance, and return
at daybreak.

Garrett and Bengt stopped on the north side of the lake, sharing a thermos of French press Bengt had brewed in the cabin.
One thing about Bengt: he made good coffee. A lot better than
the cowboy variety Garrett made on his own. They'd been out
here minding the traps together for a month. Mostly this meant
waiting around for a gulo to get stuck, then retrieving its GPS
collar to record the data. Even teamed up, it could be lonely
work. Rae Karnes, from the veterinary clinic, had come out once
to do a radio implant on a yearling, but that was the only human
they'd seen.

Bengt yawned, though he'd gotten to sleep through the
night. He was a rock climber who did not happily take to land.
Sometimes Garrett got up to pee in the wee hours of the morning and saw his hands moving around in the dark, as if scaling an
invisible ladder.

"I heard you after you got back," Bengt said. "You were talking to your sleeping bag."

"I couldn't sleep."

"Funny—neither could I."

"What was I saying?"

"I think you were telling it jokes. About what a lazy excuse for
a bag it was. Always sleeping."

"I guess I miss my daughter."

"She likes your jokes?"

"*Loves* them," Garrett said. "It's the only way I can get her to
bed—by promising to tell her one."

"If it's any consolation," Bengt said, "she must be an idiot."

He handed the thermos to Garrett. This was the closest he'd
come to friendship since college: with Bengt, Minkoff, who-

ever his field partner was. The particular partner almost didn't matter. Sometimes, joking with Bengt, Garrett would think of Charlie—not the weird Happy Husband who'd invited them to the Margolises' last July, bent on impressing them, but the *real* Charlie, the one who'd pretended to slip on his ass in front of Professor Yamamoto's class, who'd turn pink if you kidded him about a girl or said something a tiny bit critical about his brothers. Garrett was surprised, honestly, by how much he missed him. It was a kind of loneliness, keen and Charlie-shaped, that no one else could fill. There were different forms of love in the world; why did the romantic kind always bully its way to the front?

"What are you doing up here," Bengt asked, "if you miss your family so much?"

"It's my job."

"There are easier ways to make a living."

Garrett shrugged. "When I'm up here, all I can think about is getting back to them. Cece and Lana. I can't live without them. And then I go back and I'm so happy to see them, overjoyed—my soul is like, *ta-da!*—but after a couple weeks I start to get restless. All I can think about is coming up here again."

"Sounds kind of miserable," Bengt said.

Garrett looked at him in surprise. "Are you kidding? This is the happiest I've been since college."

Bengt studied him through his goggles, as if trying to picture him as an undergrad. It seemed to exceed his powers of imagination.

"If it wasn't for Cece," Garrett said, "god knows where I'd be."

"In a warm bar?"

"Probably dead."

Bengt nodded seriously, doing his best to understand. When he wasn't chasing animals, he was living like one, bivouacked on the side of a cliff and crapping in a bag. "Come to think of it, most of the climbers I know are the same way. The middle-aged ones, I mean."

"What way?"

"Dead."

"You do realize I'm only thirty-nine, right?"

"Like I said. Middle-aged."

Garrett warmed his face in the steam from the thermos, worried about his frostbite scar. "I'm glad it's my last day up here. So I can start to miss you again too."

They headed on. The sunrise was in full bloom now, embering the clouds over the mountains and turning the sky a Martian red. Probably Garrett was just tired, half-tripping from exhaustion, but the red sky seemed to flatten for a moment, flap sickeningly like a flag. He blinked the tears from his eyes and it returned to its three-dimensional self. He hadn't had a real episode in years. Not like he used to have: snowfall in August, the people turned to bouncing phials of goop. He'd eased off on most of his meds: just ten milligrams of Lexapro, which, compared to Garrett's old regimen, was like popping a Flintstones vitamin. He'd dropped the therapist he'd been seeing in Kalispell, who'd cost a fortune and seemed to think global warming was a hoax—or at least a symptom of "catastrophic thinking." Only when Garrett was in the field like this, exhausted from trap checks, did his brain get up to its old tricks; even then it was just a glimpse, like the flash of a monster's tail.

Garrett tried to appreciate the sunrise, since this was his last day up here, though to be honest he'd gone a bit wolverine himself and had to remember it was beautiful. This required a mental step, a waste of thermal energy. He thought of the day he'd met Cece, on Charlie's dock, when they'd admired the sky together. Had he really asked her about Australopithecuses? What a pretentious ass! Still, pretentious or not, it struck Garrett as a decent enough question. Admiring the sky served no evolutionary purpose whatsoever; in the Pliocene epoch, it might even have been dangerous. So who was it that first stopped in their tracks at the sight of a sunrise? Thought, *Holy crap, that's a beautiful thing?* And supposing you were this person—or caveperson—what would you make of it? Probably it would frighten you, fill you with strange new feelings, a loneliness that made you feel special, because you might not survive the day and the sky seemed to know this about you: it was showing you exactly what you'd miss. You'd want to freeze it somehow and capture its beauty. So you would paint it, maybe, in your cave. The sunrise would be there, for admiring whenever. But it wouldn't be enough. It wouldn't measure up to the image you had in your head. You'd want to create something worthy of this image, to exorcise the useless longings it stirred in your heart—longings that had nothing to do with eating and hunting and making sure your children didn't die. Even the sunrise you'd seen, the original, paled in comparison to what was in your head. Eventually you'd give up trying to copy it. You'd want to experience it firsthand. You'd learn how to fly like a bird, to go right to the source of the longings, in gigantic steel vessels that released great quantities of heat-trapping gas.

As soon as you started to admire something, to love it, you spelled its doom.

At Fishercap, they stopped well short of the trap and clicked out of their skis, then Garrett switched off the flashing safety light he'd set up in the middle of the night to keep P2 distracted. It seemed to have worked. The trap was more or less intact, only a loose pole brace where P2 must have rammed the lid repeatedly with his head. At the moment, though, he seemed to have given up and was listening to the crunch of boots in the snow. Garrett took a couple steps toward the trap, to see if this would piss him off. Sure enough, the box started to growl.

Garrett prepared the syringe while Bengt grabbed the jab stick from his pack, then the two of them approached the trap. The growling got louder, then louder still, amplified by the log box. An unholy sound, like something possessed. Garrett cracked the lid to look inside, shining his headlamp around the trap, or at least around the part of it they could see: P2 had shredded one of the inside walls, trying to claw his way out. Garrett should have been used to it by now, but the ketone-y stink of wolverine musk made him gag; even after a laundering, his backcountry clothes smelled like they'd been washed in cheap scotch. The animal himself, still hidden from view, had gone silent. Not even a hiss. Garrett took a moment to collect his nerve. Trembling, holding the jab stick like a spear, he signaled to Bengt, who cracked the lid another inch or two: the wolverine leapt suddenly at Garrett's face, roaring viciously.

Bengt dropped the lid just in time. Garrett took a step back. The animals' ferocity never ceased to amaze him. Again Bengt cracked the lid, but P2 lunged immediately, attacking so savagely he almost got loose. You could hear him panting inside, the log box steaming like a smokehouse. By the time Garrett managed to jab him, on the seventh try, his thermals were soaked with sweat.

He sat in the snow and waited for the tranquilizer to reach P2's bloodstream. All this just to get at the animal's GPS collar, so they could download the data points from the chip inside and find out exactly where he'd been the past couple months. Biologists understood very little about gulo behavior, even now. Dispersal patterns, mating habits, why the hell they occasionally decided to travel *forty miles* in a single day, and through rugged relief . . . sometimes Garrett wondered if he knew anything about them at all.

Garrett put his hands in his armpits to keep them warm. They had to do most of their trapping in fall and winter, when the grizzlies were hibernating; otherwise baiting the traps would be a death wish. Recently, the bears had begun to emerge earlier than ever, in mid-March, coaxed from their winter sleeps by the warming weather. As the winters had gotten less cold—less *snowy*, Garrett always clarified, because really it was all about this dwindling resource—P2 and his friends had been forced to travel higher and higher, many of them crossing the Divide into Canada. And it seemed like more and more mortality signals were getting radioed in every year. The animals were caught in bobcat traps, or crushed in avalanches, or shot because they'd ventured into the Blackfeet Reservation. Sometimes Garrett got so discouraged—so despairing, really—that he felt like giving up completely. Buying a grill for the backyard, so he could enjoy the early springs with Cece and Lana.

When P2 was good and zonked, Garrett laid a space blanket on the snow and lifted him carefully out of the trap and then sat there beside the blanket, holding the wolverine in his arms. Forty pounds? Thirty? How much smaller he seemed in Garrett's lap: no bigger than a collie. It was during these sedations, when the animal's ferocious strength was at its most mysterious, idling deep inside it, like some kind of motorless motor, a monster in repose, that Garrett occasionally touched the brim of something. It was a strange feeling, as if his lungs had turned to glass. He thought of his own father, the day that he'd died at the hospice. It had been three months after his stroke; his heart had simply given out, unable to keep the struggling mechanism of him alive. Garrett had seen him take his final breath. He'd expected it to be long, or remarkable in some way, but it was no different than any other one he'd taken. The last thing his dad had done was cup a hand to his forehead, suddenly, as if shielding his eyes.

Holding P2 in his arms, Garrett could feel the faint squirm of the animal's heart. He felt winded by grief. He didn't know why. It didn't really have to do with his father. It had to do with the stillness of P2's body, or maybe just with P2 himself, who seemed more alone than ever, lost in the wilderness of his dreams.

After her shift, Cece walked down to Big Sky Pizza to meet Garrett and Lana. He always took Lana out to dinner his first night back from the field. It had become a tradition, in the sneaky way things tend to when you have a kid and do something more than once with them. Cece tried not to worry about how much it would cost. She'd had a shitty night at the restaurant—shittier than usual even. Some drunk lech at a four-top had grabbed her ass while she was bent over the wine menu, helping his wife find a "nice white that she could drink with steak." Cece had fled to the ladies' room, shaking with rage. Why hadn't she said anything? Stabbed the fucker's eye with a fork? The bussers sometimes retaliated against customers, farting when they walked by their table—"crop-dusting," they called it—but she hadn't even done that. She'd hid in the restroom for five minutes, waiting for her blood pressure to reenter the atmosphere.

Even in her furry ushanka hat, Cece's ears stung in the cold. Global warming had begun feeling like a sane human response to Montana winters. (She'd said this to Garrett once—a joke!—but he was not amused.) Cece touched the tip money in her jeans, feeling it through her mittens—or what was left after tipping out the host and bartender and bussers. A hundred and forty-six bucks. Hard not to think of it as hush money. She'd always imagined she was special, destined to do something original with her life, maybe even become someone great, and this, ironically, was what had drawn her to Garrett in the first place. Running away with him, as far as she'd thought about it consciously, was meant to be part of this becoming. And yet what had she become?

Lana waved at her through the window of Big Sky Pizza, looking like she'd crossed into the witching hour. It was past her bedtime; they'd pay for it tomorrow. Garrett, who spent half his life in the wilderness, getting up in the middle of the night when a wolverine trap was triggered, seemed to regard time as a pesky human invention you were free to disregard. A bore.

And maybe you were. But boringness, it seemed to Cece more and more, was a luxury item, available only to the rich. How boring she'd seemed to herself, in med school. And how attractive, sometimes, this boringness seemed to her now.

What wasn't boring? Getting sexually assaulted at work. Groveling for money from your dad and stepmother, at age thirty-six, so you could send your daughter to summer camp. Being greeted at Big Sky Pizza by this same daughter, who was wearing fake hillbilly teeth.

"I have general herpes in my lungs!" she screamed, in some kind of demented YouTube voice. She reeled off laughing before Cece could collect herself. Their lives were like this now: filled with absurdist memes. Meeting Charlie's kids last summer had tugged on a loose thread of insecurity, made her wonder whether she was failing as a mom.

"I think she means 'genital,'" Garrett said.

"Where the hell did she learn that?"

He shrugged. A clutch of vending machine eggs, embryoed with little toys, was lined up on the table. As usual, he'd plied the kid with quarters. "She had too many Cokes, I think."

"Cokes *plural*?"

"Free refills," Garrett said. "It's tough to police."

Cece frowned at him, unzipping her coat. Of course he got to be the fun parent, the lenient one, who came down from the woods smelling like an OSHA event, armed to the gills with wolverine stories—grizzly encounters! newborn kits!—and then packed up the truck again a few weeks later, Lana Denver-booting herself to his leg to prevent him from leaving. Cece knew the girl merely pretended to be mad at him; she'd be angrier, in fact, if he never went away. It was Cece who resented it. She tried not to, tried as hard as she could to be supportive—it was his life's work, his calling, he was ostensibly saving animals—but being a full-time mom who waited tables for a living didn't make it easy. Millions of women had fought for equal rights so she could do what? Drop out of med school and become a married single parent? How had this happened to her? She'd made these choices herself.

But when Garrett was in the field, it was easier to blame

him—easier and more satisfying. Inevitably, after about a week of running herself ragged, rushing home from work with visions of Lana facedown in the house, zapped to death from fussing with a plug, Cece began thinking of escape. Her dreams lifted themselves off the couch. She'd given up finally on the idea of getting a PhD: at her age, she couldn't imagine seven years of grad school, which was how long in parent years? *Ten*, probably. Lana would be in college by the time she got her degree. Instead, Cece imagined a bookstore in LA, some charming little place in a hip neighborhood, Eagle Rock or Atwater Village, the sort of shop that had a rescue cat wandering around and window displays curated by local artists. She was not only the owner in this fantasy but lived in a beautiful apartment upstairs. The patrons were smart and well-read and relied on her for recommendations. She hosted lectures, literary salons, maybe even got authors to curate a Favorite Books table, complete with witty handwritten endorsements. Where was Lana? Reading in one of those cozy swivel chairs in the back, which she did every day after school (no latchkey kids in this daydream!). Oh, and there was a Russian literature section because . . . why not? It was her store. Just picturing this made Cece intensely happy. By the time Garrett got home from the mountains, smelling like a musk ox, he had to contend with a fantasy he knew nothing about.

Cece picked up a business card from a stack someone had left in the middle of the table: "WIN A FREE AR-15" it read above a picture of an assault rifle. The Christian Family Fellowship Church, advertising their weekly gun raffle. On the flip side, above an inventory of firearms they'd be giving away each Sunday, was a quote from John 14:27: ". . . my peace I give unto you . . ." Good god. Had she really chosen to live in this place? To raise a family here?

Lana, who'd drifted over to the arcade area, was watching some teenagers play a video game called Tropocalypse, which involved decapitating zombies. The game seemed to take place at a resort. The zombies, built like *Penthouse* models, were wearing bikinis. Cece bounded over and grabbed Lana by the arm, leading her back to their table.

"You're not allowed to watch that," Cece muttered.

"Why not?"

"Because it's sick and deranged!"

Lana leaned forward, as if she wanted to tell Cece a secret. "I'm *ammosexual*," she lisped in her ear.

Cece recoiled. "What the hell does that mean?"

"Someone who loves guns," Garrett said. "We saw it on a T-shirt."

Cece turned to Lana. "I don't want you to say that again, do you hear me?"

"Say *what* again?"

"You know exactly what."

Lana peeled back her upper lip, like a horse eating a lump of sugar, and bared her hideous teeth. "That I was born ammosexual and God still loves me?"

"Shut up!" Cece hissed at her. "Shut up or I'll rip those things out of your face!"

For a moment Lana looked at her in amazement, the teeth half-falling from her mouth. Then she burst into tears. Cece, stricken with remorse, began to gather trash from the table and pile it on a tray. People were looking at her. She could feel Garrett's eyes on her as well, judging her from across the table.

"You owe me a hundred bucks," he said angrily.

"What?" She could barely speak.

"From the bet we made. Hiking at Glacier."

Cece glared at him with hatred. She had never felt such loathing. She stood up from the table without saying a word. Then she pulled the wad of bills from her pocket and threw it at Garrett's face; before they could reach their target, the bills exploded in midair, fluttering in all directions.

The table looked like a Monopoly tantrum. The only

sound—other than the video games, their dueling ostinatos—
was Lana's crying. Garrett stood quietly and began to pick up
the twenty-dollar bills from the table, the bench, the laminate
floor. He was calm and businesslike. She expected him to make
some kind of joke, something that would fan her hatred into an
exquisite blaze—"Now, this is what I call *collecting* a bet"—but
he didn't. He just gathered the bills one by one, as if they were
playing cards. Everyone in the restaurant watched. The flame of
Cece's fury blew out, as suddenly as it had ignited.

"I'm sorry," she said miserably. "Lana, I didn't mean that."

Lana wouldn't look at her.

"Sweetie? Please. I didn't mean to say that."

Lana sniffed at the table, refusing to acknowledge her. How
many times had Cece told her she loved her? But of course the
girl would remember this, the time her mother had threatened
to rip her teeth out. Helplessly, Cece turned to Garrett, who
cracked open one of the see-through eggs on the table and
handed her a pair of fake teeth. Then he hatched another pair of
teeth and stuck them in his mouth. Despite how yellow and mis-
shapen they were—one of the canines was basically horizontal—
the teeth looked surprisingly real. Cece put hers in too. They
waited for Lana to look up and notice them. When she did, she
grimaced reflexively, revealing her own hideous teeth.

"General Herpes," Garrett lisped, introducing himself.

Cece laughed. God, how could she love and hate someone so
much?

"And this is . . ."

"Private Gonorrhea," Cece said.

She stuck out her hand, but her daughter refused to shake it,
her eyes still red from crying.

"From now on," Garrett announced, "if any of us start to
fight, or feel like yelling 'shut up' at each other, we're going to
all three of us put these in our mouths. These fake ugly teeth.

Thereby making us too ugly—too utterly ridiculous—to take seriously."

"Very funny," Lana said.

"I'm serious. I want us to take a pledge. *I, member of the Herpes-Gonorrhea family, do solemnly swear, in times of anger or rage or murderous wrath, to wear these novelty teeth.*"

The three of them raised their right hands and repeated the pledge, drooling all over themselves. It was the opposite of a bet—or maybe a bet they were on the same side of, that they would win or lose together. They dropped their hands. Everyone in the restaurant was staring at them. Sheepishly, Garrett and Lana removed their teeth, replacing them in their eggs, but Private Gonorrhea had lost her container and didn't know how to turn back into herself.

SIXTEEN

A typical LA evening, cooling suddenly as the sun went down, as if into another season. Charlie helped Angeliki set the table outside, under the fig tree that got mobbed by parakeets every fall. Even in December figs were scattered on the lawn, rupturing into little pink geodes. A few lonely grapefruit, too, from the oro blanco tree shading the hill that ran down to the neighbors' bamboo fence. Charlie, who didn't much care for figs or grapefruit, admired his shady yard nonetheless and thought about how he'd fallen in love with it at first sight, when he and Angeliki were house hunting. She'd been pregnant with Téa at the time, and mostly what he'd dreamed about was exactly this: the four of them having dinner outdoors, on the rare night he wasn't working or on call, Charlie and Angeliki picking fresh fruit to feed to their children. He'd shared this Edenic fantasy with Angeliki at the time. What he hadn't shared with her was the other fantasy drifting through his brain: the look of envy on Cece's face if she were to ever somehow visit them in LA. She loved the fruit trees in Montana so much.

He'd meant to take her to the orchard last year, when he'd asked Cece and Garrett to the lake—to rub it in? dazzle her with apples?—but the sight of her had knocked him sideways, turned his elaborate plans for the day to mush.

"Charlie," Téa said, raising her arms to him. She had Angeliki's green eyes, pupils ringed with little brown specks, like the inside of a kiwi. He picked his daughter up and put her on her booster seat.

"Why do you call me that?"

"What?"

"Charlie. Instead of 'Dad.'"

Těa shrugged. "Mom calls you 'Charlie.'"

"It's sweet," Angeliki said. "You're her best friend."

Charlie nodded, though he knew this wasn't the case. Secretly, he worried it was because he worked too much. He wasn't around enough to be a dad. Not that Angeliki didn't work hard too—she was in high demand these days, often juggling two or three design projects at once—but she was out of the house every afternoon by three thirty, in time to get Těa from preschool. He turned to Jasper, whose eyes were on him from across the table.

"Hi, Chuck," Jasper said to him, then burst out laughing. Těa smiled along.

"See, it's a conspiracy," Charlie said.

How lovely it could be when the kids didn't fight. They ate their hamburgers in the exact same way, Těa copying Jasper's technique, peeling her bun off so that a white gauze of bread stuck to the meat before eating the burger separately. Not very many things felt magical to Charlie—he was a doctor, a gospeler of science—but a peaceful dinner came close. You expected it at any moment to collapse, but by some extraordinary luck the kids were both in good moods, generous with each other, calm and grateful and uncompetitive. It was like reading a book about your family, one of those novels that make you long for the expensive life inside it, where the father comes home from work and dazzles his kids with jokes and presents. They drank wine in these books and never got mean or tired. Maybe they ate a quince in the dappled light.

One of the herons nesting in the sycamore by the garage began to bark like a demented dog. Charlie wasn't sure what conservationists were doing to the LA River—"revitalizing" it somehow—but recently a heron family had moved onto their property, waking them up at dawn and dropping half-eaten meals in their backyard. Often Charlie had to clean up a giant carp head from the lawn or risk pureeing it with the mower. Were herons endangered? Was it normal for them to be living in the middle of the city, reclaiming their ancestral lands, like the coyotes you sometimes saw jogging down the middle of the street? Or was this the beginning of the end, an omen of the apocalypse? He'd been meaning to ask Garrett about it, but every time he picked up the phone to call, he remembered his performance at the lake last summer and blushed with shame.

Of course, he thought of the mother osprey in Montana, that time he'd scared away an eagle and saved her chicks. Except he'd done it for Cece: he was just following orders. The truth is, the herons were annoying, they kept him awake sometimes after an all-nighter at the OR, they made a god-awful racket and smelled up the yard. A shotgun, now, might have come in handy.

Doing the dishes, Charlie blasted a dumb song he'd loved as a kid—"Just What I Needed" by the Cars—and was abducted by happiness. He started to dance. Well, that might be overstating it, to call it dancing. It was more dance-adjacent. The kids came in from the yard and saw him doing something nonessential with his legs. *Daddy!* Jasper said, pretending to be embarrassed but clearly thrilled. It had never crossed their minds that their father would try to dance. He might as well have turned into a bear. He was a tired man, wonderful when he was around but often on his way to work or bed, stage-hooked by phone calls, prone to falling asleep on the floor of their room when he was supposed to be playing Legos. He always seemed like he'd just gotten back from another planet, too rocket-lagged to stand up.

But here he was, singing along to the stereo while swiveling his hips. A well-rested father is maybe the best thing in the world. The kids started to dance too. When Angeliki came in from the porch, they were all three bent over shaking their asses.

"Catch an egg and shave it," she said, wide-eyed.

This was a Greek expression that didn't translate well, or at least Charlie had never really understood it. Much of the mystery left in their marriage revolved around her childhood Greek. Angeliki turned down the music.

"What's going on in here?"

"They told me to get funky," Charlie said gravely.

"We did not!"

"They did. They said: 'Father, we would like you to shake your moneymaker.'"

"We didn't!"

"They said: 'If you don't shake your moneymaker, we're going to shave an egg.'"

"Daaaaaad! We didn't! Dad started it!"

Afterward, Charlie and Angeliki got the kids ready for bed. This was a major production, partly because Charlie had riled them up: Jasper wouldn't stop moving, stripping out of his pajamas as soon as Charlie managed to get them on and running around the house, penis-proud. You forgot sometimes that every bit of fun was like lighting a fuse. Eventually Charlie had to yell at him, to threaten not to read to him before lights-out—though probably this would bum Charlie out more than it would Jasper—and the boy calmed down enough to join him in the old spindle bed where Charlie and Angeliki slept. *The Trumpet of the Swan.* Téa climbed into bed too, so that Charlie had a child on either side of him, like cubs, some deep animal thing done for warmth. He'd loved *The Trumpet of the Swan* as a boy, particularly the part where Louis gets rich playing in a band, but it wasn't the sentences that moved him now but the fact that he was saying them to his children, the same sentences his father had said to him. In fact, he was hardly aware of the sentences at all. He worked hard all day and sometimes all night, lucky to get five hours of sleep in a row, pumping people with potassium so their hearts could be revived or fixed or even replaced, anything to grant them a bit more time on earth, except it wasn't merely for these people that he worked so hard: it was for Téa and Jasper. He wanted to shelter them from loss and heartbreak. Not from the fact that these things existed—he'd devoted his life, for better or worse, to staring them down—but from the idea that they were anything to fear. That he, a cardiac anesthesiologist, feared them himself. Except he couldn't tell his children this. He couldn't tell them that his job as their father was to make them as *unafraid* as he could, for as long as humanly possible, because god knows he was afraid for them, sick with fear really, it was what kept him up in the middle of the night even in his exhaustion: how they would grow up soon and get into cars driven by shitfaced boys or dive into swimming pools from strangers' roofs or maybe even have a bad LSD trip, a truly life-scarring terror bath, and this time in bed together was Charlie's way of saying that he would be there to protect them, that bad acid trips were just a worse version of what already assailed them on a nightly basis, the creepiness that haunted bathrooms and mirrors and quickly-turned corners, portents that *the world wasn't what it seemed to be*, impervious to the "nightmare traps" Jasper built out of stuffed animals and placed around his bed. But what Charlie hoped to say by reading to them was that the world was *exactly* how it seemed, it had light and meaning and shelter, he would protect them from internet stalkers and active shooters and pervy men in gym shorts. He would trap all their nightmares—not just now, but forever. That's what his job was: to lie and lie, for as long as they would swallow it.

"Tell us a doctor story!" Jasper and Téa said after he'd finished reading to them. Somehow Charlie had begun telling them bedtime stories about famous medical anomalies. How this had begun—or why—Charlie could not remember. Their thirst for them was an act of rebellion, a way of pushing against his campaign of deception.

"Okay. A quick one. Tarrare?"

"Yes! The man who ate the baby!"

"Tarrare, Tarrare, let's see . . . ," Charlie said, pretending to have forgotten the story. It was their favorite, though it had been a while since he'd told it; he could never remember which details he'd left in or out. Tararre was an eighteenth-century French man, renowned for being constantly hungry, who could eat a quarter of a cow in a single day. Hyperthyroidism, they think he probably had. He ate so much he drove his parents to ruin. "So he had to become a street performer, eating live cats and puppies."

"Alive puppies?" Téa said.

Charlie glanced at Angeliki, who was standing in the doorway. "Oops. Maybe I left that out before. On purpose."

"Was he practicing for the baby?"

"Let him tell it!"

"Thank you, Jasper. They put him in the hospital, to try and cure him, but Tarrare was so hungry he kept drinking the other patients' blood. Also, sneaking into the morgue to eat dead people. Yes, corpses. Oops, did I leave that out last time too? I'm thinking from your mom's face maybe I did. Like maybe I'd had fewer glasses of wine when I told this before. Yes, your mother's nodding at that. Now she's walking away."

"What about the baby?" Téa said.

"Finally they kicked Tarrare out of the hospital because a baby disappeared, and they thought he'd eaten it."

"Yay!"

"Was it alive when he ate it?"

"I'm not sure. Great question."

Afterward, Charlie took Jasper to bed and zipped him up carefully in the down sleeping bag he insisted on using every night. He was such a sweet, tender, sternly philosophical kid after his fuse had run down.

"Dad?"

"What is it?"

Jasper's eyes fixed on the ceiling, as if there were something of great interest on it. Charlie knew what was coming: a thought experiment of some kind. There was a new one almost every night. Last night he'd wondered what color your blood would be if you suffocated in outer space, since there would be no oxygen to turn it red. He rarely seemed satisfied with Charlie's answers, and Charlie suspected he was really asking something else, some larger question he hadn't managed to formulate or perhaps didn't even know he wanted to ask.

"That baby that Tarrare ate," Jasper said. "Did his family think he went to heaven?"

"Probably, yes. I'm sure they did."

"So they thought he'd be like that forever? A baby? 'Goo goo ga ga—I want milk'?"

"Hmmm," Charlie said. "I don't know. That's a good question."

Jasper appraised him coldly. There was something in his face Charlie had never seen before. Was it—hard to believe—*condescension*? "He's not a baby forever," Jasper said softly, "because heaven is a crock."

Charlie, startled, sat on the edge of the bed. "Who told you that heaven is a crock?"

"That girl last summer. In Montana."

"*Lana?*"

"I didn't know if it was true or not till just now. When I saw your phase."

Charlie frowned. The boy must be exhausted. And yet he was sure his son had said "phase"—not "face." He touched Jasper's hair, stiff as straw with the day's sweat. "No one really knows if it's a crock, bud, or what happens when you die."

He was worried that Jasper would ask him what he *believed* happened, but the boy didn't. Charlie told his son he loved him, and his son said "I love you, Dad" back in a way that seemed like the refinement of something sloppy and oblique, a paraphrase of what they'd been saying to each other all evening. There was no feeling like it, really. So why did Charlie sometimes get the impression, once the kids were in bed, that his real day was just beginning? Despite the wine he'd drunk at dinner, he poured himself a scotch and went back outside while Angeliki sent emails and sat on the deck overlooking the reservoir a few blocks away, which looked like the implausible desert puddle it was. He sipped the scotch and listened to the sound of his own brain, a luxury these days. He felt so pure and silent, so much like himself at last—so far from the man who'd been dancing like a robot in the kitchen—that he wondered if he really even wanted to be a father at all. It terrified him, how easily he could come unmoored from his kids, as if one's deepest connections in life meant nothing. Why had he devoted so much energy to them? Was it all a tragic misunderstanding? In med school he'd dreamed of being a great doctor, an important one even, someone who might *revolutionize the way we think about pain itself.* Dreamed of finding an antagonist for the CB1 receptor in the brain, something that could block pain in a way that made opioids, and their addictiveness, obsolete. But greatness was cruelty, it was passion, it was Self at the expense of everything else. Sometimes he wanted to freeze his own heart and go about the world like that, to see what would happen. What great things he might do. What if this life he'd built, this life of "times"—tummy time and screen time and family time, quiet time and Medieval Times—was just a sentimental trap?

Cece had done this to him: made him wonder if the world, if everything he cared about, was a trick. He had been good, he had loved her with the purest of hearts, and look what had happened. He'd lost her anyway. When she'd first told him what she'd done, that she was wasn't coming back to LA, Charlie had gone berserk. He'd cried and begged and made some shameful threats about killing himself, trying to blackmail her with guilt. Later, he'd dreamed of flying back to Montana and grabbing his grandfather's old shotgun from the cellar and hunting Cece and Garrett down first, killing them in cold blood. For a week or so, he'd played the fantasy out in his head. Surprising them in

Garrett's bed, the shock and terror and pleading for forgiveness. Brains painted all over the walls. Then he'd shoot himself, of course. One of those revenge killings/suicides you read about on the news. He had never imagined anything like this before in his life, never even imagined himself *capable* of imagining it. When he caught himself researching plane tickets to Kalispell, hunched over his computer at three a.m., Charlie came to his senses and found someone to cover his shift the next day and prescribed himself a Triple-A Ball (Ambien, Ativan, Ardbeg), trusting he would emerge from his hibernation as a human being again.

Of course, he would never kill anyone. Not in a million years. But killing *himself* was another issue. This was the durable fantasy, the one he couldn't get out of his head after what had happened. Putting the gun in his mouth, fingering the trigger. The taste of metal and mildew. Charlie would lie in bed and think about it, caressing every detail in his mind, the way a violinist might think through the notes of a cadenza. It was all new to him, this longing for oblivion. Even as a teenager, he'd never had the remotest urge to kill himself. Life had seemed to him like one of those long summer days at the pool where you don't ever want to get out, you want to stay and swim forever, but then feel so exhausted by the end of it that you climb out, half-willingly, and hobble home. When Garrett had dropped out of college, Charlie had sympathized with him without really understanding it. He'd grieved terribly for Elias, of course—in his weakest moments, had even blamed Garrett for his death—but he'd never felt that life *itself* was the problem, that Elias's death was anything but a horrible accident that had deprived him of something precious. Now Charlie began to understand what it was like to see life as *unprecious*, to feel so crushed and despondent that you didn't want to leap out of bed in the morning and annoy people by waking them up too. *Rise and shine!* Why had he ever leapt out of bed to begin with? What did he imagine he might miss? He started smoking again, for the first time since college, buying Viceroys in bulk at Sam's Club and enjoying them (for lack of a better word) in the tobacco den of his room. He'd been a social smoker at Middlebury, but now he understood what cigarettes were designed for. Like death, you did them in bed. They were a kind of dress rehearsal. The sick day from the hospital became a sick week, which became a sick month, which became a leave of absence.

What would he have done without his family? His mother, his brothers, even his valetudinarian dad? They'd swooped in and reclaimed him as their own, nursing him back to health, forcing him out of bed since he wouldn't leap out any longer. Jake had even moved in with him for a bit, forcing Charlie to go to the gym with him and making sure he was eating something besides frozen taquitos. Without Jake, he might have lost his job. He might have become an ex-cardiologist chain-smoker. And he had Jake to thank, too, for eventually introducing him to Angeliki. She'd been hired to renovate the lobby of Jake's office; Jake had set them up on a blind date. Charlie had fallen in love with her—not instantly, thank god, but slowly, watchfully, over a period of months—and then asked her to marry him. It was a lovely California wedding; no one had become sick; Angeliki had gotten pregnant within six months. The human capacity for survival was amazing. The suffering in Charlie's past became a kind of crucible, paving the way to his current happiness. Life was a voyage, and heartbreak filled the sails.

Except that he still thought about Cece. Her face appeared to him while he was driving to work or riding the elevator at Cedars-Sinai or surfing the webpages of his mind while he was drifting off to sleep, as vividly as if he were seeing a photo in his head. A stranglehold of longing and anger would choke him for a second. It was worst in Montana, vacationing at the lake, where she seemed to rise out of every nook and cranny of the house like a ghost. He'd thought inviting Cece and Garrett to the lake last summer would somehow immunize him: it seemed ridiculous to avoid them for the rest of his life, given that they lived ten miles away. The truth was, too, that Charlie missed them. Not just Cece, but Garrett as well. His best friend in life; there had been no replacement. Charlie imagined he was a big enough man, a happy enough man, to invite him back into his life. It had been nine years. They had families of their own, they were fathers.

But then Charlie saw her. She got out of the car, a little heavier in the hips but basically the same way he remembered her, and he knew right away he was lost. He smiled, he fawned over Angeliki and the kids, but it was like waking up from some shrewdly convincing dream and trying to pretend you were still in it. Seeing her had not been an inoculation at all. It had been an infection.

A few days after Jasper's question about heaven, Charlie had to get the boy dressed for school; Jasper was too tired to do it himself. Or so he claimed. He wouldn't eat any breakfast either, declaring he wasn't hungry. Angeliki was out of town, working on a new admissions office for a fancy prep school in Oregon, and so Charlie was covering the mornings while she was away, trying to get Jasper and Téa off to school and preschool. (A tag team of babysitters was picking the kids up.) The third morning that Jasper wouldn't get out of bed, Charlie snapped at him, too tired and stressed out to gently badger him downstairs. When the boy fell asleep again, Charlie shook him angrily. Later, he got a call at the hospital from the school nurse. Jasper had fainted during recess. He seemed to be okay. Charlie, transforming into Dr. Margolis, grilled the nurse with questions, making sure she'd elevated Jasper's legs and properly hydrated him, as if she were some half-wit who'd ended up with her job by mistake. But that was his role as dad. When it came to your children, you were supposed to be an asshole.

"Are you ready for bed?" Charlie asked that night, after getting Těa to sleep. The babysitter had kept the kids up too late, whether by mistake or laziness he couldn't tell.

"I'm wearing my boofrobe."

Charlie laughed. "Your what?"

"My boofrobe."

"You mean your *bath*robe?"

Jasper looked at him strangely. It wasn't like Jasper to be goofy like this, at least before bed. Charlie touched his son's forehead—no fever—then untied the sash of Jasper's robe. The boy closed his eyes but took his arms from the sleeves, slow as could be, then lay there on his robe as if it were a beach towel.

"No questions tonight?"

Jasper cracked his eyes, as if he were watching Charlie from a distance, then rolled over suddenly and faced the wall, guarded by his fairy ring of stuffed animals. Was he already asleep? It seemed like it. They must be driving him into the ground at soccer practice.

Maybe it was the oddness of Jasper's behavior, but Charlie slept fitfully that night, troubled by strange dreams. In the morning, Jasper seemed fine enough at first, sliding out of bed as soon as Charlie woke him up and getting dressed by himself. A bit docile, maybe, but more or less himself. Charlie made him and Těa scarf down some frozen waffles and then loaded them into the Audi and zoomed them off to school, only a minute or two behind schedule, Jasper riding up front instead of in his usual spot in the backseat. As always, this was scandalous to Těa, who tended to view the world as a swamp of injustice. "Charlie, I get the front!" she yelled. Typically Jasper basked in her envy and crowed about getting to ride shotgun—Angeliki made him sit in the back, because it was safer—but today he ignored Těa's pleas entirely, leaning his head against the window as if he'd been awake all night.

Charlie stopped at a light on Hyperion, his heart brisk with worry. He said Jasper's name. The boy farted indifferently, like an old man at the drugstore.

"Charlie! Jaspy tooted!"

"I'm your dad!" Charlie snapped at Téa. He turned to his son. "Jasper? Jasper! What's going on?"

Jasper peered at him without lifting his head from the window. Charlie pulled through the red light, veered to the side of the road. Téa was crying in the backseat. He picked up Jasper's arm—how limp and clammy it was!—and checked the boy's pulse. A wallop, hard enough that Charlie flinched. He waited for the next beat. Nothing. The nothingness seeped into Charlie, filling him like a gas. A frozen deep-space terror. Had the boy died while he was taking his pulse? Wonderfully, dreadfully, the next beat arrived, thumping against Charlie's fingers, so long after the first one that it felt like a different heart.

Bradycardia.

Forty beats a minute? No, thirty at best. He'd seen seventy-year-olds with heart rates this slow, but never a child.

It must be some kind of joke. A cosmic prank.

Or maybe Charlie was responsible somehow; he'd caused it to happen.

He grabbed his phone to call 911, then thought better of it. Rush hour. Might take twenty minutes for an ambulance to get here. Better off driving to Good Samaritan himself. He'd get Jasper to the ER; they'd see if he was in peri-arrest, dose him with epinephrine if need be. Maybe even use pacer pads on him.

He'd be fine.

This was Charlie the Father thinking.

Charlie the Doctor thought: *Fifty percent chance.*

Instantly, both Charlies disappeared. He peeled from the curb, tires chirping, almost sideswiping some douchebag in a Tesla while forcing his way into the lane. This was a third Charlie, the skiing one, who sometimes coaxed himself down runs by imagining himself on fire. Flooring the gas, he slalomed through the traffic on Hyperion, thinking only *Good Samaritan Good Samaritan Good Samaritan*. Another red light approached. This being LA, there were no pedestrians, so he jumped the curb and straddled it with two wheels on the sidewalk and raced along tilted like a catamaran before rounding the line of cars waiting for the light and jolting back into the street at the empty intersection. Cars honked, people screamed, but Charlie didn't hear them. He was driving seventy on a residential street. At the next stoplight, he veered into the opposite side of the road— miraculously free of oncoming traffic—then swerved back suddenly to avoid head-on–ing a Vespa and turned onto West Temple and threaded his way up the middle of it, creating a fifth lane of traffic, blaring the horn so that people had no choice but to steer out of his way. Moses, parting the red sea of brake lights. He was aware of this thought, that he was Moses—just as he was dimly aware of Téa's crying, which had turned into a panicked keen—but it seemed to come from outside him, like the voiceover in a movie. Charlie himself couldn't think. He couldn't think, but he could feel, and what he began to feel was that he was skiing through a glade of trees. Yes, the cars were the trees, and he was swooping between them. It was impossible to keep a line, the trees being random and unpredictable, sending him this way and that, nearly to his death, but Charlie did his best. Garrett carved the way ahead of him, making effortless turns. The bastard could ski anything. Charlie was chasing him. He actually imagined Garrett up there in front of him, weaving through the cars and trucks of West Temple and then making a daredevil turn on Alvarado, spraying a rooster tail of snow. And as it did when they were skiing, weaving through actual trees, a strange invincibility seemed to descend upon Charlie: a sense that he could do anything, bend the very slope of the earth to his will, so long as he didn't stop.

SEVENTEEN

Lana went down to the lake by herself. She wasn't supposed to—her mom had forbidden her to cross the busy road alone, made Lana repeat what she'd said out loud, as if she were an imbecile—but Lana went anyway. She was eight years old. She could cross a stupid road. And Jasper was driving her up the wall. Like all boys her age, at least the ones who weren't secretly girls, he was boring and annoying and wouldn't stop spazzing around, as if everything he touched were slingshotting him across the yard. What was wrong with him? With *all of them*? Talk about elbows or shoulders or belly buttons, and life marched along sensibly enough, but say the word "balls" and they just about wet themselves laughing. If they weren't giggling about balls, they were shooting themselves with toy guns, making embarrassing *pew-pew* noises with their mouths.

In truth, Lana felt a little bit sorry for him. She suspected he'd gotten the short end of the stick IQ-wise. The kid could barely even read. It was painful to watch him sound everything out, reminding himself that b's have bellies and d's have diapers. She'd had to watch him do this, because Jasper's father had made him read aloud to everyone at lunch. From *Mouse Soup*. The poor dingus had actually seemed proud of himself.

This was no fault of Jasper's mom, who was beautiful and didn't seem to own shoes and had told Lana in the kitchen that she had "natural presence."

Lana stared at the luscious water lapping the beach. She was dying to swim, but her mom said she couldn't go in the lake by

herself either, that she had to wait till the grown-ups had cleaned
up from lunch. Lana had had a recent revelation about grown-
ups. The revelation was that they were actually children. Some
nasty trick had been played on them, trapped them in adult bodies, and now they couldn't get out. Of course they didn't want
you to have fun; they were jealous. Sometimes Lana would catch
her mother picking her nose, or popping some Bubble Wrap in
the kitchen, but she didn't know how to free her and turn her
back into a girl.

Delicious water! It slurped at the dock, inviting her in. What
a waste, to own a beach like this and be too chicken to use it. She
almost went in anyway, a quick dip, but it wasn't worth risking
her mother's wrath.

Lana decided to go back to the house, where everyone surely
missed her. *Where's Lana?* they were probably saying. *We miss
her natural presence!* She walked back up the boatshed lawn and
then ran across the highway and slipped on some gravel that had
spilled from a truck and fell down hard in the road, ripping the
knee of her jeans. Her hands stung with pain. She looked at her
palm: it was raked and bloody, bits of gravel embedded in her
skin, like the silver balls on a Christmas cookie.

Tears scratched at her eyes, but she refused to let them out.

As she was raising herself on all fours, getting ready to stand
up, a white car cleared the bend ahead of her. Lana froze. The
car sped toward her, aiming straight at her face. She couldn't
move or stand or scream. Her brain was jammed, out of service.
She closed her eyes just as the tires began to screech. When she
opened them again, the car had come to a stop in front of her,
calm as a house, the heat from its grill warming her eyeballs.
It smelled like burnt carpet. The engine hummed politely, as if
waiting for her to crawl out of the way.

A man stared at her from the driver's seat, gripping his phone with two hands. Lana had heard about cars that could stop them-selves. The thing had sensed Lana, down on all fours in the road, and had braked automatically. Had decided, no doubt, she was an animal.

The man—who seemed of all things angry at *her*, Lana—said something. At least his lips were moving. Ignoring him, Lana stood up and walked toward the house, expecting everyone to run out and greet her, deranged with worry and concern—but the front yard was quiet. No one seemed to have noticed. They were all inside, clearing up from lunch. Lana felt very strange. Everything looked new and cheap and plasticky. Her eyes were like windows she'd only just cleaned. A mosquito landed on her arm, then stabbed around a bit with its tiny straw before flying away unquenched. She felt like an empty milkshake. She told her legs to move, to walk, but it seemed to take longer than usual for them to get the news. She stopped on the first step of the porch, hidden from the grown-ups inside. Rock music—the prehistoric kind, with real live instruments—drifted through the screen door. She heard someone laugh, so loudly it sounded like a recording. "Well, color me impressed," her father's voice said.

She wanted to tell her mother that she'd almost died and left the world forever, but her mom would probably scream or some-thing, making the whole thing even more embarrassing than it was. Plus Lana would have to explain what had happened. The only thing more embarrassing than dying was being mistaken for a deer.

Also, she'd get in trouble. Cosmic, *teenager* trouble. Her mother would never let her do anything again.

Lana wandered around the side of the house to the patch of weedy grass leading to the orchard, hardly noticing where she was going. Jasper was lying in a hammock. The hammock drooped between two pine trees, low enough to the ground that his head brushed the dandelions. She felt certain Jasper would notice the fact that something had happened to her, something vital and important, but he just looked at her the way he had all morning, as if she were more interesting than a grown-up and less interesting than a Mountain Dew. This made her feel even stranger. She thrust her bloody hand in his face.

"I was almost just run over by a car," she explained.

"Sure, right."

"It's true! See, look: my pants are ripped. Didn't you hear those tires screeching?"

He shrugged.

"I basically just died."

"You did not *basically die*," Jasper said angrily.

Lana, surprised by this outburst, ogled him from above. She vaguely remembered something her mom had told her a while ago, that Jasper had had to go to the emergency room at the hospital for some reason; Lana didn't remember the details, only that her mother had gotten that weird look she always got when talking about Jasper or his dad, peering *behind* Lana instead of at her, as if she were watching a movie and Lana was blocking the screen.

Jasper yawned at her, revealing an advent calendar of missing teeth. From above, his face looked especially flat, his slender nose poking out of it like a handle. It looked like you could maybe slide it open and take out a frozen treat. Contemplating it, Lana felt the need to inflate her own value.

"You know my mom and your dad are more than just friends," she said.

"What are you talking about?"

"They actually got married."

"Ha ha," Jasper said. "Very funny."

"I'm serious. They had a wedding and everything. But then my mom ran away with my dad and left your father bereft."

"That's not true."

"'Bereft' means 'lonely and abandoned.'"

"You're making that up."

"I'm not. He almost drowned himself," she lied.

"My dad hates drowning. He won't let me in the boat without a life preserver, even if it's on the lift."

"Ask him yourself, if you want."

Jasper looked at her resentfully, as though wondering whether to believe her or not, then turned his attention to the sky. Lana climbed into the hammock with him, which basically set them on the ground. He lay there stiff as a board, staring at the twiggy tops of the trees while she examined his face. She'd discovered only recently that faces had a way of growing more appealing the longer you looked at them, especially if there weren't any others around to compete with them. Boys' faces, she was talking about. Anyway, he let Lana stare at him. It felt like an autopsy.

"Did you know your face kind of looks like a door?"

Jasper scooted a bit farther away from her in the hammock— or tried to. He was both almost her brother and not her brother at all, which made her feel squirmy and amiss, as if she'd put on something backward.

"I just feel kind of weird right now," she said. "Since I almost died."

"You were weird before that too."

Lana ignored this. She reached over and grabbed Jasper's nose.

"Cut it out!" Jasper said.

"I can't be the first person to grab your face," she said, letting go of him. "It was basically designed for it."

"At least I don't have a thing on my lip."

"That's not a thing. It's a beauty mark."

"Looks like a mole," Jasper said.

"You should look up 'mole' in the dictionary. Once you can read."

"Why are you shivering like that?"

"I don't know."

He regarded her suspiciously, then stared back at the treetops. Lana, who really didn't understand why she was shivering so much, worried that she'd been killed for real on the highway and *had actually become a ghost.* Why else would that mosquito have rejected her arm? It didn't help that Jasper found it so easy to ignore her.

"What's so interesting about those stupid trees anyway?"

"They're not stupid," Jasper said. "They're dying."

"So what?"

"See all the needles missing up there? They're being suffocated by pine beetles. We'll have to chop them down soon."

"You only know that because your dad told you."

"I know everything because my dad told me."

He said this openly, without shame. Lana had to respect this. Maybe he wasn't as immature as she'd thought. Also, most boys her age didn't give a flying crap about trees, especially dying ones; definitely they didn't spend their time gawking at them for no reason.

"Geez, stop shivering, will you? You're making the whole hammock shake."

Lana scooched over so that her arm was touching Jasper's, feeling the warmth of his body. She felt slightly better. She scooched a bit farther, then a bit farther, using him like the warm sand on a beach. The hammock tilted perilously to one side, threatening to dump both of them on the ground and tipping Lana more or less on top of him. But that wasn't the actual crazy part. The actual crazy part was how she felt being there. It was a little bit like lying on top of herself. He was sort of what could have been her, if Lana's mom had married the person she was supposed to.

She felt something against her ear, up near Jasper's collarbone. A lump. "What's that?"

"Nothing," he said.

"There's something beneath your shirt."

Jasper lay there like Gulliver on the beach, gripping the hammock with two hands. Lana pulled down the neck of his T-shirt and saw the outline of something under his skin, a little bulge with rounded corners, like a cigarette pack rolled up in someone's sleeve. It was the first interesting thing a boy had ever shown her.

"I like it," she said.

"You do?"

Lana poked it. Jasper stopped gripping the hammock so hard—or seemed to. There was a scar, pink as an earthworm, above the lump. Lana touched this too.

"It's a pacemaker," he said defiantly.

"Will I mess it up?"

"Only if you wave a magnet at it. Or a chain saw. Chain saws make it confused."

"What disease do you have?"

"It's not a disease! I can do everything you can."

"What not-disease do you have?"

"Sick sinus syndrome," he said, glancing at her. "The nonsurgical kind. It's extremely rare in children."

Lana creaked with envy. She asked him what the syndrome felt like, and Jasper told her how he'd started fainting for no reason, like in the middle of recess, then how on the way to school one morning his heart had slowed down so much that it had nearly stopped and his father had had to race him to the ER. So he was a ghost too. *Sick-sinus-syndrome*, Lana repeated to herself, like a poem or a spell. The sound of it did something to her day. It made her ambitions for it seem kind of pointless. Her dad had promised to take her to the pet store in Kalispell, to get a bearded dragon—she'd been so excited she couldn't sleep—but now bearded dragons suddenly seemed like a scam. They were lizards that ate cockroaches. She kissed Jasper on the cheek, and then, when that failed to live up to the song in her head, she moved on to his mouth, imagining that she was saving his life. She was giving him CPR. Jasper's mouth tasted like

Mountain Dew and for some weird reason those little tabs they make you bite on at the dentist during an X-ray—Jasper so stiff and motionless it seemed like he really was dead—and it felt to Lana when she closed her eyes like she was falling inside his face, possessing him even, kissing him from within instead of without, as if she'd have a life with this boy who could have been her and another one with everyone else, even though they barely knew each other. She'd had one life up to this point, and now she would have two. Already she knew this life would be long: that they'd see each other next summer, and the next. A woodpecker drummed somewhere nearby—*tok-tok-tok-tok-tok*—like a clock going at triple speed, and Lana would come to think of this as summertime, or rather summer *time*, which operated by different rules entirely, so that the days she spent with Jasper at the lake every summer seemed somehow continuous—just seemed to magically pick up again where they'd left off. They moved through Summer Time, in which days were really years.

Lana opened her eyes. They were lying on the ground, between two mossy stumps. There was nowhere to hang the hammock but they'd still ended up here, on their favorite bed of dandelions. Jasper's braces were barnacled with gunk. A blush of pimples stained one cheek. He had his shirt off, one arm stretched above his head, and you could see the weedy slick of hair in his armpit, giving off a rank new smell. They weren't supposed to be outside—the Air Quality Index was in the red—but they'd snuck out the back door anyway, eyes stinging so badly they had to squint. Glacier was on fire, as well as part of Jewel Basin. The sun was like a flashlight through a blanket. But they didn't care. They'd been waiting for this basically all year long. They'd emailed and FaceTimed and even sent each other actual live packages, filled with stupid things meant to remind them of the lake—cherries and Monopoly money, splinters and bug spray and skipping stones—knowing they'd get to see each other in person only once a year, like they had the past five summers.

Once a year. For a few days at a time. She thought of Jasper and herself as those pretend cosmonauts, the ones who went into space at light speed and returned to find a world of strangers who'd aged without them. The strangers were themselves, when they weren't together.

Lana rolled off Jasper and lay beside him in the dandelions. A swirl of tiny umbrellas ascended, *Mary Poppins*–style, on the breeze. "I wish we had our own house," she said, staring at the dim bulb of sun. "Then we could visit each other whenever we wanted to."

"Where?"

She shrugged. In truth, she couldn't imagine them anywhere but where they were. "Somewhere without smoke."

"Equatorial Guinea," he said. "I did a presentation on it in fourth grade."

Lana took out her phone and googled houses for sale in Equatorial Guinea, keeping it away from Jasper's pacemaker in case it caused electromagnetic interference. She'd gotten the phone on her thirteenth birthday and was still besotted with it, as if someone had given her one of those magic objects in a children's book: a knife that cuts through worlds. Still, it seemed ridiculous to think it could do anything to Jasper's heart. Sometimes she forgot he had a pacemaker at all. The thing was harder to see than it used to be, maybe because he was less skinny—just the back end of it sticking up a bit near his collarbone, like a tiny car sinking into a lake. The scar was less visible too, except when Jasper got too much sun and it turned a kind of beautiful scarlet. Lana found it beautiful, at least. She still liked to touch it, imagining the scar was something she could unzip. She wanted to reach inside of him and grab some deep forbidden prize in her hand. Lana understood this was not a normal thing to want. She understood, too, that it was entirely possible she didn't want this at all, possible that the scar actually wigged her out a bit, because saying it to herself—*I want to reach inside of him*—was not necessarily about what she truly wanted but what she *wanted* to want, or at least wanted the eccentric version of herself who was listening to think she wanted.

"Kiss me, brother dear."

This was their joke to each other, that they were some kind of pervy siblings. Jasper kissed her on the lips for a while. His tongue was slimy and amphibious, but at least he moved it around now instead of jamming it halfway down her windpipe as if he were getting a throat culture. They'd been kissing every summer since they were eight. It had become a kind of calisthenics. Lana wondered if they'd ever do anything more. She was bleeding again—every month, she prayed she wouldn't, that it would miraculously skip her the way the angel of death had skipped the Israelites—and could not imagine ever getting used to the strangeness down there or feeling bored enough to allow foreign objects inside what had come to seem more and more to her like a wound. Did anybody want that?

"You're getting better," she lied. "Have you been kissing other girls?"

"No."

"Boys?"

He shook his head.

"I bet the guys in your class are jealous of you."

"Why?"

"Because you've got a Zephyr 600."

This was the name of his pacemaker. Jasper looked at her suspiciously. "Why do you always want to talk about that?"

"I don't."

"Actually, they make fun of me sometimes. They call me 'C-3PO.' Once, I had to be skins in soccer practice and these guys were all like pretending to be robots behind my back."

Lana frowned. She wished he hadn't told her that. She felt

both closer and less attracted to him at the same time. She had no trouble picturing the boys in her class making fun of him, but she had the idea that people in LA were more enlightened.

"Is it scary?"

"What?"

"Having a pacemaker. Knowing it's keeping you alive."

Jasper shrugged. He wouldn't look at her. Lana had the astonishing impression she was the first person ever to ask him this. Why were the most important questions precisely the ones people never asked?

"I get scared all the time," she said conversationally. "Sometimes I'm lying in bed, after the lights are out, and I think about what it's going to be like to be dead. To be nothing. It makes me feel like one of those frogs that hop around even after their heads are crushed." Just talking about it made her skin ice up.

"You won't remember what it was like not being nothing."

"Exactly!"

"It's stupid to even think about," Jasper mumbled.

"Tell that to my brain."

He looked at her finally. He did not wear glasses, but sometimes it seemed as if he'd been wearing some and had just taken them off. "When my heart almost stopped, they put me on pacer pads. In the ICU. They're like two halves of a bun with you inside it. They jolt you over and over, to keep your heart going."

"What did it feel like?"

"Imagine you're a door and someone's trying to kick you in. As hard as they can." He looked away again. "I still have nightmares about it."

"Do you wake up screaming?"

"I wish," Jasper said. "I can't even talk."

Lana had an exotic feeling she identified as shame. She'd never thought about what it would actually be like for your heart to slow down, or to have a *syndrome*, or to need a pacemaker for the rest of your life. She put her arms around Jasper, not in a kissy way but in the way you might hug someone after a night-mare. He was trembling, which surprised her. It might have been Lana's imagination. She couldn't tell where the trembling ended and she began.

She let go of him. Jasper made a cartoony face—a dead one, his head flopped back and his eyes crossed—and Lana laughed. He was the only thirteen-year-old more interesting to her than her own loneliness. She made a dead face back. Jasper made a worse one, a real death-by-Medusa face, and then Lana returned the favor. Why was this a million times better than kissing? She used to think that having a boyfriend was about curing it, your loneliness, because that's what she'd read in books. But maybe it wasn't about curing your loneliness. It was about *doubling* it.

"You're the only one I ever take my shirt off in front of," Jas-per said. "Except my parents, of course. I mean, to be born with a normal body, and then suddenly not to—to be embarrassed all the time about it. You don't know what it's like."

"Oh yeah?"

Lana stuck her hand into her shorts and underwear, past her pad, then pulled it out again. Her finger was quilled in blood. Jasper looked at her in alarm. She wrote her initials over his heart, the real one, using her own blood. *LM.* It took a couple attempts. She tried to do one thing every day that nobody had done before, at least in Montana.

Jasper was trembling for real now—with admiration or dis-gust, Lana couldn't tell.

"Let's do something *historic*," she whispered.

"What do you mean?"

"Something we'll talk about when we're old."

"I know where my dad keeps all his wine and stuff."

"Where?"

"In the basement."

They stood up together and headed back to the house, quick with purpose. Lana had never drunk alcohol intentionally before, though she'd once had some eggnog by accident at a Christmas party and felt a strange giddy supermarket feeling like her mother was looking for her but didn't know where she was. Jasper was bare-chested, leading the way, sweatshirt tied around his waist. Now that he'd admitted he was ashamed, he seemed to want to prove himself wrong. They walked around the side of the house, where Ziggy, the Margolises' dog, came bounding up to them, leashed to a fence post. Jasper bent down to quiet him, but the dog seemed mostly interested in the blood on his chest, sniffing hungrily at it, as if he wanted to eat Jasper's heart.

She followed Jasper around the porch and then through the door to the basement, which was kept perpetually unlocked. Nobody from Montana kept their doors unlocked, but Californians *believed* they did, which inspired them to buy homes here and leave them open to intruders. Jasper led the way into the dank cavern of the basement, past the sporting-good shelves; past the boiler, where cobwebs drizzled her face; then turned the corner where Lana supposed the wine was kept. Her heart thumped in her chest. Her brain was in constant rebellion, but her heart was still an obedient organ that craved her parents' approval. It lounged in the prison of their trust. She hoped there were enough bottles that the Margolises wouldn't notice one was missing.

Jasper stopped suddenly. Some people were there already, blocking the door to the wine closet. Lana's mom and dad. Except it wasn't her dad. It was Jasper's. The two of them were hugging. Lana pulled Jasper behind the boiler, where they could peer around the metal duct without being seen. Her mother and Mr. Margolis just stood there, clutching each other without moving. Her mother's back was turned but Lana could see Mr. Margolis's face, which looked new to her, groggy and doll-like, the way people look groggy and doll-like underwater. He was gripping her mother's shirt—had fistfuls of it in his hands, as if he were holding on for dear life.

Lana and Jasper backed away and then left the basement and ran around the house in the direction they'd come. They didn't speak or look at each other or in any way acknowledge what they'd seen. Ziggy jumped at Jasper again and tried to lick his chest, but Jasper grabbed the leash and yanked the dog away hard, sending him yelping. Lana followed behind, Mr. Margolis's face still shining in her brain. It was creepy and ridiculous-looking and his eyes were closed. She hadn't seen her mom's face, but Lana was willing to bet it was just as creepy-looking, still as a mannequin's. That was the worst thing: how still they were. They'd both looked frozen, as if they'd been like that for years and were waiting for someone to unlock a spell.

Lana and Jasper were like that too: under a spell. Years went by, and also no time at all. Their bodies changed when they blinked. At one point the world literally stopped—they didn't see each other at all that summer, Covid numbers were through the roof—and then it started up again, presto, as if no one had died and nothing especially noteworthy had happened. Lana followed Jasper across the orchard and through the crazy neighbor's property and then into the forest behind the house, where they weren't supposed to go even when the air was clear. They weren't wearing masks. How strange it felt, after wearing one for so long. Strange and erotic. She'd come to think of her face, approvingly, as obscene. To be honest, she'd kind of liked wearing a mask, getting jeered at by maskless men in pickup trucks as they drove down Main Street—*baa-aa-aa*, they'd bleat at her, to tell her she was a sheep—because it confirmed that Lana was a different species than they were. She didn't belong in Montana at all. Sometimes she dropped to all fours and baaed back. It wasn't the mask that bothered them, Lana suspected, but the fact that she was carrying a concealed weapon, one whose value they couldn't appraise.

Lana spread the velvet blazer she'd been wearing on a patch of fleabane, not too far from some bear scat Jasper hadn't seemed to notice, and they lay down on top of it. A ridiculous thing to wear to the lake, but she'd wanted to seem new and exciting. *Remodeled.* Anyway, she was relieved to put it to practical use. Lana hovered over him, mooning him with her face. She could have licked his nose. She had not been this close to anyone for a long time, Jasper or otherwise; it felt like maybe the sexiest thing she'd ever done.

"Sneeze in my face," she commanded.

"Why?"

"I want you to. We're vaccinated. Then I'll sneeze on yours."

Jasper didn't seem too crazy about the idea. Nonetheless, she closed her eyes and waited for his sneeze. It was a bit anticlimactic: more wind than rain. Still, it felt like a baptism. To repay the favor, Lana took a deep breath through her nose, cocking it with a fake sneeze, and then something miraculous happened. She sneezed for real. Jasper, on the receiving end, got drenched.

"Hey!" he said, afraid to open his eyes. He looked like he'd just hatched from an egg.

"Do you believe that your face is the Son of God?" Lana intoned. "That it died and was raised back to life?"

"What the fuck," Jasper said, wiping his face with his T-shirt. "Why do you have to be such a freak?"

He took off his shirt and threw it in the fleabane, as if disgusted by it. He was no longer embarrassed by the scar on his chest and in fact you couldn't see a bump at all, since he was on a rock climbing team and always working out. This was the excuse he'd given for not texting Lana back sometimes: he was too busy, though when she'd googled his climbing gym in LA it seemed to be closed. Or had been, like everything else. When he wasn't supposedly climbing, he was writing songs on his acoustic guitar and then posting videos of himself singing them on You-Tube. Lana found the songs touchingly bad, filled with dopey platitudes and one-syllable rhymes, like "brain" and "pain." A lot of them seemed to be about his dad and what an asshole he was. In one video—"Sensory Isolation," 316 views—he'd played the entire song with a pillowcase over his head, as if about to be executed.

Jasper had smuggled some edibles on the plane from California, and they shared a gummy bear without speaking, Lana decapitating it with her teeth. She was wary about eating too much on an empty stomach. Also, there were strange people in the house, some friends of the Margolises who'd come along with them from LA. The strangers included Mr. Margolis's new girlfriend, who had adult braces; Lana's mom had made sure to mention this little detail to Lana, grinning like she'd been popping gummies herself. Her mother always acted kind of moose-tits when her dad was away. If she wasn't talking about people's teeth, she was crying over some book she was reading. Lately it was *Like Leaves, Like Ashes*, which Lana called *Like Twigs, Like Acorns* because it drove her mom nuts. Last night she'd caught her mother staring at the author's photo on the book jacket, as if the author, Gail Tippler, were hosting a Zoom.

Jasper seemed sort of distracted, or at least focused on something that wasn't Lana's face. To get his attention, she undid the knot of his swim trunks and reached under the waistband and felt him unlatch in her hand. He had hair on his chest, faint vortexes of fur around his nipples. Lana wasn't sure where the hair had come from—it had just appeared, like a werewolf's—but she liked it, just as she liked the curdled-mushroom-soup smell coming from his armpits. It didn't matter if he'd swum all morning or sat around playing those dumb killing games on his phone, the smell would be there, making her a bit crazy. She'd heard about someone who was so poor and hungry he tried to eat his own fingers. She'd been with other people too—okay, two girls, and a boy with death-metal acne—but their smells did not make her want to eat her own hand.

"Do you like that, dear brother?"

"Yes," he said in his lovely deep voice.

Lana pulled his trunks down and took him into her mouth. She'd watched a number of blow jobs on her phone, but it had not occurred to her a real one would be so dimensional. It was more slobbery than she'd imagined, and closer to throwing up, and though it turned her on somewhat there was also a trace of far-from-home despair she tried to ignore. Jasper groaned and thrust into her. Lana wanted him to feel the best he'd ever felt, and then maybe even better than that. She'd seen a clip on the internet where a guy, a porn star, died while getting a blow job. It had become infamous, at least among her classmates in tenth grade. One of those awful demented clips you vow not to watch and then do. Somehow the guy's heart had stopped right in the middle of a scene, except the people making the porno didn't know that. They just thought he was doing some understated blow job acting and kept right on filming. Eventually the woman in the clip—the starlet—realized he was dead and completely wigged out.

Lana let herself imagine what it would be like to make Jasper feel so wonderful that he died. To kill him with pleasure, his Zephyr 600 exploding like a bomb. He'd already had the battery replaced once, which was why his scar looked bigger than it used to.

Afterward, Jasper put his fingers inside her and made her go on a sunken journey. It was like heading deeper and deeper into a fiendish maze, wanting to get lost forever. She bucked against his hand and emerged only when he stopped, his fingers half-broken. At the age of sixteen, he'd already had five girlfriends. He texted Lana about them sometimes from LA. Somehow he'd become cooler, more sexually experienced, than she was.

"Is your dad coming over later?" Jasper asked.

"Nope—just Mrs. Wolverine. He's in the field."

He frowned. "I like it better when your dad's here too."

"He always does the same thing before he leaves. It's like a shtick. He winks at me, grandpa-style, and says *Be back before you know it*."

"At least he doesn't sneeze in your face."

"If you think about it, though, it's kind of a weird expression. He used to say it in the car too, when I was a little girl. *We'll be home before you know it*. It kind of creeped me out. Like he was going to wave a wand and we'd be home somehow, ta-da, before I even realized we were there. But then this one time it actually happened! I must have fallen asleep or something, because I woke up the next day in my bed, poof, like totally astonished to be home."

"What on earth are you talking about?"

Lana blushed. What she wanted to say was there was magic in the world, people got sick and died but they felt wonderful sometimes too—that even though she felt bored and lonely a lot of the time, so ugly even the dogs she saw pitied her, she felt astonished sometimes and Jasper made her feel that way too, when he put his fingers inside her. (Just last week, wandering through the park on a windy day, she'd seen a Frisbee fly out of one tree and get stuck in another.) But she got the sense that Jasper didn't understand her as well as he used to. She'd felt this even before the pandemic: that he didn't look forward to the lake quite as much. Or maybe it was just his parents' divorce that had changed things.

"What's your dad's new girlfriend like?" Lana asked.

"Horrible."

"Why?"

"You met her in the house. She's dumb as a rock. You know that song 'Beast of Burden'? She thought the lyrics were 'I'll never leave your pizza burnin'.'"

"A mondegreen," Lana said.

"What?"

"It's called a mondegreen. When you mishear a song. Like

when people think 'a girl with kaleidoscope eyes' is 'a girl with colitis goes by.' "

"Why are you defending her?"

"I'm not!"

"I just don't see how he can stand her."

Lana shrugged. "Maybe he likes her breasts."

Jasper scowled and rolled out from under her. He retied the strings of his swimsuit into a dainty bow. "Is *everything* just a stupid joke to you?"

Lana's eyes stung. She hadn't meant to be funny. It was just a statement of fact. It seemed obvious to her that some men married women because of their breasts, in the same way that swallows chose a mate based on the length of its tail feathers. But she was beginning to realize, more and more, that she couldn't tell anyone what she really thought. Even Jasper. People didn't really want the truth. Especially boys. They wanted to be agreed with, or soothed, or made to feel like folkloric beasts, dangerous but adored.

"Anyway, he's more interested in her face," Jasper said.

"What are you talking about?"

"Didn't you notice how much Becky looks like your mom?" He eyed her almost accusingly.

Lana laughed. "She does not!"

"She's even got that stupid dimple thing on her chin."

He made a face, as if he'd eaten something gross but didn't know where to spit it out. The truth was, Lana had noticed the resemblance herself, at lunch, though she hadn't fully processed it at the time. Their coloring was different—Mr. Margolis's girlfriend had freckles on her shoulders—but they had the same build and the same Sharpie-thick eyebrows and, yep, now that she thought about it, the *same stupid dimple on their chins*. Lana had always been glad to have her father's chin, but now she wondered if she was somehow missing out.

She picked a burr from Jasper's trunks. They'd never talked

about what they'd seen in the basement that one time. Not even once. Sometimes Lana wondered if it had actually been a dream. But clearly it had not been a dream to Jasper; it was as real as her mother's face.

"Anyway, my dad's a fuckhead," Jasper said. "They deserve each other."

"He seems so . . ."

"Nice?"

Lana nodded. She was going to say "shipwrecked."

"Ha. Tell that to my friends in LA." Jasper glanced toward the house. "I snuck out one time during Covid, when we were supposed to be sheltering in place. Met up with some friends on the beach to do acid. My mom called my dad, and he went completely apeshit. Drove out to Hermosa Beach in his scrubs and found us. Told everybody I had a pacemaker, that they were endangering my life. Imagine tripping your balls off, it's a deserted beach, and someone in a face shield starts yelling at you—a face shield and *goggles*—calling you a murderer." He pulled another gummy from the pocket of his trunks and popped the whole thing in his mouth. "None of my friends' parents even cared that much."

Lana thought: *But none of your friends have a Zephyr 600. Your dad was just scared. Also: acid? Also: Do you really need another gummy bear? Aren't I stimulating enough?*

"Did he know you were on drugs?"

"*On drugs?*" Jasper said, laughing. "What are you? A public service announcement?"

Lana flushed with shame. Who was this person, whose penis she'd just had in her mouth? The far-from-home feeling she'd had earlier, its nip of forlornness, had spread into her limbs.

"What's the matter?" Jasper asked, staring at her. "Are you stoned?"

"I'm just feeling some *hiraeth*."

"What does that mean?"

"It's Welsh. For a particular kind of feeling. There's no word for it in English."

He snorted. "Come on. There's a word for every feeling."

This was such a profound misunderstanding of the human condition that Lana was taken aback. Speechless, really. In fact, her speechlessness—tinged with the peculiar kind of sadness she used to feel as a girl, watching a helium balloon disappear into the sky—had no real translation. *Hiraeth*, she thought. *Fiddelsküt etch-wilder schadensplat.*

"Think we'll still be doing this when we're seventy?" she asked, trying to blunt the feeling.

"Doing what?"

"Meeting once a year. Fooling around."

Jasper shrugged. "We won't be vacationing in this dump."

"Why not?"

"I'll be famous."

Lana laughed, thinking this was a joke—but Jasper seemed to be serious. "What kind of famous?" she asked.

"You know how Bob Dylan won the Nobel Prize?"

"Ha ha. Good one."

"It's true!" Jasper said. "I'm going to be the next singer-songwriter to get one."

Lana, who had only a vague idea who Bob Dylan was, stifled another laugh. Jasper rolled away from her and lay on his back, scowling at a tree branch wagging in the breeze, as if it were a hand he refused to shake.

"What's your dad think of your videos?" Lana said.

"Are you *kidding*? I don't even show them to Tĕa."

"I wonder what we'll look like when we're old," she said, changing the subject.

Lana opened the AgeUp app on her phone and took a selfie, then selected the year 2080. She tapped the little twinkling wand and . . . presto! A gray, wrinkled woman. She shook the phone and it switched between the two Lanas: old and young, young and old. Her stomach lurched a bit every time. Lana never got tired of this; in fact, she was a little bit addicted to it. Her phone was crammed with pictures of herself at various ages, as if she'd lived a full life already and were merely retracing its steps.

She studied her seventy-four-year-old face, its gray mutant eyebrows and lopsided smile. Maybe she looked more like her mother than she realized.

She scooched back and took a picture of Jasper, whose face looked less doorlike than she remembered, as unremarkable as a regular boy's. Like she couldn't open it even if she tried. Lana selected 2080, feeling strangely gun-shy, and then tapped the magic wand. The screen froze. Went completely black for a second or two before the whole app crashed.

"It doesn't like you," she said, laughing. She reopened AgeUp to try again.

"Don't."

"It's just a game. To see what we'll look like."

"I said cut it out!"

Jasper snatched the phone away from her hands and tossed it in the weeds. He refused to look at her. What the hell was his problem? Lana lay there on the ground, stranded between her two favorite things on earth. She was about to crawl over and retrieve the phone when something snapped nearby.

"Who's there?"

She sat up. Jasper did too. Was it one of her Older Selves? Lana felt their presence sometimes, come to check up on her. Sure enough, somebody giggled.

"Hey!" Jasper said. "Come out of there."

Téa emerged from behind some stinging nettles, smiling innocently at Jasper. From behind her crept Pranavi, the girl who'd come along with her on vacation. They were suppos-

edly best friends. Pranavi was wearing ballet flats and some kind
of beaded, pint-sized dress she must have filched from a costume department. Also, bohemian feather earrings. Also—was it
possible—lipstick?

"Were you spying on us?" Lana said furiously.

"Only for a second."

"What did you see?"

"Nothing!"

This had to be true. They were too young to be perverts,
though Pranavi, staring at the shirtless Jasper, looked like she'd
been clunked on the head with a brick. Clearly she had a crush
on him; hence the evening wear. Somehow he'd gone from
being a reject-droid on the soccer field to being some kind of sex
object—at least to eleven-year-olds.

"Hello, my little wild prawn," Jasper said to Pranavi. He
made no effort to put on his shirt. In fact, he had a funny sort of
look on his face, as if he'd only just noticed her for the first time
and was imagining what she might look like in four or five years.
Lana, who tended to believe that other people's lives resumed
only when she entered them, the way you might flick on a TV,
realized she'd stepped into a drama that had already been happening, while the TV was off. It was Pranavi's parents who were
in the house; the two families had traveled here together.

"Dad and Becky had a fight," Tẽa said. "She threw a gin and
tonic at him."

Jasper grinned. "What were they fighting about?"

"Becky thinks we're spoiled. We never put anything away and
she stepped on a little Battleship boat."

Jasper's face hardened. It was like he was trying to turn himself into a horse, beginning with his nostrils.

"She made us stare at her foot," Tẽa said, "where it broke the
skin. She's got plantar warts."

"My mom had athlete's face once," Lana said, because no one
was paying attention to her.

Jasper turned on her. "Not everything's about your stupid mother, okay?"

Lana stared at him. She thought maybe he was kidding. Was he kidding?

"She also threatened to take away my phone," Tĕa said. "We're not supposed to use devices in Montana. Devices are reprogramming our brains. Are we using the device, or is the device using us?"

"What did you do?"

"I said she was using a rhetorical device, which was strictly verboten."

Jasper laughed, shedding his horse face. Who was this girl? His actual brainy sister, which ruined everything. Probably she'd just learned about rhetorical devices in school; she'd been waiting to use that line for weeks.

Lana began to feel a larger threat at work, a mobilization of forces. She touched Jasper's leg, proprietarily, but he stiffened in a way that made her pull her hand back. Something got in her eye. A bug maybe. How was it that one minute you were giving someone a blow job and the next minute you couldn't even imagine holding their hand, so faraway did they seem? You might as well cross the isle of death.

"Also, we stole Becky's phone," Tĕa said. She pulled an iPhone from the pocket of her jeans and showed it to them.

"Holy shit," Jasper whispered, as if it were the Crown of Lombardy. Printed on the back of the case, in Edwardian-looking font, were the words GIRL BOSS. "How did you get it?"

"It was locked in Dad's bedroom, right next to Dad's. Did you even know the door locked? I climbed the extension ladder and got in through the window."

"If only we knew the password," Jasper said.

"Try Dad's," Tĕa said. "It's our street address."

"They're not going to have the same one!" Lana said with disgust.

"I know the password," Pranavi said in a too-loud voice. It was the first time Lana had heard her speak.

"You?"

"She let me use her phone on the plane."

"Wild Prawn," Jasper said, smiling in a way that showed off his expensive teeth. He reserved them for special occasions, like a flasher. "Have I told you how wonderful you are?"

Pranavi blushed through her ridiculous makeup. She told Jasper the password, and he opened Becky's phone with a flourish. "We're in," he said in a movie voice, and Pranavi giggled. Lana stewed while they discussed various modes of sabotage. She suggested programming a new passcode so Becky couldn't use her phone. Téa said that was useless; Becky could just erase her phone and make a new one. Jasper nodded, as if the opinion of an eleven-year-old were superior to her own. Lana was beginning to feel like she had when she was eight, after almost getting hit by a car. Like she'd turned into a ghost.

She scowled at Téa, who had Jasper's thin-nosed face but none of its attendant beauty. The girl looked even plainer standing next to Pranavi. Lana hated them both. Especially Pranavi, whose red lips looked like those wax ones you could eat. Her dress was sliding down one arm, probably because there was nothing happening body-wise to keep it up.

"Let's send a greeting to Charlie Margolis," Jasper said, opening Becky's messages. He tapped on his father's name. "What's the worst thing you can text somebody?"

"That you're dumping them," Téa said.

"How about 'I've got AIDS'?" Pranavi said.

Lana regarded her gravely. "Do you know how many people have died of AIDS?"

"She's just joking," Jasper said.

"What about Covid? Or *brain cancer*? Is that funny too? Because my grandmother died of that before I was born."

"Everything isn't always about *you*," Jasper said, his eyes like cuts. "Why don't you go inside and wait for your mom?"

Lana gawked at him, speechless. Was he really sending her into the house? Throwing her into the weeds like her phone? She turned to Pranavi, baby skank, who glanced away quickly. Jesus, was there *sympathy* on her face?

"It's got to be believable," Jasper said, returning to Becky's phone. "Not too extreme. Like something that will make her look cringey."

"I know a cringey song," Lana said quietly.

She snatched the phone from Jasper and looked up his You-Tube video, the one with the pillowcase over his head. Jasper was too surprised to react. Lana turned up the volume, then held the phone at arm's length for Téa and Pranavi to see. It was even worse than she remembered. Jasper sat on a chair in an army jacket, strumming a slightly out-of-tune guitar, the corners of the pillowcase poking from the top of his head like the ears of a Chihuahua. *I scream but nobody can hear me*, he sang. *Everything inside me comes out queerly.* It was like a mondegreen, but on purpose.

"Oh my god," Téa said. "Is this a *joke*?"

Pranavi giggled. "Is he talking about his poop?"

"Maybe if he took the sack off his head, people could hear him better."

The chorus arrived—*Command me, reprimand me / Just don't seek to understand me*—and the girls clutched at their hearts. Téa pretended to shoot herself in the head.

Meanwhile, Jasper had gone perfectly still, as if an insect were crawling on his face. Or rather: like his own face was an insect. He didn't want to awaken it. Téa, noticing him for the first time, must have put two and two together, because she froze and went insect-faced as well and looked at the ground. Pranavi—still grinning, lipstick smeared across her teeth—dropped her hand from her chest.

Lana stopped the video and stuck the phone in her pocket, even though it was Becky's. No one seemed to mind. She felt very strange, inside out, as if her heart were beating into a microphone and everyone could hear it. Jasper retrieved his shirt from the fleabane and put it on, refusing to look at her. Lana picked up her velvet blazer, which was warm from his body. It smelled like sperm and BO. No one met her eye, not even Pranavi, and yet Lana had the Instagram-y feeling of being watched, as if the woods were crawling with people. Her Older Selves. They'd escaped from her phone all at once. She would live this moment again and again; it would never be over; she would return to it throughout her life.

The sprinklers in the orchard switched on, abracadabra, because they did that.

Lana headed through the orchard, trying not to get soaked. She didn't know what she was going to do—only that the phone in her pocket didn't belong to her. She would put it back where it belonged. If she did that, if she restored it to its rightful place, somehow everything would go back to how it was. Jasper would adore her again. Out on the lake a speedboat buzzed past the dock, towing a water-skier who was struggling to get up on his skis, dragging his ass across the lake. He looked like a dog with worms. What might have struck her as funny yesterday, or even an hour ago, seemed as repellent as she was.

Voices drifted from the porch, the loudmouth laughter of grown-ups who'd been drinking. She hurried around the side of the house, skirting the compost, then stopped at the ladder still leaning against the second-story window. Lana looked at it grimly. She had her mother's fear of heights. Someone shouted her name from the orchard. Jasper. His voice sounded funny, both loud and not loud, as if he'd swallowed something harsh.

Lana mounted the ladder and began to climb. She'd never been on anything higher than a stepstool before. The ladder shifted under her, as if it wasn't anchored to the ground—which, being a ladder, it wasn't. Lana tried not to think about this, or about the fact that she was basically climbing the wall of the house, if the wall were balanced on two feet and doing yoga. A mosquito whined in her ear. Lana let go of a rung to wave the thing away and the ladder tipped toward her, leaving its point of contact with the roof.

It stood there straight as a pole. Balanced on nothing. Lana held her breath, afraid to disrupt the miracle. She couldn't look down. The ladder wobbled, tilting one way and then the other, as if trying to make up its mind. Clutching the rails of the ladder for dear life, she looked down at last.

Someone was moving it. Jasper. He held her straight up in the air, gripping the ladder with two hands, as if he might shake her down. Though of course he wouldn't. Would he? She felt suddenly unsure. His face was red, splotchy, contorted by the stiff cords of his neck. He looked like a stranger. And yet he wasn't a stranger. He was her summer ghost-brother, who'd told her about his nightmares and once trembled in her arms. She knew things about him no one else did: that electric fences terrified him, that he liked breaking the smooth top inside a new jar of peanut butter, that once on a school camping trip he'd jerked off into an empty bag of Cheetos.

She wanted to make a face at him, a cartoony dead one, but he was too far away. Did he even remember doing that together? Whatever was wrong with him seemed bigger than Lana, a whole lot bigger, immeasurably big.

Lana closed her eyes, awaiting her fate. Uneventfully, the ladder tilted back to the house.

Jasper called to her, his voice softer now, but she climbed into the room where Mr. Margolis and Becky slept, pulling herself through the window by walking on her hands. Lana rose to her feet, shakily, then closed the window and locked it, afraid Jasper might follow her up the ladder. She'd been in this room several times before, back when Mr. and Mrs. Margolis were still together, and it had always looked like the rest of the house:

appealingly ransacked. Now it looked like a B & B. The comforter was tucked under the mattress of the bed, as if ready for inspection; on the dresser, piles of neatly folded sweaters had been sorted by color. Rather than stinking of mothballs, the place smelled "April fresh," like the restroom of a dentist's office. Through the air vent in the floor, Lana could hear Pranavi's mom talking about someone's girlfriend, who was in a "nude skydiving club."

Something rattled outside—the ladder?—but she didn't go to the window to check.

Mr. Margolis's phone was sitting beside a glass of water on the bedside table. At least Lana assumed it was his. She set Becky's phone carefully beside it. Mr. and Mrs. Phone. They were back where they belonged. Lana felt a surge of relief that surprised her. It occurred to her, maybe, that climbing up here and returning the phone wasn't only about Jasper. There was the song of your life and then there was the mondegreen of it, politely known as adulthood.

She sat on the Margolises' bed, suddenly exhausted. How weird life was. Weird and sad and schadensplat. Trees played catch.

She was maybe feeling the gummy more than she'd thought.

Mr. Margolis's phone buzzed. She thought about looking at it—what had Tēa said? That his password was their address—but resisted the temptation.

There was a noise outside, like a pebble hitting glass. Lana returned to the window. The ladder was gone, removed entirely from sight; in its place stood Pranavi, half-soaked from the sprinklers, staring up at Lana from the dappled shade of a pine tree. In her hand was a cell phone: Lana's own, which she'd left in the weeds. Pranavi proffered it in the air. How small she looked from the window! Just a little girl, wishing desperately to be older. Her feathered earrings flickered in the breeze. Lana wanted to comfort her, to ask why she was in such a rush to grow up—because it would happen, ta-da, *before she knew it.*

EIGHTEEN

Cece checked her phone one more time, rereading the text Gail Tippler had sent her this morning. *The* Gail Tippler! Author of *Like Leaves, Like Ashes*! Who was reading tonight at the bookstore, because Cece had lured her to Salish!

> How beautiful it is here! The mountains hardly seem earthbound. I keep thinking they're in mid-launch, headed for the moon. How lucky you are to live here.

The words were even lovelier—*chummier*—than she remembered. Cece's heart did a paradiddle. Just having Gail Tippler in her contacts was like, well, an act of God. Cece had been scared to text her back—what if she wrote something stupid?—and so had left the text unanswered, preserving its perfection. Anyway, she didn't want to disturb the woman while she was driving.

Cece wanted to ask Garrett whether to text back or not, but of course he wasn't here. He was in the mountains. She respected Garrett's need for solitude—respected and admired it. Truth be told, she often looked forward to his stints in the field. At least a little bit. She liked the time alone with Lana, liked being able to sleep through the night without wearing earplugs or waking to a tug-of-war for the blanket. Liked focusing on the bookstore without Garrett's needs and preoccupations man-spreading in her brain. Her life seemed to swing into focus, to fill the viewfinder of her thoughts, as if Garrett had been blocking it somehow. She was surprised, then, by how much she always missed him. That was the weird thing, the paradox of marriage she hadn't banked on: that he blocked her view of him, of Garrett, as well.

This past week, however, Cece had barely given him a thought. She'd been too distracted by Gail Tippler's visit. She'd reread *Like Leaves, Like Ashes*, maybe her favorite novel that wasn't written by a dead Russian. It opens with—what else?—a dead mother, her twelve-year-old daughter peering into her open casket just as a fly happens to crawl up the mother's nose. The girl imagines being the fly, entering "the haunted mansion" of her mother's head. The whole book was like that: an endoscopy into the mind of grief. Cece had written Gail Tippler a fan letter, or email rather, and amazingly—astonishingly—Gail Tippler had written her back. To thank her. And when Cece told her she owned a bookstore, and that this bookstore was in Salish, Montana, Gail Tippler had written back *again*, mentioning that she was going to a wedding in Missoula in July, her first time visiting Montana. She was flying out from Portland, where she lived. And somehow, against all odds, Cece had convinced her to drive to Salish for a reading, even *to have dinner with her afterward at the Trout & Tackle*.

And then the lovely text, extolling the beauty of Montana. All morning, running errands for the reading—picking up cheese and crackers, scouring the wine aisle of the IGA for some half-decent prosecco—Cece had seen the town through Gail Tippler's eyes. How quaint it was! And how majestic, really, was the mackerel sky over the lake! It was the same smoke-free paradise she'd fallen in love with years ago, at the Margolises' house. Even when she'd run into Tori Wiggins, owner of Huckleberry Gifts, out walking her dog; even when Tori Wiggins had given her advice on how to spruce up the window dressing of the store; even when Tori Wiggins's Australian shepherd had strained at its leash and she'd told the same joke she'd told for the past five years—"I think someone here needs to check his pee-mail!"—

Cece had not been filled with secret despair. She'd laughed politely, even graciously. Indeed, she was lucky to live here.

Cece sniffed her armpits. She was already nervous. Eight years ago, after that terrible night at Big Sky Pizza—the night she'd thrown her tip money at Garrett's face—Cece had decided she needed to do *something:* she couldn't wait for a divine miracle to befall her so she could open a bookstore in LA. And so she'd opened a bookstore here, in Salish. It had taken a long time, but she'd done it. Not just opened one, but convinced her favorite living writer to grace it with her presence. She'd written an intro—labored over it for days, as if she were writing the Gettysburg Address. She worried it was too gushing. What if she embarrassed herself? Got tongue-tied and aphasic? *The only thing worse than a bad speech is bad speech.* She had an image of herself at the podium she'd borrowed from Salish High, spouting aphorisms.

In the bathroom, Cece rummaged through the medicine cabinet and grabbed Garrett's beta-blockers, which he used when he had to give a talk at a university or an Ecological Society of America conference, then popped one at the kitchen sink. She immediately felt better. She was smart and capable and charming. At least med school had taught her how to creatively self-medicate.

She walked into the living room, where Lana was streaming something on her laptop. The girl liked to watch things on mute, following along with the closed captioning, because it made her feel like she was "hanging out at the Stagger Inn." How the hell she knew what it felt like to be at the Stagger Inn, the local dive bar, Cece didn't ask. She sometimes did strange things when Garrett was out of town. Last month, Charlie had found the girl *locked inside his bedroom;* this was at the lake house, when Charlie was visiting with his hideous new girlfriend. Lana had sneaked up there on a ladder and couldn't get down. "Probably a dare," Charlie had said, though his girlfriend seemed much less understanding about it, looking sternly judgmental of Cece's parenting, her lips sealed tight to conceal her braces. (The worst of it was on the ride home, when Lana suggested that Cece and Tinsel Teeth looked something alike.)

"What on earth are you watching?" Cece asked now.

"*Most Bizarre Plastic Surgeries: Animal Edition.*"

"Please don't watch that."

"It's awesome. These crazies try to look like their favorite animals. This one guy's turning himself into a lizard."

"Why does he want to be a lizard?"

Lana shrugged. "Why does Dad want to be a wolverine?"

"Did you leave a window open?" Cece asked, watching a carpenter bee bump along the ceiling, where the paint was stained brown and flaking from water damage. The thing was like a honeybee in a fat suit.

"Possibly."

"I told you not to! Now we've got those awful things buzzing around the house."

"Bombinating," Lana said.

"What?"

"That's what bees do. They *bombinate*."

"What am I supposed to do?" Cece said. "You father won't let me call the exterminator." It was a recurring spat between them. Garrett refused to have the bees dusted, though neither had he come up with any solutions to prevent them from drilling a maze of Lilliputian caves in their house and salting them with eggs. They were destroying the place, the insides of the walls turning to pumice.

"We could get plastic surgery. You know, to look like carpenter bees. Then we could all just share the house, like an intentional community."

"Actually, Kayla's on her way over," Cece said. "To pick me up. She said she'd help me get rid of them—knows some kind of 'folk remedy.' "

"Where are you guys going?"

"To the bookstore! It's Gail Tippler's reading tonight. I've told you a zillion times."

"The book club thing?"

"It's not a *book club thing*! It's Gail Tippler!"

"Geez, Mom. Take a breath, okay?"

Cece did as she was told. "I mean, yes, I made the club read her book, because it's *amazing*. Also, to make sure we have a good crowd tonight." She glanced at her watch. "I bought all that prosecco. Oh god. What if Gail Tippler's an *alcoholic*?"

Lana regarded her with something. Concern? In any case, she'd paused the lizard man on TV, who was having his tongue surgically forked.

"It's going to be great, Mom," Lana said sincerely. "Don't worry."

Cece smiled at her, feeling a rogue wave of love for this strange child on her couch. She was a sweet girl, inside the haunted mansion of her brain. Lana unpaused the laptop and resumed her trance. What would you call this trance? It was called growing up in Salish and being bored out of your skull. It was called having brainpower to burn—and then burning it, intentionally, because what else was she going to do? It was dead fuel, along with her acting talent. Because the kid could act! Cece would never forget seeing her do *Romeo and Juliet* in eighth grade, the one and only time Salish Middle School had done Shakespeare; the other kids mumbled red-faced to themselves, staring at the ceiling as they tried desperately to remember their lines, which clearly made as much sense to them as Swahili, and then Lana came out as Juliet and there was an actual sigh of relief. It wasn't just that she understood what she was saying; it's that the words seemed *natural* in her mouth, chitchatty and alive, as if she spoke that way in real life as well and just happened to stroll onstage midverse. Watching her interact with the boy playing Romeo was startling, almost cruel, like watching Fred Astaire dance with a zombie. But what was her daughter supposed to do with this talent? Star in the kids' production of *Seussical* at the Lutheran church? Cece and Garrett didn't have the money to send her to arts camp out of state. Nurturing her talent wasn't in the cards; they'd have to wait till college and pray for a scholarship.

In the meantime, Lana spent her days on the couch, doing crosswords on the computer, or hanging at the Swan Creek swimming hole with Riley, her best friend from school, a pimply girl whose evangelical parents wouldn't let her wear tops without sleeves or go trick-or-treating on Halloween. Cece wished Lana had more friends like Jasper. It had unnerved her at first when they'd become close—not just close, but thick as thieves, long-distance confidants, fusing Cece and Garrett to Charlie and Angeliki in a way that felt slightly perverse. After a while, though, the kids' friendship came to seem natural to Cece, or at least no stranger than the fact that she'd reconnected with the man she'd married and abandoned a week later. And to be honest, it gave her an excuse to keep in touch with Charlie, to return to the lake house every summer. To play tourist to the life she'd given up.

Maybe it was inevitable that something would restart between them. She couldn't sightsee forever. Cece explained it as a kind of muscle memory, a postmortem spasm, something that happened once a year when she and Garrett and Lana visited the house. Once she'd bumped into Charlie in the orchard, where she'd gone to pick cherries: they'd clung to each other for five minutes, as if frozen in time. It seemed like a joke—anyone seeing them would have giggled—but it wasn't. He was deadly serious. They both were. All the crucial moments in life were close to being funny but weren't funny at all. Another time it was in the cellar, where she'd gone down to use the bathroom; Charlie had surprised her when she'd come out. (Of course, she'd expected it, hoped for it, she hadn't been surprised at all.) It wasn't about desire. It was about stillness. Being pulled underwater and staying there, down deep, unable to move or talk or breathe. She and Charlie never discussed these encounters, or why they wanted them to be like this—they just were; it became an expectation, a thrill, because nothing had been talked about, the clutching seemed almost beyond their control. Cece thought of it as a kind of *angel lust*. She'd learned about this in med school: what they called it when men sometimes got erections after a violent death. Sometimes after these encounters Charlie would email her for a while, using her old med school account—but he always stopped eventually, after a week or three, when Cece didn't respond.

If only Garrett were so wrapped up in her. No, that wasn't fair. When he got back from the field, Garrett was everything she could hope for in a partner: horny and loving, worshipful and funny, quite a bit funnier, actually, than Charlie—what joy it was, all her doubts evaporating in a second! But after a couple weeks he'd revert to his usual abstracted self, some black fog seeping between him and the rest of the world. It wasn't that he took her for granted, exactly; it's just that his mind tended to drift to other things. To what was happening to the earth, the evil stupidity of people who were letting it happen. It wasn't that Cece didn't worry about these things as well or know them to be true—she wasn't evil or stupid—but dwelling on them did nothing to prevent them from happening. If the world was ending, the last thing Cece wanted to do was talk about it all the time. She wanted, sometimes, to chat about movies. To feel flattered and adored. To be selfish and alive and not give a shit.

She'd thought true love was about being *understood:* about finding that person who could see the sadness in you, the peep show of crazy you kept from everyone else. But what if it was better to be *mis*understood? Not to be reminded all the time, just by looking at your partner's face, that the peep show was there? What if love wasn't about sharing yourself completely, about yoking your secret sorrow to another's, but about finding someone who made you forget yourself?

When she wanted to see herself—the gunk in her soul—she had books. She had Gail Tippler. At least she turned it into beauty.

The doorbell rang. Cece left Lana to her lizard man and went to answer the door. Kayla was there, dressed up for the reading in a flouncy shirt and earrings shaped like miniature books. No: *actual* books, with pages and everything. Her lipstick was askew, as if it had been kissed onto her by someone else. As usual, she looked like someone who'd just run off on her family and had no regrets.

"Ready to kill some bees?" Kayla asked. In each hand, for some reason, was a tennis racket.

"We're going to play tennis with them?"

"They're squash rackets."

"I don't care if they're croquet mallets," Cece said. "So long as we get rid of the bees. They're destroying our house."

Kayla snorted. "A croquet mallet would be next to useless. Carpenter bees are less than half an inch in diameter."

"I didn't mean—"

"See these gaps in the strings?" she said, holding up a racket. "Exact diameter of the bees. Strips their wings right off. They drop like pebbles. You couldn't patent a better weapon."

Cece accepted this as a fact, because really that was all you could do with Kayla. She had a solution for everything, one of those competent women who wasn't averse to flouncy shirts but could split wood and replace an engine filter and maybe even kill something with an arrow. She wove her own snowshoes for the hell of it. Cece admired her greatly. When she wasn't making her own snowshoes, she worked for a title company, investigating property histories—a lucrative business in Salish. They'd met at the bookstore, after Kayla had wandered in looking for a field guide to edible plants.

Cece took Kayla to the guest room upstairs and popped out the screen before leading her onto the roof of the porch, where carpenter bees bombarded them from all directions. Kayla handed her a racket and began swinging at the air like a lunatic. Sure enough, bees dropped to the roof right and left. They looked fuzzy and companionable without their wings, like little pom-poms. Cece joined in the slaughter, imagining Garrett's face if he saw her out there swatting bees with a racket. Soon the bombardment had ceased and Kayla and Cece eased into a more discriminate bloodbath, targeting stray bees on opposite ends of the roof, as if they were actually playing tennis. Cece glanced up and saw the youngest Washburn kid watching them from the trampoline next door.

"I feel like I'm always doing these things with you," Cece said.

"What things?"

"Things that would seem crazy to me if anyone else was doing them."

"What's crazy about this?" Kayla asked sincerely. The tiny books danced in the sun.

"I guess it's no crazier than when we went swimming in December."

"Was it December?"

"Yes! You talked me into it. The lake was forty degrees."

Kayla shrugged. "I thought it was January. That's when the real fun starts."

Cece rested for a minute, trying to ignore the dead bees scattered at her feet. Some rain clouds had gathered in the distance, over Salish Lake, but it was so hot out the rain sublimed before it reached the water. Garrett called it this, "subliming," which Cece loved. You could see the wisps of rain dangling halfway to earth. She would have to point this out to Gail Tippler—both the virga themselves and the wonderful verb "sublime."

"I hope that doesn't turn into a real storm. I'm counting on a good turnout." Cece brushed a wing off her shirt. "We'll have the book club at least."

Kayla forehanded a bee, conspicuously silent.

"What?"

"Well, I wouldn't count on them entirely. Brandy's husband's sick. So she's got to watch the twins. And Corrine had to drive to Missoula; her mom's lost her mind, been digging holes in the front yard."

"What about Thea?"

"I think her boyfriend's in town. A surprise visit."

Cece stared at her. "Wait. *None* of them are coming?"

"You publicized it, right? I saw all the flyers. I'm sure you'll get a good crowd."

Kayla hit a few more shots. Cece felt suddenly tired. Not just tired: totally drained, as if she'd swum a bunch of laps and were trying to hoist herself out of a pool. What if no one came to the reading? What if this was a huge fucking mistake? What if, dear god, she'd dragged Gail Tippler here from Oregon, simply to humiliate her? No, Kayla was right—she'd put up flyers all over town. People had promised her, to her face, that they'd be there.

Just thinking about it—a stream of curious faces, crowding into the bookstore—made Cece smile. She loved the store, even though it was surrounded by cheesy souvenir shops, situated on a pedestrian pier that jutted into the lake. She'd converted it from a gallery selling "Western art," which seemed to mean a lot of bronze sculptures of Native Americans sternly evoking noble virtues. Cece was happy to see the gallery fail and even happier to convert it into a bookstore with books about urban life, life in LA and New York and Paris, Delhi and Istanbul and Tokyo, bringing the big bad world of "cultural elites" to Salish, Montana. It had not been easy to string together the capital: sucking up to her dad, getting him to cosign the loan, then convincing the SBA office to insure the debt and hand her a 504 on top of it. What high hopes she'd had! The Light at the End of the Dock, she'd called the store, investing six hundred bucks in a neon-green sign, proud of her own wit, the way she'd wedded the literary to the literal, not caring (or pretending not to care) that few people caught the reference. Of course, she'd been sure to devote a section to the American West, eschewing the white-men-who'd-rather-be-fishing club in favor of James Welch and Willa Cather, Louise Erdrich and Leslie Marmon Silko. (Why were so many novels set in Montana about taciturn ranchers and gambling addicts living in trailers? Most of the Montanans she knew had jobs and families like everyone else. They also talked up a storm.)

The trouble was, she hadn't sold any books. Baldwin languished on the shelf, as did Woolf, Wolfe, and Wolff. In fact, the only books that sold, infuriatingly, were the ones Garrett had curated: the hiking guides for Glacier and Jewel Basin, or sometimes the ones with endangered animals on the cover. Things had gotten so financially dire that Cece had revamped the whole store two years ago, paring the Literature offerings down to a few classics (*Anna Karenina*, semper fi!) and dicing the stacks into a Zeno's paradox of more and more sections: Cookbooks, True Crime, Thrillers, Romance, Pets, and the dreaded Self-Help & Relationships. "At least I don't have a Wedding section," she told Garrett, before adding a Wedding section. One day, after selling two mysteries in a row that featured a cat detective named Fussypants, Cece got so depressed that she closed the store for the rest of the afternoon. When the pandemic hit, she had no choice but to shut the store down completely; she never would have survived if her landlord, Wayne—a widower with a bit of a crush on her, or so Cece suspected—hadn't given her so much rent relief. Anyway, it was an effective wake-up call. What had she been smoking, opening a bookstore like this in Salish? Thinking Tove Jansson would fly off the shelves? Cece came very close to pulling the plug on it for good.

Instead, she started thinking of herself as an entrepreneur, not an evangelist, which washed her immediately with relief. ("An evangelist for what?" Paige had asked, and in fact Cece had no answer.) She'd invested her life savings into the store—or at least the small inheritance her grandmother had left her—and she couldn't bear to see it go up in smoke. Anyway, she enjoyed running her own business, even if it sold cat mysteries. Certainly it was a million times better than waiting tables. She discussed business models with Paige, who helped her come up with some "R & D strategies" to improve her "product-market fit," and focused on catering to local bibliophiles, or at least to readers, or at least to souvenir shoppers on Main Street who wanted "a quick read for the plane." If she managed to hand-sell a Jansson novel occasionally, that was icing on the cake.

At least she'd move some Gail Tippler novels. So long as it didn't rain. *Sublime!* Cece yelled at the rain, threatening it. Well, she did this in her head, not out loud, though she was so tired she could barely think. Something was wrong with her. Her legs felt like noodles. A carpenter bee flew into her shoulder. Probably it was looking for its dead friends. It blimped around, wondering where the party had gone to.

She swung her racket at the bee, which screamed. Cece heard it quite clearly. An awful sound, like someone being tortured. The wounded bee stared up at her from the asphalt. It had the face of an actual carpenter. Specifically: Jesus. "Your ass is grass," it said to her, quite clearly.

"What's wrong?" Kayla said.

Cece shook her head. She should have hired an exterminator, outsourced the genocide to a professional. Kayla helped her back through the window. She wobbled at the top of the stairs, and Kayla grabbed her arm. My god, was she dreaming? She could barely walk. She felt like she was on another planet, a humongous one, where the gravity was off the charts. In the kitchen, Lana seemed to be having a staring contest with the refrigerator, whose door alarm had started to beep. Cece dropped her racket on the breakfast table and slumped into a chair.

"Who won?" Lana asked.

"Your mom's not feeling well," Kayla said. "I wonder if it's the heat."

She brought Cece a glass of water, which Cece contemplated at length. How strange, the idea of pouring this into her stomach, a part of her body she'd never seen. She had no proof it even existed.

"Did you take one of these at lunch?"

"Take what?"

"A zolpidem." Kayla held up Garrett's bottle of pills.

Cece laughed. "Those are beta-blockers."

"No, Mom, they're Ambien," Lana said, looking at the label. "The generic kind."

Cece felt sick. Oh god, had she grabbed the wrong pills? Was she looped on Ambien? She was supposed to be at the bookstore in an hour. Gail Tippler, winner of the Djuna Barnes Award, was meeting her there. She was *introducing her*, for fuck's sake. She thought about canceling—she could avert disaster while simultaneously taking a nap—but worried that Gail Tippler would never forgive her. She'd come all this way, just for Cece. It meant something to Cece, the reading, that she couldn't fully explain.

"Maybe you should lie down," Kayla said gently.

"Yeah, Mom. You look like the walking dead."

"Like a zombie?" Cece murmured.

"No. Like a dead person, except you're still moving for some reason."

"I can't lie down! Are you out of your minds?"

Somehow, Cece managed to take a shower—a cold one, which helped raise her from the dead—and then changed into a dress, a designer color-block thing she'd ordered from LA. She couldn't have done it without Kayla. Lana, bless her soul, helped too. They shepherded her to Kayla's truck and then helped her into the passenger seat, making sure her seat belt was securely fastened. Everything would be fine. It was just a matter of staying awake. And the best way to stay awake was to do awake things, like stick your head out the window of a moving truck. No one had ever fallen asleep with their head out the window of a moving truck. It would be like falling asleep in a hurricane. Kayla turned onto Echo Lake Road, the wind whipping Cece's hair so that it lashed her face. It sounded kind of inviting, didn't it? A little hurricane nap. Someone grabbed her from behind and yanked her inside.

"Jesus, Mom! You actually fell asleep?"

"Of coursen't."

"You'll get decapitated."

Cece smiled. How sweet it was, not just for Lana to come along—crammed into the little-ease of the backseat—but to keep her from getting decapitated. Cece slapped herself awake. Talking was a bit of a challenge—the words seemed to sublime on the way to her lips—so she focused on keeping her mind busy. This was easiest with her eyes closed. When she opened them again, rain was pecking at the top of the truck. Thunder rolled in the distance, like children roughhousing in an attic. They stopped in the middle of the road.

"Did we run out of gas?"

"We're here," Kayla said. "At the bookstore." She touched Cece's leg. "Are you sure you want to do this?"

Cece nodded. She felt a bit better. Not awake, exactly—but promisingly semiconscious. Kayla grabbed the box of prosecco from the back of the truck, refusing to let Cece do it herself. Lightning flashed over the Mission Mountains. Inside the store, Meadow was sitting behind the counter with her eyes closed, holding a book called *The Radical Mind: Buddhism and the Illusion of Being.* Cece waited for her to look up and notice them—the door had jingled, after all—but she was frozen in place.

"Is Meadow on Ambien too?" Kayla whispered.

"That's just her natural state," Lana explained.

Cece, who felt literally at sea, skippered herself toward the front counter. On Paige's suggestion, she'd hired someone to work the register two days a week so that Cece could focus on "digital marketing." Somehow she'd ended up with Meadow, a first-generation Salish hippie, who put crystals in her drinking water because she believed they recharged her energy levels. (Chakra Absorbers, Garrett called these people.) At least Meadow was a voracious reader, not to mention a trusty resource when it came to stocking the New Age & Alternative Beliefs section.

"What are you doing?" Cece asked enviously, because Meadow's eyes were still closed. The woman seemed Sphinx-like, ageless, untroubled by the havoc the sun had wreaked on her face. Cece admired this about her. Increasingly, she had the feeling she could learn something important from the woman, even life-altering, if only she could figure out what the hell she was talking about.

"Trying to see if time is emergent," Meadow said.

"I see."

"It's hard to grasp. Our consciousness isn't large enough. You're supposed to turn off the movie projector of your brain and think of every moment individually, like it's a door—*visualize the picture of a door, eternal and separate*—and then eventually you'll be able to walk through them. Through *it*."

"And go where?"

Meadow shrugged. "Into the moment."

"Sounds lovely," Cece said, because it did.

"This isn't the easiest place to turn off your brain. People keep coming in looking for books." Meadow opened her eyes. "That reminds me: can I get next weekend off? I'm doing some journey work on Friday night and need time to integrate."

"Journey work," in Meadow-speak, meant doing drugs—though of course she called them "sacraments." Cece looked at Lana, who smiled into the book she was flipping through. They would have fun talking about this later. Sometimes Cece won-

dered if she kept Meadow on just so she and Lana would have
something to bond over.

She let Meadow head home early, wherever that was—a commune? a UFO?—and they busied themselves with setting up for
the reading. Or Kayla and Lana did. Cece sat guiltily behind the
counter, too woozy to work, watching them carry foldout chairs
from the storage closet and arrange them in front of the podium.
Rain battered the windows. It was pouring now, coming down
in sheets. Cece tried not to despair, counting on the citizens of
Salish to brave a little rain. These were the same people, after
all, who got their kids to school in two feet of snow. In a *blizzard*.
Snow days were as exotic to Lana as they'd been to Cece growing up in LA.

Cece pulled out her phone and saw that she'd missed a text.
From Gail Tippler. She was running late because of the storm.
Cece tried her best to text back—proms lemongrass, she wrote,
among other cryptograms—and then gave up trying to outwit
autocorrect. It was like using a Ouija board. She mustered her
strength and wobbled over to the card table Kayla had set up,
helping her plate an assortment of crackers, trying to make the
store seem homey and urbane at the same time. It wasn't the
bookstore of her dreams. There was no LGBTQ+ section, no
endcap devoted to books in translation. Occasionally drunks
stumbled into the store, attracted like moths to the neon, and
then yelled at Cece when it wasn't a bar. Still, it was the best
bookstore in Salish, the only one she knew of where you could
buy a Christian romance novel from an ayahuasca enthusiast
who thought you could walk through time like a door. They'd
just started to break even last month. She was proud of it, in
all its down-market glory—proud of *herself* for keeping it in
business. She liked chewing over the publisher incentives, writing shelf talkers for books no one bought, even managing the
invoices that piled up because she couldn't afford a bookkeeper.

Just seeing the sign from the street, its beckoning green light, filled her with a sense of accomplishment.

As did the arrival of Gail Tippler, prizewinning author, who entered the store in a green suede jacket that somehow made the rain seem trifling. (Had she worn green, oh my god, *on purpose?*) Even with wet hair, she looked effortlessly elegant, her glasses the kind that immediately make all other glasses seem out-of-date. A perfect braid draped over one shoulder, like a scarf. She was even more attractive, somehow, than her author's photo. She hugged Cece and then did that European thing where she air-kissed Cece's cheeks. Cece, flustered and delirious, or half-delirious, lifted the hem of her dress and curtsied. Her pre-ballet teacher, Ms. Zarelli, would have been proud.

"I'm sure more people will show," she said. "They're on Montana time."

Gail Tippler smiled graciously, perching her glasses on her forehead to defog. "Oh, are Montanans usually late?"

"Constantly," Cece said, though this wasn't true in the slightest. They were no later than anyone else. She offered Gail Tippler a plastic cup, hefting a bottle of prosecco, and the elegant woman pretended to dither before snatching the cup from Cece's hand, as if she were dying for a drink. Cece laughed boisterously.

"Love your snatch!" she said, filling her cup.

Gail Tippler gave her a strange look and then glanced around the store. "What a great store this is. Have you had it a long time?"

"I don't think so."

Gail Tippler stared at her.

"I'm sorry," Cece said. "For missing your text."

"I'm just relieved I made it."

"I was on my roof. Killing bees." She mimed swinging a racket back and forth.

Gail Tippler sipped her prosecco. "Do you mind if I . . . use the restroom?"

"Yes! I mean no. I'd be honored."

Cece escorted Gail Tippler to the bathroom, which was harder to find than usual. The woman followed her around the store. Cece felt like she was bombinating, on the verge of collapse. She found the bathroom—a stroke of luck!—then chugged a cup of prosecco. Had she told her favorite author that she loved her vagina? Was that possible? And were the chairs empty, glaringly bereft of people—except for her daughter and her best friend, who was wearing earrings in the form of tiny books? Had she lured Gail Tippler out here to, well, humiliate them *both*?

Cece prayed for someone to arrive. Anyone. Tori Wiggins. A barfly in search of a drink. Amazingly, the door jingled and a man with an umbrella came in. An actual umbrella! In Salish! What's more, he wore glasses and a blazer and was carrying one of those Moleskine journals with the little wee-wee of a ribbon peeking out the bottom. He shook his umbrella and then sat in the back row, clutching the journal in his lap. He had a book with him too—Cece couldn't see the cover—and he flipped through it deliberately, as if hunting for a particular passage. *Like Leaves, Like Ashes*? Cece thought about approaching him, one Tippler fan to another, but didn't trust herself not to scare him off.

She did her best to summon further patrons into the store, but the door failed to budge. The Light at the End of the Dock was just that: a waste of electricity. The empty chairs made it look especially desolate. Gail Tippler, who'd emerged from the bathroom, seemed newly resigned. Her manner had changed: polite as ever, but the warmth of her earlier hug had cooled, as if she'd been tricked into cleaning up someone else's house. She treated Cece like a stranger, which of course she was.

"I'm so sorry," Cece said, on the verge of tears. "It must be the rain."

"Let's just get started," Gail Tippler said.

Cece got up to introduce her. Did she have legs? If so, they'd forgotten the principles of movement. She made it to the lectern somehow and pulled her intro from her pocket. She read whatever was on the paper, which might as well have been in Klingon. Only when she'd sat down again, teleported there somehow by chance, did Cece realize she'd forgotten to flip the paper over. She'd only read half of her introduction.

Unfazed, Gail Tippler walked to the lectern, applauded by Kayla and Lana and the well-dressed fan in the back row. She thanked Cece without looking her in the eye and then began to read the opening to her novel, the one Cece knew practically by heart. She was an excellent reader, her voice clear and relaxed and full of feeling. Still, the sentences refused to communicate. They were like packages Cece couldn't open. Her brain was too tired to do the work. She closed her eyes, pretending to follow along. Maybe if her consciousness were larger. She tried to gum up the projector of her mind, to visualize each second that passed as a door she could step through. On the other side was a secret place, eternal and separate, where the words all lived. The words were throwing a party, so delighted were they to have escaped their books. They wanted to dance around and do drugs, not tell stories. They weren't Gail Tippler's bitch. Long live gibberish! Down with fascist authors! Cece stepped through the door and joined the party. How liberating, to leave past and future behind. To not string one moment to the next, in hopes of creating *events*. Because true life was drivel. It was a word disco. Nothing was asked of you, no choices were demanded, you could live in two places at once . . .

Someone was shaking her leg. Kayla. She tipped her head toward Gail Tippler, who had stopped reading, it seemed, and was awaiting instructions. Cece leapt up from her chair. She felt strangely refreshed. She thanked Gail Tippler for a wonderful reading, then asked if anyone had any questions for her.

The man in the back row raised his hand, holding his journal aloft.

"Yes?" Cece asked gratefully.

"Is it my turn now?" the man said.

"What do you mean?"

"Is it my turn to read? I've been sitting here patiently for an hour."

Cece gaped at him. Possibly he wasn't real. A product placement, engineered by Moleskine. "This is a literary reading. With a featured author. She came here from Portland."

"I respect that. But she should give other people a chance."

"What are you, a moron?"

"Hey now," Gail Tippler said. "Okay."

"This isn't an open mic night! It's a reading by Gail Tippler! Winner of the Djuna Barnes Award!"

The man didn't seem angry so much as righteously offended. He left the store, forgetting his umbrella. Kayla grabbed it for him, then ran outside to chase him down, as if eager to escape herself. The rain had stopped during the reading, and the damp sidewalk through the window, grained with mica, sparkled like a jewel.

Gail Tippler, who'd gathered her things, squeezed behind the table they'd set up for signing books and removed her jacket from the chair.

"Weren't we going to dinner?" Cece said.

"It's a ways to Kalispell. I'm visiting Glacier tomorrow."

"I made a reservation. It's not the French Laundry— Laundrette?—but it's the nicest restaurant in town."

"I don't think so. The drive up wiped me out." Gail Tippler leaned in for a second, as if to kiss Cece goodbye. Her glasses seemed photochromatically darker, or perhaps it was her eyes themselves. "Anyway, I might bore you so much you'd fall asleep."

Cece looked at her. She wanted to explain about the Ambien, how even now she couldn't be sure she wasn't dreaming—how else to explain the way the evening had gone, except as a nightmare?—but Gail Tippler zipped her green jacket and exited the store, nodding politely at Lana as she left. Cece stared at the stock she hadn't signed. Twenty-four books, which Cece would have to return to the publisher in New York.

Lana said something, trying to be helpful, but Cece ignored her daughter and walked to the back of the store and locked herself in the bathroom, which smelled like Gail Tippler's perfume. She sat on the toilet lid, staring at the engorged penis some asshole had etched into the paper towel dispenser. Who would do such a thing, in a bookstore? By this point she knew the penis intimately—could draw it, probably, with her eyes closed. It wasn't inconceivable she'd see it on her deathbed.

Once, when she was ten, a kid named Mindy Godofsky had told her that everyone in fifth grade hated her savagely because she smelled like farts. She'd actually said that: *savagely*. Cece felt a little bit like that now. She started to cry. If only she hadn't raided Garrett's pills. But of course the Ambien wasn't the problem. Montana was the problem. There wasn't a person in Salish who'd ever read a real book. If they had a choice of reading a book or carving a penis on its cover, they would choose the latter.

Cece hated it here. Savagely.

Her phone buzzed. Was it Gail Tippler? Wanting to go to dinner after all? Cece wiped her eyes with a streamer of toilet paper, then pulled her phone out of her pocket.

Just got into town for a mental health break. Are you around? I could use a drink—or 2.

Charlie, of all people. The phone buzzed again.

Garrett doesn't answer his phone. Assuming he's in the field?

Then:

Okay. I've had a drink already—or 2. ⅄

Cece stared at the texts. Stared and stared at them. The dots at the bottom of the screen bubbled silently, blub blub blub, like someone trying not to drown.

NINETEEN

The great god Ullr, patron saint of skiers, had covered the earth with snow to protect it from harm. It was a great idea—one of the best ever. Why not pack the world in something soft? And it wasn't just for the earth's sake that Ullr covered it in snow. He wanted people to ski on it. He was a skier himself and couldn't keep a secret. He carved planks out of trees and strapped them to his feet and schussed across the sky, leaving a trail of stars behind him. Ancient Norsemen looked up and saw this and stopped drinking from their ox horns and felt strange and giddy and boring. They wanted to feel like Ullr did. And they did—they taught themselves to ski. They zipped after elk and boar, using their weapons as poles. They felt like gods. Ullr was proud and flattered. He rewarded them with snow, tons of it, dumping it from the sky for a thousand years. Before long millions of people were skiing, all over the world, not to hunt elk and boar but because they were sick of gravity.

But now Ullr was old. His knees hurt. He stuck to the blue runs. People prayed to him, begging for snow, but he was hard of hearing. Half of the Alps' glaciers were gone. Snowpack in the Rockies had declined by 40 percent. Snow lines were receding uphill, more rapidly than anyone had predicted, making the bases of the world's ski resorts look like mud baths.

Last night, however, Ullr had listened. It had dumped all night, a foot of fresh powder, and was still going strong. Charlie took credit for this. He'd prayed to Ullr before bed. They used to do this in college, the night before ski trips: *Brave Ullr, friend of winter, bestow upon us the Snow of the Nine Virgins and we will repay you in hacksilver.*

"You realize the Vikings didn't invent skiing?" Garrett said.

"They didn't?"

"The Sami people invented it like eight thousand years ago. They brought it to Scandinavia from central Asia."

Charlie frowned. "Is there anything I love that white people didn't rip off and pretend to invent?"

Garrett shook his head. They were sitting on a chairlift at Alta, snowflakes pelting their ski pants and sticking there perfectly intact, like sequins. It was ten degrees out. They couldn't feel their toes or fingers. Also, the visibility was shit: close to a whiteout. In other words, heaven.

"How are the rental skis?" Charlie asked.

"Fine. A bit chattery. It's the boots that are the problem."

"They hurt?"

"No, not in the least. I could play tennis in them."

"That's a problem?"

"I'm not used to feeling comfortable."

Charlie laughed. "Remember how your big toenails used to fall off?"

"Every year," Garrett said.

"It's how we knew it was spring."

The ski patrol was still blasting and had yet to open Catherine's, the Backside—basically anything worth skiing. Charlie was disappointed, but Garrett felt secretly relieved. It was the first time he'd been to a resort since before Elias's death. He did not pray for snow anymore, except as a way of keeping wolverine kits safe. Groomers were one thing, a bowl of fresh powder another. The thought of dropping into one on downhill skis made his head feel wobbly, as if his helmet were too big.

He was still trying to figure out why Charlie had invited him out here, or why he, Garrett, had consented to drive the nine hours from Salish to spend the weekend at a resort. He suspected that Charlie wanted him there for moral support. They were supposed to be skiing together, the three of them, but Jasper had made a single run, then headed into the lodge with an upset stomach. Charlie had rousted them from bed at seven a.m., like a camp counselor, then shepherded Garrett and Jasper out of the time-share he'd rented and up to the Goldminer's Daughter for the buffet. Even after everything that had happened to him, the guy was all about greeting the day with a breath of fire. He was like one of those inspirational coffee mugs—worse, because he could talk. Jasper—a twenty-year-old college student, less handsome than his dad but with the same heartthrob hair, thick as paint—had devised a strategy of pretending to be dead. He received food and put it in his mouth, but with as little exertion as possible. He might have been eating a shoe. Charlie studied him carefully, as if examining him for clues. *You know what Robert A. Heinlein said? The science fiction writer? One should not attend even the end of the world without a good breakfast.* Having lived with Charlie in college, Garrett couldn't imagine being his son.

Poor Jasper. He'd transferred to the University of Utah and was living in Salt Lake City, away from Santa Barbara, where he'd been in rehab. A clean break. It was easier to stay sober out here, among the Mormons. He'd gotten into some trouble in high school: drinking related, mostly, which according to Charlie had been standard-issue hijinks. He'd gone easy on Jasper because of his heart condition—relieved, even, that he was having a normal American childhood. At least he'd told Garrett this. But then at UCSB, away from home and no longer pinballing between parents, Jasper had gotten into harder stuff: Adderall, like everyone else, then benzos and painkillers. He was stalking kids who'd had their wisdom teeth out and stealing Vicodin from their backpacks. By the end he was holed up in his dorm room, smoking heroin three times a day. At least he wasn't injecting, Charlie had said, one of those "at least"s that was like saying "at least it isn't stage four." He'd sounded heartbroken, confessing all this on the phone. Garrett, surprised and honored by his old friend's confidence, hadn't known what to say. He wasn't sure he deserved it. Was he being absolved? Obscurely blamed? Helping wolverines wasn't easy—seemed, much of the time, to be a fruitless endeavor—but at least Garrett knew how to try.

Both Garrett and Charlie had done their share of drugs in college, but only on special occasions. Also, they didn't have a pacemaker. Also, the drugs seemed quaint to him now, almost picturesque: weed, shrooms, the rare bump of coke after finals were over. It wouldn't have occurred to them in a zillion years to do heroin, or where to find it if it had.

"I hope Jasper's feeling better," Garrett said now, watching the snow accumulate on his skis. *Refills all day!* he would have said once, when skiing was about life to him and not death, a dream you dreamed only by doing it. Somehow the source material had been lost.

"He loves to ski. You'll see. He really opens up on the mountain."

"That's good. Because he seems kind of, I don't know . . . quiet."

"He never got over the divorce," Charlie said.

"With Becky?"

"No! God. He hated Becky. I think he and Těa popped champagne when we separated. Could never understand what I saw in her."

Welcome to the club, Garrett thought, but of course kept this to himself. He'd met Becky only once, soon after she and Charlie had surprised everyone by getting married in a civil ceremony. Garrett had insisted on having them over, to celebrate: a depressing evening, as it turned out, largely because Charlie seemed to dislike his new bride, gritting his teeth whenever she opened her mouth. Cece, for her part, seemed downright hostile, prodding Becky to talk about her belief in UFOs, which it was obvious Charlie found nutty. (To be fair, Becky spent much of the meal complaining about the Margolises' house, miffed at having to spend her honeymoon in Montana.) The surprise wasn't that they'd gotten divorced but that they'd lasted a year.

"Jasper's mother, I'm talking about. Spouse number one." Charlie clacked his skis together, shelling the trees below them with snow. "Angeliki doesn't help matters. The bitch fills his head with lies. Typical Greek, like her parents—can't keep her fucking mouth shut."

Garrett looked at him in surprise. As far as he could remember, he'd never heard Charlie call anyone a "bitch"—let alone traffic in ethnic stereotypes. It was so churlish and unlike him that Garrett didn't know what to say. Clearly, the morning camp counselor had beat a hasty retreat. What was Angeliki telling Jasper? That his father was still hung up on Cece, after all these years? Was this true? Possibly. Garrett didn't know, because of course he and Charlie never talked about this—just as they never talked about Garrett's betrayal of him, the trespass that had upended his life. Not even once. Incredible, but true. It was like a chest they were afraid to open, worried they might awaken a curse. Which wasn't to say it wasn't there all the time, hexing the air between them. God, if only Charlie would mention it! Garrett longed for this sometimes, just to clear the air for a moment. (Dreaded it, too, in equal measure.)

Still, he felt grateful to be able to talk to him at all. What a staggering choice it must have been: To invite them back into his life. To swallow his pride, his bitterness, and reach out to them in friendship. Whatever selfish motives there were, it was a gesture of forgiveness as well. Garrett recognized this. Charlie couldn't have Cece the way he wanted, or Garrett either, and so he'd taken them the only way he could. He'd welcomed them back into his life. Why? But who knows why? The brain has a hundred billion neurons, but they might as well be asleep.

The chairlift had stopped for some reason. Was swinging gently, in fact, high above a ravine. They must have been a hundred feet off the ground. Cece would have absolutely lost her shit.

"My fingers are numb," Charlie said. He slid his poles under one leg and began to bang his hands together.

"No wonder. What are those, gardening gloves?"

"They're Hestras! I've had them for twenty years. Sven and Garfunkel, I call them."

"Why?"

Charlie shrugged. "I think Téa dubbed them that. When we used to ski together. God, we had so much fun on those Mammoth trips—me and the kids."

Garrett had on his full wolverining gear, including Arc'teryx gloves that had cost him a week's pay. The things were like armor gauntlets; he'd blown one of the thumbs out last winter but sealed it with roof-repair tape. "This isn't California," he said. "You'll get frostbite in those things."

"Too late," Charlie said.

"Jesus. Really?"

"I don't know. My fingers feel funny."

"Let's have a look."

Charlie pulled one hand from a glove to show him. The fingers were red at the tips.

"Just frostnip," Garrett said.

"You're the lay doctor."

Attempting to put his glove back on, Charlie dropped it off the chair. The two of them watched it fall. Down it went, down down down, then vanished into a tree well.

"Garfunkel!"

This wasn't a joke. Charlie looked genuinely bereft. He stared at the spot where the glove had vanished, as if it might reemerge from its hole.

"You really will get frostbite now," Garrett said. The chairlift, still out of service, creaked in the wind. "Here. We can share. Stick your hand in my glove."

He lifted his arm, offering up one of his gauntlets. Charlie wriggled his hand into the cuff, which was big enough to accommodate them both, then stuffed it inside as far as it would go. His icy fingers touched Garrett's hand. They sat there like that, wearing the same glove. Garrett thought of his father, how lonely he must have been before he died.

Was the lift broken? Charlie began to shiver. Garrett told him not to worry about Garfunkel, that they could buy some warmer gloves at the base. This was a new thing—being the bright-sider in the friendship—but he did his best. He wondered again why he'd been invited out here. Maybe it wasn't all that complicated. Maybe Charlie just missed skiing with him, with Garrett, back when dropping a glove off the lift wouldn't have expressed anything but itself. Garrett missed those days too.

A skier in the chair in front of them began to shout. *Ullr! A little help!* Then someone else: *Ullr! Get this thing moving!* Soon everyone was shouting to the heavens. Men, women, even what sounded like a kid. *Ullr! We need you! I want to ski!* It was a Wednesday on a powder day. The lift was packed with locals. They were sitting in chairs in the middle of the sky. *Ullr, you fucking Jerry! Deliver us from prison!*

Garrett laughed. He shook his fist at Ullr, which meant Charlie did too. The appeals to Ullr died down and then a new prayer took its place, rising toward them from below, passed from chair to chair as in a game of telephone. It got louder and louder, an echo in reverse. *I'm in love with you, Mia Clapsaddle! Pass it up!* By the time it reached Garrett and Charlie, Garrett felt weirdly nervous, weak with responsibility, as if he were holding someone's heart.

"I'm in love with you, Mia Clapsaddle!" he yelled, cupping his (and Charlie's) hand to his mouth. "Pass it up!"

The words were conveyed up the mountain, though they themselves were not.

"That can't be a real name," Charlie said.

"She's real!" Garrett said, drunk with happiness.

Charlie stared at him. His goggles had reflective lenses, which meant that Garrett saw his own startling face.

"You're a lot different than you used to be," Charlie said.

You too, Garrett thought, but did not pass it on.

———

Charlie had to ski down with his hand in his jacket, like Napoleon. So far, the day had not been going as well as he'd hoped. He was frozen and a bit altitude sick, and losing his glove had made him weirdly depressed. It seemed related somehow to other things he'd lost. He held his poles in one hand, refusing Garrett's help. Being one-gloved was humiliating enough—he didn't want someone schlepping his poles for him.

At the base, Jasper was sitting in a plastic chair in his sweat-shirt, turning obliviously into a snowman, even though the four-hundred-dollar shell Charlie had bought him for his birthday was sitting in his lap. The boy did not look happy to see him. On the other hand, he didn't look particularly *unhappy* either: just mildly bored, as if he were waiting for a bus to arrive and take him someplace interesting. He stared at Charlie's hand, still concealed in his jacket, but didn't seem curious enough to ask about it. He'd been such an inquisitive little kid, so full of endless crazy questions. How exhausting it had been at the time! Charlie had longed sometimes for the kid to shut up. Now he'd have given anything to field a question about the color of your blood in space, or whether dogs, if they knew how to cook, would happily eat each other.

"Sorry, buddy," Charlie said, and Jasper frowned. He chafed at being called this—though Charlie couldn't seem to stop himself. "Our lift got stuck. Is your stomach better?"

"A little bit."

"Your father lost Garfunkel," Garrett explained, stepping out of his skis. "He fell off the chair."

"Who's Garfunkel?" Jasper said.

"You don't remember?" Charlie took his naked hand out of his jacket, which looked not only nipped but possibly bitten. "Garfunkel and Sven?"

Jasper stared at him blankly. He seemed to have lost interest. His phone chimed, and he pulled it out of the pocket of his ski pants. "He's, um, okay?" he mumbled, staring at his phone.

"Sven?" Garrett said. "Oh, he'll be all right. Once he gets over his survivor's guilt."

Jasper paid no attention to this, busy reading something on his phone. Charlie had hoped the three of them would hit it off, now that Jasper was sober, a survivor of his own brush with despair—three men, doing something outdoors that they loved—but his friendship with Garrett, its jokey undergrad cosplay, didn't interest Jasper at all. More than that: seemed to annoy him. And why not? Jasper had never much warmed to Garrett, no doubt because of his connection to Cece, whom the boy had always had it in for—or seemed to, anyway.

Sometimes Charlie wondered if Jasper knew about him and Cece. Not the night they'd slept together, after some disastrous reading at her bookstore, but the rest of it: the secret mother-dough of hope that Charlie nurtured and that Cece had kept alive, or that they'd kept alive together, just enough to make sure it didn't perish. Even now, some part of him held on to it. Waited cruelly for a text, despite Cece's having freaked out and blocked him from her phone. Rejected him, it seemed, for good. It had been four years now since they'd really talked. (And thank god for this, right? Thank *someone*. He wouldn't have married Becky—would have spared himself that gallows farce—but would have probably in the end lost Cece and Garrett both.)

He often wondered what it was about Cece Calhoun. Why her in particular? Why? She was just a woman, one among billions. Angeliki was more beautiful than her; even Becky, in a pageant, would probably squeak out on top. Was it only that she'd wounded him so terribly? No—there was more to it than that. It was mysterious, and yet when he thought of Cece it didn't seem mysterious at all. What he came back to, again and again, was a moment she probably didn't even remember: their third or fourth date, when they were both still at Hopkins and Charlie had taken her for a picnic at Prettyboy Dam. They'd brought a single apple to share between them. Charlie had gone to pee; when he'd come back, five minutes later, Cece had eaten the whole thing. She'd looked at him sheepishly, and then—without a word, mouth so full of apple she couldn't speak—offered him the core. Charlie had cracked up, and then Cece had too. It had seemed like the funniest thing in the world. Had he ever felt so happy? As if he'd burst into flight.

And now he'd invited his old friend out here, with the vague idea of helping Jasper somehow. The two of them might bond over their struggles, seeing as Garrett had gone through some dark times himself at that age. They'd both dropped out of school; been hospitalized too, though of course for different reasons. That was the idea anyway: for Garrett and Jasper to hit it off. But now that they were here, Charlie realized how naïve this fantasy was. Not just naïve: boneheadedly sentimental, like one of those TV shows where people called each other "champ." *You know what, champ? I'm here to tell you there's light at the end of the tunnel.* An afternoon special.

My advice for you, champ? Steal someone's wife.

Jasper put his phone away, zipping it carefully into his pants. God, if only the boy took care of himself—his own body—as lovingly as he took care of his phone. At least covered in snow he seemed less fragile somehow, protected from damage. Something had happened to Charlie that day he'd driven Jasper to the hospital, when the boy's pulse had slowed to a crawl; it was like stumbling upon something he couldn't have imagined, even in his dreams. A new kind of terror, vast and unnavigable. Charlie was deeply acquainted with death. You had to be in his line of work. It wasn't just a casualty of the job; it was his livelihood, his bread and butter. It was as natural to him as life. Even Elias's accident, as devastating as it was, hadn't rocked his sense of life's meaning, its essential value.

But Jasper had been a child. *His* child. When he realized Jasper's sinus node was fucked up, that he would need a pacemaker for the rest of his life, Charlie had locked himself in his office and cried, wondering if the defect was somehow his own fault, longing for something to be wrong with his heart too. How unfair it was! Even when the pandemic hit, when he was watching people get smothered by their own lungs, pleading for death because they couldn't get enough air, breathing as if through a cocktail straw, even when Charlie was proning people who were panting forty times a minute, or intubating them because they couldn't even manage that, or doing tracheostomies because they'd been on a ventilator so long their larynx was getting scarred—even when he was doing these things, he escaped to Jasper and Téa, played a kind of movie clip in his mind, a crowd-pleaser of Charlie dancing with them in the kitchen before they knew anything was wrong with Jasper's heart. He must have played that clip a hundred times in his head. Early in the pandemic, they'd lost a girl, a teenager, perfectly healthy when Covid got to her. She'd been in the ICU on her sixteenth birthday. Her parents had Zoomed in and sung to her, squeezed into the dollhouse window of an iPhone; the girl, intubated, had no idea they were there.

The next day, she'd died.

Charlie had shut off the ECMO circuit himself. The girl had coughed once, then labored shyly for breath before giving up. It was appalling. He'd been appalled. He'd gone outside for a smoke break—he'd started smoking again during the pandemic, even as people's lungs were choking them to death—and half-expected to see the streets turned to lava, angels falling from the sky in flames. But he also knew he could endure this—could endure almost anything, in fact—so long as his own children were okay. He repeated it to himself, after every pointless death. His secret weapon. *This isn't Jasper, this isn't Jasper, this isn't Jasper.*

Now Charlie touched the boy's head, relieved he didn't stiffen like he usually did. The tiniest breakthroughs counted as a triumph. Or maybe Charlie's hand was just too numb to feel it. He propped his skis on the rack, explaining he had to go buy some new gloves. "It'll be a minute. Can your stomach handle a hot chocolate?"

Jasper shrugged. Charlie took out his wallet, fumblingly, and offered him a ten.

"I'm twenty years old, I can buy my own drink," Jasper said, but then snatched the money before Charlie could put it back.

Garrett bought Jasper and himself a hot chocolate—the boy didn't offer to pay—then sat with him in the cozy bedlam of the lodge. Garrett took it in happily. He'd missed the stupid pleasure of this: the funk of skiers, the burn of thawing toes, a hot drink warming your hands until you couldn't tell cup from fingers. The grins on people's faces when they came in stomping their boots. There was no way to describe it. Life was a long, incompetent search to get back to a feeling you had when you were six.

"How's it taste?"

Jasper shrugged. The snow in his hair had begun to melt, trickling down his sideburns. Hunched there among skiers on a powder day, perhaps the happiest human beings on the planet, he looked like a pallbearer. Garrett felt like he owed it to Charlie to try to connect. Also, he sincerely wanted to help the kid, whom he'd known for years somehow without managing—or perhaps daring—to befriend.

"You know, I was hospitalized too for a while," Garrett said.

"Rehab isn't a *hospital.*"

"A treatment center. Whatever. I dropped out of college as well."

"My dad told me," Jasper said. "Because of your friend dying in an avalanche."

"Elias, yeah. He was a big part of it."

Jasper looked at him, possibly for the first time. "I'm amazed you're out here skiing."

"Me too," Garrett said.

Was Jasper criticizing him? Hard to tell. The boy took a sip of cocoa, which left a heartbreaking mustache on his lip. Garrett fought the urge to wipe it off with his napkin.

"My point is that it helped," he said. "I got better. It took a long time, but it happened." Garrett looked at the table. "I mean, if someone had told me I'd have a beautiful kid, a family, I never would have believed them. I didn't even feel *human.*"

"Sounds pretty good."

"Which part?"

"Not being human."

"It's not good," Garrett said. "It's terrible."

"Look, you can spare me the heartwarming speeches," Jasper said. "I know my father put you up to it. Part of his 'Save Jasper' campaign."

"What's wrong with that?"

"I'm not one of his fucking patients."

Garrett studied him carefully. He understood Jasper's anger on some level, just as he understood a wolverine's trying to bite off his face. The boy had never asked to be saved.

"Your father's an extraordinary person," Garrett said finally. "His love, his kindness. It can be hard to live up to."

Jasper laughed. "You think he loves you?"

Garrett blinked at him. "It's complicated," he said. "But yes. Yes, I do. We've been friends a long time."

"Sometimes he wants to murder you."

"He does?"

"He told me sometimes he wishes *you* were the one in the avalanche. That you'd died instead."

Jasper finished his cocoa, still sporting his chocolate mustache, then headed off to the restroom. Garrett tried to buckle his boots, but his fingers were trembling. He couldn't get them to work. Of course, there was no reason to believe Jasper, whose anger would make him say anything. He barely knew the kid anymore. Or was this actually a fantasy of Charlie's? God knew what lurked in his friend's soul. There was a whole other world, as Éluard said, and it was in this one. Garrett looked back at the windows, but the fairy-tale snow looked strange, artificial, like the paper kind they use in movies.

Braving the snow, the three of them collected their skis and poles and headed back up the mountain. The visibility had improved somewhat; you could see whorls of snow dust wisping from the trees. Jasper sat on the inside of the chairlift, legs pressed tightly together, as if he were squeezed into a church pew. Even in his ski clothes, dressed for fun, he gave off a microclimate of anger. Charlie modeled his new gloves, split-finger ones that made him look like a sheep, half-hoping Jasper would make fun of him. Anything that might acknowledge he existed.

"Remember that time in Mammoth you flew clean out of your boots?" he asked Jasper. He turned to Garrett. "Jasper hits a patch of powder—fifty degrees out, it was like cement—and all I see are these smoking boots, nobody in them. Like a cartoon."

"Dad, *please*," Jasper said.

"What?"

"I'm here, okay? We're skiing together. Isn't that fucking enough?"

Charlie looked at Garrett, who glanced quickly away, the scar on his cheek cindering in the cold. The empty chairs on the down-line dangled above them, high as birds. They approached the spot where Charlie had dropped his glove. The hole had filled with snow. Charlie felt suddenly morose. The trip he'd planned so carefully—his sugarplum visions of reconnecting with his son, coaxing him back to health by rekindling his love of skiing—was a bust. A fucking *ski trip*? *Seriously?* He pulled one of his new gloves off with his teeth, then took Sven from his pocket and dropped it off the lift like the other.

"What are you doing?" Garrett said.

"I thought they should be together," he said with difficulty.

"Don't talk! You'll lose the new one too."

Charlie put his cloven hoof back on. For a quick, pure moment, he wanted to push Garrett off too. He'd tried so hard to be as good as people thought he was, he'd invited Garrett and Cece back into his life—a little bit in love, certainly, with his own forgiveness—but sometimes it felt like a giant ruse.

When they got to the top, a ski patroller was opening the gate to Catherine's traverse. Skiers were lined up at the rope, like patrons outside a nightclub.

"Holy shit," Charlie said. "They're opening it!"

"Good timing," Garrett said in a strange voice.

They got off the lift and headed for the queue of skiers, who'd begun skating through the gate and then taking off their skis to boot up to the traverse. Most of them were whooping or battle-crying or generally making a nuisance of themselves. In the falling snow, the noises sounded louder than they were. Charlie ushered Jasper in front of him, then looked behind him for Garrett, who'd stopped about ten yards from the gate, as still as a post.

"What are you waiting for?"

Garrett stared at Charlie without speaking. He didn't look so good. Looked, in fact, like he might throw up. Was this why Charlie had invited him out here? To test his PTSD? Garrett shook his head, mechanically, like one of those animatrons at Disneyland. "Meet you at the bottom," he said, then kick-turned and took off down the groomer they'd been skiing all morning. Charlie watched him go, too giddy to feel remorse.

"I guess it's just you and me," he said.

Jasper shrugged, unsmiling. They skated through the gate, then took off their skis when they couldn't skate any farther and hitched the brakes of their bindings together and hiked up the boot-prints that had been made in the snow, balancing their skis on one shoulder. When they got to the traverse, Jasper was breathing hard. He looked a bit pale. Still, he'd climbed up here with Charlie. He was doing it. They scraped the snow from their boots, then snapped into their bindings and followed the tracks that had already been made on the traverse, watching skiers ahead of them peel off without stopping, whooping into the beautiful white bowl like paratroopers jumping from a plane. A good twelve inches, light as flour. Except for the cries of joy, it was as quiet as a church. Charlie sidestepped past some people futzing with their boots, grinning stupidly at them, and traversed far enough that he was knee-deep in powder and snowshoeing on skis, then stopped at the top of a glade on the far edge of the bowl that no one had touched. A perfect tree run.

"It's all yours," he said to Jasper.

All avid skiers shared a secret: they were selfish pricks. They'd shove their own kid into a tree if it meant getting to make first tracks. So it was a gift Charlie was giving his son. He was saying, *I know you're pissed at me, you're sullen and defiant, but I'm letting you have this: A glade of fresh powder. The first line.* And Jasper seemed to realize this. He nodded at Charlie—if not in gratitude, then at least with some acknowledgment of what it cost. Not just this tiny little sacrifice, but all the powder days Charlie had missed in order to teach him how to ski in the first place, stuck on the bunny slope while skiers ate hero snow for lunch. This was the real sacrifice: giving up your own joy, the thing you maybe loved to do more than anything else on earth, so that your kid might experience it someday too. Might feel a bit of this joy himself.

And sure enough, once Jasper pushed off, dropping into his first turn, he seemed to become someone else: all of his awkwardness, his sullenness, vanished in an instant. He floated through the trees as if it were his natural state, the only one in which he really made sense, as if loneliness weren't a burden to him but the best thing in the world. He kept his ass low, skiing just like Charlie. Their styles were identical. The same slalom-y crouch; same way of planting his poles, high-poised and precise, as if he were spearing fish. The boy had grown up chasing him, matching his turns, so this shouldn't have surprised him. Still, it moved Charlie to see it. Watching Jasper bob through the trees, graceful as a dolphin, he had a strange feeling that he wasn't there. That he himself, Charlie, was dead. And here was this other person, this man who skied just like him, making lovely tracks in the snow. He was gliding down a mountain at ten thousand feet. There was more to us than we thought. We left things in the world; we were more than just a body.

Charlie dropped in and followed Jasper through the trees, crossing his son's tracks, which had its own kind of thrill to it. Snow sprayed his face. He was eating it like candy. Emerging from the glade, he could see Jasper watching him from the bottom of the bowl, a dopey-looking grin on his face. He was actually smiling. What relief! Charlie's heart surged. This was life too. This was happiness.

Jasper leaned on his poles, still catching his breath once Charlie had stopped in front of him. He was severely out of shape but continued to smile—smiled though he thought he might puke. In truth, Jasper didn't care about skiing. He was cold and miserable and felt like a worm stranded aboveground. But he wanted his father to think he was enjoying himself. It was easier if his dad thought he was okay. It made Jasper's life easier. So he smiled big, feeling the wind on his teeth.

His father, beaming like a toddler, leaned in to hug him. They were both on skis—they had to lean toward each other, like the leaves of a drawbridge—but Jasper let him do this. He had not hugged his father in a long time. Years, probably. He was so angry at his dad, so fucking pissed off all the time, and he couldn't even say why. The guy had saved Jasper's life, rushed him to the ER when his heart was slowing to a stop. The truth was, Jasper sometimes wished he hadn't. That he'd let him die. What if his heart was his true self, which had given up long ago? Jasper was keeping it alive against its will.

His father let go of him finally, wobbling on his skis. With his dorky new gloves, his red helmet and parka, he looked a bit like a lobster. What did this lobster want from him? It would follow him to the ends of the earth.

"Where to next? The Backside? Should we see if Gunsight's open?"

"Sure," Jasper said. He touched his stomach.

"What? Is it bothering you again?"

He nodded. "I shouldn't have eaten that omelet."

Jasper avoided his father's eyes, trying to remember if Gunsight took them to the lodge. Had he left the pen tube in the men's room? There was still some resin on the foil, enough for a hit. Jasper could practically smell it in his pocket: the harsh, vinegary stench. He clutched his stomach, groaning a bit, because his dad had been hugged, he was a happy snow lobster, he would believe anything.

III

COMPASS ERROR

TWENTY

1.

Garrett and Cece were on the way to Charlie's house, for the reunion. Brig had brought about the reunion by having a stroke. It wasn't a funeral, thank god, but definitely not the nostalgia-fueled bacchanal he'd envisioned.

"Can he talk?" Cece asked from the passenger seat.

"I don't think so. Not very well."

"So it was a full ischemic? Where was the clot?"

Garrett shrugged. Sometimes he forgot that his wife had gone to med school, that she'd ever imagined she wanted to be a doctor. "I don't know. It's the right side of his body, I think, that's paralyzed."

Cece looked out the window. The reunion had been Brig's idea to begin with. He'd been emailing all of them for years. Still, it took his having a stroke to mobilize everyone, for the reunion to become a Thing. They were doing it for Brig now. Charlie offered up the Montana house as headquarters. Next thing you knew it was planned, the whole gang was convening for four days in Salish: Brig, Johnny, Marcus, Garrett. They'd brought their wives, turning the trip into an excuse for a vacation.

Garrett, who'd dropped out of college over thirty years ago, often wondered why the most durable friendships in his life were with some smartasses he'd managed to impress at the age of eighteen. Maybe it was college itself that did this to you: trapped you in a hammerlock you couldn't escape. Sometimes he envied Lana, who'd managed to dodge it completely, leaving the Uni-

versity of Montana after her first semester and hightailing it to
LA. Garrett had assumed the acting thing was a pipe dream—a
naïve Montanan fantasy—but it seemed, against all odds, to be
working out. She sounded so young on the phone, so much like
her old jokey girl self, that he had to remind himself she was
twenty-three.

"I wanted to go out to dinner," Garrett said now. "On our
anniversary."

"It's okay."

"I just wish they'd planned this whole thing for another
weekend."

"Are you losing your voice?" Cece asked.

"A little bit."

She frowned, as if this affliction were somehow his fault.
"Gets worse every summer."

Garrett drove past the Salish post office and crested the hill
leading into town—normally their first view of the lake, but they
could barely make out the boat slips in the marina, so thick was
the haze of smoke. It was a terrible time for a reunion. The AQI
had been in the three hundreds all week, so high that they were
warning you not to leave the house. There was a local fire in
Finley Point—several, too, in the Bob Marshall Wilderness—
but mostly the smoke was from farther west, from Oregon and
Washington, blowing eastward on the jet stream. Secondhand
smoke, they called it around here, joking about migration from
"Commiefornia," by which they meant the entire West Coast.
(*Even the smoke wants to move to Montana.*) July and August were
the worst. It was like huffing an ashtray. Your eyes burned; you
could taste the smoke; just driving to the store might give you a
migraine. Recently, on top of losing his voice—and though he'd
never had asthma in his life—Garrett had begun to wheeze, feeling the ghost of his father. No doubt all those summers in the
field had taken their toll. The only plus side to the smoke was
that the tourists had thinned out a bit, deciding it wasn't worth

leaving Seattle or Portland for a week spent indoors, huddled around the air purifier—health-wise, they were better off in New Delhi—though of course there were always locals determined to recreate on the lake no matter what, blasting music from pontoon boats or doing donuts on their WaveRunners, shrouded in a yellow-gray fog of smoke. Astonishing, what people learned to live with.

But then, out of nowhere, a storm would blow in and clear the air overnight, dropping the AQI into single digits, and the gorgeous world you loved and remembered would be magically restored, Kansas transforming into Oz. It was hard to imagine they were the same place.

You were at the mercy of the gods, or at least the elements. So you planned things—dog walks, college reunions—and prayed for the best.

Though it was over a hundred out, Garrett turned the air-conditioning down, worried it was draining the VW's range. Some time ago he'd sold the Forester—gifted it to a neighbor's daughter, basically, for five hundred bucks—and bought this Hail Mary of a car, an EV, which had a nifty *Consumer Reports* score of 86. God, how much time had they spent researching it together? Then finding the perfect used model, exactly three years old, because that was the Goldilocks age of value versus features? They'd sat side by side in bed, computers on their laps, hours of his life—of his marriage—that he would never get back. Meanwhile, the earth burned.

Now he glanced at Cece as he drove, wanting to tell her that he'd bought her an anniversary present—a vintage solar system model he'd ordered on eBay, which hadn't arrived on time—but found that she was out of earshot. Not literally, of course, but that's the way it felt. They'd been married twenty-four years, to the day, and yet these spaces still widened between them, ones they didn't have the energy to cross. Why did they happen? There was no cause to them, really—they were just a feature of living together, like leaky gutters or joint tax returns. And yet if Garrett thought about them too much, he could pitch into despair. They'd chosen to spend their lives with each other. It had not been easy; it had been the easiest thing in the world. They'd raised a daughter together, struggling at times to stay afloat. He'd held Cece after her grandmother died, when she'd cried so hard it sounded like she'd stopped working, an engine turning over and over—and then again after her father died, of a heart attack, when she hadn't cried at all. He knew what her snot tasted like. He knew that watching someone eat a banana, even on TV, made her gag. He knew about her fantasies, the sweet ones and the scary ones and the deep dark perverted ones. He knew about the memories that disturbed her sleep, the things she still felt guilty about, like the time in seventh grade when she and Paige called someone named Gretchen Winkelstein and said it was the dog pound and started to bark.

Garrett knew all these things, and countless more. Then out of the blue—on their anniversary no less—he discovered he couldn't speak to her properly, or really at all. He might as well have married a plant. It was heartbreaking. It broke Garrett's heart. Sometimes marriage felt like a dazzling present they didn't want to soil or scratch, didn't have the courage to *actually use*, and so they'd locked it up in the garage where neither of them could touch it.

At Charlie's house, it was like a rainy day at camp, everyone crammed inside because of the smoke. Garrett found himself doing that thing men his age seemed to do at reunions, which was to pair off like dance partners and gawk when the other wasn't looking. At least Garrett and Marcus were doing this in the kitchen: stealing glances, pretending they weren't sick to their stomachs—half-nauseated with fear, with the bends of rocketing through the years since they saw each other last—while transferring beers to a cooler. An old friend's face was like a mirror; worse, because it showed you how the mirror had been lying to you.

"You're bald!" Marcus said when Garrett took his cap off for a second to air-cool his head.

"Not completely. I shave it off as a public service. So I don't look like Arthur Schopenhauer."

Marcus stared at him with concern. "Your voice. Are you losing that too?"

"That grows back. After fire season." Garrett closed the fridge. "You're old, too, in case you hadn't noticed."

"I don't feel old. I feel eighteen."

"In that case, you look terrible."

In truth, he looked younger than any of them; except for the hair at his temples, which had turned to fleece, he could have passed for forty. Marcus took out his phone and held it in front of Garrett so he could see the wallpaper. A baby—an infant—with pudding-y folds under its eyes and a wrinkled-up forehead. "Speaking of bald, look at this little fellow."

"You have a newborn?" Garrett asked in astonishment.

"A grandson!"

Garrett did his best to hide his shock. He had not imagined he was *that* old: that his friends would begin turning into grandparents. But of course he *was* that old. Fifty-five. He might have been a grandpa, too, if Lana hadn't decided to mainly date women—might even have had one of those terrifying names: Boppa, PawPaw, Gramps.

He'd never seen a baby with wrinkles before. It looked like a bell pepper forgotten in the fridge.

"Isn't he a cutie?" Marcus said.

"Did you really just say 'cutie'?"

"Maybe. Yes. You can say that as a grandpa."

Johnny entered the kitchen, carrying a can of Diet Pepsi. Marcus showed him the picture on his phone.

"Whoa. Is that one of those bog mummies?" Johnny said, then glanced up at Garrett and Marcus. His face fell. He examined the photo again, sliding his glasses down his nose. "Hey now. Very cute. I'm still getting used to these progressive lenses."

"Want a beer?" Garrett asked, changing the subject.

"I'm saving my brain cells for science," Johnny said, hoisting his Diet Pepsi. The can was ergonomically crumpled, as if he'd been carrying it around for a while. Johnny nudged past the cooler and disappeared into the bathroom.

"Am I hallucinating," Garrett said, "or did Johnny just refuse a beer?"

"The guy's in recovery."

"Since when?"

"Oh, like *ten years* ago," Marcus explained. "You need to spend less time in the wilderness."

This news saddened Garrett, though whether it was because he was so out of touch with everyone or because the hilarious exploits of Johnny's youth had turned out in hindsight not to be hilarious at all, he couldn't say. Certainly Johnny had fared better than Brig, who was sitting on the porch in a wheelchair, smoke be damned. Garrett watched him now through the window. He looked okay at first glance, at least with sunglasses on, but on closer inspection things started to unravel, his mouth strangely out of place, as if it had been turned a squeak too far with a screwdriver. He'd collapsed last February after a morning jog, forced to crawl up the front steps of his Tudor revival. The whole journey—sidewalk to house—had taken an hour. Garrett had heard all this from Charlie, who'd heard the details from Soledad, Brig's second wife. She'd found him scratching at the door, like a cat. Six months of physical therapy, and still Brig's toes were curled up, his speech a drunken slur only Soledad could interpret. Brig Latin, she called it. She was a brisk, fearless woman, a commercial airline pilot, who treated Brig's tragedy as if it were a smoking 737 she had to steer safely to the ground.

In other words, a godsend. Soledad had put some marbles on the deck and was making Brig pick them up with his toes and drop them, one by one, into a bowl. She'd brought the marbles from New Jersey, to make sure he practiced.

"Thank god for Soledad," Marcus said, watching as well.

"Where the hell did he meet her?"

"Airport bar, where else?"

"Poor woman," Garrett said. "She certainly didn't know what she was getting into."

"I don't know," Marcus said. "It's part of the contract, isn't it?"

"What do you mean?"

"Marriage. It's a whole-life insurance policy. Especially at our age."

"*That's* why you married Gabby?"

Marcus glanced behind him. "To be perfectly honest? I'd be lying if I said it hadn't crossed my mind." He popped a beer from the cooler and toasted marriage, mortality, possibly both. "And it will be *us*, not them, who cash in first."

"Speak for yourself."

"Anyway, it's not Brig I'm worried about," he said.

Marcus nodded at an old picture, enshrined on the fridge, of Charlie and his kids on the dock. Garrett knew the picture well; he'd taken it himself, maybe fifteen years ago. "Two ex-wives," Marcus said. "At least one of them riding the alimony pony. His daughter refuses to talk to him at all. And his eldest, Jackson—"

"Jasper."

"*Jasper.* First the heart stuff, bad enough—and now what? Kid's an addict? What a nightmare." Marcus swigged his beer. "I mean if someone had asked me which one of us would have ended up old and alone . . ."

"You would have thought it was me," Garrett said. "I know."

He continued loading the cooler, sticking beers into the ice. It was the same, no doubt, for all their friends. They wouldn't admit it, probably, but they'd never really forgiven him. Somewhere in the depths of their hearts they blamed him, Garrett, for Charlie's woes. The failed relationships, the prodigal children, the whiff of despair that seemed to follow Charlie around like cologne—it was all because Garrett had stolen his wife away from him, a quarter century ago.

Garrett grabbed beers for Cece and Charlie, meaning to join them in the living room. How enlightened it was that the three of them could do this now—that they'd been doing this for years. At least his best friend, the guy whose life he'd destroyed, had forgiven him long ago. And in fact Charlie looked okay from the doorway. Better than okay. He sat on the couch next to Cece, tanned and smiling, fiddling with one of those watches big enough to eat off—every inch the kind of doctor who could absorb two ex-wives and still spend a month every summer away from home. You'd never know his son was doing his second stint in rehab up near Whitefish, at some wilderness treatment center, or that Charlie had left a silent voicemail on Garrett's cell phone last month at three in the morning, purporting the next day to have dialed him by mistake.

And yet there was something awkward about him too, a forced heartiness. He leaned into Cece's every word, laughing too loudly at her jokes. Did he know about their anniversary? Garrett had decided not to make a fuss about it, once he'd realized the reunion had been scheduled for the same weekend; the date of their wedding was probably not something Charlie chose to keep in his head.

It was nothing, two old friends chatting. So why couldn't Garrett move, struck by a familiar disquiet? Even now, after so many years, he could still feel this vague, radioactive misgiving. Cece pointed at Charlie's teeth, which must have had some food stuck in them. To help him find it, she slid a fingernail between two of her own teeth; Charlie copied her, as if staring into a mirror.

Cece made up an excuse—she wanted to track down her drink, though she didn't have one—and fled the living room. Even in Charlie's loneliness, there was always a force that tugged at her, some chink of possibility that yawned into regret. But she knew that Garrett was watching from the door of the kitchen. After a quarter century together, Cece could sense him in the next room, like a phantom limb.

It seemed impossible that he'd never suspected anything, but of course he was away so much, stalking animals with his radio receiver. Looking for other kinds of signals. If Lana knew anything, she had never told her father.

He didn't know Cece had come a hair's breadth, at least in her own mind, from leaving him. Just picturing the bed upstairs terrified her. She was afraid to go near the staircase, as if a sudden wind might blow her up it, might sweep her into Charlie's bedroom against her will. How she'd hated Montana that night at the store, still zonked on Ambien: hated the life that felt to her like a wrong turn, a compass error. Seven years already, since that fiasco with Gail Tippler. It didn't seem possible. The memory still mortified her. She'd sent Lana home with Kayla, telling them she needed to scan some books on Edelweiss, then had taken a Lyft to the Margolises' house. Charlie had been waiting for her on the porch. Ten minutes? Eighteen years? Thicker in the middle than he used to be—every man's curse to turn into his father—but the breadth of him had felt good to her, nestlike; it had felt like comfort. It was as if she'd never left him, as if they'd gotten married last week. He'd even smelled the same. They'd gone inside the house, ducking under the lintel on their way upstairs. So easy, so natural, like stepping back into her youth.

Afterward, Charlie had gotten up to use the bathroom, and Cece had listened to the splash of urine in the toilet, feeling wide awake for the first time in hours. She thought helplessly of Garrett. How, when Lana was a baby, he'd get up in the middle of the night to pee and actually sit on the toilet like a woman, worried the sound of it might wake her. Number one and a half, he'd called it. At some point his go-to lullaby for Lana, "Goodnight, Irene," changed to "(You Make Me Feel Like) A Natural Woman."

It was the ease of it that had frightened Cece away: how easily it reopened for her, this enchanted door, as if the most momentous years of her life had never happened, vaporous as a dream. She'd gotten dressed while Charlie showered and then escaped downstairs, hiking up Route 35 a ways before requesting a Lyft.

Cece felt suddenly claustrophobic, trapped inside on a summer day. She joined Brig and his new wife on the porch, braving the smoke, which had turned the boats on the lake into flat gray silhouettes, like the targets at a shooting gallery. One hundred and four, was it? It just got hotter and hotter. Even the birds were lying low. The only sign of life was a plastic owl perched on the crossarms of a telephone pole, meant to scare away ospreys from nesting there, though it had been years since Cece had seen a nest.

"The smoke doesn't bother you?" she asked Soledad.

"Brig has trouble with crowds. He gets overwhelmed."

Cece walked over to Brig in his wheelchair and smiled at him, but he gave no reaction whatsoever, focusing on the bowl of marbles at his feet. Her heart sank.

"He can't see you from that side," Soledad said.

"Oh?"

"It's called 'one-sided neglect.'"

Cece looked at her helplessly. "Better than two-sided, I guess?"

"Now we're discussing my childhood." Soledad, laughing at her own joke, flapped a hand at her. "Come over here, to the right side of him."

Cece did as commanded. Sure enough, Brig's face lit up with recognition: the hidden stagecraft of a smile. It was like the changing of sets behind a curtain. He garbled something that Cece didn't understand.

"He says it's good to see you," Soledad said. "You haven't changed a bit."

"You understand everything?" Cece asked, after Brig had wheeled himself inside for a drink.

"If I don't, he sings it."

Cece stared at her. She seemed to be serious. "Sings?"

"It's one of those things—mysteries of the human brain. He can communicate perfectly that way."

"Wow."

"Apparently it's pretty common."

"Garrett and I have enough trouble communicating. I can't even imagine."

"How long have you been married?" Soledad asked politely.

"Twenty-four years! It's our anniversary today, in fact."

Soledad seemed impressed. "Congratulations. That's a real accomplishment."

"Well, I'd rather not think of it like *that*."

"Did you get him a present?"

"It's right here in my carryall," she said, choosing not to elaborate.

Eventually, the smoke was no match for a cooler of beer, or at least nine half-drunk vacationers cooped up inside, forty yards from the deepest lake in Montana. Marcus was the first to change into his suit, and then Johnny did too, singing "Smoke on the Water," though his wife, Cynthia, seemed more worried about swimmer's itch, which with the record temperatures had become a scourge. The last time they'd gone swimming together, she'd gotten blisters on her legs. Brig said something in response, but even Soledad had some trouble understanding it.

"Why don't you sing it, honey?" she suggested, slipping off his sunglasses.

Brig looked at her. He seemed embarrassed. He turned to Johnny and opened his mouth, silencing the room. Outside, the wake from a speedboat splashed faintly against the dock.

"Your first two wives," he sang to Johnny, *"were allergic to you too!"*

He had the voice of a country star: deep and sonorous. Everyone was speechless. It was like an Old Testament miracle. Brig sat there impatiently, waiting to be insulted back.

"How many beers have you had?" Johnny sang back at last, in a dreadful voice.

Brig's eyes lit up. *"You don't need to sing too, you dumbass!"*

Brig wanted to go swimming with everyone else, so Soledad took him into the bedroom to get changed, confessing to Cece—who helped her find the way—that she didn't know how to swim. Cece offered to help out. She changed into her swimsuit and led the partygoers down to the lake, as if she lived there herself. The smoke burned her eyes. No one whooped or joked or threw off their shirt. It was too hot for it—or maybe they were just sheepish about their bodies, the love handles and biopsy scars and herniated belly buttons. Soledad had some trouble getting Brig to the water, struggling with the wheels of his chair, which bogged down in the stones of the beach. His legs were as white as a baby's.

Cece took a swig from her water bottle. She carried it everywhere now, because of the heat. What was the term they used in med school? *Insensible loss.* The evaporation of water from the body, a loss you can't feel.

"It's hotter than the hinges of hell," Soledad said.

"How long can a heat dome last?" Johnny said.

"Maybe it's a permanent thing," Marcus said. "Like the Astrodome."

"The *Houston* Astrodome? Does that still exist?"

No one could answer this. Like other totems from their childhoods, it seemed like a figment of their imaginations.

Soledad got Brig into a life vest, one arm at a time, and then Cece hoisted him out of the wheelchair—how little he weighed!—and walked him carefully into the water, carrying him like a sleeping child fetched from the car. The hard stones of the lake bottom hurt her feet. He was still a lot to manage, the vest bulky and hot from the sun, and Cece was worried she might slip. She'd never liked Brig all that much—of Garrett and Charlie's friends, he'd always seemed the most obnoxious to her, most obliviously *privileged*—but holding the diminished banker in her arms moved her strangely. She was sure this was a preview of some kind: a sneak peek from the future. Already Garrett had lost his voice; god knew what all that smoke, those fire seasons, had done to his lungs. Dressing your husband every morning, making him pick up marbles with his toes, wiping him no doubt when he used the toilet—Cece wasn't sure she'd be capable of it. It would be like getting turned into a saint by mistake.

Cece waded into the lake, nearly stumbling from the burden in her arms. It was appalling, what love expected of you. She wasn't sure she'd have the courage to do it. Not just the courage: the *desire*. She was not yet done with her own life. Life! People talked about it all the time, as casually as the weather, but Cece suspected they were as confused about it as she was. It was supposedly right in front of you, speeding by—something to be *gotten*, to be *grabbed bravely by the horns*—but she'd never mistaken this daredevil thing for Life. Life was something else entirely. She'd gone on a hike once with Garrett, some unmarked route he'd found on a satellite map—Hidden Meadow, it was nicknamed—and they'd wandered a buggy spur trail for hours, searching for their destination. Life seemed like that hike to her sometimes: forever peering through the trees, waiting for a glimpse of flowers. Where was it? Where? She was beginning to suspect it didn't exist.

Brig began to float, buoyed by the life preserver, then drifted from Cece's arms, pitching gently in the waves. He glanced at

Soledad—for reassurance?—but seemed to be enjoying himself, grinning his offstage grin. A wave from a pontoon boat splashed over his head. Cece sneaked a look behind her, where Charlie and Garrett were watching from the lawn. Her husband's face, hidden behind an N95 mask, was inscrutable.

The water was too shallow to jump into, at least safely, so Marcus waded in behind Cece and took over with Brig, propelling him around the lake like a kickboard. Cece dove underwater— it felt like a heated pool, nothing to whoop about—then swam out to rescue an inflatable raft drifting past the dock. The lake was so crowded now that relics often washed up on the Margolises' beach. Cece did not swim the raft to shore, as she'd planned, but instead scrambled on top of it, looking for an excuse to escape Garrett and Charlie. She was suddenly sick to death of them both. Why hadn't they just fucking married *each other*? They clearly belonged together. Loved and hated each other, like any couple.

She was not supposed to sunbathe at her age—who in their right mind would want to, in this smoke?—but Cece indulged herself anyway, floating through the yellowish haze. Her throat burned, not unpleasantly. It reminded her of smoking a joint. She hadn't smoked one in years. *Buzz, buzz* went a Jet Ski, invisible as a mosquito. Somewhere a tuber yippeed, like a cowboy, but lost to the fog of smoke the cry sounded ghostly and forlorn. Cece drifted away from the dock. It occurred to her that she might get killed by a watercraft, sliced in two like the fish that sometimes washed up on the beach—or used to. Despite the heat, the sun was no brighter than the moon. She could look right at it. It was orange and lurid and round as a dodgeball.

Cece's eyes itched. It was more than just the smoke. She was in mourning. The summer was gone. Not just this summer: but the next one, and the next. The smell of cherries. The blue skies that almost squeaked. The leaps off the dock and the fairy-tale raspberries and the sun flickering through the pines. That feeling she got just looking at the lake, a kind of treehouse freedom, like a breeze from childhood . . . So long, spacious skies! Cece floated in the smoky haze. "Smaze," they called it. The word offended her. And yet also—how weird, how fucked-up—Cece was in no hurry to get out of it.

They'd had plans to barbecue—eight pounds of hamburger meat!—but Charlie scrapped them because of the smoke and ordered pizza instead. Everyone gathered around the TV to stream the latest episode of Lana's show, which was called *Houdini, PI.* (Watching it was Garrett's idea, though he pretended it wasn't.) The premise of the show was that Harry Houdini comes back to life after being cryogenically frozen and decides to devote his life to solving crimes. It was as stupid as it sounded, but Lana had a bit part in several episodes, playing a tenant who lives in Houdini's apartment building and keeps encountering him in odd places after he's performed one of his magical, death-defying escapes. The encounters were typically played for laughs. The part wasn't going to win Lana any Emmys, but she was still young.

Garrett left a spot open on the couch for Cece, but she perched next to Soledad instead, on the arm of the recliner. Had she actually snubbed him? He couldn't say. Anyway, it was just as well: she got so nervous waiting for Lana's brief appearances that Garrett was just as happy sitting apart.

Though Lana had told them, neither Garrett nor Cece could remember when she was supposed to come on, so they watched for a good twenty minutes or so before she finally appeared onscreen, whistling to herself as she pushed one of those rolling laundry hampers into the elevator; Houdini popped his head out of her dirty clothes, his mouth covered in duct tape, and Lana's character screamed in fright. Everybody at Charlie's house laughed and cheered. Garrett hadn't watched TV for years—basically thought shows like this were the nuclear dust of capitalism, softening people's brains while the world ended—but felt ridiculously proud of her. He beamed and beamed.

The only one who didn't watch was Charlie. Garrett spied him sitting on the porch by himself, smoking a cigarette, which shocked Garrett less than the fact that he didn't seem to care if anyone saw. Even in college, there'd been a furtiveness about it, sneaking Viceroys on the roof. Garrett wondered if it was painful to think about Lana, if she reminded Charlie of Jasper. The kid was a dropout too, but not because he was following his childhood dreams: he'd flunked out of the University of Utah, his second stab at college, then moved back in with his mom, who'd kicked him out after he'd stolen some of her jewelry. And so he'd moved in with Charlie, whose condo looked like a nursing home. He'd taken all the doors off their hinges and stored them in the garage. There were puzzles on the table, a schedule of activities on the fridge. Cece and Garrett had gone to see them in LA, the last time they were visiting Lana. Charlie had begun talking in the straw-grasping argot of the damned, claiming that Jasper's pacemaker might actually be a good thing. The kid was at greater risk of infection, sure, but it ironically might save him from OD'ing—or at least lower his chances.

Now the boy was in rehab again, at age twenty-three. Charlie, Garrett knew, had sacrificed a lot for him—passed over a division chief job at Johns Hopkins so that he could stay near Jasper, avoid destabilizing his son's life when his hold on it was so precarious to begin with. Recently he'd left research behind and gone into private practice, partly to help pay for Jasper's treatments. He'd wanted to be a great doctor, even a famous one—in college he'd talked about making "a permanent contribution"—and yet he'd turned out to be just another anesthesiologist. Well respected, wealthy, obscure. No one rewarded you for that, least of all your own children. In the end, they might even hold it against you.

What had Garrett been thinking, showing Lana off to their

old friends? In Charlie's own house, no less? He hadn't been thinking at all.

He walked onto the porch to see if Charlie was all right, but his old friend was busy prising a beer from a six-pack at his feet. A tidemark of gray stained the part of his hair. It wasn't the gray that perturbed Garrett but the fact that Charlie had been dyeing it to begin with. His eyes took a while to focus on Garrett's face.

"Hey, how many of those have you had?" Garrett asked.

Charlie shrugged. "I can't drink a drop when Jasper's at home. Nothing in the house at all. This is like Rumspringa."

"How's Jasper doing?"

"No idea. Won't let me visit. That was the deal I made, to get him into treatment out here: I'd leave him alone. Doesn't mean you or Cece can't drive up there." He popped the beer in his hand, which sprayed all over his shirt. "In fact, I kind of told him you would."

Was he serious? Garrett, whose inpatient memories still drunk-dialed his dreams, did not relish the idea. "I looked it up. The website. Looks like a terrific program."

"Better fucking be. Forty-five grand. For *six weeks.*"

The cigarette dangled from his lips, as if he'd forgotten it was there. Charlie tried to suck the foam off his beer with it in his mouth, then resolved the quandary by removing the cigarette. He peered into the blowhole of the can, as if daring it to spray him again.

"Not enough smoke in the air for you?" Garrett asked.

"Have a Marlboro," Charlie said, offering the pack.

"No thanks. I shouldn't even be out here without a mask on."

"Come on. Don't be a doormat."

"I haven't smoked since your . . ."

"My what?"

"Bachelor party."

Charlie jerked his hand back, as if he'd been bitten. *Finally,* Garrett thought, *it's coming.* They'd talk about it at last. The wedding; Garrett's betrayal; the whole dreadful mess. Garrett had been rehearsing this moment for years. But Charlie merely peered into his beer can again, smoke venting from his nostrils. The moment, if it had ever existed, was lost.

"This used to be a sleeping porch. My grandparents would come down here to sleep when it was hot." Charlie dropped his cigarette into one of the beer cans at his feet. "Now everyone wants to sleep inside, where the A/C is."

"It's the American way," Garrett muttered. Central air was a new phenomenon up here; animals sometimes mistook the condensers for free housing and got chopped up by the blades. Weasels, ground squirrels, you name it. People came home from the grocery store and their entire house smelled like death.

"Remember hood ornaments?" Charlie said.

"On cars? Yeah, of course."

"Where did they go?"

"Same place as sleeping porches."

"You know what I milly riss?" Charlie asked.

"Milly riss?"

"Car keys. You had to stick them in the door and actually *turn*, remember? Once I got stuck at LaGuardia because my car doors froze and the lock wouldn't turn. In the long-term parking lot. It was like zero degrees."

"That was the *Burlington* airport. Sophomore year of college. I borrowed Johnny's car and drove out there to pick you up. I saved you from freezing to death. Believe me, you didn't find it so charming at the time."

"Maybe that's what I miss. You coming to pick me up." Charlie glugged some beer, tilting his head back. "What do *you* miss?"

Garrett shrugged. He didn't want to play this game. He stared at his friend's beer-soaked shirt, feeling a junk punch of despair.

"Wait, let me guess," Charlie said. "Mountain rhinos."

"Black rhinos, you mean?"

"Whatever. The one that's extinct. Who can keep track?"

"Mountain rhinos might have some trouble leaping between rocks."

Charlie threw his empty beer can at the corner of the porch. "What else are kaput? Sea turtles?"

"So far just the hawksbill."

"Poor hawksbill. See you on a stamp."

"Jesus. Do you *want* them to be extinct?"

"Of course not," Charlie said. "On the other hand, does it really matter?"

Garrett looked at him. "Of course it matters."

"Face it—no one gives a shit about rhinos. Or hawksbill turtles. Or *wolverines*." Charlie opened the cooler for another beer, and Garrett shut it with his foot. "In fact, we *prefer* them extinct."

"What the hell are you talking about?"

"Don't tell me you don't feel a little bit relieved. Poor hawksbill turtle, what a tragic loss! Nothing to be done! On the other hand, nothing to be done! We're finally off the hook. We can remember them how we want to, without all the guilt. Just look at the dodo bird."

"Is that supposed to be funny?" Garrett said angrily. "Because it's not."

"I couldn't agree more."

"We're driving evolution back four million years."

"I know. I watched your TED Talk. Or whatever it was." Charlie mimed like he was driving and then pretended to do something: bump over roadkill? He dropped his hands without meeting Garrett's eyes. "Do you honestly think you're making the slightest bit of difference up there, chasing wolverines around? How many years have you been doing it now? Twenty?"

"Eighteen."

"Wouldn't that time have been better spent, I don't know, with your *wife*?"

Garrett stared at him. He had not expected this, such viciousness. Or rather: he'd been expecting it for years but had been tricked into letting down his guard, thinking he'd been forgiven. Charlie bent over to get another beer. Garrett left him alone and went inside the air-conditioned house, which felt like entering heaven—or maybe a Starbucks. Seething, he stood by the air purifier for a minute, breathing deeply, detoxing not so much from the smoke outside but from Charlie's bitterness. Garrett questioned his life's work every day. One look at the news, its blithe inventory of outrages against the earth, and he felt seasick with discouragement, as if he might actually throw up. Last thing he fucking needed was Charlie questioning it for him.

Soledad noticed Garrett by the door and beckoned him into the living room, where everyone was still gathered around the couch. They'd decided to play a game of Charades, the old-fashioned kind with actual slips of paper. This was Soledad's idea. She liked party games. They called Charlie in from the porch, oblivious to his mood, then broke into teams and wrote down the names of movies or books or TV shows and folded the answers into a bowl, which they gave to the opposing team. It soon became clear that couples who'd managed to end up on the same team were at a distinct advantage, having learned telepathy long ago. Cynthia guessed Johnny's right away, just as Johnny guessed hers. Even Soledad seemed to rely on Brig, who sang out the answer to her pantomime, *Blade Runner*, before anyone else. While acting out *The Norton Anthology of Poetry*—what asshole, *sadist*, had come up with that?—Garrett found himself feeling weirdly forlorn, trying not to interpret Cece's baffled silence as some kind of verdict on their marriage.

When it was Charlie's turn, he rose stiffly from the couch and walked to the middle of the rug, puffing his chest out like a rooster's and taking short deliberate steps. Garrett felt a stab of foreboding. Charlie fumbled into his shirt pocket and pulled out some reading glasses. Garrett wondered for a second if he'd forgotten where he was, so transfixed did he seem by what was written on his card, but then Charlie looked up and found Cece in the crowd, staring at her for so long that people shifted in their seats.

Eventually he stuck the card in his pocket, and Cynthia flipped over the plastic hourglass they were using for a timer. After making the book sign with his hands, Charlie pretended to grip something in his fingers and then brought the pretend something to his mouth.

"You're drinking a beer," Marcus said.

Charlie ignored this, repeating the motion.

"Okay, you're brushing your teeth," Soledad said.

"Oh my god. No. He's performing fellatio."

"Multiple fellatios!"

"Steve Jobs!"

"It's a *book*, you idiot."

Charlie staggered around, bumping into things.

"Is he pretending to be drunk?"

"He's actually drunk."

"*The Lost Weekend.*"

"It's like a what-do-you-call-it," Johnny said. "A Buddhist koan."

"*Under the Volcano!*"

"Oh, oh, are you the Shakespeare guy? *Merry Wives of Winter?*"

Charlie stopped in the middle of the rug, swaying in place. He lurched up to Cece and began pointing at her face, jabbing the air with his finger. His face gleamed with sweat. Everyone watched him, speechless. Marcus, who'd been filming Charlie, lowered his phone. Cece seemed as stumped as everyone else. Glaring, as if he'd been saddled with the stupidest teammates in the world, Charlie held up a finger—"First word"—and tugged at his earlobe. Then he walked over to the ceramic lamp next to the couch and swatted it to the floor, where it shattered. Garrett shot up from the couch. Charlie admired the shattered lamp for a second, a look of gaudy satisfaction on his face. He was panting.

"Disaster," Charlie said.

"I'll say," Gabby said.

"*The Master and Margarita*. It's Cece's favorite book. Tell them, Ceece!" He looked at her desperately. "Her favorite drink too: margaritas."

Cece wouldn't meet his eye from the couch. Garrett, who'd never seen her drink a margarita in her life, wondered if this could possibly be true. Charlie stared at her, rocking gently on his feet.

"She doesn't like cocktails," Garrett said finally.

"No one asked *you*."

"Also, that's not her favorite book."

"How about we play something else," Marcus said.

"Tell them, C," Charlie said. "In med school, at that Mexican cantata place." Someone laughed, which seemed to bewilder him. His reading glasses were askew, as if he'd just stepped off a roller coaster. "Where was it, on Fleet Street? You used to down them like water."

Cece shook her head.

"Tell them!"

"I don't like cocktails," Cece said without looking at him.

Charlie stared at her in disbelief.

"Maybe it's time for bed," Soledad said to him.

"What?"

"Do you want some help upstairs?"

"Okay, Mom. Are you going to change my diaper too?"

Charlie grinned at the room, as if he thought he was being funny. It seemed to dawn on him, gradually, what he'd just said. His eyes snagged eventually on Brig, who was staring at him from his wheelchair.

"Merrily, merrily, merrily, merrily," Charlie yelled at him.

"Okay," Garrett said, grabbing him under the armpit. "Okay."

He expected Charlie to put up a fight, but he seemed to deflate as soon as Garrett touched him, as if whatever spell had been cast on him had suddenly evaporated. Garrett helped him upstairs to bed, where he lay in the position in which he'd been dropped, one hand thrown over his heart, like someone taking the Pledge of Allegiance. What a pigsty his room was! The drawers of the dresser were pulled out, sagging in their runners; draped over them, as if migrating upriver, was a pair of red sweatpants. In college, he used to fold his clothes when they were *dirty*, laying them carefully in the hamper though he knew they'd be stuffed into a machine.

The poor guy was breathing in that way that drunk people do, like a Doberman after a walk. Garrett had a vague memory of what this was like. Why on earth had they ever confused it with fun?

"What was that story about the guy?" Charlie demanded, without opening his eyes. He sounded even drunker now. Garrett hoped he wouldn't remember any of this tomorrow.

"What guy?"

"Dammit, the guy! Who carried the finger in his mouth like a Jolly Rancher?"

"You mean the vet up at Waterton?"

Charlie nodded. Garrett had no idea why he was thinking of this now. It was one of those war stories that wildlife biologists tell, to impress people; Garrett had to search his brain to remember it properly. Two volunteers on the project had been building a wolverine trap, using a chain saw to cut up logs, and one of them had slipped and taken off a finger. The injured guy had gone into shock. And Henderson—that was the wildlife vet's name—found the finger and put it in his mouth and kept it there for two hours while they waited for an SAR copter to come. It was a way of keeping it clean, or cool, something like that. Garrett didn't recall the reasoning.

"That's what I call friendship," Charlie said. He opened his eyes and stared at Garrett—accusingly, it seemed.

"You should apologize to your guests in the morning."

"Would Cece suck on your member? If it was dismembered?"

"There's something wrong with you," Garrett said seriously.

"No shit, Dr. Freud." Charlie scowled. "Anyway, guy's an idiot. The human mouth has more bactria than a toilet."

"Bacteria?"

"*Bacteria!*" he said, snapping his fingers in Garrett's face.

Some laughter drifted upstairs, a burst of applause. Someone had put on a Prince song. Charlie beckoned to Garrett, who leaned over him carefully, thinking Charlie wanted to whisper something in his ear. Instead, Charlie reached up with both hands and seized him gingerly by the throat. A stranglehold. Reluctantly, Garrett played along and did the same to Charlie, clutching his windpipe. Garrett would humor him: enact this dopey thing they used to do in college, a pledge or promise or test of love. They hugged each other's throats. And in fact, feeling the long-lost sensation of Charlie's hands on his throat, their clumsy drunken squeeze, Garrett felt transported for the first time that night, freed from the larger game of Charades he'd been playing all day, pretending to be joyously reunited with his friends and not saddened by how old they looked, how tame and befuddled—by the feeling that even though Brig hadn't died, they'd all found themselves at a funeral anyway. Charlie squeezed Garrett's throat harder, choking him a little bit, and so Garrett squeezed harder too.

2.

After dinner—served at five thirty, because apparently addicts were toddlers—Jasper walked down to the stables with his therapy group. He liked to think they were worse off than he was, though maybe that was one of his patterns of denial. *Minimization*, they called it. Still, he couldn't help comparing himself favorably to the other residents. One of them, a former Miss America contestant, had fallen down the stairs while holding her baby. One of them had been Narcanned so many times his parents had started planning his funeral. One of them was so hooked on Oxy that he'd stuck his hand in the garbage disposal, hoping a doctor would write him a script. These were his pals at Whispering Pines Ranch.

As for Jasper, golden boy of the ranch, he'd never even injected. There was always a line he wouldn't cross. He'd started by taking benzos. Then Vicodins. Then Roxys. Only twenty milligrams, but no more. Then, okay, forties, but not eighties. Then, when the high wasn't quick enough, he was rubbing the coating off eighties and crushing them up to snort. Then he was snorting heroin—buying sniffer bags in Isla Vista—but not smoking it. He wasn't an idiot. Anyway, it wasn't serious: an ice cream habit. Then he was smoking it, but no needles! Needles were for burnouts, the walking dead. Then, surprise surprise, he was skin popping. But he'd never stuck a needle into an actual vein, not even once!

It wasn't until he'd shared all this in group, seen the familiar haze of sadness and concern on everyone's faces—mixed with a pitying scorn for the pride he felt at not injecting—that he recognized how ridiculous it was. His sense of superiority.

You'd think since this was his second stint in rehab, he would have learned his lesson: he belonged with the desperate fuckups of the world.

The sun never seemed to go down in Montana. It warmed Jasper's face in that way that felt weirdly cold at the same time. A goose-pimply kind of heat. This was a new sensation, or a new-old sensation, one of many he'd rediscovered since detoxing. He stopped for a second to wipe his face, which was drenched in sweat. The Suboxone did this to him, particularly after dinner. His roommate had started calling him Old Faithful. Compared to being dopesick, a walk in the park.

They hiked along the gravel road to the corral, where the horses were grazing in their pasture, silent as ghosts. Their chestnut flanks rippled in the sun. The smoke had magically cleared—a brief rain, it seemed to come in cloudbursts up here—and the funk of manure was stronger than usual. Just smelling it lifted Jasper's spirits. He'd grown to enjoy equine therapy, the one part of the day he looked forward to. Every morning he was woken at six, greeted by a schedule that had been slipped under the door. Yoga, therapy (group), therapy (individual), lunch, therapy (CBT), therapy (art or music), dinner, therapy to process the therapy you had in the morning. The horses they saw when they could, depending on the smoke. The general philosophy was: NO ESCAPE. You were supposed to confront yourself, your own addiction, twenty-four/seven. It was like being stuck in one of those mirror mazes all day long. How Jasper longed sometimes to sneak back to his room and take a nap!

But he loved Nutmeg, the horse he'd been matched with, drawn to her from the start: a mare with a white diamond between her eyes, symmetrical as the one on a playing card. *She can sense your heartbeat from ten yards away*, the equine therapist had said. Jasper found this hard to believe, but then Nutmeg had done something startling. She'd come right up to Jasper and nuzzled his pacemaker. Sniffed at it through his T-shirt. That first time he'd met her, Jasper had done everything wrong; he'd tried to bridle Nutmeg but she'd seemed nervous and skittish, ducking away from him and pinning her ears. He'd laughed it off, turned his crummy horsemanship into a kind of comedy routine. Later, when they were integrating in circle, Shauna—a woman in his group—had said watching him try to bridle Nutmeg made her sad. Jasper had been completely absorbed in himself, his own failure, when it should have been about *Nutmeg's* experience. He needed to subjugate himself to her needs.

After that first encounter, he was slow and patient around Nutmeg, and the horse warmed to him abruptly. He felt a calmness—an effortless click—that he never felt around people. She demanded nothing from him, never asked him to love her back or remember her birthday or feel sufficiently grateful for the amazing wondrous life he'd been given. Currying her down sometimes, leaning one hand on her coat while he circled the comb, Jasper felt something inside her he couldn't explain. A force bigger than himself. Once, when he was a little kid, he'd heard his grandpa use the word "horsepower" while mowing the lawn and had had no idea what it meant. He'd imagined something magical, a godlike thing, like "higher power" but in the form of a horse with glowing laser-beam eyes. And that's what he felt sometimes inside of Nutmeg. Not the superhero eyes, but a Horsepower, a great lonely strength telling him he was there. He was real. It couldn't be faked.

Today they were doing Horse as Mirror. Everyone paired off with their "healing companion," dispersing across the pasture and approaching them like eighth graders at a mixer, sparks of grasshoppers shooting from the grass. Jasper volunteered to go first. The idea was that Nutmeg was an emotional Einstein, more attuned to his feelings than he was himself. Jasper believed it. The mare watched him approach, whinnying softly. There was nothing so flattering as a hello from a horse. She sniffed at the legs of his jeans, which were soaked from the damp grass of the pasture. He waited for Nutmeg to rest her head on his shoulder. Maybe even blow on his face, her sign of affection. Instead, she eyed him carefully, swishing her tail.

Babs, the equine therapist, asked him to describe Nutmeg's behavior.

"She's feeling wary," Jasper said. "Suspicious."

"Why do you think?"

"Maybe because I'm tense."

"And why are you tense?"

He looked at Nutmeg, as if she might tell him what to say. "My dad's in town. In Salish, I mean. He called me during Phone Time."

"Did he say something to upset you?"

"He's throwing a party. As we speak. The Movie Star's parents are there."

Babs, who had red hair and the kind of freckles people find adorable on little kids but disfiguring on adults, seemed intrigued. She propped her sunglasses on the brim of her cap. She generally stuck to the script—most of the staff did, in their vaguely Christian, tour-guide-of-the-soul way—but this had piqued her interest.

"Who's the movie star?"

"A girl I know. *Used to.* Her parents are planning to visit me."

Babs laid a hand on his shoulder. Probably she thought Lana was a user, an ex who'd gotten him hooked. "It's entirely in your rights to refuse visitors."

"My dad asked them to. He loves them. Particularly the Movie Star's mom."

"Do you have to do what your dad wants?"

"Well, he's paying for rehab." He gestured at the grazing horses. "For *this.*"

Babs didn't answer him. This was a popular strategy at Whispering Pines. He looked at Nutmeg, who seemed to be warier of him than ever—another thing his dad had mysteriously ruined for him. "I feel like it's the least I should do."

"You're *shoulding* on yourself again," Babs said. "If you're doing something out of obligation, not because you want to, you start to resent yourself, others, the whole idea of staying clean. We know what that leads to, right?"

Jasper nodded, though he couldn't remember what particular thing this led to. *A victim mentality? Negative self-talk?* He couldn't always keep them straight, though he knew he was supposed to be using coping strategies. One of these was not to say Lana's name. He called her the Movie Star. Or sometimes the Vampire Star. This was something he'd learned about in college, in Intro to Astronomy. (He'd wanted to be an astrophysics major, even declared it on some form or another, which seemed hilarious to him now.) Sometimes you get these two companion stars that are kind of like siblings—they're actually called that, "sibling stars"—except one of them ends up feeding off the other, sucking all the energy out of it and using it for fuel. It does this for many years. The vampire star gets big and fat and powerful, while the other, the fed-upon star, dwindles into nothing. You can barely even see it.

It didn't seem just. *She* was the weird one, the one who'd called him "brother dear" and drawn her initials in menstrual blood on his chest, who'd seemed to have a crush on *his fucking pacemaker.* If anyone belonged in a facility, it was her.

Of course, it wasn't really fair to blame Lana for all that, for making a success of her life. For the fucking shitshow—shit *carnival*—that was his own. Babs would have called this "a pattern of distortion." Or was it "a pattern of blame and shame"? (Jasper had patterns coming out of his patterns.) He hadn't exactly been a model friend himself, had he? It's just that they'd lived in that special place, that perverted sibling land, for so many years. They were going to be famous together, move to a fishing village where they could grow old in peace. They weren't supposed to leave each other behind.

It was her mom that he hated. The helpless dying-trout face his dad got whenever she was around, like he was waiting to be thrown back in the water.

Jasper had brought all this up in group once, god knows why, but no one seemed to get what he was talking about. Probably he hadn't explained himself very well. They were supposed to write a letter to their addiction, breaking up with it, but he'd spent a whole page of the letter talking about the Movie Star and the whole thing that had happened between his dad and her parents, how his dad had *actually invited them back into their lives*. Her parents had done this awful shitty thing, a quarter century ago, and his dad was too much of a chump to cut them off. Why couldn't Lana's family just leave them alone? Her mom had already ruined his parents' marriage—wasn't that enough? He was so sick of paying for things people had done—to each other, themselves, the entire fucking planet—before he was even born.

Or maybe his dad was just obsessed: with the Movie Star's mom, obviously, but also with some vision of how things were supposed to have panned out for him. He wanted to have had a different life completely. The whole thing made Jasper feel like he should never have been born. He'd tried to explain this to his addiction counselor—that he felt like a ghost sometimes, like he didn't really exist—and his counselor had thought he was talking about being an addict. "Do you want to spend your life like that, walking around in a dream?" But life had already felt like a dream to him, well before he was using. Everyone on their phones all the time; grown men spraying people—kids!—with machine guns; the whole planet burning up and no one seeming to care . . . it had never seemed fully real to him. A machine, a dinky little battery, was keeping him alive. (He still had nightmares about the pacer pads in the ICU, waking with a coppery taste in his mouth.) Coasting on heroin was the one time the dream made sense to him, when he felt like he was in the same state as the world.

He approached Nutmeg again, who still seemed a bit uneasy, stiffening when he touched her withers. How afraid she was! He tried to scratch under her chin, her favorite spot, but she jerked her head out of reach. Jasper felt rejected—bereft even. His eyes glazed with tears. Of course, the horse could read his mind, knew he was filled with thoughts of the Movie Star, who'd left him behind to rot. But he missed her. Oh god. He missed her too. She'd done something to him, when they were kids: found his loneliness and turned it into a place, a shelter, a hideaway in the woods.

He closed his eyes. Nutmeg snorted in the heat. He was supposed to reframe his thoughts, use one of the mantras they'd taught him in CBT. *I am capable of change.*

He was going to a sober house in Palm Springs in two weeks. Palm Springs! The place with the golf courses. He was going to stay clean this time, it was a hundred percent in his power, because he was stronger than his addiction.

Jasper kept his eyes shut, waiting for Nutmeg to approach. Her heart, Babs had told him, was enormous. Weighed as much as a one-year-old girl. If he could regain her trust, this thing with the girl-sized heart, then his hope was real. There was love and light in him still. Yes, he could feel her approaching. Was that her in front of him? Her warm grassy breath? He raised his face to her, waiting. *The past does not define me. The past does not define me.*

3.

Charlie tightened his grip on Garrett's throat. Garrett, whose back was killing him from leaning over the bed, returned the favor. Charlie seemed encouraged by this, as if Garrett were giving him an excuse to continue. Was the man finally, at long last, going to kill him?

"I slept with Cece," Charlie said in a pinched voice.

"I would hope so. You were engaged to be married."

"No! I mean after that. Seven years ago? While you were off being Jeremiah Johnson." Charlie looked at the dresser. "Only once. One time," he said proudly. "I swear to God."

Garrett stared at him. A price tag was poking out of the neck of Charlie's shirt, as if he'd bought a new one just for the party and neglected in his nervousness to cut it off. What shocked Garrett, more than Charlie's confession, was that he wasn't shocked at all.

If anything, he felt a strange electric calm. What was wrong with him? He had no idea. The hairs on his arm seemed to move, tickled by a breeze from the A/C.

Charlie closed his eyes, as if he were waiting for Garrett to punish him—to strangle him for real. Eager for it even. And Garrett should have felt that way: furious and betrayed.

He let go of Charlie's throat. Charlie, ashamed or just shit-faced, rolled to the other side of the bed, turning away from him. Another song came on—"Only the Good Die Young"—and the guests downstairs cheered. Garrett could hear Cece singing along, accompanied by Brig's beautiful baritone. She had a terrible voice, was in fact irredeemably tone-deaf, but this fact had never once occurred to her. She sang lustily in the shower and the car and while doing the dishes. Sometimes, to Garrett's embarrassment, she belted along to the old-time bands that played at the Wild Mile Café, startling even the musicians. It touched him deeply: not the singing itself, but the self-deception she'd managed to cling to for fifty-two years and that even marriage had failed to set straight.

Charlie had fallen asleep, snoring the way Elias had in college, like bathwater suctioning down a drain. (Elias! He was always lurking.) Garrett covered Charlie with a blanket. Then he turned off the lights and went downstairs to join the party, remembering not to brain himself on the lintel though the ancient duck drawing had faded to a petrograph. In the living room, Cece was dancing with Soledad and Gabby and Marcus, doing that thing with the pointer finger of each hand where she wiggled them in the air like antennae. It should have been ridiculous, but somehow Cece managed to make the move graceful, sincere, *even sexy*. Her hair, tinseled with gray, swung back and forth as she danced, whipping her face. Her face! How young and beautiful and unfamiliar it looked, bright as a stranger's. Somehow Charlie's confession had transformed her. That lovely freckle on her cheekbone, shaped like a top hat. He hadn't noticed the

freckle, it seemed, for years. Was this possible? Garrett bumped
Gabby aside in a way that made Cece laugh and they danced
together—"Just Like Heaven" was the song now, because you
never grew old on Spotify, you were always sixteen—and she
smiled at him, tenderly, in that affectionate mocking way she did
when he tried to dance. *Strange as angels, dancing in the deepest
oceans.* He remembered singing along to this on the radio once,
thinking the lyrics said "deep explosion," and Cece laughing at
him so hard that Diet Coke sprayed out her nose. Now the floor
was covered in popcorn, which crunched underfoot. Midtwirl,
Cece grabbed a handful from a bowl on the coffee table and
stuffed it into her mouth, dropping half the kernels on the floor.
He stuffed his face, too, raining popcorn. When was the last
time they'd actually *danced*?

Between songs, Garrett grabbed Cece's elbow and pulled her
into the guest room, where Mr. and Mrs. Margolis used to sleep.
The sun was setting, the windows beginning to turn off like lanterns. They sat on the bed together. Garrett wanted to give voice
to the feeling inside of him. To say it in a new way, just as Brig
had managed to express himself in song. It seemed to require
that—a new voice—but he only had one of them, the same old
voice she knew to death, worn to a rasp now from the smoke.

"I'm sorry we didn't get to go out on our anniversary," he said
lamely.

"We *are* out," Cece said.

"I meant somewhere special."

"We *are* somewhere special. The place where we met."

Garrett looked at her.

"Anyway, I brought these."

She reached into her pocket and pulled out a Ziploc bag,
inside which were three sets of novelty teeth. Garrett laughed.
They each put a set in their mouths, ceremoniously. Everything
that had seemed newly beautiful about his wife vanished in a
second. She looked like a syphilitic pirate. Garrett kissed her, or

tried to, but his teeth bumped into hers and her mouth was full of drool. His love for her could not overcome his disgust.

Cece took out her teeth and peered around the room. "You know, I don't think they'd be very happy about our being in here."

"Who?"

"The Margolises."

"Luckily, they're both dead," Garrett said.

This hadn't come out exactly the way he'd intended it to. Cece looked at him: a bit sadly, a bit happily. Never one without the other. If she'd been a simpler person, easier to love, probably he would have been bored a long time ago.

"We'll be dead too someday," she said.

"That's true."

"I don't know why we get like this. Like, I don't know . . . we can't even see each other."

"Maybe that's a good thing? I mean, with *our* teeth."

"You always joke," Cece said defeatedly. She put her novelty teeth back inside their bag. "Maybe you were right about marriage all along. 'The only adventure open to the cowardly.'" Frowning, she grabbed the teeth he'd been wearing off the bed—squeamishly, between two fingers—and dropped them in the bag with the others. "I wanted us to have a happy anniversary."

"I *am* happy," Garrett said.

It was true. She'd cheated on him with Charlie, most likely in this very house, and yet the news had . . . *made him want to dance?* In fact, it had not felt like news at all. Perhaps he'd known for years—known that something had happened between them—but hadn't admitted it to himself, the way you might feel all the symptoms of a flu before piecing together that you were sick. He hadn't wanted the burden of being wronged.

He should have felt that burden now. So why did he feel the opposite? *Unburdened*, as if a weight had been lifted?

They were even at last. Him and Charlie. Or at least *more* even. He could stop feeling so fucking guilty.

And Cece had returned to him. Chosen Garrett once again. What's more, he'd had nothing at all to do with it.

"I got you a present too," he said, remembering the vintage orrery he'd bought. "It hasn't come in the mail yet."

"What is it?"

"It's a surprise."

She frowned. "Give me a *hint*."

Garrett laughed. Classic Cece: she'd be mad if he told her— furious, really—but would spend the whole time before it came trying to get it out of him. "It's sort of like a clock, but for the universe."

"A clock?"

"Yeah. You move the hands yourself."

TWENTY-ONE

Lana had been getting the texts for a week, from a number she didn't recognize:

Childbirth is nonconsensual.

Then, a couple days later:

A desert island is no tragedy, neither is a deserted planet.

Then this morning:

You're imprisoned in evil matter.

Lana went to the bathroom and looked at herself in the mirror. Yes, well, it might have been evil. More likely it was simply in its thirtieth year on earth and feeling a little bit tired, being carbon based and all. Those Montana summers had begun to take their toll. The skin above her chest looked splotchy. The "beauty mark" on her lip had tipped decisively into mole. Some faint lines had begun to appear on her forehead, like a cold front moving north. Lana knew the lines would get deeper, and she'd have a harder time getting parts, and then even if she grew an Oscar out of her fucking head and pranced around like a unicorn, no one would give her a second glance.

Still, she did not really wish to be imprisoned in anything else.

She cleaned up from breakfast and then went out to sweep

the balcony, not bothering with her respirator even though the smoke stung her eyes. The San Gabriels were on fire again, as were the Santa Susanas; from her balcony, Lana could see the charred remains of the Griffith Observatory, its domeless rotunda looking weirdly forlorn, like an egg cup without an egg. Of course, the observatory had burned last October, in the Cahuenga Peak fire—but the feeling, at least, was of a single fire, one that never fully went out. The planes flew all year round, dumping pink clouds of slurry. Everyone just accepted it now, like they accepted the respirators and the controlled blackouts and the water tax. Even when the Hollywood sign had burned, the steel letters curling like Shrinky Dinks. How shocking the footage had been at first, then sort of freaky-cool in a Burning Man way, then ironic-iconic enough to put on a T-shirt. A new sign was supposed to go up by Christmas. Everyone just shook the ash from their hair, drove their Tesla down Sunset with their air filter on, as if nothing were wrong.

Lana was no different. She did this too (minus the Tesla). What choice did they have?

She swept the ash from her balcony, then watered her potted geraniums with the leftover water from a wineglass in the sink. The Santa Anas were blowing, the palm trees across the street sculling in the wind. Her phone vibrated again. Was actually ringing. Why hadn't she blocked the unknown number from her phone? She'd dealt with celebrity stalkers before—well, okay, *one* stalker, but she'd had to get a restraining order when he started showing up at her apartment building dressed like Houdini.

She wrestled the phone from her jeans: a 323 number, different than before, though one she failed to recognize. She forced herself to answer it.

"Lana, it's Charlie Margolis."

"Mr. Margolis!" she said, then felt ridiculous. She was a grown woman. Still, what was she going to do? Call him Charlie? Sometimes she had to remind herself she wasn't a little girl.

When she thought of her childhood, she pictured those rashes she used to get after she'd been hiking all day in Glacier or Jewel Basin, through innocent-looking weeds, the kind you don't even think about being noxious until it's too late and your legs are aflame. She was still trying to wash it off.

"It's Jasper," Mr. Margolis said, sounding worried. "He's moved to the desert. Joined some kind of antinatalist thing."

"Antinatalist?"

"Church of VEX, they call themselves. Short for 'Voluntary Extinction.' They think humans should stop having babies and die off—the sooner, you know, the better. It's a save-the-planet thing, I guess."

"He's living there?"

"Yep. Yes, he is. My only son." Mr. Margolis cleared his throat. "The website? It's pretty, um, extreme. What scares me is the talk of euthanasia."

"Like mass suicide?"

He didn't answer. She realized now that the texts must have been from Jasper. Some part of her had known this already. And yet something—fear? protectiveness?—prevented her from telling Mr. Margolis about them.

"I heard he was in rehab again," Lana said.

More silence. Had he hung up on her?

"Which 'again' do you mean?"

"Fourth?"

"Fifth time was last spring. Actually he's been great. Working at a climbing gym in Palm Springs. On Subs, exercising every day. His dream was to be a route setter—whatever the hell that is. That's what he told me over Christmas. I thought, *Thirty years old, he's finally found his calling.*" Mr. Margolis cleared his throat. "Then he met some eco types on a climbing trip. Joshua Tree, I think. Extremists. They recruited him. You know those guys who, like, promise to solve all your problems? I'm not sure if they're kooks or just, I don't know, your dad on acid."

"I'm surprised he'd join something like that," Lana said, though in all honesty she wasn't. The boy had never liked his own family much. How tragic, at his age, to still be looking for one. "Are you asking for help?"

"I've called and called. He won't pick up."

"Did my parents ever tell you about visiting Jasper at that place near Whitefish?"

"I barely remember it. They said he was 'difficult.'"

"That's one way of putting it," Lana said. Apparently, he'd called Lana's mom a whore.

"I just thought—you know, you guys were so close. He adores you."

Lana was not at all sure that Jasper adored her. Quite the opposite, in fact. She hadn't seen him since that summer they were sixteen, when she'd played the clip of him singing with a pillowcase over his head. Humiliated him in front of his sister and her friend. He'd stopped speaking to her after that. No, that wasn't completely true: he'd called her once seven or eight years ago, in the middle of the night, after she'd debuted in *Houdini, PI*. He'd been out of his gourd, talking a mile a minute, as if he were leaking like a balloon and had to get the words out before he deflated. *You're a shit actress and should go back to Montana.* Lana had hung up on him. For all she knew, he was still trying to shake her off a ladder.

Or maybe not. Not long after the phone call, an envelope had arrived in the mail, one of those Priority mailers with no return address. No note inside: just some Monopoly money, a splinter of wood, a chapati-flat stone, perfect for skipping. Lana had never responded to this sentimental gesture. Oh, she'd *wanted* to: written two different emails to Jasper, apologizing for betraying him when they were sixteen. Because she thought of him sometimes, parched with guilt. Okay, more than sometimes. A lot. You might even say she *dwelled*. She knew this guilt was self-aggrandizing; he hadn't turned out the way he had solely because of something she'd done when they were kids. She was but one point on a plane. Still, he'd wanted to be a singer-songwriter, a famous one, and she'd gone out of her way to crush his dreams.

"Okay," she said to Jasper's father.

"Okay?"

"What is it you want me to do?"

———

A week later, she sat in the passenger seat of Mr. Margolis's car, heading through the Mojave Desert on their way to Twentynine Palms. The view from Route 62 was flat and atrocious, an endless sandbox speckled with creosote bushes. Lana loved it. In Montana, everything was so beautiful that it made you feel ugly inside. Ugly and deformed. There was a smugness about it, a spiritual superiority. She'd never forget the first time she drove through the High Desert, on her way to LA, the gust of kinship she felt looking at the suffering plants. The land itself seemed to be in distress. And the Joshua trees! Those contorted arms, twisting this way and that like an actual Joshua she knew, a kid in a wheelchair she used to tutor for Volunteer Hours in twelfth grade. You'd only grow that way if you were in pain.

Mr. Margolis stared straight ahead as he drove, focused on getting to the collective where Jasper was living. That's what he called it, a "collective," as though calling it a cult would turn it into one. And wasn't a collective, like, a *farm*? What could they possibly be growing out here in the desert? Lana might have asked Mr. Margolis these questions, but they hadn't spoken much since he'd picked her up at her apartment in Los Feliz, sporting a salt-and-pepper beard that might have looked distinguished if not for the yarn-y fiber of banana dangling from it. This was perfectly okay with Lana, who hadn't slept well last night—stewing, as she was wont to, on the state of her life.

"What did Jasper say when you told him we were coming?" Lana asked now, partly to wake herself up.

Mr. Margolis glanced at her, then returned his eyes to the road.

"Tell me he knows we're coming," she said.

"How would he? He doesn't answer my phone calls."

"Oh my god. You haven't spoken to him at all?"

"Actually, he wrote me a letter. When he first moved out here. Maybe six months ago? He said they had a one-legged dog on the farm named Ouroboros. I'm assuming he meant to say *a three-legged dog*. A slip of the tongue. He signed the thing 'Better off dead, Jasper.' Instead of 'love' or 'sincerely' or whatever." Mr. Margolis fiddled with the air-conditioning vent. "That was about it. It was a short letter. I wrote him back several times, but he never responded."

He smiled at her, the thread of banana in his beard trembling like a worm. His hand was trembling as well. Lana had noticed this when he'd fiddled with the air-conditioning vent. Mr. Margolis's decline, from Lana's perspective, was a distant tragedy related to her birth. It didn't really concern her. He'd never liked her very much, at least that was Lana's sense, as if she were somehow proof of the world's unfairness.

Lana stared out her window, annoyed she'd been roped into an ambush. She thought about demanding they turn around and drive back to LA, but the truth was she had nothing else to do. She was between jobs, between girlfriends, between meal kit deliveries. She hadn't had a callback all spring. The last shoot she'd done was for a VR game called *SpacePaladins: Omega Rising*. She'd played someone named Starbreath, who ends up getting decapitated by a knight riding a dragon. That was last fall. Since then she'd been to twelve auditions, all of which had amounted to squat. Lately, when she called Fehmeeda, her agent, there was a longer and longer gap between when Fehmeeda's twenty-year-old assistant answered and when Fehmeeda got to the phone. Lana had a bad feeling she was being ghosted, but delicately, as if her agent were backing away from a bomb.

"Your dad's father used to have a three-legged cat," Mr. Margolis said. "Can't remember his name."

"Barnabas," Lana said.

"Yes. He could walk on a fence."

"He died before I was born. Eaten by a coyote, they think."

"Right, of course," he said, darkening. He studied the road. "Your parents would have inherited him."

"You and Mom had an affair, didn't you?" Lana asked suddenly.

He glanced at her in surprise. Lana was as surprised as he was. It had just come out. Mr. Margolis reddened. Even his beard seemed to glow. What had her mother seen in this man, too fair-skinned to keep his emotions to himself? He was handsome in a textbook sort of way. The eyes and nose and mouth were all pleasantly proportioned, like a poem that rhymed. But there was something missing. A force, maybe—a confidence?— holding them together.

Reaching across her, Mr. Margolis fished around in the glove compartment and took out some wraparound shades, the cyborg-y kind with mirrored lenses.

"Let me tell you something," he said finally, now that his eyes were hidden. "Your mother blocked me from her phone a long time ago. Cut me off completely." He looked at Lana—or at least his sunglasses did. "She's a good person."

Lana frowned. It had seemed outrageous to her as a girl: her mother's unhappiness. The woman had everything she needed. Namely, Lana herself. How dare she be unhappy? And how dare she cheat on her marriage, imagining she could solve it?

But now Lana wondered if she'd ever truly cared about this, or if it was just another way of siding with her father, who was gone half the time and therefore easier to adore. To be honest, Lana didn't give two shits about marriage. It was an ancient relic, like monogamy itself. Why would she care about something invented five thousand years ago, as a kind of burglar alarm to protect a man's most valuable property? It astonished her, in this day and age, that anyone would agree to something called "wedlock." Anyway, it made no room for mistakes. Life was hard; people fucked up in all sorts of indefensible ways. Maybe her mother would have been happier with this man with ridiculous sunglasses, who cared more about people than about wolverines. Who believed—even now, after she'd ditched him twice—that she was a good person.

"Do you hate me too? I'm sorry."

"No," Lana said truthfully, wondering at the "too." It saddened her more than anything else he'd said.

On the outskirts of Twentynine Palms, or somewhat before the outskirts, the car's GPS told them to turn up an unmarked dirt road and follow it for several miles. The road was so washboarded that Lana worried she might chip a tooth. She braced her hands against the dashboard, feeling like an egg shaker full of bones. Eventually they reached the end of the road, where a mangled bicycle, missing both wheels, was chained to a ramshackle gate. The bike had clearly been there a long time. A homemade sign was posted to the gate.

CHURCH OF VEX, it said in permanent marker, then below this, in smaller print: WE'RE ALL TRESPASSERS HERE.

Charlie got out of the car and opened the gate, which meant dragging the mangled bike along with it. They drove farther. Someone had planted quotes or slogans along the side of the road, in the manner of old-fashioned Burma-Shave signs: HAPPINESS IS FOR PIGS; MAN IS THE CANCER OF THE EARTH; THE GREATEST LUCK IS NOT TO BE BORN . . . BUT VERY FEW PEOPLE SUCCEED IN IT. Before long they reached a small compound of abandoned buildings: squares of white stucco, austere as a barracks, crumbling at the corners. They looked like sugar cubes. Some of them had cacti or sunflowers out front, potted in old paint buckets or planted ambitiously in the ground. In front of one building, impaled on garden stakes, was a colonnade of doll heads.

Lana, who'd been calm up till now, started to feel a bit scared. The air smelled of manure, or perhaps human shit; she wondered why this pungent smell was a relief to her, then realized there was no trace of smoke. Chickens gabbled somewhere nearby. Mr. Margolis pulled up to the last house on the right, which was larger than the rest and whose corrugated roof jutted over the front door like the brim of a hat. A dog was lying in the shade of the roof. Jasper, in fact, had described the thing correctly. It sat there in a tray, one-legged and obese, like a rump roast stabbed with a meat thermometer. The woebegone creature barked at them, then began advancing toward the car, using its leg to propel the tray, which turned out to have little wheels attached to it.

Someone appeared in the doorway of the house: a dreadlocked white woman, so immaculately sunburned she looked like she'd been pulled out of a scalding bath. "Boros!" the woman yelled at the dog, who stopped barking.

Lana and Mr. Margolis got out of the car. "Good morning," Mr. Margolis said, though it was well into afternoon. He took off his glasses, as if the woman might recognize him. "We were looking for Jasper Margolis."

"And who might you be?"

"I'm his father. Charlie. And this is Lana, Lana Meek, an old friend of his."

"Oh, Mr. Rise and Shine!" the woman said with delight.

"Excuse me?"

"We've heard all about you. The noble doctor. You used to wake him up every morning. 'Rise and shine!'" The woman laughed uproariously, as if this were the funniest thing in the world. Her teeth had tooth-sized gaps between them, like the studs of a Lego. "Oh god. I'm going to enjoy this little reunion."

"What does that mean?" Mr. Margolis asked politely.

"Nothing. We've just been starved for some entertainment."

She glanced at the sun, idly, the way you might glance at a watch. "Let's see how the fiend reacts to Dr. Frankenstein's pursuit."

Mr. Margolis stared at her. "Dr. Frankenstein?"

"You brought him into this life, didn't you? Nonexistence never hurt anyone," the woman said sententiously, "but existence always did."

"We read your signs on the way up," Lana said, frowning.

The woman, ignoring her, turned toward the adjacent building, whose front door was cracked as if someone were peering out of it. "Jasp! You've got visitors!"

The door opened and a shirtless man with a shaved head came out, squinting in their direction, a fanny pack girdling his waist. He had a little homemade broom in his hand, like the kind you might use to brush off a suit. He peered at them for some time, then bent over carefully and swept the ground in front of his bare feet with the little broom before taking a step. He hunched toward them this way, sweeping the dirt before him as he walked. Lana wondered if he was clearing a path for Jasper's appearance. Was Jasper king of this wretched cult? Some kind of extinction pooh-bah, getting the red-carpet treatment?

The man who'd been clearing the path stopped sweeping and stood up straight and astonished Lana by smiling. She recognized the face, of course, gaunt as it was, but only felt a hundred percent sure when she saw the bulge of the pacemaker below his collarbone. Lana hugged him, instinctively, but Jasper just stood there, the broom handle poking her in the stomach. It was like hugging a tree. A tree that stank to high heaven. Were her eyes watering because of the smell? Mr. Margolis seemed to be in shock, staring at Jasper as if he didn't recognize his own son.

"What are you doing here?" Jasper said.

"What are *you* doing here?" Lana said. She looked at his broom. "Are you, like, the janitor?"

Jasper laughed. He was tanner than she would have thought

possible: alarmingly tan, in that charbroiled way that made you think about being made of meat. If she hadn't known his age, Lana would have pegged him for forty. His forehead was mapped with wrinkles, old-person ones, and he had that look that addicts seemed to get, that crooked-face thing, as if it had come slightly off its hinges. Rousing himself, Mr. Margolis tried to hug him too; Jasper stepped back and left his father stranded there for a second with his arms out. If Jasper felt guilty for doing this, it didn't show on his face.

"It's a monastic broom," he said defensively. "An *ogha*. Jain mendicants use them."

"You're, like, a *Jainist monk*?"

"God no. We don't pretend to be Jains. For one thing, we don't believe mankind can be saved. Or in the path of four jewels." He rolled his eyes at her, as if she had the slightest idea what he was talking about. "But we do find their daily practice inspiring—particularly when it comes to ahimsa."

"Well, you've got the smell down. You've definitely practiced that. When's the last time you had a shower?"

Jasper smiled at her.

"Never mind. Don't answer that."

"Like Jains, we believe all forms of life are sacred, no matter how minute. It's why we don't step on insects." He held up his little broom. "Man is a scourge. Just by being born, we've done irreparable damage. The least we can do is spare other creatures." He said this last bit woodenly, even with a kind of boredom, as if he were reading it off a teleprompter.

"Jasp," Mr. Margolis said hoarsely.

Jasper, ignoring him completely, peered at his father's car. "Hey, did you bring anything to eat?"

Mr. Margolis glanced at Lana and the woman with dreadlocks and then walked over to the Audi and rummaged through something in the backseat before returning with a bag of Doritos. Jasper looked elated. He snatched the Doritos from Mr. Margolis's

hand without looking at his face. Jasper handed Lana his broom
and ripped open the bag right then and there, shoveling chips
into his mouth. Boros, the one-legged dog, trundled his way
over to Jasper's side in search of crumbs, punting himself along
with the pole of his leg. The woman with dreadlocks watched
Jasper stuff his face with a look of disgust, then snatched the bag
from his hands before he was finished.

"Maybe you should give your visitors a tour." She looked at
Lana and Mr. Margolis. "I'm sure the celebrity actress is a busy
woman. Unless they're planning on joining the congregation?"

"My back is killing me," Jasper said, staring at the bag of
Doritos in her hand.

"Step mindfully. You can give the broom a rest for an hour."

Jasper nodded. The woman had some power over him that
felt unnatural. Lana didn't like it. And how did she know Lana
was an actress? Lana handed the little broom back to Jasper, who
stuck it in one of his belt loops. Stepping gingerly, he led them
back along the path he'd swept and along the side of the building where he presumably lived, its windows glinting in the sun
so that you couldn't see inside. A pane in one of the windows was
broken; someone had taped a piece of paper over it that doubled
as a sign. A PERVERSELY DISTRESSING INTERVAL OF CONSCIOUSNESS,
it read. Still ignoring Mr. Margolis—pretending, in fact, that he
wasn't there—Jasper led Lana to the rear side of the barracks,
where a hidden menagerie was sheltering from the heat. There
was a pen for sheep and another one for goats, most of whom
were lying in the shade cast by a barn made from recycled pal-
lets; the chickens were a bit more active, or at least vocal, one
of them bobbing up the little UFO ramp that led to their coop.
There were even some peacocks roaming about, dragging their
green trains through the dirt.

Lana nodded at a man in a sleeveless T-shirt who was tinker-
ing with an electric dirt bike flipped upside down—but he just
stared at her with a tube of something in his hand. Jasper made

no effort to introduce her. He led them past the goat barn to a foul-smelling garden stockaded by hay bales, lush with squash and tomato plants, from which an elderly woman was pruning branches; the woman stared at Lana from under the brim of a cowboy hat, frozen in midprune. Mr. Margolis waved at the gardener and said hello. Like Dirt Bike Guy, she failed to respond, merely gazed at them curiously, as if they'd invaded her ancestral village. Upon seeing Jasper she seemed to rouse from her trance, enough to say, "Hey, Seahorse," and blow him a kiss.

"Did she call you *Seahorse?*" Mr. Margolis asked.

Jasper continued to ignore his father, treating him like he wasn't there.

"Are you, um, involved with that woman?" Lana asked.

"No. Ha. I mean, aside from the occasional cuddle puddle." Jasper said this with a straight face. "Anyway, we're all celibate here."

"You are?"

"It's not worth the risk."

"Of emotional fallout?"

"Of procreation!"

He led them past the vegetable garden, around the far side of the goat barn, where Lana was startled by the sight of a naked man sitting on the toilet. The man stared at her nonchalantly, as if he were waiting for a movie to start.

"Here's our composting toilet," Jasper said, explaining how they used "humanure."

"There's no door?"

"The goats don't mind. I think they appreciate it."

"It has two toilet seats," Lana said.

"Yep, you can sit side by side. Shoot the shit, in more ways than one!"

She had nothing to say to this. When had he started talking this way? Like some demented hobo? Lana felt sick inside.

It wasn't a normal sick, but the way you might feel after visiting someone in the hospital, realizing they were worse off than you'd imagined. Jasper pointed out the pit mine in the distance, cut implausibly out of the enormous layer cake of a mesa: an old iron mine, though it hadn't been in operation since the 1980s. The walls of it were terraced, like one of those Incan farms. It was impressive, even kind of beautiful, in the way Lana imagined an expressway might look to a Martian. She wondered if Jasper's church had bought the land or was merely squatting. She'd begun to feel like she was squatting herself—not here, on this particular strip of land, but on the earth itself. It was because they were walking so slowly.

"Where are we going?" Lana asked.

"To see Nautilus."

It sounded like something from *SpacePaladins.* "Is that a person?"

"We make the pilgrimage once a day. For inspiration. Are you familiar with Anekantavada, the principle of many-sided reality?"

"Of course not," Lana said.

"What we think of as reality is only a taste," Jasper said. "A teensy little part. Most of what's here we don't experience at all." Again, he seemed half-bored by his own words, as if he were being forced to listen to himself. "It's best, given the vastness of our ignorance, not to interfere."

"Are you planning on living out here forever?" Mr. Margolis asked. His beard glistened with sweat. He looked angry—furious, even—though not at his son. Jasper continued to ignore him. "Jasper. Jasp! I'm talking to you."

Still nothing.

"Seahorse!"

Jasper spun around, the swiftest he'd moved all afternoon. "Don't call me that," he hissed. "What are you even doing here?"

"I'm worried about you."

"I didn't ask you to meddle in my life."

Mr. Margolis removed his sunglasses again. His eyes were like sores. "I'm your father."

"Exactly," Jasper said, as if Mr. Margolis had admitted to drowning puppies.

He spun back around and led them toward the ruins of the mine looming at the edge of the pit. He moved faster now that they were away from the barracks, shielded from view by a cluster of crumbling brick buildings. An abandoned transfer tower sat rusting in the sun, its long conveyor encircled by catwalks; it looked like one of those kids' toys with the racing penguins, doomed to ride the same escalator forever. Jasper ignored the tower, his eyes fixed ahead of him. Lana wanted to tackle him to the ground, wanted to lie in the dandelions together and sneeze happily on his face—anything to shock him back to the kid he used to be. Instead she asked him who this Nautilus person was, if they lived down here in the rubble, and he explained a bit condescendingly that yes, she lived down here, striving for zero impact, though the real question might be what we even mean by "live." We say so-and-so "lives" in a house, or in Cincinnati, Ohio, but what we really mean is that they consume resources, the very least of which is physical space.

"How does she eat?" Lana asked when he was done lecturing her.

Jasper shrugged. "Alms, I guess you'd call them. We make sure that she's well fed." He unzipped his fanny pack, pulling out a handful of radishes. "I should warn you she's sky-clad."

"Sky-clad?"

"That's what Jains call 'naked.'"

They stopped at an abandoned railway cart parked outside of a pair of tunnels reinforced with corrugated steel. You could hear the wind siphoning through the tunnels: a phantom roar, like the sound of a seashell. Painted on the wall between the tunnels were the words:

RAYBURNE MINING
CORPORATION

Digging

Toward

Tomorrow

Jasper directed them toward one of the tunnels, which smelled like urine; peering into it, Lana could see a person sitting in the middle of the tunnel, about halfway toward tomorrow. The person gazed—cross-legged, perfectly still—at the opposite wall. A brown sleeping bag was rolled up beside her.

Jasper handed Lana the radishes in his hand, then urged both her and Mr. Margolis inside. It didn't occur to her to resist. They were guests in this strange country; you did what the natives asked. The sound once she'd stooped inside the tunnel was considerably louder, a low-pitched organ-y drone that seemed to come from nowhere, or rather everywhere, as if she'd stepped into a didgeridoo. The person sitting in the tunnel was part of the sound, was maybe even creating it herself, the way a whale makes sounds without opening its mouth. Lana trained her eyes on the halo of light at the other end. Her sneakers crunched on the gravel, but the woman in the tunnel failed to move or look up. Even when Mr. Margolis sneezed—it smelled rancid in there, eye-wateringly bad, like a latrine—the naked woman failed to acknowledge it. Her body, unlike Jasper's, was white as a bone. As thin as one too: you could see the actual cage of her ribs. Her head, shaved nearly bald, was covered in insect bites.

Lana crouched down and dropped the radishes in her empty

bowl, but the woman didn't glance at her or move so much as an inch. Lana's heart seemed to have stopped moving too. It occurred to her that the woman might be dead. But she wasn't dead; she was sitting there with her eyes open. A living statue.

Lana backed away from the woman. Something radiated from her, the kind of heart-whistling emptiness Lana used to feel as a girl grabbing laundry from the basement or questing to the bathroom in the middle of the night. A similar fear snaked through her now: ancient and terrible, realer than she was somehow, as if everything true and good in the world—everything she'd thought would protect her, love and kindness and sanity— had turned out to be a hoax. Lana hastened back to the entrance and then stumbled free of the tunnel, feeling like she'd narrowly escaped with her life. Mr. Margolis, who'd emerged alongside her, seemed spooked as well, trembling as he put his sunglasses back on.

"Where's Jasper?" she asked.

Mr. Margolis glanced around helplessly. He patted the front pockets of his jeans, frisking himself.

Lana's throat went dry. "Tell me you have the key for your car. The fob."

"I left it in the cupholder, I think."

"Shit," Lana said, fearing the worst. She lived in Hollywood and knew plenty of recovering addicts. They retraced their steps through the abandoned mine—moving much faster this time, practically jogging—and returned to the barracks, startling some peahens pecking at the dirt. Sure enough, the Audi was gone. In its place sat the woebegone dog on its little dolly. The dreadlocked woman was there too, looking much less friendly. In fact, she looked like she wanted to cure the earth's cancer, starting with Lana and Mr. Margolis. In her hand was the half-eaten bag of Doritos, which she threw at their feet.

"The fiend has escaped."

They called a ride-share, a woman named Josefina, who took them into Twentynine Palms and then agreed to drive them around for a bit, Mr. Margolis paying her directly from his wallet. A rosary dangled from her rearview mirror, tilting to one side when she turned. It was a tiny town, the kind of place where the main street is as wide as a football field and no one seems to get out of their car even to eat. Rows of palm trees flamed in the wind. They passed a visitors' center, a food pantry, a casino that looked like a Walmart. The driver, who was very talkative—in fact, seemed to believe she was taking them on a tour of some kind—explained that the casino was owned by the Twenty-Nine Palms Band of Mission Indians, who were really Chemehuevi Indians; if they were interested, there was a Chemehuevi burial ground on Adobe Road.

"Where do people go to buy drugs?" Mr. Margolis asked.

The driver didn't answer him. In fact, she stopped talking to them at all. Nonetheless, she took them past some motels and divey-looking bars and then out beyond the center of town to where the road became highway again, unbroken by traffic lights; a guy was walking his bike along the shoulder, a jumble of plastic bags swinging from his handlebars. The driver pulled over abruptly. Mr. Margolis offered her fifty dollars to wait for them, and Josefina nodded unhappily, glaring at Lana, who debated staying in the car and letting Jasper's dad go on without her. She'd already endured far more on this trip than she'd bargained for. But she had that parched feeling in her throat, a kind of hangover-y thirst, as if everything they'd witnessed that day—Nautilus, the one-legged dog, Jasper's making off with his dad's car—were somehow her fault.

Lana grabbed one of the water bottles from the door pocket and followed Mr. Margolis outside, peering into the crater between the highway and some railroad tracks. Spreading across a scrubby strip of sand, under a canopy of stars, was an encampment of tents and tarps and dugouts rigged up with poles and cords and scraps of scavenged plywood, describing an inventive miscellany of shapes. A few of them had solar panels propped in front of them. The panels shone in the moonlight, like TV sets.

Mr. Margolis glanced at Lana, then took off his watch and stuffed it in his pocket. The man with the bike headed down a trail to the encampment, bags jostling as he walked; Lana and Mr. Margolis followed him, picking their way through broken glass. You could see the seam of mountains in the distance, lit pinkly by the Milky Way, which hovered over the tallest peak like a genie escaped from a bottle. When they reached the bottom of the berm, the guy with the bike turned to greet them, inquiring in a friendly Southern twang if they needed help. His hair was wet, slicked back behind his ears.

"We're looking for a boy," Mr. Margolis said. "A man, I mean." He described Jasper as best he could.

"Can't help you, I'm afraid. I've been at the Circle K, performing my ablutions." The man posed as if for a photograph, grinning. He was wearing a T-shirt that said MISSISSIPPI STATE. How far away from home he was—they all were.

"Is there a particular . . . spot for addicts?"

The man laughed. "Take your pick."

Lana and Mr. Margolis snooped around for a while, using the flashlight on his phone. They called Jasper's name, poking their heads into tents and tarps and shacks, even descending into a literal hole in the ground, an enormous burrow Lana might have mistaken for an animal's except for the two-by-fours bolstering the ceiling. She would not have imagined yesterday that she'd walk into a human fox den, let alone in the middle of the night—would not have imagined it, frankly, in a million years—and yet here she was doing it, of her own free will. Most everyone they looked in on was asleep, zipped into a sleeping bag. The smell, the poverty, the sense of general trespassing:

it didn't seem that different from Jasper's commune. The more Lana looked around, the more natural it all seemed to her, inevitable really, as if the truly unnatural thing was living in an apartment, a house, pumping water through the ground—through an aging labyrinth of pipes—so that someone could spray herself with it and take a shit indoors. That ancient fear snaked through her again, tingling her scalp; she could almost hear the didgeridoo sound in her ears. She had the eerie feeling—roaming these homes built from nothing, from the earth's surfeit of debris—of having emerged from the other end of the tunnel.

Eventually they came to a glowing plywood shack with a tattered American flag stuck to the top of it. Inside was a woman cooking something on a camp stove, squatting next to a framed replica of *The Blue Boy*, though in the replica for some reason the boy's outfit was green. Mr. Margolis asked her if she'd seen Jasper.

"Skinny guy? With a face?"

What did this mean? Lana had no idea. Nevertheless, they followed the woman's directions, walking around an open pit of trash and finding their way to a small tent not far from the train tracks. A guy sat in a lawn chair outside the tent, illuminated by one of those rechargeable lanterns and surrounded by what looked like the contents of a storage unit: lamps, golf clubs, a vacuum cleaner with a red bow tied around its neck. Death metal roared from a radio in his lap. The guy had his eyes closed, nodding softly to the music as if it were Vivaldi. Mr. Margolis asked him if he'd seen Jasper, and the guy dropped the radio in his lap and took off running, hopping over the train tracks and vanishing into a ditch on the other side.

Lana poked her head inside the tent, where a shirtless man lay facedown beside a pile of boxes, shivering as if he had a fever. In front of him was a cookie of vomit. He tried to lift himself up on all fours, using his elbows for leverage, like a baby doing tummy time.

"Jasper?" Lana said.

"Dad," he said, paying no attention to her. Mr. Margolis had crawled inside the tent and was kneeling beside him. "Where are you?"

"I'm right here."

"Dad. Dad Dad Dad Dad."

Jasper began to cry. Still kneeling, Mr. Margolis shone the flashlight right into his eyes, inspecting his pupils, then grabbed one wrist to check his pulse.

"Heart rate's okay. Do you need Narcan?"

Jasper shook his head. "I was just dreaming about this animal. The godflow. It's like a wolf dog, get it? But it experiences time backward. It gets smaller and smaller and then gives birth to its parents. When it's a pup. Of course, to him, the godflow, they're actually his children."

Mr. Margolis helped him out of the tent and then steadied him as he wobbled upright on one foot, holding him around the waist. Jasper put his head on Mr. Margolis's shoulder. Lana switched off the radio. She offered Jasper the bottle of water, but he ignored it completely, clinging to his father. He had no interest in her whatsoever. One of his feet, black with dirt, seemed to be bleeding.

"You didn't bring shoes?"

"I lost my fanny pack," Jasper said, patting his waist.

"Where's the car?"

He shrugged.

"You have no idea where the fucking car is?" Lana said.

Mr. Margolis shot her a look. "We'll find it *tomorrow.*"

"What?"

"We can stay at a hotel or something."

"I need to go back," Jasper whimpered.

"I saw a Days Inn. On the way into town."

"No, Dad! Please. They'll throw me out!" He started crying again.

"Okay. Shhhh. We'll figure it out in the morning."

Lana stared at Mr. Margolis. "I'm not spending the night in that creep-show cult. It's like Jainstown out there."

Mr. Margolis pulled the watch from his pocket. "At this point, it's practically sunrise." He seemed transformed, lighter somehow, as if Jasper were supporting him and not the other way around. "Let's get him dried out first. Back at the collective. I don't want him climbing out a motel window, looking for his fellow seahorses."

Jasper couldn't walk—his foot hurt too much—so Mr. Margolis hoisted him onto his back, gripping him under the legs and carrying him like that, as he must have done a thousand times before. It was a long walk back to the highway. Jasper's foot was dripping blood, or so it looked like in the dark. Lana resisted bringing up the path of four jewels, whether he'd strayed onto it by mistake. She was hungry and exhausted and pissed about the car. Mr. Margolis, on the other hand, seemed happier than she'd seen him all day—or at least more vivid and alive, tearing purposefully up the trail to the road, Jasper bouncing on his back like a little boy.

They couldn't all fit in the backseat, not with Jasper perching his foot on someone's lap to keep it elevated, so Mr. Margolis offered to take the front. Jasper seemed okay with this. He leaned back against the door, eyes invisible in the dark. He surprised Lana, on the ride back to the commune, by reaching for her hand.

"I'm sorry," she said quietly, staring at Jasper's foot in her lap. It smelled like roadkill. She felt her eyes tearing up again, though not from the smell.

"What for?"

She wanted to say, *For not realizing how much trouble you were in.* "You sent me those things in the mail," she said instead. "I never even emailed you back."

"And you can't forgive yourself."

She nodded.

"Poor sibling star," Jasper said, leaning toward her. She could smell the puke on his breath. For a second, his eyes flaring in the approaching headlights of a truck, Lana wondered if he might hurt her. She almost wanted him to. Instead he made a face at her, a gruesome one, the kind they used to make as kids, lolling his head to one side and crossing his eyes. Lana couldn't bring herself to make one back.

Jasper and Mr. Margolis shared the only mattress. There were no cushions to be had, not even a pillow, so Lana lay on the cold floor of the barracks and balled up the blanket Jasper had given her and slipped it under her head, shivering in the breeze from the broken window. It was like trying to sleep on an ice rink. Not that she planned to sleep anyway. She didn't trust these freaky insect worshippers. Her shoulder ached. Also her head. Also her heart.

Mr. Margolis was telling a story about some crazy French guy who ate a baby. Jasper had insisted he tell it. Begged him, as if his life depended upon it. Mr. Margolis had sighed, but Lana could tell he was pleased—or at least pleased to be spending the night this way in some creepy desert commune, telling bedtime stories to his strung-out son. He really was depressed, if this was the best thing to happen to him in a while. It made Lana miss her own father, the way he used to tell her about the wolverines he'd been tracking or make up funny stories about the Washburns next door. Her mom, too—though she drove Lana crazy sometimes. She'd been unhappy for so long, her mother. Though Lana was beginning to think it wasn't unhappiness her mother suffered from so much as *happiness*, or at least an idea of it that didn't exist. If she admitted to being happy, what would she aspire to anymore? The last time she'd visited LA, her mother had complained the whole time about "the jerkwaterness" of

Montana—the lack of art museums, of ethnic food, of footwear that wasn't waterproof—then seemed secretly relieved when it was time to fly home.

It was like that Russian movie with the magic room in it, the one that supposedly grants you your deepest desire in life. But what if your deepest desire in life was *not* to fulfill your deepest desire in life? What if it was, simply, to keep on desiring it?

What would be in Lana's magic room? Sleep. A bed that dissolved her into a puddle. Lana listened to the sound of Mr. Margolis's voice, its reedy rise and fall, anything to put her mind off the scorpions she imagined were setting up camp in her sneakers. If only her agent could see her now, how guilty she'd feel. What was this agent's name? Lana didn't remember. Her mind wasn't working. Mr. Margolis's voice feathered away like smoke, leaving Lana alone in the dark. Except it wasn't dark. A light hovered in the distance. She must have been dreaming, because she was in that tunnel again with the naked woman, the woman who refused to move. The bowl at her feet was full of popovers, the kind Lana's mother used to make on Sunday mornings. They smelled like Montana. Lana approached the woman, very slowly, no longer scared but trembling with joy. The light in the distance blinded her, like the beam of a flashlight. That was where the room was. The hidden room, the room with the rain inside of it. She didn't want to look at the woman, but her legs, thin as a lamb's, were in the way. They were spread open, exposing the woman's vagina. It was the biggest vagina Lana had ever seen. There was something being mined in there. That was the sense Lana had: that something was being pulled out of the woman, something old and not of this earth, maybe even older than the solar system itself, like the diamonds found in meteorites. "The celebrity actress doesn't have all day," Nautilus said suddenly, in the voice of the awful woman with dreadlocks.

Lana woke up with a jolt. Goats bleated outside. How long

had she been asleep? It felt like a minute but had clearly been hours. The window was pale with light. Jasper and Mr. Margolis were asleep, brought face-to-face by the sagging mattress.

Lana sat up slowly, still half-submerged in her dream. *The celebrity actress doesn't have all day.* Okay, fair enough. No argument there. Lana stared at Jasper, whose face in the brittle light looked like it had been crushed and smoothed out again, like a piece of paper rescued from the trash. If she died tomorrow, what could she say to justify being born? That she'd been in a couple dumb TV shows? Acted in a video game, for which she'd been painted turquoise? Been in love with a few women, then driven them away with her neediness, her sleeping around? None of these seemed to justify bumping the population by one, the damage she caused simply rolling out of bed every morning.

What on earth had she been doing? Literally: what, on this earth, had she been doing?

Something sounded from outside. Footsteps. Lana sat there on the floor, listening to their approach. Her heart was pounding, though she couldn't say why. You could live out here, pretending to be dead, or you could make a fucking impact. Make sure the earth remembered you. Anything in between was a waste of space. A peacock screamed from somewhere: a dreadful sound, like a leprechaun being murdered. The light in the window darkened. And then a familiar voice, the one from her dream:

"Rise and shine, Jasper's maker! Rise and shine, Lana Meek! Rise! Shine!"

TWENTY-TWO

Garrett hiked up Canyon Creek, trying to get to a good prospect of the valley, where he could point his radio antenna and hopefully get a signal. He'd been signal-less for a week and a half. Not even a cheep. It was June, an unseasonable eighty-two degrees in the park. But everything was unseasonable these days. That was the problem. Garrett had seen martins, a band of goats, even some moose tracks near the defile of the creek. But no wolverines. Every so often, he stopped and rubbed a deer leg he'd scavenged from roadkill on the scree littering his path, trying to create a scent trail. Anything to lure Q14 out of hiding. It was an act of desperation more than practical science. Best as anyone could tell, there were only four gulos left in the park—the rest had died, or fled to colder climes, or been marked down as "fate unknown." Soon, if you wanted to find a wolverine in the US, you were going to have to fly to Alaska.

Near Cracker Lake, Garrett veered through a boulder field and climbed a talus slope so he could shoot the transmitter down into the drainage. He wheezed a bit on the ascent. The AQI was in the low hundreds—these days, they got smoke from Oregon starting in May—but it was enough to bother him, squeezing his throat so that it felt like he was breathing fire. The wheeze revved into a cough. Garrett had to sit down for a minute and let the cough run its course: a bit of a shaggy-dog thing, long and disjointed, with several trick endings that left him hacking again, harder than before. He'd turned into his father at last.

Incredibly, Garrett had outlived him. He was sixty-three.

It felt good to rest his knee for a bit. To the west, below Piegan

Peak, he could see the cirque basin that held Piegan Glacier—or had for seven thousand years. It was bald now, as gray and snowless as the desert. It still took him aback to see it like that: a tug of grief. Of course, they were almost all gone now, the glaciers, melted to nothing or dwindled into snow patches. At this point only Blackfoot was left, and Harrison, both in rapid retreat. Garrett tightened his knee brace to relieve the pain. Charlie had warned him not to get surgery, but Garrett had done it anyway, refusing to believe that he had osteoarthritis and couldn't be helped. But of course he did, and couldn't.

Carefully, he stood up again and unfolded the Yagi antenna and plugged it into the receiver. He turned the gain up to MAX, searching for signals near and far. He moved the antenna back and forth, slow as a metal detector. Nothing. Static. Story of his days. Increasingly, Garrett felt like one of those kooks out looking for a beast that didn't actually exist. A cryptozoologist, tracking the Yeti. He hiked farther up the talus and pointed the antenna toward the south bank of the drainage.

Remarkably, the receiver began to cheep. Garrett's heart lurched. The yearling had been MIA for fifty-three days. Garrett, an atheist, had begun praying for her survival; just last night, lying in his cot in the ranger station, he'd whispered, "Please, God, let me know Vincent's fate." He'd named Q14 this—Vincent, after Vincent van Gogh—because she'd had her left ear bitten off while fighting a grizzly. Actually, Garrett had no idea if it was a grizzly who'd wounded her, but he'd begun to mythologize the animal for reasons he couldn't explain. He'd always had a curious thing for Q14. They'd trapped her as a kit in her mother's den, when she was still white as a polar bear, and even then she seemed scrappy and resourceful, trying to bite through the stitches where they'd implanted a radio. Garrett had lain awake all night, worried about the incision coming unglued, her tiny insides spilling out.

It was an Adam and Eve situation really. Vincent and P19, the last breeding wolverines in the Lower 48, needed to mate. They needed to find each other and get on with it, or it was sayonara to the gulos in the park. This would be the final generation.

Garrett checked the receiver again, because there was something strange about the signal, something he was just now wrapping his mind around. It was cheeping double-time. The mortality alert. The radios were programmed to do this if the animal hadn't moved for a long time.

The radios malfunctioned all the time. In hot weather, like today, it probably meant that Vincent had gone swimming in a creek, or maybe in Cracker Lake, and the thing had gotten cold enough that it short-circuited. Past a certain temperature, the radios liked to slip into mortality mode.

Plus the bearing for Vincent kept bouncing around, as if she were moving. It was hard to tell. She was so far away—almost two miles—that it was hard to get a fix. Garrett turned down the gain on the receiver, trying to get a more precise reading, but the cheeps faded into static.

He hiked back to the truck, then drove to the ranger station to tell Piper what he'd found. Piper reacted to the news appropriately. She screamed. She jumped up and down. They'd been looking for Vincent for a long time. She stopped jumping when he told her about the mortality signal, though Garrett emphasized that he believed the radio was on the fritz. The wolverine seemed to be moving around—though it was possible, too, that the readings were faulty.

"In other words, she might be dead."

"She's not dead," Garrett said.

"But it's called a 'mortality signal' for a reason."

"Look, I know Vincent. I've known her since she was a week old. She likes to keep us on our toes."

Piper looked at him doubtfully. What did she know? A grad student from Missoula, volunteering for the summer! Of course, he was a volunteer too. At this point, everyone was. Funding for the project had dried up many years ago; they'd kept it limping along for a while, squeaking by with micro-grants from private donors, but eventually they couldn't afford the running expenses it took just to man the traps. GPS collars, alone, were three thousand bucks apiece. Park officials ended up pulling the plug, unhappy with how little hard data they were seeing and with how much the researchers were handling the animals. That was the explanation anyway, but from Garrett's perspective it looked a lot like giving up. The population was dying out anyway; why waste the park's resources on something hopeless?

In the end, he'd used a small chunk of Cece's inheritance and started the study up again himself. His wife had offered the money, and he had accepted it. "Why wolverines?" she'd asked him once, in the early years of their marriage, and Garrett had not been able to answer her. He'd told her that if he was sixty and still obsessing over them—if people started calling him, say, "the wolverine guy"—she had his permission to strangle him. But that's exactly what had happened. Not the homicide part, but the rest of it. Incredibly, he was in his sixties; a recent article in the *Billings Gazette* had referred to him as Mr. Wolverine; he was still chasing after gulos, luring them into traps in order to try to figure out where they'd been and understand them an iota or two better than before. To be honest, Garrett couldn't really explain it himself. Certainly there were bigger problems in the world than the disappearance of an animal most people couldn't identify from a photograph. He might just as easily have ended up devoting his life to lynxes, or bull trout, or yellow-bill cuckoos. But no: he'd mistaken the world's Quick-Pick lottery for fate. And then of course he'd had to spend the rest of his life justifying it, convincing himself it was meant to be. Like Cece and her baboons.

In darker moods, of course, he saw his vocation differently. It did not seem like a fluke at all but a life sentence, masochistically imposed. He could have picked an easier animal to track. But he'd chosen wolverines, the stealthiest animal in the park. Cece called them his "invisible friends." Which meant a life, basically, of searching.

Hunting for something in the snow.

Garrett drove the pickup out to Canyon Creek, then hiked the trail with Piper through the benchland, taking reading after reading, trying to pinpoint Vincent's location. Piper watched him sweep the antenna back and forth, perhaps sensing, rightly, that she shouldn't interfere. She was not beautiful—she was too tall and gawky and fretful for that, hunching around the great outdoors as if she were being bombarded by bats—but there was always a transformative intimacy that arose when you were sharing a cabin with someone. The quirks of their appearance began to seem less quirky and more inevitable, more like an accurate representation of the beauty inside of them. How strange someone's face is, until it's not strange at all. You look at each other and laugh; you start to feel a bit drunk all the time; you excuse the things—habits, opinions—that would ordinarily bother you. You feel like the last two people on earth. In Garrett's case, the intoxicant could be a woman or a man; it had happened with both. In the past, he'd combated this feeling by imagining he had a GPS collar on. He actually did this. He pictured himself with a radio on, then did some mental telemetry and imagined he could track himself a month later, after he'd gotten back from the field. That had always been his strategy: to point his antenna into the future, a month from now. And he could never imagine a scenario, once he'd returned to the world, in which he'd rather be somewhere else than in his own house—rather be with a research partner than with his own family. With Cece and Lana. Not even close. It was a way of sobering himself up. Because that's the way you lived 90 percent of your life, if you wanted to avoid hanging yourself: sober. Even when he found out about

Charlie and Cece, he'd kept his imaginary collar on, resisting the temptation to fuck someone else. Why? Because he didn't want to. He needed Cece more than she needed him.

Garrett hiked up a skid trail a ways to get another reading while Piper stayed behind, leaning against a krummholz fir. She stooped against the wind, her hair flagging in the precise tilt and direction of the tree's branches. Of course, Garrett was far too old for her anyway. The days of intoxication were over. He was no longer of breeding age. He walked back down to where Piper was standing, ignoring the pain in his knee. According to his triangulations, Vincent was lurking on the other side of Canyon Creek, hidden among a forest of young spruce.

"She's not moving," Piper said, watching him repeat his findings.

"Might be localizing for some reason."

"In June?"

"Anyway, she was moving before," Garrett said. "I tracked it from Cracker Lake."

"I thought you said the signal was unreliable."

"No, no, it was pretty clear. Unambiguous. She was up and moving."

Piper gave him a curious look, as if he were a teacher who'd misspelled a word on the board. "Do you think you might be, um, biasing your readings?"

"What are you? Twenty?" he asked.

"You know how old I am. Twenty-four."

Garrett, who'd been fighting a burr in his throat, began to cough. He turned his back until the attack had passed; when he spun around again, Piper was looking at him with a note of pity. He saw himself, suddenly, through her eyes: one of those sentimental Doolittles, the kind who anthropomorphizes his subjects and begins treating them like pets. Whose data gets compromised because he starts leaving trap-bait out to help them through the winter.

"I've been doing this a hell of a lot longer than you," he said. "I know a fucking live gulo when I hear one."

Piper failed to respond. Garrett led the way back to the truck, which he drove down to the knickpoint of Canyon Creek, where it cascaded down an escarpment before entering the woods. He was being an asshole, but so what? He didn't care. He got out of the truck and began to traverse the escarpment with the receiver in one hand, listening to Vincent's frequency, which came from every direction now, cheeping more and more loudly as he switchbacked down to the tree line. Piper followed behind him, keeping her distance. Garrett's heart was pounding. It should have been even hotter at the tree line, below the alpine zone. Certainly he was sweating. Was he shivering too?

The radio signal was coming in too strong. He turned the gain down all the way but still couldn't get directionality. To lower the sensitivity, Garrett disconnected the Yagi and tracked with the receiver only, creeping into the forest, his boots crunching softly on the duff. He followed the signal across the creek, wading through knee-high water to a stand of larch on the opposite bank, where the cheeps from the receiver jumped an octave. Soon the meter was going bananas, showing full bars. He felt parched and strange and sick with fear.

Snow began to fall—huge flaked, evil—swirling all around him. It was over eighty degrees.

"Onion?" Piper asked.

Garrett looked at her helplessly.

"Do I need to call 911?"

"No. It's not that." He handed her the equipment. She was right, of course: he could hear the flies from here. "I just . . . I don't think I can look."

IV

THE HIDDEN MEADOW

TWENTY-THREE

Cece did not remember exactly when the whispering had started, though she remembered what she'd been doing at the time: walking Aristotle on the forest road behind the house. A human voice, frail but urgent—or so it sounded. She'd stopped in the middle of the road to listen. She'd imagined plenty of things in her life, usually when she'd had trouble sleeping and felt like she hadn't fully decamped from her dreams. But this was different. The whispering did not spring from her head, she was sure of it, though neither did it seem to spring from anywhere else. It was just there at her ear, private as a secret. Cece couldn't make out the words: only the sound itself, *wish wish wish*, like someone muttering in their sleep.

She'd heard it again last weekend, hiking in Jewel Basin. Maybe this was why she'd taken a wrong turn on a trail she'd hiked fifty times before. Or maybe it was something else entirely. In any case, she'd gotten lost. She'd meant to stop at Picnic Lakes for lunch, a painless four-mile loop, but had somehow hiked past them without noticing; when she tried to retrace her steps, she ended up on a trail she'd never seen before, switchbacking into a burned-out ravine overgrown with fireweed. She was almost out of water and hadn't thought to bring a map with her. Cece sat in the fireweed and tried not to panic. She'd felt this way as a girl once, separated from her parents at Disneyland: as if she'd stepped through a door somehow, into a perilous alien world. She could die in this world. It was September and beginning to get cold in the mountains—though not as cold as it used to get, when you had to pack for surprise snowstorms—and Cece could see her breath. It misted in front of her, vanishing almost as soon as it appeared.

She got up again and wandered for a long time before encountering another hiker, a park ranger, who shared his water with her and escorted her back to Picnic Lakes. She'd met the ranger before, through Garrett—but Cece was too humiliated to bring this up. By the time she got back to the trailhead, it was an hour past dark. Garrett, waiting for her at home, had been about to go out looking.

This wasn't the first mistake she'd made. It was the second or third. There had been the morning she'd yelled at Garrett for losing Aristotle's food dish, even though Cece was the one who fed him twice a day and gave him his pills. Well, turns out she'd put the dish, full of kibble, in the fridge! Who would do such a thing? Or the time she was making Moroccan chicken for dinner and couldn't seem to follow the recipe, as if it had transformed itself, maliciously, into an algebra problem. She got so tangled up in the steps that she felt like crying.

But it was the hiking fiasco that had made Garrett insist she call the doctor. She hadn't even told him about the whispering. But she'd called and talked to her general practitioner—or at least her GP's receptionist, who'd set up an appointment with someone new. Her old GP, who for years had been telling her to get more flavonoids into her diet, flavonoids this and flavonoids that—Cece and Garrett had called him Flavor Flav—had apparently died.

"Oh my god," Garrett said. "How did he die?"

"Pancreatic cancer. Very sudden, she said." Cece looked at him. "What?"

"Nothing."

"You were about to say something about flavonoids, weren't you? Make a joke."

"I wasn't," he said. "I wouldn't."

"You and your wolverines!"

What did she mean by this? Even Cece didn't know. He'd basically retired—hadn't gone wolvering in several years. Garrett ended up driving her to the doctor's office; not only that, he insisted on accompanying her to the lobby and waiting like a concerned parent while she had her appointment. Dr. Plattner, her new GP, found Cece in an examination room. The doctor was young—fresh off her residency, it looked like—and had the sort of freckled outdoorsy face Cece associated with ski lift operators, people who thought being a birth coach someday would be super rewarding and maybe found couples over sixty "cute." That was the vibe Cece was getting. A kind of snowboarder-with-a-heart-of-gold thing. She wasn't being fair, but Cece didn't care. It had been hard enough to admit to the receptionist why she'd wanted an appointment; now she had to repeat the story about getting lost in the woods to this thirty-year-old Patagonia model. She found herself downplaying it, failing to mention the whispering or the fact that she'd run out of water. Turning it into an anecdote, a funny thing you might tell at a party. At some point, Cece realized that Dr. Plattner had already heard the story from her receptionist and was perhaps weighing the discrepancies between the two versions.

"Is there a history of dementia in your family?"

"No," Cece said before explaining how her mother had died. "My grandmother lived to be eighty-seven, sharp as a tack. And my dad died of a heart attack . . . at sixty."

"And his parents?"

"I'm not sure. He was estranged from them. His dad was kind of bonkers."

"Bonkers?"

"Head trauma, they think—got mugged on a trip to Europe and was beaten with his own umbrella . . ." She trailed off. Dr. Plattner was staring at her. Only now did it occur to her that this story might be suspicious: a way of explaining something less fathomable.

"What I'd like to do is give you a short three-part test," Dr. Plattner said. "But it's important not to jump to any conclusions about the results. It's not a diagnosis or anything, just a way of seeing if maybe we should investigate further."

"What kind of a test?"

"It's called the Mini-Cog."

"As in 'miniature cognition'?"

"I believe so," Dr. Plattner said, smiling.

Cece was showing off. Of course, this whole thing was absurd. So why was she so nervous? Her hands were trembling.

Dr. Plattner asked her to repeat three words. "Apple," "house," "chair."

Cece laughed. "That's it?"

"Please repeat them if you can."

"Apple, house, chair," Cece said genially. She felt a wave of relief. Dr. Plattner handed her a pen and some paper, then asked her to draw a clock.

"A clock?"

"A clock like you might see on the wall. Draw it so it says eleven ten, please."

"A.m. or p.m.?"

"Good question. Hmmm. I guess it doesn't matter, does it?"

Cece drew a circle, then hesitated. When was the last time she'd seen an actual clock? They didn't have one at home. And she'd never worn a watch in her life. Cece wrote in the numbers no problem, beginning with the "12" at the top and working her way around full circle, 2-3-4, etc., all the way to 11, but when it came time to draw the hands she had some trouble picturing their positions. She drew the long hand pointing at the 11, then realized it would be the short hand, then realized it would have to point not directly at the 11 but somewhere between the 11 and the 12. And the long hand would be at the 10. No, the 1.

No, 2! By the time she'd finished, she'd drawn so many hands that the clock looked like a bicycle wheel.

"I'm sorry," she said, flustered. Her heart was pounding. "It's been a very long time since I looked at an actual clock."

"Of course. Anyway, you did fine."

"How is that fine?" Cece said, close to tears.

Later, Dr. Plattner asked her to repeat the three words she'd told her to memorize earlier.

"House, apple . . . ," Cece said. "House, apple . . ." Something curdled in her throat. What was the third one? Jesus Christ, hadn't she been paying attention? Her tongue felt strange in her mouth. "Could you repeat the words?"

"I'm afraid not, sorry," Dr. Plattner said.

"Ha, right. It's just that it took a lot longer to do the clock than I thought. It distracted me from what you said earlier." She looked at Dr. Plattner, realizing that that was the whole point of the clock test. Or one of them. The examination room, with its charts and strange instruments, had started to look unreal, almost sinister. "Thing is, I remember so many things. Almost everything. Random facts I've learned. Like in World War I, if a soldier lost his nose in battle—did you know this?—if a soldier lost his nose somehow, like in a blast, surgeons would sew one of his fingers to his face. Attach it to the place where his nose used to be. Then, when it grafted to his face, they'd cut off his finger and leave it there."

Dr. Plattner stared at her.

"You don't believe me?"

"It just sounds, I don't know, far-fetched."

"It's *true*," Cece said.

Dr. Plattner jotted something down on her chart. Infuriatingly, she was still smiling. "I guess plastic surgery's come a long way."

"Rhinoplasty, yes. Leaps and bounds." Cece blushed. Why was she talking this way? Dr. Plattner scribbled something else in her chart. "I don't know why I mentioned it. Still. Just funny to think about. Like I wonder if their noses were . . . ugh, what do you call it? Able to grab things? Like an elephant's trunk."

Dr. Plattner nodded at her. Then she said she was going to refer Cece to a neuropsychologist. The results of the test didn't mean anything at this point. It was important to remember that. But she thought it would be a good idea to see another doctor, a specialist, for further evaluation. She handed Cece a pamphlet, explaining that it was about ways to keep her brain healthy. The pamphlet was called *The Six Pillars of Alzheimer's Prevention*.

"I want a different doctor," Cece fumed after she'd walked with Garrett to the car. The computer display on the VW was black again, failing to respond at all; they waited for it to reboot. Who was giving the car cognition tests? Humiliating it for no rhyme or reason? She crumpled the pamphlet, unread, and threw it on the floor.

"What did she do?"

"Made me draw a clock!"

Garrett looked at her.

"I mean, when's the last time you even saw a clock? Anyway, I know how to draw one. It's just that I got flustered. More and more flustered. And I kept fucking up. I told her, 'We don't have any wall clocks at home!'"

"That's true."

"I told her about the nose thing, how they used to replace soldiers' noses with their own fingers in World War I. Didn't they used to do that?"

"Why in god's name did you tell her that?"

"I don't know!" She started to cry. "And then I couldn't think of that word. I was joking about having a nose like a finger. One that you could move around. But I couldn't think of the name for it. For an elephant's trunk—you know, how it can grab things on its own?"

"Prehensile?"

Cece stiffened, as if he'd somehow betrayed her. He was her life's companion. Her mother had died and she'd landed somehow at his feet. She'd seen a comic strip once of a doctor snipping an umbilical cord: the baby gusted around the delivery room losing air, like a balloon deflating.

"I forget words like that all the time," Garrett said.

Dr. Plattner emerged from the building with another white-coated woman, perhaps on their way to lunch.

"Look! There she is. God, I fucking hate her."

"Which? Putting on sunglasses?"

"I could strangle her with my bare hands," Cece said.

Garrett looked at the pleasant-looking woman in sunglasses crossing the parking lot. He was scared—a cold, embryonic fear—but he didn't tell Cece that. He had a pathological need to cheer her up. To make her laugh. It was not the opposite of fear but its demented companion. It was marriage. He put his hand where his nose was, hiding it with his fist, then lifted one finger slowly, flipping Dr. Plattner the bird.

Before this—before she'd gotten lost in the wilderness and then failed a stupid test at the doctor's—Cece had been waking up with a feeling of sunshine on her face. Not sunlight through the window, but bona fide sunshine. She'd lie there for a bit while Garrett slept, feeling that pleasant tingling warmth on her face, like a mask you never want to take off. It was nothing like the sun actually felt these days, its oven-y scorch. No, it was a feeling from her childhood, back when she and the sun were friends. That old approving warmth in her body.

Cece wondered if this meant she was happy. Who knew? She'd never really understood what was meant by it, happiness, except in relationship to being unhappy. Sometimes she'd lie in bed and imagine the mysterious warm feeling was coming from the little sun in the orrery on her dresser, the one Garrett had given her for their anniversary. She used to move the miniature planets around every day, for no real reason—though she hadn't in years and the brass arms had rusted fast, or at least Earth's had. It had gotten stuck where it was: isolated from the other planets, like a reject at school. Cece loved the orrery but particularly the reject Earth. It was painted like a tiny globe, with continents and everything. They'd had a cat for a while—Bucket—who used to hang out on the dresser and lick the meticulous planets, especially Earth, which for some reason tasted the best. Perhaps he mistook it for prey. This went on for a long time, weeks, before Garrett mentioned the paint was probably full of lead.

Bucket was with Lana now, enjoying a lead-free retirement. Sometimes Cece thought of the two of them in LA, sheltering in Lana's Spanish Colonial flat, and missed Lana so much her heart grabbed. She could visit any time she wanted to, of course. Cece used to love going to see her, insisting they spend every second soaking up the city, going to restaurants or bakeries—real tacos! real croissants!—or catching movies that would never make it to Salish. Lately, though, she found herself insisting Lana fly to Montana instead. The traffic, the constant fires, the haze of hipness that seemed more and more like the punch line to a joke everyone had forgotten. After a day or two, she'd find herself longing for their humble house in the country, the crunch of gravel under the VW's tires and Aristotle's bulleting out of the gate like a racehorse, the view of Mount Aeneas in the distance making whatever you'd just bought in town seem slightly foolish, even perverse.

Provided it wasn't a red-alert day and you could see the peak at all. Cece often felt guilty for feeling happy—or whatever you wanted to call it—given the state of things. You couldn't read *The New York Times* without despairing at the latest drastic revelation and also somehow feeling like it was redundant, like you knew about it beforehand. Heat deaths in London? Devastating monsoons in Pakistan? Hundred-year floods, wreaking havoc in Lima and Dar es Salaam? Another fascist prick here in the

States, riding the migrant crisis to power? Everyone knew these things would happen, smart people had been predicting them for years, and yet the world—or at least the assholes running it—seemed uninterested in stopping them. So she'd given it up: the news. She wouldn't even listen to it in the car.

This summer, instead of fires, they'd been battered by storms. Everything would be calm and clear and lovely, the world as tranquil as a picnic, a few dark clouds lounging in the distance, then Aristotle would start to whine and cower and circle the porch, the sky darkening like an eclipse, the clouds gathering into a mass, thundering impatiently, beginning a cavalry charge toward the house, and then boom: ninety-mile-per hour winds. This was the real news, delivered to your doorstep. Rain would machine-gun the windows, flooding the house. Cece and Garrett would spend the next couple hours wringing out towels, trying to keep the rain from pooling on the floors. Never before had they so much as leaked, the windows, but everyone said this now: never before, never before. Never before had so many trees come down. The force involved! Two-hundred-foot spruces and pines, ripped out of the ground like weeds. It was no longer a matter of whether a power line would be taken out, but how many lines. There'd been so many blackouts this year, Cece had lost count. They seemed to last longer each time, which meant the well pump was out of commission sometimes for days; Cece and Garrett would run around the house like the Marx Brothers, slipping on rain-flooded floors, filling every container they could find with water before the pressure dried up.

Now, after failing Dr. Plattner's test, she dropped Garrett at home and drove into town with Aristotle in the back, feeling guilty for blasting the air-conditioning. Eighty-five degrees. Yesterday the high had been fifty-one. Cece stopped at a red light outside of town, behind a van with the logo of a smiling house on it. A cleanup service, for water and fire damage. You saw more and more of these trucks: a booming industry.

She parked in the lot behind the bookstore, next to the gas-powered Jeep that Lexie had inherited from her parents. The Jeep was mosaiced in bumper stickers that Cece didn't understand, derived—she suspected—from internet memes. A unicorn with a marshmallow impaled on its horn. SUBMIT TO THE KUMQUAT. An Adam and Eve with their genitalia transposed, which Cece guessed had to do with genderism, or Christofascism, or both. Probably this didn't make Lexie's life easy in Salish, though of course the girl didn't live in Salish—she lived in her phone.

"How's it going?" Cece asked. It was Monday, a notoriously slow day for customers.

Lexie did not look up from her Origami, which she'd unfolded to the size of a greeting card. Cece tried not to be offended by this. She used to tell Lexie to turn off her phone, until she realized that no part of the command was legible to her. Nobody turned their Origami off; it was impossible. Also, no one under the age of forty called them phones. "Did you know that moths drink the tears of sleeping birds?"

"According to whom?"

"According to science," Lexie said. "To moths."

"I did not know that."

Cece waited in vain for a report of the morning, watching Lexie fold her phone into a pyramid and perch it delicately on the counter. Of course, this was where she'd heard the thing about the finger-replacement surgery: from Lexie herself. The girl sometimes seemed less like a human being and more like a backup drive for her Origami. She was lovely and thin as a heron and quite possibly a lunatic. When she wasn't reading her phone, she was whitening her teeth. You could basically see by them at night. Cece wondered if maybe she loved her Origami so much she was trying to turn herself into one.

Naturally, from Lexie's perspective, Cece was the one who was insane. Why else would she own a bookstore? Sometimes Cece wondered this herself. And yet the place was still in business, despite an endless parade of salesclerks: Meadow, the Buddhist, who'd vanished one day and then sent Cece a cryptic email from Peru; Guthrie, sweet lunk of a river guide, whose favorite book was *The Essential Calvin and Hobbes*; Nisha (wonderful Nisha!), who actually knew something about literature and could quote Roland Barthes; Dwindle Grimes, of the Dickensian name, which somehow sounded the way he made the employee bathroom smell; and now Lexie, twenty-year-old college student, home for the summer to visit her phone. (Cece had hired her largely on the basis of her bumper stickers.) Somehow the Light at the End of the Dock had survived them all—was, in fact, doing better than ever, even though it hadn't changed much since Meadow worked there. Sure, Cece had made some minor adjustments: there was now a Used Books section, surprisingly lucrative in Salish, where the dearth of trash collection was a boon to used-good purveyors of all stripes. But it seemed that the dire prognoses for all things analog, for all things brick-and-mortar, had not come to pass—that maybe the book was an invention that couldn't be improved upon. It folded in two ways: open and shut.

"I need you to place an order for me," Cece said, ransacking her pockets for a book title she'd written down and handing the slip of paper to Lexie, who peered at it as if it were an artifact of a lost civilization.

"Who for?"

"Townsend at the coffee roasters. He asked me to get it in."

"You mean Townes?"

"That's what I said." Cece stared at the glowing pyramid on the counter. On each of the three sides was the picture of a different guy, mugging drastically for the camera. One of them was shirtless—possibly naked. "I only popped in for a minute. Aristotle's in the car. Imagine being a Newfie in this weather."

"You could serve him a bloodsicle," Lexie said.

"What is a bloodsicle?"

"A frozen blood Popsicle. It's what they serve lions and tigers on very hot days."

"Lexie, where are you getting all this from?"

Lexie shrugged. It wasn't coyness: she sincerely didn't know. Facts were leaking out her ears.

"Go ahead and close early today if you want. Seems slow."

"Like when? Four o'clock?"

"Sure," Cece said, glancing at the clock above the travel section. Yes, of course: the clock. On the wall of the bookstore. Cece saw it every day she came in. Something lodged in her throat, like a bone.

Back at the car, she picked the crumpled-up pamphlet off the floor and smoothed it across the steering wheel. She read it carefully (or tried to). She felt sick enough that it was hard to focus. Tucked among the list of behaviors meant to forestall Alzheimer's was an anecdote about Catholic nuns; someone did a study of 678 elderly nuns, looking at essays they wrote as novitiates, when they first took their vows. The nuns who wrote the most fluent essays—using long, sophisticated, syntactically complex sentences—were the least likely to get Alzheimer's. Idea density, the scientists called it. Journaling, therefore, was the answer! The more you journaled, boosting the density of your ideas, the less likely you were to get Alzheimer's. But wasn't it just as likely that there was something about the nuns' brains to begin with, some congenital edge that impelled them to write longer sentences and ensured as an added perk that they wouldn't ever go nuts?

And the poor nuns who got it! After all those years of worship. If marrying Jesus couldn't keep you from going batshit crazy, then what good was a pamphlet?

Still, she folded it carefully and stuck it in the pocket of her coat.

Cece drove to the Salish River lookout and took Aristotle for a walk along the Wild Mile. It was hot and muddy on the trail, but Aristotle didn't seem to mind, running ahead to scare up animals or find the perfect rock to pee on. Far below them, roaring like static, brimming from all the storms they were having, the river along the Wild Mile boiled and frothed; just last week a kayaker had brained himself on a rock. Aristotle, splattered with mud, flushed a ground squirrel out of a shrub. Cece remembered what the trail used to be like when they'd first moved here, teeming with butterflies in particular. Cabbage whites. Whole clouds of them, rising from the ground like snow in reverse. And the birds! Aristotle would have had a field day. It wasn't unusual to see a ptarmigan strutting across the trail.

When's the last time she saw a ptarmigan here? Or, for that matter, a butterfly? Now it was mostly ground squirrels, and even they were dwindling, it seemed. She thought of the verse from Genesis she'd memorized in Sunday school, the one that had struck a gong of terror in her heart. *And the earth was without form, and void, and darkness was upon the face of the deep.* How could she still remember this, and not the word after "house" and "apple"? It wasn't death that scared her so much as oblivion, the face of the deep, that missing word that she'd never retrieve. One after another, the words going poof. Not a sudden death, but a gradual one, an accretion of losses, one you were in denial about until it was too late, the way the ptarmigans and butterflies had vanished somehow without her even noticing.

Maybe the world had it too: a memory problem. The density of its ideas was in freefall. She and the earth were in this together.

Indescribable, the dread she felt. As if she were going up in smoke.

Cece followed Aristotle into a patch of June grass between the trail and the river: a much calmer stretch of water, before it funneled into the mouth of the canyon. A fly fisherman had climbed down to the river and was whipping it with his line, oblivious to their presence. Cece sat in the grass while Aristotle caught his breath, panting with his tongue out. She lay down beside him. It smelled like warm earth. The whispering started up again in her ear, near and distant somehow at the same time. She could make out the voice now, what it was saying to her. "Come closer," it said. Yes, no doubt about it. Clear as a bell. *Come closer.* But it wasn't her mother's voice. It was like a voice from another room—or maybe from the front of the car when you're half-asleep in back. Cece closed her eyes. She had the oddest feeling, as if she were moving up and down.

———

On the way home, she passed another one of those cleanup trucks—or maybe it was the same one she'd seen earlier. They were everywhere. A slogan was written across the barn doors of the van.

LIKE IT NEVER EVEN HAPPENED.

———

That night, in her dreams, she flew around. The birds cried and cried in their sleep. She was very thirsty.

She woke up late, the parched feeling still in her throat. Garrett was already up. Cece parted the curtains and saw him in the front yard, kneeling at the edge of the grass and planting some bulbs along the fence, his brown head glowing in the sun. Aristotle lay in the grass beside him, like a tipped-over pommel horse. Garrett stopped for a moment and wiped his forehead on his sleeve. How like an old man he looked, digging in his garden. It was nice to see him outside without a mask on: rare these days, at least in the summertime. He spent most of his life indoors now—exactly what he'd been afraid of, when he retired—though honestly he'd probably still be up there with his Yagi if there were any wolverines left in the park. That was the real reason he'd stopped: there was nothing to find. The search was over. Cece would never tell him this, but she was secretly glad that they'd disappeared. She liked having him around, and not merely because she got lonely without him; there was a relief to it, even a novel hint of shyness. A sense that they were left only with each other. Call it sadness or surrender. She opened the window.

"What are you planting?" she called to him.

"Money!"

Cece laughed. For some reason—no reason, really—they called daffodils this. They'd become "duckbills" long ago— surely Lana was involved—which had turned into "dollar bills," which had evolved etymologically into "money." (The joke, of course, was that they never had enough and so had to grow it themselves.) And it wasn't just daffodils: they had their own secret language. Coffee had become "Carmichael," mysteriously enough, just like sex had become "draining the tub," dating from when Lana was small and they'd had to come up with a way of explaining why they were in the shower for so long. Cece had read about the Wixárika people in Mexico, who performed a renaming ceremony before harvesting peyote; they called the desert "ocean," the moon "sun," in order to enter a different world than their own. Maybe marriage was like that. Gradually you renamed the world and created a new one, one only you could enter. You turned flowers into money, took the lullaby of unexciting days and called it happiness.

Cece made some coffee for herself, then checked for texts on her old museum-piece of a phone. Lana called it her "ham radio," presumably because it didn't fold into shapes. Cece decided to call her. She needed to hear her daughter's voice. She used it like a compass sometimes, the way you might orient a map.

"Mom, I'm at the studio. I can't talk."

"Working?"

"We've got to finish the assembly cut by Friday."

"This is the film about whatever it's called? Transpersonism?"

"Transhumanism!"

"Right. About the people trying to become computers."

"Why can't you ever remember the name of it?"

"*The Daedalus Project*," she said proudly, then felt stupid. What was she, a game show contestant? Anyway, her daughter hadn't been asking if she remembered the name of the film itself, which after all Lana had been working on for four years. Somehow the girl had reinvented herself: gone from being a character actor in video games to a filmmaker, a documentarian, and an acclaimed one at that. Her first film—or at least her first feature-length one, about a homeless encampment out in the Mojave Desert—had won several prizes. *The New York Times* had called it "profoundly moving, even visionary in its way, as if Frederick Wiseman had teamed up with Tarkovsky." Whenever she learned of Lana's accomplishments, Cece of course felt extremely proud and happy—though there was also, if she was completely honest, a slight queasy feeling, a jab of envy. Lana had gotten herself to LA, bent on making her mark. When one life hadn't panned out, she'd jumped boldly into the next. And it had worked. Her boldness had paid off. She'd been more ambitious than her parents, or at least her mother, whose one true act of boldness—or what she'd mistaken for it—had revolved around love.

Marriage, the only adventure open to the cowardly.

And now here she was, feeling proud of herself for remembering the name of her own daughter's film! "I've got a transhuman you might want to interview. Lexie, at the bookstore? She's turning herself into a pho—an Origami."

"Mom," Lana said dismissively. "That's not really what it's about."

Cece bristled. Clearly Garrett hadn't mentioned anything to Lana—about the doctor's visit, about Cece getting lost—or else Lana wouldn't be talking this way to her. The fact that he'd kept it to himself made Cece even more frightened. Someone coughed in the background, then said something she couldn't make out.

"Is someone there with you?" Cece asked. "I thought you were working."

"Hello, Mrs. Meek," the voice in the background said.

"It's Mrs. *Calhoun*."

"Luciana brought me lunch."

"Is that your girlfriend?"

"She wants to know if you're my girlfriend," Lana said.

They both laughed. Seemed to find this quite funny. Cece couldn't keep track of the women—and occasional men—Lana was dating. Or sleeping with. Or whatever the appropriate term for it was. Monogamy seemed to be a thing of the past, a quaint dorky custom regarded by Lana's generation with pity and amusement, like check-writing or going to church. Was that partly Cece's problem? That she'd been born in the wrong era? That she'd spent her life, say, *collecting stamps*, without realizing they were obsolete?

"Did you know that moths drink the tears of sleeping birds?"

Silence. "You called to tell me that?"

"No. I mean yes. I just called to talk."

"Mom, I really have to go. I'll call you tomorrow."

"Okay."

"I love you, Mom."

"What?" Cece said, though she'd heard her perfectly.

———

Even though it was her day off again, Cece went by the bookstore and picked up several boxes of donations. She did this every month: thinned out the shelves of used books to make way for better ones—okay, maybe "better" wasn't the right word, given that Edith Wharton might lose out to, say, James Patterson, but "marketable"—then delivered the culled books to Lakeview Village, the nursing home on 93. Now that he was retired, Garrett usually helped. The boxes were heavy, and Cece found that loading them into the car by herself had recently become impossible, just as other things she used to take for granted—climbing the ladder to the attic, pulling volunteer saplings up from the yard— had become physically perilous. Today she let Lexie and Garrett do the lifting while she watched from the curb. Ever since her appointment with Dr. Plattner, she'd had trouble meeting Garrett's eyes; it had been like this when she'd first left Charlie, as if looking Garrett straight in the eye would turn them both to stone.

"Are you sure you want to get rid of *More Great Pantyhose Crafts*?" Garrett said, snooping through the box they'd just loaded.

"I have no idea where that came from."

"Well, you must have bought it from someone, right? A pantyhose crafter?"

"What's a pantyhose?" Lexie asked.

Cece looked at her, smiling. "God, I envy you."

At Lakeview Village, they dropped the boxes off at the assisted-living wing, which had its own library. It wouldn't have been a terrible place to end up, provided you had nowhere else to live. There was an enormous birdcage with chattering parakeets, a cozy gas fireplace blazing all year round, even a billiards table where Cece had once seen a palsied man and woman trying to sink balls, as if on a date. It was hard to imagine that people were dying in their beds—but they were, of course, if not here, then elsewhere on the premises. They died, and then the bodies had to be carted away so new people could take their rooms. There was a waiting list.

On the way back from the library, Cece stopped in front of a locked door that led to the memory care wing. Vintage Gardens, it was called. You needed a code to enter. Cece stared at the door.

"What are you doing?" Garrett asked.

"I want to check it out."

"Don't be stupid."

"I'm not being stupid. I'm being the opposite. Seeking knowledge."

He shook his head, keeping his distance.

"Okay, go back to the car then," she said.

"You're being silly."

"What are you waiting for? I said go back!"

The man spent his life around animals that wanted to rip his throat open, and here he was acting like a little sissy. Worse: a hypocrite. Wasn't he the one always ranting about the future and our refusal to face it? Humans blindfolding themselves to disaster? Cece peered through the window in the door, just in time to see a guy with a tool belt beep himself through.

She grabbed the door before it closed and stepped inside, not expecting Garrett to follow. But he did. He slipped in behind her. Together, they walked down the hall into a beige communal space that resembled the lunchroom of a country club, if the country club were maybe going out of business. No billiards tables here. The walls were bare except for a few paintings of trees done in an array of styles—realist, impressionist, expressionist—like options in a catalog. Cece suspected they'd been printed off the internet. A woman in a wheelchair sat in the middle of the room, waving one hand in the air and yelling, "Help! Help me! Help!" to a nurse behind the desk, who ignored her completely. Despite being snubbed, the woman kept on yelling for help. It seemed to be expected of her.

Cece chose not to intervene, partly out of respect for the nurse and partly because she felt like a trespasser. No one paid the slightest bit of attention to her; it was as if she and Garrett didn't exist. Gathered around a staff member, arranged in a semicircle, sat a group of five residents in varying stages of alertness. Each of them held a swimming pool noodle in their lap. Were they going for a dip? No, it was an exercise class. The staff member, a guy in a Lakeview Village shirt, was palming a balloon in one hand. "Look alive now," he said—apparently without irony—and tossed it to one of the more alert residents, who batted the balloon with her Styrofoam noodle, keeping it aloft. "It's all yours, Marybeth!" the staff member said to a different resident. Marybeth grinned at the sound of her name but made no effort to hit the balloon. It settled to the floor at her feet. Undaunted, the staff member picked up the balloon and turned to a different resident, a man with an intelligent face and bushy eyebrows, black as Stalin's. He might have been a distinguished professor of economics. The staff member tossed the balloon at the man, who stared intrepidly ahead as it bounced off his face. He didn't even flinch. Just sat there with his mouth open, like a beanbag target. Cece turned to the woman yelling for help, sensing that the woman's eyes had fastened on her.

"Yes?" Cece said.

"Do you know when we dock in Rotterdam?"

"Dock?"

"My son's coming to pick me up at nineteen hundred hours," the woman said, tugging Cece's shirtsleeve. "What if I get off in Hamburg!"

Normally, Garrett drove when the two of them were in the car, but on the way home Cece insisted on taking the wheel. She wanted to drive. Be in control for a change. She had no desire to talk to him. They rode home in silence, Garrett sipping some coffee he'd filched from the kitchen while Cece stared at the road, terror hollowing her veins. The hands on the steering wheel felt disconnected from her, otherworldly almost, as if they were someone else's. Were they trembling? To the west loomed the recurring dream of Salish Lake, as blue as aquarium gravel. The view astonished her. She'd lived here most of her life.

Something lumbered into the road. Cece slammed on the brakes, spilling the coffee in Garrett's hand. A black bear. It loped across the highway, clumsy almost in its lazy mechanical strength—or maybe not clumsy so much as golemlike, as if it had been born out of clay and were still mastering its limbs. Two cubs crashed out of the pines and trotted along behind it, ignoring Cece and Garrett completely. Their fur, sleek as oil, rippled in the sun. Cow and cubs took their sweet time crossing—they seemed to form one thing, the way that a comet has a tail—then disappeared into the trees on the other side of the highway.

Cece let out a breath. Weirdly, they never paid the slightest bit of attention to you, these bears. Like you weren't even there. It was why you felt so strange afterward.

How many bears had she seen in her life? *Fifty?* Most people saw exactly none. Cece turned to Garrett, whose lap was soaked.

"Are you all right?" she said, frightened he'd hurt himself. "Did the coffee burn you?"

"Nope. It was cold to begin with."

Cece pressed the gas again, edging back up to speed. The road was straight and deserted. "I want an Origami," she said after a bit.

"Why?"

"I just do. I want one tomorrow."

Garrett nodded, choosing to accept this. A small thing—and not small at all. Unfathomably, she started to laugh.

"What is it?"

"I don't know. Just thinking about those poor zombies with their pool noodles."

"Maybe don't call them 'zombies,'" Garrett said.

"Did you see that guy take a balloon in the face?" Cece said. "He didn't even blink."

"On the other hand, he was one of the few people who made contact."

Cece looked at him.

"You ought to see him play baseball," Garrett said innocently.

Cece laughed: a gust of relief. As long as they could still joke, everything would be okay. Ashamed, she thought about her outburst in the nursing home, when she'd yelled at him to go back to the car. Why had she been so pissed at him? Anyway, it didn't matter. She wasn't going to end up like those zombies, those people, doing balloon aerobics. If she was sure of anything, it was this. She would do everything the pamphlet prescribed. Exercise regularly. Start lifting weights. Cut out sugar, white flour, TV. Keep a journal every day, like those Catholic nuns. Learn a foreign language. No, two foreign languages. How lame was it that she couldn't speak French? And she'd always wanted to learn Russian, to read *Anna Karenina* in the original. Life mattered. It had dignity and purpose. There was some part of her—a Self, an essential Cece—that was immutable. Safe from corruption. The part of her that loved to swim; that came up with dorky aphorisms; that couldn't hear a song from her childhood, no matter how cloying or obnoxious, without leaping up to dance . . . What was life, if she lost that?

She wouldn't allow it! She'd do what the pamphlet said: Become a detective. Observe the world so closely, glom on to it so fiercely, that she'd never unglom. The important thing was to record and remember.

Practice the five W's, the pamphlet said. *Keep a "who what when why where" list of all your activities.*

Back at the house, Cece turned off the car while Aristotle barked at them from the yard, his muzzle wedged between the pickets of the fence. They sat there for a minute in the last light of day. Maybe it was the aftereffect of the bears, but everything looked different to her, seemed to glow damply of its own accord, as if Aristotle's walrus face and the hydrangeas drooping over the fence and the dogwood Cece and Garrett had planted themselves thirty years ago had just plopped into the world, naked and unseen. Increasingly she had this feeling: that the world was baring itself to her for the first time.

Garrett's head, brown as an almond, skimmed the roof of the car. He looked bigger somehow in the passenger seat: an overgrown child, knees wedged against the dash. A lamp was on in the bedroom window upstairs. Garrett was staring at it. Had she left it on herself? She was militant about conserving energy, always swept the house before they went anywhere, flipping off switches. Sometimes, out of instinct, Cece switched the lights off while Garrett was still in the room, trying to read. It drove him nuts.

He got out of the car, face bent toward the ground. Was he trying to avoid showing it to her? Of course not. Probably his knee was acting up again. He was simply minding where he stepped. Cece watched him walk, a bit haltingly, to the gate.

Who: Garrett Meek.

What: Her husband.

When: Till one of them dies.

Why: God knows; every reason; none at all.

Where: Salish, Montana. Home.

TWENTY-FOUR

How unlikely it is, to befriend anyone. The average person meets eighty thousand people over the course of their lifetime, nearly all of whom vanish without a trace. Good riddance in most cases—but also bad riddance, calamitous losses. We're lucky if we die with one or two close friends.

Garrett drove the road he used to skin up on skis, trying not to jostle Charlie too much, who was checking the air quality sensor on his wrist. It was February, but the snow was so thin—a twenty-one-inch base—that the road was more mud than slush, banked by scattered islets of snow. Fifty-eight degrees, warm enough to open the windows. The sun cooked Garrett's arm as he drove. He'd slathered it in sunscreen, as per his doctor's instructions, but still needed to be careful. He'd had three cancers removed already. All that time in the wilderness, slogging around outdoors, had done more than damage his lungs. Last year, Charlie had had a kidney scare that took him off salt for six months, but other than that he seemed remarkably fit. He'd quit drinking after Jasper died. For a while there, Garrett had worried he might tip in the other direction. It was one thing to be living alone at age seventy-four, another thing to be *grieving* alone—especially something like that. But Charlie seemed healthier than he had in a long time, physically, at least, and in fact had cut back on his drinking well before the tragedy.

Some of their friends had not been so lucky. Brig, amazingly, was still going strong—had even learned to talk again, more or less—but in general the old gang had not fared well. Johnny was dead from colon cancer. Marcus had had a heart attack three years ago, gotten a triple bypass. Gabby, who had macular degeneration, was going blind. Yet Garrett for some fucked-up reason—or, more likely, no reason at all—had gotten off okay. A gimpy knee, some basal cells. True, he struggled to breathe half the year—even indoors he got laryngitis, what Lana called his "smoky voice"—but he was hardly alone in that.

Garrett parked in front of the ski hut he used to backcountry at as a boy, not so different from the hut where they'd spent the last night of Elias's life. It looked twice as tall as he remembered it, probably because there was so little snow on the ground. Someone had redone the windows recently, installed solar panels on the roof. People used the hut for backpacking trips now, since you could hike all year round—or almost all year—and in fact the website barely mentioned skiing, cross-country or otherwise. Garrett had looked it up this morning. *Access a hundred miles of pristine hiking trails from your front door,* it said, and then under it: *OUR SINCEREST APOLOGIES BUT WE CANNOT REFUND MONEY BECAUSE OF SMOKE.*

Charlie zinced his nose, as fastidious as ever about sun protection. The AQI was only thirty-three, typical for winter, so Garrett left his respirator in the glove compartment and eased out of the car, feeling the old joyful diminishment he'd felt his entire life in the mountains, that sense of grateful irrelevance. A relief, really, from being human. In the distance, sharp as a dream, soared the craggy arrowhead of Mount Aeneas. The bowl was already half-bare, brown patches showing through the snow, like cigarette burns in a sheet. Mostly Garrett had skied around Missoula, in the Bitterroot, but occasionally he and his friends would drive all the way up here, crash at his grandfather's for a night before hitting the backcountry. A few diehards still skinned up to the bowl occasionally, after a high-season dumping—or so Garrett had heard. But it was like skiing a rock garden. You had to be rich enough not to care about trashing your skis.

The sport was dying: resorts drying up, even in the Rockies. It pained him to read about them. Whitefish was still hanging on—half of the mountain, anyway—though the season was only three months long. Garrett felt ashamed mourning it, given everything that was happening: the refugee crises, the water shortages in the Middle East, the ocean die-offs and vast boneyards of coral. Still, it was something he'd loved.

Why hadn't he skied more while he could? He'd spent half his life on Nordic skis, tracking wolverines—but it wasn't the same. He should have enjoyed himself more, his only youth.

They went for a short hike on the Alpine Trail, wending their way up a switchback of marshy snow. Garrett walked slowly, letting Charlie take the lead, partly because his knee was acting up again and partly because he didn't want to talk to him about Cece, what was happening to her. They hiked in step, surrounded by a balmy silence. How strange it was to be up here in fifty-eight-degree sunshine and not hear a sound; Garrett had still not gotten used to it, just as he had not gotten used to the absence of insects in his mouth when he went for a bike ride or the eerie stillness of the lake, no fish jumping at dusk and wrinkling the water. In the old winters there had been a churchy silence, not unlike the one now, but it seemed in keeping with the whiteness over everything, and even then on a windless day you could always make out a pika scampering over the snow, a woodpecker knocking against a tree. Garrett listened now and could hear nothing, no peep at all except for the crunch of Charlie's steps.

They stopped at the top of the pass, admiring the view. Charlie glugged from his water bottle, looking a bit shaky, and Garrett wondered why his old friend had wanted to come up here in the first place. The hike had been Charlie's idea—important enough to him that even Lana, who'd flown out for the week, had picked up on it, offering to watch Cece at the house while the two of them drove up to Jewel Basin. It was the first time since Jasper died that he'd wanted to do much of anything; the first time Charlie had been to Montana in a while, preferring the condo he'd bought in Corona del Mar, despite the drowning beaches. He liked to quote a line from *The Magic Mountain:* how young men preferred the mountains while old men preferred the sea. (In fact, the line was from *Buddenbrooks,* and Garrett himself had been the one to discover it in college.) Charlie's divorce payments had long ceased; he had plenty of money. He'd had a serious girlfriend for a while, more serious at least than the others—much younger, a speech pathologist he'd met online—but the relationship had gone bust soon after Jasper's death. No doubt his grief had proved too much for them. Garrett often tried to imagine what it would be like, to get that call from the police. To learn that your son had been living only ten miles away, squatting in an apartment in Glendale, and that you could have easily driven there—and then to drive there, to the morgue, to ID the body. To flip over the photograph. Not to know if your son had killed himself or finally OD'd, or in the end if there was any difference between the two.

They talked about the married couple who'd bought Cece's bookstore, how it was struggling now to survive. Cece had had something—a gift.

"How's Téa doing these days?" Garrett asked. "Have things gotten any better with you two?"

"It's the one good thing to come out of Jasper's death. What's that line you used to toss around? 'A deep distress hath humanized my soul.' *Two* souls, in our case. She always took her mom's side—thought I was enabling him by letting him live with me. *Supporting* him. When I knew he was using, I mean." Charlie took his hat off, airing it in the breeze. "Now she comes to visit me every week, with the kids. In Corona del Mar. I take them to the tidepools. I even drive up to Eagle Rock sometimes and babysit. Prue, Téa's youngest, calls me G-Pa."

"That's wonderful. You didn't tell me."

The zinc on Charlie's nose had begun to drip. Lines etched

either side of his forehead, from hairline to brow, as if his face were in quotation marks. Garrett did not remember seeing them before. Probably Garrett looked just as old—*older*, since Charlie had his hair—and yet he still felt twenty inside, as young as he'd been when Elias died. He thought of the frostbite scar on his cheek. Both of them, now, had been marked by death.

"You always used to tell me, about Elias . . . how many times? That it wasn't my fault."

Charlie looked away. "And it never sank in, did it?"

"Not for a long time," Garrett said. A lifetime, actually, though he didn't say that. He still had those dreams occasionally—digging in the snow, the frantic time-bomb panic—but no longer saw Elias's face watching him through the ice. Even awake, Garrett had trouble picturing it vividly. "Remember all that stuff you said at our reunion thing? About it being a secret relief when, I don't know . . . the *hawksbill* went extinct?"

"No," Charlie said.

"Well, I sort of get it. The relief part."

"What's a hawksbill?"

"A turtle," Garrett said. The names seemed more and more inadequate, like translations from a language no one spoke.

Charlie put his hat back on. "Lana looks great, by the way. How's she doing?"

"Wonderfully," Garrett said, then joked that if she flew to any more film festivals to claim awards, he was going to make her donate to the biofuel industry. Her new film, about a funeral home in Amish country, was doing especially well.

"I'm surprised she hasn't made a film about *you*," Charlie said.

"I never told you? She went into the field with me one summer, back when I was chasing gulos. Should have seen the gear she was lugging around. *The Last Wolverine*, she was going to call it—except we never spotted any."

Charlie laughed. "She'll have to change the title."

"I suspect it referred to me."

Charlie laughed again, then gave Garrett a look that seemed to say, merely, *It's late.* Not in the day—it wasn't even noon—but in a way that seemed to include the islands of slush, the mountains around them, the fact that they were standing there at all. He thought of the day they'd met in college, when the campus was encased in ice. Not a world under glass, but made of it.

Garrett tightened his knee brace, preparing to head back down. But Charlie didn't move. He just stood there dripping zinc. He looked at Garrett, nervous with determination, like a kid working himself up to ask for a dance. So it was finally coming. After all these years. They would talk about it, at last, because it was too late not to. They would clear the air. Amazing, how perfectly—*immaculately*—this was communicated before Charlie had even opened his mouth.

"I still hate you sometimes," Charlie said.

"I know."

"I have a fantasy where I kill you in your sleep."

"Strangling?"

He shook his head. "With a pillow. I get to watch you flop around."

"I'm glad we're not spending the night."

Charlie didn't smile. He was in no mood to joke. Clearly he had a script in his head, one he'd rehearsed beforehand; he would not be sidetracked. "The thing is, I know it was for the best. She would have been unhappy with me."

"Stop it!" Garrett said.

Charlie stared at him, startled.

"No lies, please. There isn't time. She would have been just as happy with you, and you know it."

"I don't think so."

"You would have made her happy and unhappy," Garrett said. "Like I did. It just would have been different."

Charlie shook his head. If Garrett thought this would console him, he'd made a grave mistake. The idea did not comfort him.

In fact it was monstrous. It meant there was no reason for her leaving him, for everything that had happened; no meaning at all.

"So no one was better off . . ."

"Don't be stupid," Garrett said. "You introduced us. *You saved me.*"

They looked at each other: the only hikers on the trail. The mountains, as old as the dinosaurs, were empty as far as the eye could see.

"We should get back to Cece, don't you think?"

The two friends zigzagged back down the way they'd come up, following the switchback toward the hut. The trail turned out to be more slippery than they'd realized. Despite the warmth, or maybe because of it, stray patches of ice lurked beneath the slush, their treachery only revealing itself on the descent. Garrett and Charlie picked their way slowly back to the car, at one point gripping each other's sleeves as they crossed a glazed patch of snow. They steadied each other, laughing at their own helplessness. How long ago it was—eons—that they'd slid across the ice.

Back at the Margolises' house, Garrett pulled up the driveway and plugged in his car. Charlie had moved out here for several months, planning to stay till fire season, mostly because of the breakup with his latest girlfriend but also to be the point person for the contractor on some renovations he and his brothers were doing. Extending the dock—the lake had shrunk so much that jumping off it was currently out of the question, the water deep as a puddle—and building a guesthouse out where the orchard used to be. That was the big one, of course, and from what Charlie had said a major investment for all three of them, but now that Bradley and Jake were grandparents, they'd started having to rent the neighbor's place in the summertime if they wanted the whole clan there at once. Which, of course, being the Margolises, they did. And anyway the orchard had dried up several years ago, along with the raspberry bushes: the combination of water rationing and root-rot fungus had killed everything. There just weren't enough cold months anymore—"chill hours," they called them. Charlie had told Garrett he'd cried, snapping his great-grandfather's apple trees into kindling.

Inside the house, Lana and Cece were huddled on the couch watching TV, one of those glossy nature shows that drove Garrett crazy. Lana was an excellent caretaker, better than he was probably, since she never seemed to get mad or impatient. Now that she was in her forties, her old thirst for attention had turned itself inside out, perhaps because she was finally getting attention from the world. It was such a relief when she flew out to help that Garrett found himself lingering in the supermarket for no reason, just to have a bit more time away from home. He suspected that for Lana her visits were also a relief, that it was nice to escape Hollywood for Salish, where no one seemed to take the slightest notice of her even though she'd grown up nearby. Garrett felt a bit bad about dragging her out to Charlie's—but of course, Lana loved the house too. Like mother, like daughter. Even now, you could tell they both enjoyed coming here, felt some unsnuffable spark of nostalgia.

Stopping at the couch, Garrett bent and kissed his wife on the cheek, which made her stiffen and purse her lips. She always seemed taken aback when he kissed her, even a little bit angry. As if he had no more right to her than anyone else.

"Well, la-di-da," she said, touching her hair.

Lana laughed, which made Cece laugh too, the same chiming, room-sized laugh that used to make people stare at them in restaurants. It had embarrassed him happily for forty-four years. Lana looked at Garrett. "When did she start saying that?"

" 'La-di-da'? It's the first I've heard of it."

"Mom, you're turning into Annie Hall."

"Speaking of hearing things," Garrett said, spying an opening, "I heard a good joke yesterday."

Lana groaned.

"Want to hear it?"

"Do I have a choice?"

"Actually, I was raving to someone about your new film. Morgan, from the Greedy Grape. She told it to me. What do you call an Amish person with his hand up a horse's ass?"

"The butt of an offensive joke?"

"A mechanic!"

Lana smiled, which was all Garrett wanted from his daughter. It was like a gift from the magi. He'd adored her his entire life, of course, but this new feeling he had for her—admiration, even a kind of bashfulness—had taken him by surprise. It was more than just parental pride. He genuinely loved her films, had the sensation watching them that he was experiencing something important, world-sharpening. *Honeycutt Funeral* was maybe the best one yet. What he hadn't told Morgan at the Greedy Grape was that it had moved him deeply: the way it begins with Clyde Honeycutt Jr. leading a customer around his showroom, past tropical-themed coffins that look like Hawaiian shirts—*We put the spendiest ones up front*, he admits later, *because the customers are drunk with grief*—and then mirrors this at the end, obliquely, with an Amish casket-maker making a simple pine box. Twenty minutes of this—an act of humble craftsmanship, unfolding in real time—and yet Garrett found himself in tears.

He suspected his daughter had made something great. Maybe even extraordinary. Had he told her this? Nope. He'd made an Amish joke.

Lana, who'd been brushing her mother's hair—something Cece seemed to love—stopped what she was doing, distracted by the sound of Charlie upstairs. Even with the TV on, you could hear him through the vent, rummaging around in Jasper's old room. For years, Charlie had kept Jasper's summer clothes in the closet, mixed with all of his cousins' things—on the off chance he might start vacationing here again.

"Are you all right?" Garrett asked.

"Just—all these pictures of Jasper."

There was one over the fireplace, Jasper doing a cannonball off the dock. Brown as a roach. He tanned in a way his father never could. "You'd think he was only ever a child," Garrett said.

"I always thought it would be his heart thing," Lana said. "That's what worried me. He was always talking about electric fences and all that, how they could kill him. But of course, that was the least of it."

Lana had said this to Garrett before, in a way that made him think she felt some guilt—though over what precisely, Garrett wasn't sure. At one point long ago, Cece had suggested to him that Lana and Jasper were romantically involved. Or at least had been when they were kids. But Garrett didn't believe it. It would have been too strange for them, for Lana, and anyway he wasn't her type. Still, they'd been very close, had helped each other survive lonely childhoods: Jasper because of his heart issues; Lana because, well, she was Lana. What a mystery your own children were. You gave them everything, and it was like tossing a coin into a well. Charlie had held a special memorial here a month after the death, had taken the Crestliner out and scattered half of Jasper's ashes in the lake. (Angeliki and Téa had scattered the other half in the Pacific.) The boy didn't have any friends left—or at least anyone willing to make the trip. Just Garrett and Lana and the Margolises, Charlie and Jake and Bradley. And Cece, of course, who'd laughed when the ashes had landed on the water, clouding it like chum.

Now, sitting there stiffly as Lana brushed her hair, regal as a queen, Cece began to hum to herself. This was a recent development, the humming. It didn't follow a tune so much as venture valiantly in search of one. Last week, Garrett had taken her to see *Fiddler on the Roof* at the Salish Playhouse, where Cece had seemed to compete, lustily, with the singers onstage. He'd wanted to get her out of the house, but clearly her theatergoing days were over. The couple seated next to them had complained to the manager, then moved to the front row.

Of course, given what had happened in January, it had been brave of him to take Cece anywhere. She'd become convinced at the drugstore he was out to get her—convinced, in fact, he was trying to kill her, to make room for his "Moroccan lover." Screamed bloody murder and wouldn't stop. They'd had to call 911 and have her restrained. The look on her face as the EMTs tied her to a stretcher, shackling her wrists with towels: Garrett would not soon forget it. The doctors had blamed the whole thing on a urinary tract infection. A common thing, apparently, in Alzheimer's sufferers. UTI-induced psychosis. Afterward, Garrett had gone back to Lakeview Village, to the special wing that they'd made fun of seven years ago, but couldn't bear to put Cece on the wait list. They'd spent forty-four years together: most of their adult lives. For better or worse, he'd loved her. Imperfectly, but maybe he wasn't the worst husband either? It was his one accomplishment in life, other than raising Lana.

Besides, what would he do with all his time?

On TV, a snow leopard was stalking a Himalayan blue sheep, preparing to toboggan down a cliff to snatch it while a mellifluous, awestruck voiceover made it seem like the starving animal was Jackie Robinson or something. It was like living in the Weimar Republic and pretending something inspiring was afoot. Lana went upstairs to call her new girlfriend (forty-two, their daughter was, and still dating) and Cece wandered away from the TV, restless as always, humming her never-ending song. Like a cat, she gravitated toward windows. Garrett told the TV to turn off and joined his wife in the dining room. They'd upped her meds after the drugstore incident; she was generally in an okay mood these days. It was still hard to rouse her from bed—

she slept till one, two in the afternoon sometimes—but once up, she tended to greet the day more heroically than he did.

There were the depressions, of course, horrible mute spells in which she sat half-sucked into the couch, head flat against the cushions, like an astronaut blasting into space. But these—knock on wood—had been few and far between lately.

"You've been up for a while then," Garrett said to her.

"Oh sure. You know me."

"Well, sometimes you sleep into the afternoon."

Cece scowled. "Very funny."

Her lips were chapped—he would have to deal with that— and her hair needed a trim, grazing her shoulders. She'd never been vain, though she'd liked to look her best. Garrett had a hard time keeping up her appearance, now that she no longer cared and resisted his ministrations. Plus she still looked beautiful to him; the beauty was mysterious, deeper than her face let on, like the invisible depth of a pool.

"You used to get so mad at me when I forced you out of bed," Garrett said. "Even if we had to catch a plane. You'd actually curse."

"That's right."

She looked at him, smiling vaguely. She didn't remember any of this, of course. It made her ashamed to pretend—he could tell—but how else would they talk at all? So he pretended too, just as he was pretending this very moment that Cece knew his name. They were double agents, from a marriage that no longer was.

He thought this sometimes: that their marriage was extinct. At other times, he thought it might be deeper than ever. They were like those fish living in the darkness, a thousand meters down. Sea devils. The male attaches to the female, their bodies slowly fusing together; he shares her bloodstream until they die.

"What beautiful tall trees," Cece said, gazing out the window. "Wow. Look at them."

"We have nice trees too. On our property."

"Nothing like this," she said contemptuously.

"Are you hungry? Did you get some lunch?"

"Oh no. Don't trouble yourself. Wow! Would you look at those trees? *Beautiful.*"

"How about a baked potato?"

"Right."

"I'm being serious. Wondering if you'd like a baked potato for lunch."

"A banana sounds good."

"You can't buy bananas," Garrett said, for the millionth time. The drought in Asia, in South America, meant nothing to her. She was still in an enchanted garden, when peaches weren't a luxury good and a bag of coffee cost less than a haircut. "I can make you a potato."

"No, I couldn't, thank you. Not on a Saturday."

"It's Wednesday."

"Wednesday!" she said, as if gripped by panic. Weirdly, she always thought it was Saturday. She'd gotten stuck there, in the tar pit of week's end, and couldn't get loose. She gazed out the window again, brightening. "Look at those trees," she said, whistling. "Have you ever seen trees like that?"

Garrett went into the kitchen, looking for evidence that Cece had eaten lunch. No plates on the table, or in the dishwasher, though possibly Lana had dried them already and put them back. It was easy to forget to feed her, since she never asked for anything herself. That was what had happened in LA, the last and final time he'd taken her to visit Lana. They'd forgotten to feed her lunch, then brought Cece to the zoo. A pleasant enough day until they'd visited the Primate House. She hadn't wanted to go in—it was hot and smelly inside, nearly stifling—but Garrett had insisted, remembering how she'd convinced herself to like baboons as a kid. Once inside, though, Cece had bypassed the baboons and headed straight for the chimpanzees, who were

lounging around their enclosure like Romans after an orgy. Cece
was transfixed. She stood right in front of the plexiglass, ogling a
gray-bearded chimp with one of those big volcano things growing out of its rear. Perhaps out of boredom, the chimp looked up
from the carrot it was eating and peered right back at her, black
eyes glimmering.

Cece tipped her head to one side, and the chimp tipped its
head as well, mimicking her. She tilted her head the opposite
way, and the chimp—sternly, with great dignity—followed suit.
A few bystanders laughed. Intrigued, people at other exhibits
came over to watch. Cece moved her head faster, discoing it back
and forth, and the gray-bearded chimp discoed its head as well,
matching her movements perfectly, like the reflection in a mirror. The crowd of zoo-goers roared with laughter. Garrett, who
was standing behind Cece, couldn't help laughing himself. He
figured she was having a grand old time.

But then Cece spun around and he saw her face. She wasn't
laughing. She looked pale, wild-eyed, deeply shaken. She
scanned the crowd frantically before spying a little girl holding a
pink torch of cotton candy.

"I do not," Cece said, grabbing the girl's shoulders, "like
this!"

The girl started to cry. Mortified, Garrett had apologized
to the girl, and then to the girl's mother, who'd snatched her
daughter away from Cece as if she were a pervert. He'd managed
to calm Cece down eventually, ushering her out of the Primate
House and back into the sun, but for the rest of the day there'd
been a faint plunging dread in her eyes, a remnant of whatever
the chimp had revealed to her.

Now Garrett took Cece outdoors, in the unseasonable warmth,
and walked her down to the road. The traffic was much qui-
eter than it used to be—all those EVs—though it made crossing the highway more treacherous, since you often couldn't hear

cars before they turned the bend. Garrett took Cece's hand and walked her across the road. The dock looked strangely misplaced, extending over the dry lake bottom, which was bleached gray as the moon. The world's oceans were rising, but Salish Lake was in retreat, dependent as it was on snowmelt from Glacier and the Bob Marshall Wilderness. They'd raised the level at the dam, but it hadn't done much to offset the shrinkage. The Margolises' boat lift hung in midair, rusting over a jumble of sticks; the Margolises had moved the Crestliner into yearlong storage. Waves lapped against the pilings at the far end of the dock, a sea at low tide.

"That certainly is a big . . . thing," Cece said, pointing at a log that had beached itself between Charlie's and the neighbors' docks. She seemed transfixed by it. All she cared about, it seemed, was trees.

"A log," Garrett said. "Yep."

They walked out to the end of the dock, where the swim ladder stopped well short of the water. Most of Charlie's neighbors had adapted already to the shrinkage. Some of them had demolished their docks and put up new ones; a few had even built new homes closer to the water, taking advantage of the increased acreage. But mostly people had just added on to their existing docks, extending them farther and farther, like tongues stretching to get a drink.

And yet the lake, if you gazed straight out from the dock, looked the same as it used to, bright as a jewel in the afternoon sun though darkening near the point under a wrack of cloud. A hole in the clouds shone a spotlight on the water. Garrett held Cece's hand, staring at it. A Jet Ski ripped to life somewhere and a column of buffleheads rose from the point, as if they were being sucked up by the vent in the clouds.

This lake had delivered her. Had brought her to him one morning, steaming in the sun. Almost everything that mattered to him in life could be traced back to that moment.

"This was where you were when I met you. The first time. You were standing right here, where we are now, because you'd just been swimming."

"Swimming!"

"I was surprised you'd been in the lake so early in the day, and you said: 'A person afraid of cold water is a bystander of life.' I remember it perfectly."

She smiled vaguely, then returned her attention to the log. "Geez, look at that. What an enormous . . . thing."

"Oh for fuck's sake!" Garrett said, dropping her hand.

He took off his boots and socks and climbed down the swim ladder until he was standing on the last rung, hovering above the ankle-deep water. It wasn't Cece's fault—he knew this, of course, it was childish to blame her—but his hands shook with rage. He rolled up his pants as best he could with one hand and then stepped into the freezing lake. His feet turned numb, throbbed almost angrily with pain, but he made himself stay there, submerged to the ankles. He wanted life. The water, gin-clear, rippled above his frozen feet, which felt so strange to him they might have belonged to someone else. Some minnows floated nearby, still as a photograph. They looked trapped in ice. Garrett stepped toward them. They didn't dart from his foot as they would have in the summer, but rather drifted away in slow motion.

Garrett had the eerie sensation that someone was behind him, about to tap him on the shoulder. He'd experienced this feeling once before, long ago, but couldn't remember when. He glanced back at the dock, but Cece was still there, staring amorously at her log. He looked back at the lake. A wind he couldn't feel scuffed the water. It slithered toward him from afar, like something moving beneath the surface.

The trees outside were beautiful. Extremely beautiful. She'd never seen such trees before. Look at them! What trees they had here! Up and up! Holy crap, they were tall. She'd never seen such trees in her life. They were enormous. And the trees! How tall they were. They certainly grew big around here, by the lake. She lifted her hair from her neck. God, what tall trees they had here! She plumped her hair, feeling a bit stucky along the neck. Stucky? Panic gripped her heart. Sad, sadder, sadder-day. They used to seal girls into churches and call them saints. Anchorite. Angkor Wat? A little window opened to their face. A squint, it was called. *How are you today? Just peachy!* They used to seal girls into churches and call them dead. Seal them behind walls, like plumbing. What seems to be the matter, Professor Plum? Pipes are a bit stucky.

Knock knock.

Who's there?

God and the angels.

God and the angels who?

Never mind! It was just the pipes!

She smiled to herself. Why was she smiling? She had no idea.

Holy shit, she was out of it. She had Alzheimer's disease. She was dying.

She felt the panic again, wringing her heart. Why? She wasn't sure. The only thing that helped was to look at the trees—or at least what she could see of them through the squint in the wall. How tall they were! She'd never seen such trees before. Or such stumps. Stumps were the graves of trees. Gravestones. She lifted the hair from her neck, feeling a bit . . . something. A bit something or other. What beautiful tall trees! Up and up! And the lake beyond! Enjoy canoeing from your backyard. This home is going to impress the *most pickiest* of buyers.

But where were all the angels? You know, *ANGELS*? With the feathers and the songs? Bird is the word. Bird bird bird is the word. Bird is a word.

She should tell _____ about the trees, how beautiful they were. Tell him before she forgot. She turned toward the lake, but _____ was nowhere in sight.

Where was he? Where was he? Where was he? Where was he? Where was he? Where was he? Where was he? Where was he?

Oh god. Oh hell. *We don't use that word here at St. Timothy.* H-E double hockey sticks.

She walked back up the yard, toward the yellow house. The windows were all lit up. Like dabs of butter. Where was _____? Probably he was inside, which was why she was crossing the river. The *road*. Panic seized her heart. She felt wrong. Cornered. Her throat was clogged. Where was he? Probably he was in the house, the yellow one, where she belonged too. She couldn't breathe right. Her throat was clogged. She was all sealed up. She felt like the dark before it was anything. Before it was "dark." There were no words in her brain, she couldn't speak, she could only grunt howl stamp point. *The earth was without form and void.* In Sunday school, they learned about Sunday. *Let there be lights in the firmament.* What's a star to a lizard? A stock exchange or a *Pirates of Penzance* or a turkey tetrazzini? Terrible! Terrible! Where was he? Why was her face wet? The earth was without.

The terror passed through her. She opened the gate to the yard. Where was he? She stared at the grass, shivering. The trees, she couldn't help noticing, were very beautiful. The flowers too. They beautied the grass. The Hidden Meadow! Filled with light! Why was her face wet? Well, she'd been swimming. Of course! She loved to swim in the lake. She was cold and wet and her husband was about to swoop out of the house with a towel warm from the line. Yes, _____ would appear on the porch any second. He was in the yellow house. They'd lived in it forever.

Lana cleaned the blood from Garrett's elbow, dabbing it softly with a washcloth. There was some talk of urgent care, but Garrett laughed in her and Charlie's faces. He was only scraped up a bit. Lana taped some gauze to his elbow with masking tape, since there wasn't anything else in the house. How worried she seemed, tending to him! Garrett remembered all the times he'd ministered to her, after the clumsy girl had hurt herself: the splinters and bee stings and skinned knees. The awful time she'd broken her finger, when Cece had slammed it in the door of the pickup by accident.

Now here Garrett was, half-naked, wincing like a child. His shirt was ruined; they'd had to throw it in the trash. How peculiar it was, to watch the cared-for become the carer.

But of course that's what getting old was. This return on your investment. He'd done the same for his own father, though his father's investment had been meager.

"Shouldn't you be wearing your knee brace all the time?" Lana asked.

"Where's Charlie?" Garrett asked, ignoring this.

Lana shrugged. "Still looking for Neosporin, I think."

"An anesthesiologist without a first aid kit."

She didn't laugh at this but grabbed one of Charlie's shirts from the back of a chair and threw it to him. "Here, Dad. Don't sit there half-dressed."

A plaid Pendleton, one of Charlie's favorites. He'd had it forever—ever since Garrett could remember. He liked to come to Salish and change into Montana Man, dressing in indigenous garments. Gingerly, Garrett pulled the ancient shirt on, taking care not to mess up the gauze on his elbow. The shirt smelled like Charlie—or rather, his deodorant, the same kind he'd used since college. Garrett did up the shirt wrong—he had to unbutton the damn thing and try again—which interested his daughter. He could tell by her face: the way its concern contained a kernel of judgment. She was worried he couldn't take care of Cece, that he was too old and feeble and prone to falling. Wondering how to force him into admitting her into a home.

He hadn't told his daughter about getting disgusted with

Cece for a moment and wading into the lake by himself, leaving her alone on the dock. About his alarm when he'd climbed out again and discovered she was gone, when she wasn't on the dock or beach or boatshed lawn, when he'd called for her and heard nothing but the hum of cars on the road. This was the real reason he'd tripped and fallen: he'd been running to make sure Cece wasn't killed by a car. In his panic, he'd slipped on the dock, his bare feet wet from the water. It had nothing to do with his bum knee at all. When he was younger, even five years ago, it would have been something to laugh about. How many times in Glacier had he eaten it on the trail, trying to keep up with a gulo?

Now it was Cece he was chasing.

Anyway, she was fine. Garrett had found her on the other side of the road, standing in the front yard of Charlie's house. She'd greeted him with a look of maddening affection on her face, as if he hadn't done anything wrong—at least until she noticed the blood seeping through his jeans and began to glance around fretfully. Garrett hid his arm from her, the elbow of his shirt torn to shreds. Probably it was lucky he hadn't broken a hip.

"Did your mother worry about where I was?" he asked Lana, who was kneeling on the floor and tending to his knee now, gingerly rolling his Levi's past it so she could clean the wound. "When Charlie and I were hiking?"

"*Yes*, Dad. Of course. She kept glancing around and asking where you were."

"By name?"

"She's totally focused on you," Lana said, avoiding the question. "She gets agitated when you're not around."

He was embarrassed by this: his need to be needed. He glanced at Cece, who was sitting on the couch in the living room, reading a Sotheby's real estate catalog. By "reading," he meant something he didn't fully understand and that in fact touched some acupoint of horror in him. She could read the same page for an hour—in fact, never flipped the pages at all. Was it just the same sentence, over and over again?

"Well, that makes sense," Garrett said. "The dependency on one person. Fixation. It's in line with what the literature says."

Lana busied herself with dressing his knee, as if refusing to meet his eye. He wondered, not for the first time, whether she knew about Cece's infidelity, whether Lana might have talked about it with her mother. The two of them were very close. Amazingly, Garrett had never discussed it with Cece, his own wife. He'd imagined they might, at some point, but he'd never felt a need that outweighed the comfort of what they had—and now of course it was too late. Sometimes he found himself wondering if that night with Charlie had even happened. Garrett's life, with no one to corroborate it, had begun to feel gauzy and unstable. He'd read all about the stages of the disease, read about what myriad devastations to expect, but no one had warned him that her dementia would start to feel *contagious*, that the very fabric of reality might begin to erode for him too. How lonely it was, to be the sole keeper of their past.

At night, feeling the strange new weather of her presence beside him, Garrett had trouble falling asleep, wondering if there was someone else watching him, if there was anyone with whom he might share the memories of his life. He'd never been a believer—was not, like Charlie, raised by religious parents—but understood for the first time why someone might give in to this other kind of marriage, in which your Partner's mind was flawless and unfading. Not by chance did religious converts talk about being *found*.

Garrett stood up, grimacing from the cut on his knee. Lana grabbed him under the arm, as if to help him walk, and he shook her off.

"I can drive home," Lana said.

"I'm perfectly fine! Anyway, we can put it on autopilot."

"Do you even know how to do that?"

"Lan, Jesus. I'm not a Luddite. I might be old, but my brain still works."

They both looked at the couch. He hadn't meant to say that. Cece just sat there inscrutably, wearing a sun visor she must have found on the porch.

"You must be starving," Garrett said to her. "It's about time we headed home."

"Yeah, right," Cece said.

"I'm serious."

"That's for sure!"

"We don't live here. This is Charlie's house."

Cece glanced at Lana. Fear skimmed her face. Abruptly, she tipped the visor down to her nose so you couldn't see her eyes.

"Ta-da!" she said, tipping the visor up again.

"Mom, you're a riot."

Garrett took his wife upstairs to say goodbye to Charlie. He'd hoped Lana might be spared the peekaboo routine, a new development. It was almost more than he could bear: watching Cece act like a toddler. Sometimes she turned to him with a mischievous look on her face and he felt sure she was going to tell him one of her dopey maxims—*A kitchen with a TV in it is a bellwether of divorce*—but then she'd pull her hat over her eyes and lift it up again, beaming, as if she'd popped out of a cake.

Garrett's eyes blurred. If only he didn't love her so much. He loved her and at the same time missed her terribly. Occasionally, even now, he'd forget about the amyloid deposits in her brain and would talk to her like he used to, asking her where the garlic press was, or if she remembered the name of some trail they used to hike on, and would be met with nothingness. He could hear it sometimes, like wind whistling through a cave. In these moments a kind of terror would seize him, an old feeling of panic, like peering at that sheared patch of snow and realizing Elias was nowhere to be seen. And yet she was here now, climbing the stairs in front of him and ducking under the low-hanging beam, accessing some lockbox in her brain where the memory of its peril was alive and well. She was gone and not gone. Holding her at night, sometimes while she slept, he let himself imagine she was the same person as always, that she'd never left.

He never touched her unless she initiated it. Otherwise, it would have been too strange, too upsetting. But sometimes Cece seemed practically possessed. Out of muscle memory, or maybe just horniness, she would pull down his pajamas and do the old things, taking him in her mouth while she touched him, and he would do the same thing for her. They'd fuck like they used to, as wildly as ever—more wildly, in fact, than they had in years. This was the dirty secret he didn't tell anyone. The Alzheimer's had restored something to her: a newness, a mystery. To watch this child-stranger turn back into his wife: it was like something from a fairy tale, the smashing of a spell. Her body at least remembered him. Think of the amnesiac from the news: the well-dressed guy who'd been found on a British beach, dripping from the sea, who didn't know his own name and curled into a ball if anyone asked him what it was—but who could plop down at the piano and play a seamless rendition of *Swan Lake*. Cece was like that, Garrett her instrument. They would come at the same time, two old people in the dark.

Upstairs, Cece wandered into Charlie's bedroom, as if this were a perfectly natural place to be, and immediately started rearranging all the knickknacks she could find, stacking them purgatorially on the bed before putting them back in places they didn't belong. Garrett watched her from the doorway. Sometimes she got mad if you interrupted one of her projects. She placed Charlie's travel alarm clock on the windowsill; a jar of pennies ended up in the trash.

"How'd you do it?" Charlie said, joining him.

"What?"

"She's finally interested in housekeeping."

Garrett laughed. "Sorry about that. We're supposed to be saying goodbye."

"Oh, let her," Charlie said. "She seems to be enjoying herself." He turned toward Garrett, noticing for the first time what he was wearing. "Nice shirt."

"What, this piece of shit?"

Charlie laughed. "Just treat it better than your own shirts, please."

"I have no idea what you mean."

"Have you forgotten my wedding day?" Charlie said. "I had to button your shirt with a stapler."

It was the first time he'd mentioned the wedding since, well, the wedding itself. Garrett felt a shock of relief, as when a furnace you'd forgotten was blasting turns suddenly off. He followed Charlie into Mr. Margolis's old office across the hall. Charlie's now, of course. It was here where they'd tried to fix Garrett's shirt—where he'd learned, with a blend of sympathy and ghoulish hope, that the groom was ill.

"I don't think I could do what you're doing," Charlie said seriously.

"What's the alternative?"

"I don't know. A nursing home. Some kind of . . . escape."

"I escaped in my twenties," Garrett said. "Didn't work out so well."

Charlie ignored this. Scattered expensively on the desk were a laptop and an Origami and some VR goggles. The laptop's screensaver was a picture of his kids at the dock: Jasper and Téa, grinning like maniacs, wet hair flat as paint. Garrett's heart snagged for a moment. How depressing to think about Charlie up here by himself during fire season, avoiding the outdoors. Lost to newsfeeds, or porn, or whatever in his case was making him disappear.

"I know everyone says this," Charlie said, "but it still amazes me. That you'd turn out to be the one, in the end, to devote your life to it."

"To what?"

"'The whole bourgeois conspiracy,' I think is the way you used to put it."

Garrett looked out the window: storm clouds flickered over the lake, like a tube light on the blink. He'd been selfish, perhaps, too circumscribed in his idea of happiness. He thought of Cece's agitation these days—never wanting to sit in one place, rearranging the house or pacing the hallway, peering into rooms as if playing a game of hide-and-seek—and wondered if it was some distillation of regret. A life's restlessness.

"You know," Charlie said, staring out the window too, "when I had to go pick up Jasper's body, make the arrangements for the cremation, the funeral director said something funny to me. I thanked him and he said, 'I'm just the travel agent, making sure his bag is all packed.' At the time I just sort of gaped at him. No, you know what? I wanted to punch him in the fucking face. *Where do you think he's flying to? Does he have one of those little harps in the overhead compartment?* But then I kept thinking about it, this idea that Jasper was flying somewhere—that he was on a plane, and I was left behind in some shit airport. And it kind of made sense to me. Like here we all are, waiting for our flights. A layover. It's not actually where we belong at all."

Charlie stepped away from the window. From across the hall, Garrett could hear his wife humming her tuneless song, chasing a melody she'd never catch. The soundtrack to their marriage.

"Here," Charlie said. "I want to show you something."

He opened the drawer to his father's old desk and took out something from deep at the back of it. A ring box. Charlie opened it calmly, though his hands were trembling. There, nestled in its velvet mouth, was a wedding ring, the one Cece had given him the day they were married. A simple band of white gold. It seemed brighter than it should have been. Garrett did not need to read the inscription. He remembered what it was.

TILL THE STARS GROW COLD.

"My mom wanted to throw it out," Charlie said. "She was so furious—furious, really, till the day she died. Just the name 'Cece' would send her into a rage. I had to pretend that you guys never came to visit."

"So why did you keep it?"

Charlie shrugged. Garrett stared at the ring. It didn't upset him, as he might have expected; if anything, he was glad Charlie had kept it. The man had been through everything, he'd lost and lost, while Garrett—for no earthly reason, and against all odds—had won. He'd turned his life around completely. Married the woman of his dreams; raised a brilliant and successful daughter. He'd killed a man, then been rewarded for it. Neither of them deserved their fate, and yet this was what life had dealt them.

Garrett gazed at the handsome ruin of Charlie's face. His eyes looked damp, or perhaps just rheumy with age. Maybe if they'd been born at a different time, if they were part of Lana's generation, none of this would have happened. They might have skipped marriage—its creaky ownership vows, its consumer talk of "taking" and not "giving"—altogether. And in fact the ring, preserved in its little display box, did seem like something from a museum. The only thing missing was a little plaque:

WEDDING BAND, 2004
*First associated with the marital dowry
and later with the promise of fidelity*

Outside the lake had begun to roar, boiling with rain. The speedboats had all gone in. Even the Lazy Bear—ordinarily blasting music at happy hour, rain or shine—was silent. How strange it was to be old. The events that had seemed so important to Garrett seemed shamefully distant, even a little ridiculous, like the plot of a movie he'd once thought profound.

Cece was still rearranging the bedroom, pulling the jar of pennies out of the wastebasket and replacing it with a bottle of nasal spray. Garrett rescued the nasal spray from the trash and set it on Charlie's dresser. He cleared his throat, but Cece was humming too loudly to notice him. From behind, with her hair woven into a single braid—Lana's doing, no doubt—she looked trim and alert, almost elegant. She bent over to pick up a pillow, and her shirt fell up her back. A girl's back, smooth as a doll's. She fluffed the pillow in her hand, playing it like an accordion, then picked up another and did the same thing.

"It's about time," she said, noticing Garrett. Frowning, she sat on the bed and closed her eyes. She had these sometimes: dizzy spells that stopped her in her tracks.

"What's the matter? Do you feel light in the head?"

"Light in the head?"

She looked at him wonderingly, as if he'd said something strange. He pulled off her shoes and helped her lie down for a minute. *Light in the head.* Yes, it was strange, wasn't it? Cece certainly thought so, too dizzy to open her eyes. She looked for it, this light, believing she was more than it was. She was tall and mighty! Up and up! But she couldn't see beyond it. The looking was the light too. She was sealed inside it, like a church.

She thought this and then immediately forgot it.

Cece stretched out on Charlie's bed, obeying the silence. For the first time all day long she did not feel restless—felt, in fact, almost at peace. Like she belonged there. *God, how tired I am.* Was this Garrett's thought or Cece's? (For a second, they had the same thought—though how would they ever know this?) She opened her eyes and stared at the man squatting by the bed, who smelled familiar. His shirt looked familiar too. She had unbuttoned that shirt, possibly even worn it.

"It's me," Garrett said. "Your husband."

Cece smiled at him suspiciously, neither agreeing nor disagreeing. He smiled back, pushing up the sleeves of Charlie's shirt. Then she began to rearrange the pillows, switching one for the other, as if she'd been doing this for years.

TWENTY-FIVE

1.

The fire began small, in the undergrowth, which was desiccated from a summer of 105-degree temperatures. It stayed low to the ground for a while, burning grass and pine needles and ferns. Eventually a wind gusted from the north and the fire crowned, spreading to the tops of the trees and passing from one pine to the next, igniting the flammable oils inside their trunks. The fire found its wings. Soon it was traveling at close to fifteen miles per hour, creating its own weather, whirling and bursting, spotting downwind to ignite additional fires. Snowshoe hares exploded. Logs catapulted into the sky. At one point, it seemed to veer into fast motion, hairpinning uphill and devouring an entire slope in a matter of seconds.

The fire fed this way for days, despite the human efforts to contain it. When there was nothing left to feed upon, the west face of the mountain reduced to ash, the flames caught a downdraft and spread downhill in search of fuel, using a creek bottom for a chimney. It headed toward some homes along the lake, which—like Salish itself—had already been evacuated. Stray horses wandered the highway. Hotshots took engines and skidgines up the fire road and fought the blaze as best as they could; helicopters dumped water from enormous buckets they'd filled in the lake. An air tanker, bleeding from its belly, doused it with slurry. Hand crews did their best to clear a line uphill from the houses, working chain saws and Pulaskis, scraping the ground to soil on the steep hillside and then using drip torches to set a backfire so that the line was even wider, trying to protect the houses with a moat of dirt and ash.

But the fire proved impossible to contain. Flames hopped the moat, not from the wind but because the blaze was so hot it caused the pines fifty yards downhill from it to spontaneously ignite. The fire consumed one house, then the next. They went up like the trees did: expertly, as if they'd been put on earth to burn. The fire swept toward the lake. It did not notice that the third house was yellow, or that it had been there for a hundred and twenty-two years, or that it was a house at all. That the house meant anything to anyone—that some old people explored it, almost nightly, in their dreams—of course never occurred to it. The timber was simply waiting to be used. It had waited a long time. The fire consumed the orchard and the house and the front yard, turning the badminton net into a gigantic spark gap for a second, then continued down to the dock and burned that up too, transforming it into smoke that you could see from space.

2.

Lana grabbed her light meter and Zoom recorder, then opened the trunk of her rental car and pulled out her old Canon C300, which she still used on scouts. The camera was hopelessly outdated, but they'd had a long relationship and she couldn't bear to replace it. Agnes, Lana's partner, observed her from the passenger seat, watching for signs of distress. Lana ignored this. She crossed the highway and waded through the fireweed that skirted the road to the place where the house used to be. Spires of blackened pines surrounded the area; the few whose crowns were still intact looked like arrows, fletched at the top with withered branches. It had rained the night before and the trees smelled dank and cindery, like burnt rope. The smell clawed at Lana's headache. She stepped over the foundation, into the Margolises' living room. It still had a feeling about it, a ghost of shelter though you were just as outdoors. The stone fireplace stood in the open air, charred but unscathed. The rest of the house had disappeared.

Seedlings had begun to sprout here and there, interspersed among the fireweed, impatient to claim the site and return it to forest. Ponderosa pines. One still had its seed coat stuck to the top, like a Christmas ornament.

Her mother had loved this place. Lana had too. One of the few things, really, they'd had in common.

Lana waited for her head to stop throbbing. She'd gone to a bar with Agnes last night, where she'd literally cried into her beer—visiting her mother always turned her into a country song—before bucking herself up with a margarita. Shakily, she took some measurements on the meter. The light was tough, but she'd be shooting flat anyway. She checked the profiles on her camera and chose neutral—she'd apply a LUT in post—then began to film the ruins, panning from the fireplace to the rubble of the foundation, half-buried in the earth like an ancient city. She was just scouting at this point, to see how it looked. She had the idea for a documentary: a kind of essay film, about her and Jasper and the summers they'd spent at the house. Something like *Sans Soleil*, narrated in the form of a letter. She imagined bringing some furniture out here and arranging it around the fireplace, stage-designing it from memory.

She recorded the ambient sound—birdsong, the buzz of cicadas—on her Zoom. Then she stepped over the foundation and headed between the poles where the clothesline once stretched and through the blackened fence where the orchard was, re-meadowing now with pioneer grass. The ancient apple trees, of course, were gone—had died well before the fire. Lana wished she could remember the names of them, the different cultivars; Sweet Sixteen was the one that came to mind, and only because Jasper used to eat them in a pervy way as a joke. If only she could ask her mother. Her father had put her in Lakeview two years ago, when she'd become a danger to herself. ("Graveview Village," he called it.) Her mother roamed the halls endlessly, vocationally, like a robot vacuum. Lana and Agnes had found her there this morning, touring the memory wing in her nightgown. She'd seemed startled to see them, almost annoyed. Her hair was white and thin—had turned to silk, like something in a fairy tale. She'd beckoned Lana over to tell her something, a secret, but when Lana bent down to listen, her mother only breathed in her ear. Seemed to have forgotten what she was going to say. Or perhaps the breathing itself was the message. The secret. She'd wanted Lana to remember it, the only news she had left.

Lana had cried on the way back to the house she'd grown up in. (She cried every day on these visits—felt, sometimes, on the plane from LA, as if she were a storm cloud preparing to rain.) She'd stopped on the porch to recover, not wanting to upset her father, whom she could see was napping on the couch, an E. O. Wilson book tented on his chest. He seemed lost without Lana's mother. Spent most of his time at the nursing home, roaming the halls with her or listening to cheesy pop songs from their youth, one of the few things that made her stop moving. Stillness at last. They'd lie in her adjustable bed together, holding hands. Her mother would hum along to Bonnie Tyler or Duran Duran, clutching the stuffed animal he'd given her. A raccoon. Why he'd bought her such a thing, Lana had no idea. But she loved it, carried it everywhere she went. Lana found the whole development—the eighties hits, the raccoon—demeaning. Sometimes when she visited, her mother would call out, "Mommy!," like a child waking up from a nightmare, and then get upset if Lana corrected her. She'd have no choice but to go along with it, singing "Goodnight, Irene" or making pretend weather on her mother's back, which seemed to put the world back into joint.

It was easier with Lana's father there. Her mother was always checking for his sneakers by the window. If they weren't there, she flipped out. Pitched a fit and threw things at the wall. It got so bad that he'd had to drive home barefoot one day, buy a second pair of sneakers so he could leave the old ones in her room. They sat there beside her mother's slippers, laces tied into perfect little knots, as if Lana's parents had been raptured from their shoes. He'd spent half his life without her, traipsing around the mountains, but now he couldn't seem to bear leaving her alone. He'd started talking about moving to Lakeview Village as well, to one of the assisted-living suites.

Her parents' marriage had always seemed like a cautionary tale to Lana, a source of heartbreak and remorse. A rash decision—a *crush*, really—leading to years of fallout. All that suffering: Mr. Margolis's, which had trickled in some pitiless way down to Jasper. And for what? An imperfect marriage, like every other. There had been good times, it seemed—but plenty of bad ones too. Lana was not at all sure it had made her mother happy.

But maybe she'd had unreasonable expectations for it. Can kids ever see their parents' relationship for what it is? Every flaw, every fallibility, feels like a betrayal, as if the only point of marriage were to keep their child happy. Above all, it wasn't supposed to look like work. But what if the *work itself* was the point?

How strange that in the end Lana's parents would be so hungry for each other's company, like newlyweds. She'd mentioned this to her dad, and he'd said "newlyweds" was a good term for it.

"What do you mean?"

"It's like she's found someone new. A different husband. I don't actually have a name."

Lana shot the orchard for a while, doing a circular pan along the fence. A stack of buckets had melted into a giant blue patty, like something expelled by Paul Bunyan's ox. She zoomed in on it, remembering how her father used to take her up here, at the Margolises' urging, to collect raspberries. They'd fill a whole bucket to take home, her father balancing it miraculously on his head. How she'd worshipped him! She used to picture him up in the mountains, chasing wolverines, and think he had the greatest life ever. As she got older, the wolverining had started to seem less glamorous to her—a bit pathetic even, as if he were using it as a way of disengaging from the world. She'd felt bitter about it. Now she felt like he'd found something small to do, to save, and had done his very best to save it. Lana admired him for it. She didn't know how to tell him this, to put it into words. He'd told her, not long ago, that his life had been a waste, he hadn't managed to keep a few dumb wolverine families alive, and she'd tried to tell him you couldn't measure a life this way, in Gulo Units. *If you look for a meaning,* Tarkovsky once said, *you'll miss everything that happens.*

Lana had thought about interviewing her dad on camera—the man's memory was startling—but he had no interest in discussing the past. Besides, his vocal cords were nearly shot. He'd literally lost his voice.

Still, she had her mother's breath in her ear. That was something.

Her head drummed with pain, an upbeat to her pulse. She walked across the orchard and through the east gate of the fence to where she'd humiliated Jasper in front of Téa and her friend. What was her name? Parvini? Lana zoomed in on the patch of fireweed where she imagined they'd sat. It was hard to tell among the graveyard of trees. They poked from the earth at odd angles, like birthday candles. Lana woke up at three or four a.m. sometimes, still plagued with guilt. Not just from humiliating Jasper on purpose, but from the years before that too, when she'd brandished her boredom like a gun and done everything she could to shock him. When she'd used him to grow up.

She could not hold the camera steady. Maybe she should have flown Izzy, her DP, out here to help. But this was part of it, of course: the trembling. The unsteadiness. It was the main story.

It was late in the day, the sun flat against her back. The shadows of the trees seemed to go on forever. She heard a snap in the woods, deep among the spires, where the fireweed was as tall as a fence. Lana froze. She remembered those prematurely aged photos of herself she used to keep on her phone. Yes, here she was; she'd returned.

Another sound, like branches underfoot. Something was there.

Lana backed away slowly, filming as she went. She had the eerie sensation—a conviction, though there was no evidence—that the camera saw something she didn't. She stopped shooting, then returned to the place where the house had stood. She found a charred log and laid it in the fireplace. Then she walked down to the lake, where all that remained of the dock were its metal pilings sticking out of the water. The sunset was outlandishly beautiful, painting the clouds over the bay a volcanic red, as if a toddler had picked up the sun and smeared it everywhere he could. The lake, too, had turned to lava. Lana put down her camera, knowing that it was impossible to film such a thing without turning it into a postcard. What was it her dad used to say? *A photo turns ugly things beautiful and beautiful things ugly.* She stared at the sunset for a while. Then she walked back to her car, where Agnes was sitting on the hood.

"Did you get what you needed?"

"Of course not," Lana said, then smiled.

"Some sunset, isn't it? It's, like, *prehistoric.*"

"It's the smoke in the air," Lana said. "The particles. They make the sunsets even brighter."

Agnes thanked the sun personally, for its lifetime of service—she was like this, a goofball—then got into the car with Lana, who drove off. The bear, who'd been watching her from the woods, wandered down to the lake in search of dead fish. Occasionally they washed up on the beach. The sun continued to do its thing, pulling out all the stops, but the bear could not have cared less. The wind smelled of trout. He roamed the shoreline, skirting a lounge chair that had melted like a crayon. A noise echoed off the lake. The bear flattened his ears, thinking for a second that the people were back—but it turned out to be nothing, or nothing worth huffing about, just an abandoned rowboat scraping against the rocks.

The people were finally gone.

V

WEDDING DAY, 2004

Cece opened her eyes and found herself in the same spot she'd been in when she'd closed them: upstairs at the Margolises' house, wedding dress pooling at her feet, as if she weren't sitting in a chair at all but melting like a snowman. What sort of person sends an email like that—a drunkmail? a *love letter*?—to a bride two days before her wedding? A crazy person. A sad fucking douchebag. Cece had decided to keep it to herself. She would tell no one, deny it ever came, pretend she'd answered Garrett's follow-up plea and deleted it unread. For an hour after reading it, she'd walked around with her head tingling, as if she'd eaten too much wasabi. It was daybreak; the lake was still as a puddle; twice in a row she'd failed to put any coffee grounds in the coffeemaker and ended up with a pot of hot water. Cece had decided to keep this under wraps as well.

She was getting married. A third of the wedding guests had norovirus—including one of her bridesmaids, Ushi—but she was getting married. What's more, people were helping her. She wanted to cry. What lovely people! What friends and family! Cece knew they were being especially nice because they felt sorry for her, but it didn't matter. Paige beamed at Cece with a foundation brush in her hand, then crouched down and inspected her face as if she'd painted it herself, which in a way she had. Akriti pinned a red rose in her hair. Cece's grandmother, crowding in to admire her, agreed she looked gorgeous, smiling her lopsided smile—what Cece's dad used to call the "Calhoun root-canal grin."

Cece did her best to smile back. Her grandmother had been

through this before, with Cece's mother, which was maybe why her eyes looked damp. She was happy and sad at the same time. Cece felt her mother's absence like a crime, an injustice, as if she'd been cheated out of a proper wedding. That was the real disaster. Three generations of Cecelias. What right did the name have to survive when her mother hadn't?

Cece began to cry. She was ruining her makeup, ruining all of Paige's hard work, which made her cry even harder. She felt like that stupid wall at Glacier. Everyone in the room gathered around to console her. *What's wrong?* they asked, but she couldn't explain it. It was her mother, her mother—and not her too. No doubt they thought it was because of the sick members of the wedding, the empty chairs. And perhaps it was. Akriti dabbed Cece's face with a Kleenex.

Then everyone stopped looking at her, because they were looking at something else. Something behind her. Cece turned in her chair and saw Garrett, literally the last person she would have chosen to perform her wedding, wearing a ridiculous tux that pooched out at the stomach. His eyes shone with pity. Cece's tears turned hot. He took a step toward her, appallingly, and she bared her teeth at him and stood up from her chair and lifted one hand, pretending she had a spray can in it. Then she did the worst thing she could think of—or maybe the only thing she could imagine that might save her—which was exterminate him.

———

At least a third of the chairs were empty; the rest were filled with people—young and old, yawning and unyawning—who'd devoted a good deal of time and effort to be here and were waiting for the opening remarks to begin. They looked at Garrett expectantly. He didn't mind. He had a newfound clarity. He'd watched the processional numbly, in a kind of trance, as if he were a sleepwalker who'd come upon it by accident. What Cece had done earlier in the house had cleared his mind completely—liberated him, in fact. She despised him. She'd read the email he'd written, knew the secret feelings in his heart, and had rejected them completely. They repulsed her, and rightly so. Garrett's heart felt dead, scoured of all illusion, as if it had been dunked in acid. The only life he'd be ruining today was his own.

On either side of him stood the bride and the groom, each flanked by the closest friends who were well enough to stand. He didn't dare look at Cece so instead focused on Charlie, who was visibly feeling ill, slouched there in his suit and swallowing conspicuously, as if he had something in his throat. Garrett, cleansed of hope, gave him an encouraging smile. Charlie did his best to smile back, staring at the pregnant bump in Garrett's shirt where he'd stapled it together. Twenty years from now, maybe, they'd talk about how ridiculous Garrett looked. Their eyes would tear up with laughter. Charlie would never know that he'd been in love with his fiancée, or that he'd sent an email hoping to steal her away from him, or that their worlds had hung in the balance.

Cece made a noise of some kind. A cough, perhaps to prompt him to get started. Garrett avoided her eyes. A drab, otherworldly calm had descended upon him. It hardly mattered what his opening words were. In his hand was the legal pad from Mr. Margolis's office, which, except for the generic preamble Garrett had scribbled at the top, was as blank as before.

"We're gathered here today," he began, "to celebrate two remarkable people, Cece and Charlie, who've decided to join their hands in matrimony."

Garrett, after reading this dismal sentence aloud, found himself staring at the blank lines below it. This did not make them any less blank. Garrett racked his brain for something to say. In the midst of his despair, he had a strange feeling. It felt like someone was standing right behind him, about to tap him on the shoulder. As if he were on the verge of being startled. He actually glanced behind him, which made people laugh. And miraculously it occurred to him, returning to the sunlit void of the page, what weddings were about. They were about promising to fill this blankness. To write a future for yourself. Precisely what his own life didn't have. He looked up from the pad, letting it drop to his side.

"That's the way these opening words usually begin. And in fact I've got a long speech written here, one that I wrote months ago, full of equally boring remarks."

More laughter. He glanced at Charlie, who was looking at him with concern. Still, if he knew he was lying, he didn't show it. Garrett poked at his stapled-together shirt, sort of trying to deflate it like a balloon, which made people laugh harder.

"But I've got a better idea," he said, extemporizing. "I'd like to say a few words about what marriage is, and what it means, because it seems to me that weddings aren't so much about the day itself. They're about the future. Because that's what a wedding is, right? A promise that the present makes to the future. It's a celebration of some other day—maybe ten years from now, maybe twenty—but a day that rhymes somehow with today. Because the future is what gives meaning to the present. Without it, you're just sort of, I don't know, *not there.*

"So let's do something. Let's all close our eyes for a second. No, I'm serious. Everyone, please, close your eyes. Let's imagine these two wonderful people's lives—or rather, the life they will have together. Some day in the future, I don't know, ten years from now. A day that rhymes with today. I have an idea of what this future life might be, having talked to both the bride and groom about it. A pretty good idea. Charlie will be a famous anesthesiologist, having invented some brilliant new painkiller— or no, he'll be on the cusp of developing it and will soon be famous. Cece will be . . . well, I'm not sure what Cece will be doing. But it's going to be amazing. She'll be famous too. They'll have two kids, let's say one boy and one girl, maybe Nathaniel and, um, Sylvia. Sylvie? Sure, why not. And Nathaniel and Sylvie will come here every summer, to this gorgeous spot, and do all the things Charlie used to do as a boy, all the things he's told me about since I first met him in college. They'll pick raspberries and cherries. They'll play games of Masterpiece and croquet and have bonfires on the beach and roast marshmallows for s'mores. They'll do funny walks off the end of the dock, pretending to be a blind person or a sleepwalker or somebody getting shot. They'll get horrendous nasty splinters. Charlie will take them in the boat to get ice cream. Cece will be the true fisherman in the family—fisher*person*, I should say—and go out trolling for trout and bring them home for Charlie to clean and cook for the family. They'll go hiking in Jewel Basin and come home and jump in the lake with all their clothes on, including their boots. The whole family will do this, and they'll grow old together, and they will always have this place, which I know that Charlie loves, and Cece too, and where we happen to be celebrating the promise of their future: not the exact one I've just described, of course not, but one just as happy, just as enviable, a rhyme for the day we are this very moment creating." Garrett found that his eyes behind their lids were growing moist, not at his own words, but out of mourning for the life he'd be missing. "Now everyone please open your eyes again. Open them. And feast your eyes on the bride and groom, who have invited you here today, asked you to meet them in this beautiful corner of the world, one that means more to them than any other place on earth, because they want you to be a part of this future too."

The guests did as he'd commanded. And what did they see? A green-faced groom, shivering in his designer suit. He seemed moved by Garrett's words. Or maybe he was just fighting the urge to throw up. Either way, his face trembled with emotion. Garrett stole a glance at Cece, who continued to stare resolutely ahead, as if looking directly at him would turn her to stone. Somehow this made her even more beautiful. Garrett realized, after today, he would most likely never talk to her again. To either of them.

Nor would he set foot on this stretch of lakefront, whose wonderfulness he'd just been extolling. His father was in the hospital, probably dying.

A woman in a coat and tie, one of Cece's college friends, got up to read a poem. Garrett did not hear a word of it. He was distracted by someone in the audience, an old woman in the second row framed by empty seats. She looked a lot like Cece. Same dimple in her chin; same jack-o'-lantern eyebrows, arrowed into a V; same expectant way of sitting, as if a butterfly were parked on her nose. Cece's grandmother, surely. She looked very old, fogged with exhaustion, as if she'd traveled an extremely long way to be here.

Only now, in the middle of her own ceremony, did Cece realize that all weddings were basically the same, no matter how many square dance bands you decided to hire. She tried to focus on Colleen's poem. Her friend had written it especially for her. It was meant to be a surprise, and a statement: a queer woman reading a poem in praise of marriage. Except that Cece wasn't taking in a word. Her brain had been reduced to a single task: not looking at Garrett. She stared at the grass, or off into the distance, or at her husband-to-be's face.

This face—Charlie's—was extremely sweaty. Sweaty and pale. He was clearly not feeling well, swaying like a drunk. Every few seconds he'd close his eyes in a slow-motion blink, as if he'd just taken a hit of something, then swallow in a way that involved his whole face. Afterward, he'd do his best to smile at her and produce instead a kind of perverted leer. It touched Cece deeply, this leer. He was trying not to ruin her wedding day. Self-sacrifice, right through to the end.

Had she really just called it that? *The end?*

And yet why couldn't he just tell her he had the virus? Why this instinct, always, to make things seem better than they were?

When it came time for the vows, Charlie gave her a haunted

look and then asked politely to sit down. Mr. Margolis pulled out a chair for him. One of Cece's bridesmaids—Ushi had been assigned this task originally; she didn't look to see who it was—handed her a folded-up piece of paper, which Cece unfolded silently, like a letter in a movie announcing someone's death. She vaguely recalled this silent unfolding from other weddings she'd attended. How ridiculous! All the planning she'd put into the wedding, her crazed efforts to make it unique, seemed absurd to her now. Even her trembling fingers seemed like part of the script. How long had she spent on her vows? Months? And yet one glance at them on the page revealed them to be bland, predictable, *mawkish*. She might as well have gotten them off the internet.

Charlie stared at her from the front row, doing his best to keep his head up. He was breathing quickly. Sort of panting in the sun, like a golden retriever. Now, a seated groom, slumped in his chair during the vows: *that* was original. Cece could honestly say she hadn't seen that one before.

She did something she hadn't expected. She laughed. And Charlie, despite how awful he must have felt, laughed too. That laugh that seemed to come from a different voice, high-pitched and whinnying, as if he'd been dubbed by a horse.

It dawned on her, for the first time, that she'd be hearing this laugh for the rest of her life. A laugh that she loved.

Cece read her vows to him—*I promise to never go to bed at night angry with you*—though honestly she didn't register a word she was saying. All she could think about was Garrett standing beside her in his terrible shirt. She had the feeling that he was trying to tell her something. Would he try to stop the wedding? Say that Charlie was too ill, that there was no way to continue, that they'd have to postpone it to a later date? Hadn't he ruined her wedding enough? Cece went on with her vows, determined not to look at Garrett, to focus on the oaths of love and kindness she was making—but the words swarmed from her mouth like bees. Now and then she glanced up at the groom, who leaned ashenly in his chair, head balanced on the plinth of one hand, looking more mystified than moved, as if he were having trouble following the words as well.

Garrett moved closer to her—she could feel this invisible step, as vividly as anything that had happened that day—and Cece looked at him for the first time. Eyes. Nose. Lips in motion. Yes, he was mouthing something at her. Something abominable. I LOVE YOU? No, something else.

SLOW. DOWN.

The same thing she'd scribbled in the margins of the paper she was holding, as a reminder.

Then she'd finished her vows, abruptly, and it was Charlie's turn. Garrett helped him out of his chair, letting him grip his shoulder while Charlie fished his vows from his pocket and read from them in a shaky voice, gripping the paper with one hand. He looked like he might collapse. By the time they were supposed to exchange rings, Garrett was supporting most of Charlie's weight. The crowd began to murmur, shifting in their seats. Cece waited in silent terror. A BB of sweat rolled down her armpit. Garrett helped Charlie fish the ring out of its box when Johnny offered it to him, making sure he had a decent grip on it.

"Charlie, as you place the ring on Cece's finger, please repeat after me: *I promise you love, honor, and respect, / to be faithful to you / and to forsake all others, / until death do us part.*" Charlie tried to slide the ring onto Cece's finger but was shaking too much and dropped it on the lawn. The crowd murmured. Garrett bent down to look for it, then got down on all fours and snooped around in the grass. "It's lost," Cece whispered, close to tears. For a minute it seemed like this was true. But then Garrett found it in a tuft of clover and held it in the air to grateful applause. He handed the ring to the groom, then held Charlie's hand to steady him while he placed it on Cece's finger. The metal band was warm from his fever. Carefully, Cece took the other ring from

Paige and promised to forsake all others and made to slide it on Charlie's finger, but he was wobbly and confused, preoccupied, it seemed, with staying upright. Garrett lifted the groom's arm, steadying it. He buoyed Charlie's hand with his own, stretching both toward Cece, who leaned forward and slipped on the ring.

———

The groom took to his bed, disappearing as soon as the ceremony was over. But the guests refused to let a good party be ruined. They ate tacos and drank beers with names like Hoppy Hedonist and did some square dancing courtesy of Rod-O and the Feckless Fiddlers, who were much better than their name. Semis, clattering down Route 35, blared their horns as they went by. Thanks to all the promenading, the do-si-do–ing and right-and-left-granding, the norovirus was passed from guest to guest, infecting every last person at the wedding. There would be projectile vomiting on several planes back to LA and New York. There would be couples in small apartments fighting over the only toilet. There would be canceled vacations and lethargic infants and middle-of-the-night visits to the ER. The DJ came on and played Top 40 hits no one had liked when they were released and yet had somehow become sacred relics of their youth. People whooped when each song came on, as if they'd won something in a raffle. The weather was glorious; the breeze from the lake smelled like cherries; people were picking them from the trees and spitting the pits at each other for no reason. Even the bride, groomless, was determined to have fun, dancing with her friends and singing along to each song while pointing at people in a way that made the pointed-at feel a tiny bit famous. She was sweaty and flushed, more real than she'd seemed all day, and even the most happily coupled guests couldn't help comparing their partners to her, wondering if they'd underestimated what life had to offer. The fiascoes of the ceremony—the sick groom, the speed-read vows, the dropped ring in the grass—had already taken on the sheen of legend, conforming graciously to a future where they would all seem harmless, even hilarious. The dancing had this sense to it too, as if the dancers had to live up to the stories that would be told about them.

Everyone agreed that the officiant's remarks were beautiful, that without his steady hand the wedding might have been a disaster—though no one could find the man himself. He'd vanished when no one was looking. Someone said that his father was ill; another remarked that she'd seen him crossing the road to his truck, right after the ceremony.

What a good friend, people said when it was reported he'd come straight from the hospital.

At some point after dark, as always seems to happen when there's beer and a lake and a large group of people, some of the guests crowded down to the pier and stripped out of their clothes, hooting as they jumped into the water. Even Cece joined them, stepping out of her wedding dress and leaving it on the dock, shivering in her underwear. She glanced behind her for a minute, as if looking for someone. But the groom was ill, he was in bed, her eyes roamed the yard for no reason. She must have known this, and yet she kept searching the crowd. She chewed her lip. Then all at once she seemed to give up; her face eased into a smile, as if she were glad—relieved, even—to be alone.

People sensed this, at any rate, though they knew of course it couldn't be true, that no bride would prefer to be single at her own wedding. Dancing with his three-year-old daughter on the lawn, Marcus Porter pretended not to look at Cece standing there in her underthings. Paige approached her from behind, still in her heels, then mimed a push before cannonballing into the lake fully clothed, red dress rippling around her like blood. The photographer, cigarette dangling from his mouth, jogged down to the beach, adjusted his flash, and then focused on the dock, hoping to catch the bride middive. He crouched there with his finger on the button. A breeze picked up, and the wedding dress at Cece's feet skated toward the house without her.

Her friends, neck-deep in the lake, cheered her on. *Come on!* they yelled. *You only live once!*

The weather was perfect. She couldn't go wrong. Still, she hesitated, savoring the moment before she leapt, as if she didn't want to ruin it by jumping.

ACKNOWLEDGMENTS

I owe a big debt of gratitude to biologist and author Doug Chadwick, who was nice enough to meet with me, back when *Dream State* was merely an idea, and whose work inspired Garrett's vocation in the novel. I'm especially indebted to *The Wolverine Way*, Chadwick's account of tracking wolverines in Glacier, which greatly informed chapters 15 and 22. It's a wonderful, important book—please read it! Research-wise, I'm also indebted to the film *Finding Gulo*, directed by Colin Arisman and Tyler Wilkinson-Ray, and to *Dopesick: Dealers, Doctors, and the Drug Company that Addicted America*, by Beth Macy.

This book wouldn't exist without the generosity of the Noel family, particularly Gordon and Margaret Noel, who invited me to their home in northwestern Montana twenty-five years ago and have hosted me and my family there every summer since. I hope the novel does the place justice. Thanks as well to Jennifer Noel, who took time out of her crowded life to talk to me from her car. A big thanks, too, to Dr. Laeben Lester, for vetting a hundred details and letting me read aloud to him in a crowded restaurant while he was trying to enjoy his food. Thanks to Emma Snyder, for getting into the weeds with me about independent bookstores (and for running such a wonderful one herself). And thank you to Kenny Wachtel and his filmmaker friends, for letting me pester them with questions.

Heartfelt thanks to the readers, amazing critics all, who helped turn *Dream State* into a novel: Andrew Motion, Danielle Evans, Tom Barbash, Scott Hutchins, and Greg Martin. This would be a far worse book without your expert advice. Thanks to

GM, too, for being my backcountry ski guide/avalanche safety expert.

Thanks to the MacDowell and Yaddo organizations, and to everyone at Johns Hopkins, for their generous support.

Warm thanks to my wonderful agent, Dorian Karchmar, for the three-hour Zoom feedback and for believing so strongly in the book, even well before its final form. (Wow, did I luck out when I called you back in 2002 for agent advice.) I'm immensely grateful, as well, to Thomas Gebremedhin, whose brilliant editing improved the novel in countless big and small ways. Thanks to Johanna Zwirner, Oliver Munday, Michael Goldsmith, Jess Deitcher, Andrea Monagle, Aja Pollock, Hilary DiLoreto, Casey Hampton, and everyone else at Doubleday who worked to bring *Dream State* into the world.

And last, first, and everywhere in between: Katharine Noel, love of my life, who helped me every inch of the way. I could not imagine writing this or any book without you.

ERIC PUCHNER is the author of the story collection *Music Through the Floor*, a finalist for the New York Public Library's Young Lions Fiction Award; the novel *Model Home*, which was a finalist for the PEN/Faulkner Award and won a California Book Award; and a second short-story collection, *Last Day on Earth*. His short stories and personal essays have appeared in *GQ*, *Granta*, *Tin House*, *The Best American Short Stories*, and many other places. He has received an Award in Literature from the American Academy of Arts and Letters. He is an associate professor in the Writing Seminars at Johns Hopkins University and lives in Baltimore with his wife, the novelist Katharine Noel, and their two children.